PHANTASTES
A FAERIE ROMANCE FOR MEN AND WOMEN

SPECIAL EDITION

'I regarded George MacDonald as my master; indeed, I fancy I have never written a book in which I did not quote from him.'

C.S. LEWIS, NOVELIST AND AUTHOR

'George MacDonald... in his power to project his inner life into images, beings, landscapes which are valid for all, he is one of the most remarkable writers of the nineteenth century.'

W.H. AUDEN, POET AND AUTHOR

'George MacDonald... could write fairy-tales that made all experience a fairy tale. He could give the real sense that everyone had the end of an elfin thread that must at last lead them into Paradise.'

G.K. CHESTERTON, NOVELIST AND AUTHOR

'Phantastes is a haunting, provocative and disquieting novel that links the dreams of medieval romance with the new awakenings of the Victorian era and – in opening a long-lost door to the realm of Faerie – stands as a daringly challenging forerunner to the modern fantasy novel.'

BRIAN SIBLEY, WRITER AND BROADCASTER, AUTHOR OF C.S. LEWIS THROUGH THE SHADOWLANDS AND THE LAND OF NARNIA

'In Phantastes we are presented with a momentous experience of spiritual realism, a symbolic perceiving of reality itself. Of its kind it is, I think, unsurpassed.'

COLIN DURIEZ, AUTHOR OF NUMEROUS BOOKS ON FANTASY LITERATURE

'Surely, George MacDonald is the grandfather of us all – all of us who struggle to come to terms with truth through fantasy.'

MADELEINE L'ENGLE, NOVELIST

'Phantastes is as close to a dreamed-world as psychological realism gets. In MacDonald's Celtic shadow land, sweet aspirations of love and bitter apprehensions of death skirl, like a sound on the wind of distant pipes, mysteriously and compellingly both within and just out of conscious reach, intertwined in such an enchanting way as to lead inexorably to the conviction that somewhere a joyous harmony is playing, beckoning us to come to its fullness.'

DAVID LYLE JEFFREY, DISTINGUISHED PROFESSOR OF LITERATURE AND THE HUMANITIES, BAYLOR UNIVERSITY

PHANTASTES

A FAERIE ROMANCE FOR MEN AND WOMEN

SPECIAL EDITION

GEORGE MACDONALD

Illustrations by Arthur Hughes
Edited with an introduction and notes by Nick Page

Paternoster:
thinking faith

LONDON • COLORADO SPRINGS • HYDERABAD

Phantastes was first published in 1858.
First published with illustrations by Arthur Hughes in 1905.

14 13 12 11 10 09 08   7 6 5 4 3 2 1

Introduction and notes copyright © Nick Page 2008
Photos on p.8, 9, 18, 20 © Nick Page

This edition first published 2008 by Paternoster
Paternoster is an imprint of Authentic Media
9 Holdom Avenue, Bletchley, Milton Keynes, Bucks, MK1 1QR, UK
1820 Jet Stream Drive, Colorado Springs, CO 80921, USA
Medchal Road, Jeedimetla Village, Secunderabad 500 055, A.P., India
www.authenticmedia.co.uk

Authentic Media is a division of IBS-STL U.K., limited by guarantee, with its Registered Office at Kingstown Broadway, Carlisle, Cumbria CA3 0HA. Registered in England & Wales No. 1216232. Registered charity 270162

British Library Cataloguing in Publication Data

A catalogue record for this book is available from the
British Library

ISBN-13: 978-1-84227-615-0

Book Design by Nick Page
Cover photo © Meg Blacker
Printed and bound in the USA by Versa Press

PHANTASTES
A FAERIE ROMANCE

SPECIAL EDITION

Contents

George MacDonald around the time that Phantastes *was written.*

INTRODUCTION

One cold spring day in March 1916, the seventeen-year-old C.S. Lewis picked up a book from a railway station bookstall. He was later to write that he had not the faintest notion of what he had let himself in for. As he read the book that night he felt as though everything had changed, as though his imagination had been 'baptised'.[1] The book was *Phantastes*, by George MacDonald.

By that time MacDonald had been dead for over a decade and, though popular and respected in the mid-Victorian era, his reputation was already on the wane. Yet Lewis recognised what many readers have since come to identify; that there has never been a writer quite like George MacDonald.

George MacDonald was born in the small Scottish town of Huntly, Aberdeenshire on 10 December, 1824.[2] His mother gave birth to six boys – two of whom died in childhood. Soon after his birth, the family moved south of Huntly, across the River Bogie, to 'The Farm', a sturdy, grey farmhouse which his father had built. There, his father ran a bleaching business, where cloth manufactured in Huntly was treated and laid out to whiten. His father, though industrious, was never wealthy. When George was only eight, his mother died of tuberculosis. The

---

1 Lewis, C. S, *Surprised By Joy: The Shape of My Early Life* (London: Geoffrey Bles, 1955) p.171
2 The best biography is Rolland Hein's *George MacDonald: Victorian Mythmaker* (Whitethorn, California: Johannesen, 1999). Greville MacDonald's biography of his parents – *George MacDonald and His Wife* (London: G. Allen & Unwin, 1924) – contains many personal reminiscences but is obviously influenced by family ties. William Raeper's *George MacDonald* (Tring: Lion, 1987) is good, although not as thorough as Hein's. David Robb's *George MacDonald* (Scottish Writers, 11; Edinburgh: Scottish Academic Press, 1987) is excellent on the Scottish background of MacDonald's life and work.

The house in Huntly where MacDonald was born.

disease was to blight the family; MacDonald later called it 'the family attendant'. George himself suffered from it; it was to claim two of his brothers, his step-sister and even four of his children.

Nevertheless he had a happy childhood, wandering the fields and countryside of Huntly, spending summers on the north coast in Cullen and Portsoy. His father remarried in 1839. George was fond of his step-mother, but the most important relationship in his life was with his father, whom he loved and respected.

The family attended the Missionar Kirk in Huntly – a strict Calvinist denomination, noted for their extreme Sabbatarianism. Calvinism with its emphasis on the sinfulness of man, the salvation of the elect and the rejection of 'works' as a means of salvation was a huge influence on George. Although he was later to reject the joyless, grim-faced doctrines of the Kirk, he did take from it a fiercely independent spirit and a sense that religion was not merely a pragmatic set of philosophies but something that determined your whole life.

From an early age, however, he seems to have felt uneasy about the teaching of the church. In the poem, 'A Hidden Life' he paints a picture of their Sabbath journey, walking across the fields to 'a little church', and their return, discussing what they had heard:

> ...And as they walked
> Together home, the father loved to hear
> The new streams pouring from his son's clear well.

The Farm, Huntly, where MacDonald was brought up.

> The old man clung not only to the old,
> Nor bowed the young man only to the new;
> Yet as they walked, full often he would say,
> He liked not much what he had heard that morning...[3]

It was, in fact, the walk home, the walk through the fields, which inspired him more. If he struggled to catch sight of God in the church, he found it easy to see the Lord in the fields and scenery around him. Some years later he wrote to his father that

> One of my greatest difficulties in consenting to think of religion was that I thought I should have to give up my beautiful things and my love for the things God had made. But I find that the happiness springing from all things not in themselves sinful is much increased by religion. God is the God of the beautiful – Religion the love of the beautiful, and Heaven the home of the Beautiful – Nature is tenfold brighter in the Sun of Righteousness, and

---

3 MacDonald, George, *Poems* (London: Longman, Brown, Green, Longmans and Roberts, 1857) p.20

my love of Nature is more intense since I became a Christian, if, indeed, I am one.[4]

Nature was sacramental, an outward sign of God's grace. In his writings, the Scottish landscape becomes mysterious, symbolic and bursting with God's presence.

In 1840 MacDonald left home to study in Aberdeen. He won a bursary to King's College, where he studied chemistry, natural philosophy, modern literature and languages. He was, to some extent, a solitary, introspective figure, who 'did not much mix with students at college, and, indeed, hardly cared to descend into the ordinary arena of emulation.'[5] Some of this isolation may have been due to poverty; he was forced to miss the 1842–43 term due to a lack of funds and the same cause was to stop him pursuing his chosen career of medicine.

It was probably during this period that he discovered the German Romantic writers – writers and mystics such as Novalis, Heine and Hoffmann.[6] Their influence on MacDonald was profound. However he was also reading British writers. *Phantastes* is peppered with references to Heine and Novalis, but also to Scotch ballads, to English Rennaissance authors such as Sydney, Shakespeare and Tourneur.

He graduated in 1845 with an MA and travelled to London, where he found work as a private tutor. He disliked the job, and the unheated room aggravated his health problems. While he was in London, however, he was introduced to the family of James Powell, a prosperous leather merchant with six daughters. George fell in love with Louisa, his

4 MacDonald, George, and Glenn Edward Sadler, *An Expression of Character: The Letters of George MacDonald* (Grand Rapids: Eerdmans, 1994) p.18; Hein, Rolland, *George MacDonald: Victorian Mythmaker* (Whitethorn, California: Johannesen, 1999) p.67

5 Hein, Rolland, *George MacDonald: Victorian Mythmaker*, p.53

6 Where he discovered them, however, is a matter of some debate. His relative Sir William Troup claimed that he spent some time in the summer of 1824 cataloguing a library in the north of Scotland where he discovered a cache of these writers. Certainly the image of a library features frequently in his novels, but his son Greville never identified the place and nor did his father, apparently, ever mention it to him. In all of his letters MacDonald makes not one reference to this event. He most likely discovered them in the library at King's College, or later in London. See MacDonald, Greville, *George MacDonald and His Wife* (London: G. Allen & Unwin, 1924) p.73; Hutton, Muriel. 'The George MacDonald Collection' *Yale University Library Gazette* 51, 1976, pp.74–85; Hein, Rolland, *George MacDonald: Victorian Mythmaker*, p.554 n.37.

third daughter. He was not a natural suitor. Louisa wrote on the back of one of the letters she received from him: 'My dearest, dearest. An overgrown baby with manners like a bear.'[7] Throughout his life he was not comfortable 'in society'. He hated the veneer, the insincerity of it all. In the loneliness of London he was drawn once again to his Bible. He wrote to his father:

> I love my Bible more – I am always finding out something new in it – I seem to have had everything to learn over again from the beginning – All my teaching in youth seems useless to me – I must get it all from the Bible again. . . . I have of late seen more of the necessity of studying Christ's character and I am in the habit of reading the gospels every day.[8]

For some time the conviction that he was called to be a pastor and preacher had grown in MacDonald. Inspired by his reading of the Bible and fired by the conviction that he had important things to teach people, in 1848, MacDonald enrolled in Highbury College to study for the Congregational Ministry. He became engaged to Louisa Powell and, in 1850, accepted an invitation to become the pastor of the Trinity Congregational Church in Arundel, Sussex. He had hardly started as a Pastor when he was struck down by a severe lung haemorrhage.

The illness forced him to travel to the Isle of Wight to convalesce. While there, he wrote a long verse-drama, *Within and Without*. The work (which was not published until 1855) tells of a monk

MacDonald in 1855, from a relief by Alexander Munro

---

7   Hein, Rolland, *George MacDonald: Victorian Mythmaker*, p.71
8   MacDonald, George, and Glenn Edward Sadler, *An Expression of Character: The Letters of George MacDonald*, p.17; Hein, Rolland, *George MacDonald: Victorian Mythmaker*, p.65

called Julian, who leaves the monastery to search for God. He marries his former lover, Lilia and fathers a child, but their love cools and they are separated. Eventually, Julian, Lilia and their daughter are reunited after death. The poem contains themes which MacDonald was to rework all his life; the obsessive pursuit of the ideal, the sense that God must be pursued in the everyday world; the idea that God is present and active all the time, and the belief that death is only the beginning. Its depiction of the monastery – a cold, rational, heartless place dedicated to money – may indicate his feelings about Highbury or, more presciently, some sense of anxiety about the church he was about to enter. That there was already some ambivalence about the move is evident in a letter sent to his brother Charles in November 1850:

> I don't quite think that I am settled here [Arundel] for life – but my business now is to do the duties of my place small as well as great – I hope either to leave this after six or more years, or to write a poem for the good of my generation perhaps both.[9]

One imagines that the Arundel congregation were unaware that they were getting a poet as well as a preacher. Louisa and George were married in March 1851 and settled in Arundel. He wrote to his father that he was 'far happier, much more at peace, and I hope learning now rapidly the best knowledge.'[10] Within a year of their marriage, Louisa gave birth to a daughter – Lilia Scott. However, this happiness was short-lived. Powerful factions in the Arundel congregation began to grow restless with MacDonald's teaching, particularly his exhortations to live more Christ-like lives. He wrote to his father:

> I firmly believe that people have hitherto been a great deal too much taken up about doctrine and far too little about practice. The word doctrine, as used in the Bible, means teaching of duty, not theory. I preached a sermon about this. We are far too anxious to be definite and to have finished, well-polished, sharp-edged systems – forgetting that the more perfect a theory about the infinite, the surer it

9   Hutton, Muriel, 'The George MacDonald Collection', p.77
10 MacDonald, George, and Glenn Edward Sadler, *An Expression of Character: The Letters of George MacDonald*, p.45

is to be wrong, the more impossible it is to be right. I am neither Arminian nor Calvanist. To no system would I subscribe...[11]

This, frankly, is not what wealthy, orthodox, utterly certain congregation members wanted to hear. His views on the afterlife were also suspiciously heterodox. In one sermon he expressed the hope that animals might share in the afterlife; in another that unbelievers may have the chance to respond to God after their death. He was moving towards universalism – the idea that all men and women would eventually turn to God and receive everlasting life. In December 1851 he privately published a small book of translations from Novalis – proof to his opponents in the congregation that he was 'tainted' with German theology. Things came to a head when they unilaterally reduced his salary by £50 per annum.[12] MacDonald struggled on for a while, but was forced to resign in May 1853. It was his only experience of the full-time Pastorate, and it left him with a lifelong distrust of 'official' religion – of denominations and creeds and doctrine. He disliked doctrinal disputes, for example, and would refuse to get involved.[13] He hated the way that people could be 'religious', or 'churchgoing', yet fail to show any real sign of being Christ's disciples.

These were troubled years. In March 1853, just before he left Arundel, George's brother Alec died, his illness made even sadder by a failed love affair. George left Arundel and moved north to Manchester where he hoped to found an independent congregation of his own. He also gave lectures on literature, science and theology. Poor, anxious, afflicted by bouts of bronchitis and tuberculosis, MacDonald and his family relied on the support of relatives and well-wishers to survive.

It was during this period that he revised *Within and Without*, which was published in 1855. In the summer of that year George was back

---

11 MacDonald, Greville, *George MacDonald and His Wife*, p.155
12 The disagreement may not have been entirely based on his orthodoxy. Louisa MacDonald suspected that 'the most influential of the deacons' did not want them leaving the house they rented from him into a larger one. Hutton, 'The George MacDonald Collection', p.77.
13 His son, Ronald, wrote: 'he hated, as a designation, the word *Protestant*. You cannot, he would say, make a belief out of a denial.' MacDonald, Ronald, *From a Northern Window: A Personal Remembrance of George MacDonald*, (Eureka, Calif: Sunrise Books, 1989) p.45

at Huntly, where his step-sister Bella was seriously ill. Just a few weeks later, in late August, she died. 'We must weep often in this world,' Mac-Donald wrote, 'but there are very different kinds of tears.'[14]

Within and Without was well-received and brought MacDonald to wider public attention. In autumn 1855, he had a massive lung haemorrhage which almost killed him. He was forced into a period of rest and recuperation, first on the south coast, then with his family in Huntly, where he did little but 'read German stories and write a few verses now and then.'[15] It was clear that he could not return to the grimy smoke of Manchester. Providentially, one of those who had read and admired *Within and Without* was Lady Byron, the widow of the poet. When she discovered the dire straits the MacDonalds were in, she paid for George, Louisa and Mary, their youngest daughter to spend the winter of 1856/7 convalescing in Algiers. He returned to England much restored in health, and convinced that the suffering he had been through had a purpose. With more help from Lady Byron the family moved to Hastings, where they found a new home and christened it Huntly Cottage. MacDonald's second book, *Poems*, appeared in 1857 but sold poorly. So he turned to something new. He turned to *Phantastes*.

The actual writing of *Phantastes* occupied MacDonald during December and January of 1857/8. He wrote to his father on January 2 saying 'I am writing a kind of fairy tale in the hope it will pay me better than the more evidently serious work. This is in prose. I had hoped I should have it ready by Christmas but I was too ill to do it.'[16] A subsequent letter reports that on a trip to London he 'put a little MSS that took me two months to write without any close work — a sort of fairy tale for grown people, into a new publisher's hands and two days after had £50

14 MacDonald, George, and Glenn Edward Sadler, *An Expression of Character: The Letters of George MacDonald*, p.102.

15 Hein, Rolland, *George MacDonald: Victorian Mythmaker*, p.182.

16 MacDonald, George, and Glenn Edward Sadler, *An Expression of Character: The Letters of George MacDonald*, p.125.

in my hands for it.' The publishers were Smith, Elder and Company and the book was published on October 28, 1858.[17]

Phantastes is a *Bildungsroman*, a story of personal development. The hero Anodos – whose name means either 'upwards', or 'pathless' – has to traverse a kind of spiritual landscape. As one character says, 'I have heard, that, for those who enter Fairy Land, there is no way of going back. They must go on, and go through it.'[18] Anodos cannot tread the same path twice, but he can revisit the same subject: each episode and encounter has a similar theme and purpose, each iteration gradually ridding him of selfhood and bringing him nearer true humility. One of the key images in *Phantastes* is the mirror. Mirrors occur with bewildering frequency. And even where there are not physical mirrors, there are events which are mirror each other. Some critics, taking perhaps the speed with which *Phantastes* was written as indicative, have described *Phantastes* as lacking structure, as being a kind of stream of (un)consciousness. In fact nothing could be further from the truth. *Phantastes* is very carefully structured, but it is structured around repetition and reflection. The 'main' story of Anodos contains many events which repeat, rework or reflect one another. And his story is mirrored in the poems, ballads and stories embedded within the text – such as the tale of Cosmo and the Ballad of Sir Aglovaile.[19] 'All mirrors are magic mirrors,' wrote MacDonald. 'The commonest room is a room in a poem when I turn to the glass.'[20] *Phantastes* itself is a kind of magic mirror, through which we see life – our life – in a different way.

Mirrors, of course, have two sides, and in *Phantastes* one is never sure which side of the mirror is which. In chapter 2, for example, Anodos wakes to find a stream running through his room; his large, green, marble basin has become a fountain from which the water is

---

17 Bulloch, John Malcolm, *A Centennial Bibliography of George MacDonald* (Aberdeen: The University Press, 1925) p.33.

18 See below, p.106.

19 This is why the poetry in the book is important, even though much of it isn't, frankly, very good. It is a part of the structure and the message.

20 See p.125.

'overflowing like a spring'.[21] In chapter 10 he finds himself in the fairy palace where he finds another overflowing basin, below a 'large fountain of porphyry'. The stream from this basin leads him into the interior of the castle where he finds an exact copy of his own room. Does his room exist in both worlds? Is the fountain in the fairy palace the source of the water in his washbasin? Has MacDonald, some thirteen years before his great friend Lewis Carroll, taken us through the looking glass?

So *Phantastes* is full of these 'mirror' events. It is a story which is many stories, all of which are the same story.[22]

It has its faults, of course. It is packed with rather uneven poetry, and features the usual Victorian twee, idealised children. But it is never less than memorable, thanks chiefly to a succession of powerful, almost primal imagery. *Phantastes* is replete with the symbols and characters which were to become the building blocks of MacDonald's fantastic fiction. There is the dream-like journey across a mysterious landscape; the culminating act of virtuous self-sacrifice; the journey through dark, labyrinthine interior. Above all there is the 'feminine' image of God; the ancient, wise woman, with the eternally young eyes.

In writing the book, MacDonald drew on a wide range of literary influences, including Malory, Bunyan, and Scottish Ballads and folktales. Perhaps the strongest literary debt, however, is to the *Märchen* of the German Romantics, particularly Novalis's poetic novel *Heinrich von Ofterdingen*, a quest story where the hero undergoes 'a progression through various spiritual landscapes.'[23] It was these books which gave

21 See p.47.

22 For differing views on the structure of *Phantastes* see Docherty, John, 'A Note on the Structure and Conclusion of *Phantastes*', *North Wind* 7, 1988; Gunther, Adrian, 'The Structure of George MacDonald's *Phantastes*', *North Wind* 12, 1993; Soto, Fernando, 'Mirrors in MacDonald's *Phantastes*: A Reflexive Structure', *North Wind* 23, 2004; McGillis, Roderick, *For the Childlike: George MacDonald's Fantasies for Children* (Metuchen, N.J London: Children's Literature Association Scarecrow, 1992) pp.51–65

23 Blackall, Eric A., *The Novels of the German Romantics* (Ithaca: Cornell University Press, 1983) p.121; Woolf, Robert Lee, *The Golden Key: A Study of the Fiction of George MacDonald*, (New Haven: Yale University Press, 1961). Woolf is excellent on the sources of MacDonald's work, particularly the German romantics, but with regard to the history his obsessive Freudian interpretation pushes him into sheer fabrication.

MacDonald a model for writing a fantasy work for adults – a 'faerie romance for men and women' as he called it.

It was not, in fact, his first attempt at prose fantasy. *Within and Without* contains a short prose fable called 'The Singer'. The tale tells of a father looking on the corpse of his son. The father recounts a dream in which he saw an assembly of godlike figures called the Immortals – 'hundreds of majestic forms, as of men who had striven and conquered'. In the dream, a young man comes to sing for them. He disappears into a deep, dark cavern ('when I looked into it,' says the narrator, 'I shuddered; for I thought I saw, far down, the glimmer of a star') and starts to sing. The father/dreamer asks one of the Immortals to explain what is happening:

> And he answered me thus: 'The youth desired to sing to the Immortals. It is a law with us that no one shall sing a song who cannot be the hero of his tale – who cannot live the song that he sings; for what right hath he else to devise great things, and to take holy deeds in his mouth? Therefore he enters the cavern where God weaves the garments of souls; and there he lives in the forms of his own tale; for God gives them being that he may be tried. The sighs which thou didst hear were his longings after his own Ideal; and thou didst hear him praying for the Truth he beheld, but could not reach. We sang, because, in his first great battle, he strove well and overcame. We await the next.'[24]

The dreamer then falls asleep again and, when he next sees a scene from his dream, the young man has returned, this time, 'his face worn and pale, as that of the dead man before me.' He has reached the end of his journey and the immortals welcome him to sing 'what songs thou wilt.'

This fragment shows that, some years before *Phantastes*, MacDonald was already dwelling on some of the key themes of the book.[25] There

---

24 MacDonald, George, *The Poetical Works of George MacDonald* Vol I (London: Chatto & Windus, 1915) p.52

25 The Singer is not in the original ms. of *Within and Without*, written in Dec-Jan 1851. It is part of the 'Corrections and Additions' added in the summer of 1854. However, in the ms. the lack of any alteration to the text of the Singer might imply that MacDonald was copying from a more finished, earlier draft. At any rate it was written no later than August 1854.

Welcome to Fairy Land. Woodland on the hills above
The Farm, Huntly, where MacDonald was raised.

is the idea of noble, 'good' death; there is the dream-world; there is the longing after his own 'ideal' and the striving for truth and there is the key idea of the protagonist becoming the hero of his own story.

'The Singer' is a dream, within a story, within a poem. In *Phantastes*, the boundary between fiction and reality is continually blurred. The book begins with Fairy Land flooding into the real world, and continues in this vein. Boundaries are porous — characters from stories appear later in real life, stories which Anodos reads he seems to inhabit. In chapter 3, Anodos reads about Sir Percivale; in chapter 6 a knight emerges from the woods who, while not Percivale, bears a striking resemblance. Anodos meets people who are descended from characters in fairy stories.[26] In the library of the fairy palace Anodos encounters books which physically transport him:

> Or if the book was one of travels, I found myself the traveller. New lands, fresh experiences, novel customs, rose around me. I walked, I discovered, I fought, I suffered, I rejoiced in my success. Was it a history? I was the chief actor therein. I suffered my own blame; I was glad in my own praise. With a fiction it was the same. Mine was the whole story. [27]

In MacDonald's philosophy, the song, the poem, the tale must be lived. Stories are transformational; songs have power to change things. In Fairy Land, Anodos, who never had the power of song before, sings songs that bring statues to life and free people from stone. *Phantastes* is not only a spiritual statement, therefore, but an artistic statement as well. It is about the power of art — especially poetry and story — to wake people from their sleep. This belief in the transformational power of stories is crucial for MacDonald, for it gave him the seriousness of purpose he needed. He had been denied the pulpit in Arundel; if he could not transform lives through his preaching, he would do it through his art.

26 See p.103.
27 See p.138.

The River Deveron, just north of Huntly.

So *Phantastes* is a self-conscious work of fiction with layer upon layer of story. But the intriguing thing is that they are all the *same* story, reflecting the same central theme, albeit from different angles. Anodos must learn to deny himself, to give up what he desires; he must learn to die. And he has to learn it over and over again. The message is that this same tale must be retold in our own lives, every day. As MacDonald wrote, 'A man must die many times…'

The idea of writing an English-language version of a German romance may have occurred to MacDonald the summer before when, as we have seen, he was in Huntly, reading 'German stories'. If so, he fused the idea with the setting, for in MacDonald's fiction, Fairy Land is Scottish. To picture the land of *Phantastes*, one only has to walk into the forests and woods of the area; dense, verdant, cool. The rivers of Fairy Land are the cool waters which flow around Huntly. When Anodos walks in the forests, he is in the woods above The Farm; when he stands on the desolate beach, he is standing at Cullen, or Portsoy, or the coast of Aberdeen.

But Huntly was not just a place of physical beauty, but of pain and grief and loss. In 1855 he was there for Bella's last days; in 1853 for the funeral of his beloved brother Alec. And this is perhaps the deepest landscape of *Phantastes*; for it is a book which travels over and again through sadness and pain and death.

Anodos falls in love with his ideal, the white lady, but she flees from him. She is eventually revealed to be the lover of Sir Percivale. He has to give her up. In the parallel story-within-a-story of Cosmo – a story about a mirror, which also mirrors the story surrounding it – Cosmo has to give up the woman he loves in order to free her. He sacrifices his own life for hers, he gives her away that she might live.

Various scholars have reflected on whether MacDonald himself was jilted by a woman, given that the scenario appears so often in his novels. There is no evidence of such an occurrence. However his brother Alec *was* rejected by a woman. When he declared his love for Hannah Robertson, a girl from Manchester, she rejected him. MacDonald's brother John wrote to George:

> [Alec] made a manly declaration of his love, telling her plainly he had nothing to depend on but his own resources. He was received in the most gentle and ladylike manner, but was disappointed in hearing that she never had the remotest idea of his attachment… Alec displayed a very fine spirit, expressed his thankfulness even his sorrow for the way he had been treated, and, without giving way to any extravagance, sorrowed deeply and earnestly… he wrote a long letter to assure her that, so far from thinking her behaviour harsh or unkind, he was most grateful for it, and that, although the trial was the deepest he had ever experienced, he believed it was a lesson from God and one of the most beautiful… he is very sad and looking ill, though perfectly quiet and patient. [28]

He and Hannah did, in fact, develop a relationship, but when Alec's health began to decline, the girl's father prevented 'all further intimacy'.[29] Alec came to Arundel in March 1852 to be nursed, but gained

28 MacDonald, Greville, *George MacDonald and His Wife*, p.169; Raeper, William, *George MacDonald* (Tring: Lion, 1987) p.90.
29 MacDonald, Greville, *George MacDonald and His Wife*, p.170.

Alec MacDonald in 1852

little from the climate and returned home to Huntly. Alec wrote to Louisa:

> She was my first love... But yesterday morning I laid it aside. I told her long ago that it was 'better to have loved and lost than never to have loved at all.' I can say so still. She tried to forget me now, and for her own sake I hope she will succeed... I have no further claim. I cannot wish to forget her, but my hopes can fold their wings now, for it is winter, and for a time at least they must rest. My fears are dead...[30]

He died in April the following year, in the arms of his father. Before he died he turned to his brother Charles and said 'Never mind, Charles, man! This is nae the end o'it!' MacDonald, writing to his father after the death wrote:

> Of him [Alec] we need never say he was; for what he was he is now — only expanded, enlarged and glorified. He needed no change, only development. Memory and anticipation are very closely allied. Around him they will both gather without very clear separation perhaps. He died in his earthly home and went to his heavenly... Let the body go beautiful to the grave — entire as the seed of a new body which keeps the beauty of the old and only parts with the weakness and imperfection. Surely God that clothes the fields now with the wild flowers risen fresh from their winter-graves will keep Alec's beauty in His remembrance and not let a manifestation of Himself, as every human form is, so full of the true, simple, noble and pure, be forgotten.[31]

It seems to me that, in the death of Alec, we see many of the events which are worked out in *Phantastes*. His reaction to the loss of his beloved is exactly what Anodos eventually comes to experience himself. When Anodos says 'I was dead and right content' there is a sense that like Alec,

30 MacDonald, Greville, *George MacDonald and His Wife*, p.171.
31 MacDonald, George, and Glenn Edward Sadler, *An Expression of Character: The Letters of George MacDonald*, pp.57–58.

he has folded his wings. And MacDonald's statement, 'He needed no change, only development' could stand as the theme of the entire book. Those who look for a real life equivalent of the White Lady and Anodos may well have been looking at the wrong MacDonald.

Phantastes then, is a tale of a journey, a journey not of change, but of development. At the start Anodos has 'fairy-blood' in him; what is needed is for him to recognise that, and to learn from the encounters which his journey brings. He has to die and emerge anew – 'expanded, enlarged, glorified'. Tolkein wrote: 'Death is the theme that most inspired George MacDonald.'[32] And 'inspired' is the word: for MacDonald viewed death as the high point of existence. It would be easy to dismiss this as wishful thinking, but we should, at least, acknowledge that MacDonald's belief in 'good death', death as the entrance to a new, fuller life, was not based on ignorance. His theology of death was forged in the crucible of loss and bereavement. *Phantastes* may be a fantasy, but is not escapist.

It received generally unfavourable reviews. The *Athenaeum* review was harsh, claiming MacDonald had 'lost all hold of reality… Anyone reading it might set up a confusedly furnished second-hand symbol-shop.' The *Spectator* described the work as placing 'us in the wildest regions of fairy and fancy, and though some of the persons or incidents appear to be allegorical, yet we can rarely satisfactorily interpret them, and sometimes not at all.' The reviewer in *The Globe* could only identify what it was *not* like:

> We know nothing with which it can be fairly compared. It is not like Fouque's *Undine*, nor Tennyson's 'Princess'; it is not like the old tales of King Arthur's 'Round Table'; it is not like the *Fairie Queen*; nor is it like the German popular and supernatural tales, yet it is not unlike all of these. [33]

---

32 Tolkien, J. R. R, *Tree and Leaf* (London: Allen & Unwin, 1974) p.59.
33 *Athenaeum* Nov 6, 1858, p.580; see Bulloch, *A Centennial Bibliography of George MacDonald*, p.33; See Raeper, William (Ed.), *The Gold Thread: Essays on George MacDonald*, (Edinburgh: Edinburgh University Press, 1990) pp.38–39.

The reception – and its poor sales – were to result in George Mac-Donald abandoning purely adult fantasy for many years. The stream went underground, until it burst out again some forty years later in a final, wonderful flowering with *Lilith*.

The reception of *Phantastes* was disappointing, but, once again, there were harder trials to bear. Neither MacDonald's father, nor his brother John lived to see its publication. His brother died in July, 1858, at the age of just 28. Some six weeks later his father was struck by a heart attack.

MacDonald did not think of abandoning writing. He had, by now moved from Hastings to London. In 1859, he accepted a post as a Professor of English literature at Bedford College, one of the first colleges for women. He held the position until 1867.

These were years of struggle, artistically. Following *Phantastes* Mac-Donald tried his hand at a play but nothing came of that, nor when he turned it into a novel. Although he was writing tirelessly, his son recalled that 'all bread was paid for by casual earnings.'[34]

In 1860 the Cornhill magazine serialised *The Portent*, a story dealing with Highland belief in the second sight. Also around this time he began a collaboration with the pre-raphaelite painter Arthur Hughes. During this period he was writing children's fairy tales: *The Light Princess, The Giant's Heart, The Shadows, Cross Purposes* and *The Golden Key* were all written in this period.[35] Remarkably, given their undoubted quality, they too failed to find a publisher. But they show how MacDonald was channelling his symbolism into children's tales. *The Light Princess* is a tale about a girl who, literally, lacks gravity – she cannot take anything seriously. She is eventually redeemed by the sacrificial love of a prince, who is willing to die for her. *The Golden Key* is one of the most remarkable

34 MacDonald, Greville, *George MacDonald and His Wife*, p.317
35 Greville MacDonald wrote that all the stories eventually published in *Dealings with the Fairies* were written 'before the end of 1863'. MacDonald, Greville, *George MacDonald and His Wife*, p.324

stories of the Victorian era.[36] It is a highly symbolic account of the male and female journey. A boy called Mossy finds a golden key and, accompanied by a girl called Tangle, he sets out to find the door which the key will unlock – the door to the land from 'whence the shadows fall'. They meet, typically for MacDonald, at the house of an old wise woman, before their paths diverge. Ultimately, both Mossy and Tangle have to plunge into a pool and 'die' before travelling on:

'You have tasted of death now,' said the Old Man. 'Is it good?'
'It is good,' said Mossy. 'It is better than life.'
'No,' said the Old Man: 'it is only more life.'[37]

The Golden Key is very close in tone and feel to *Phantastes*, but if anything the imagery is even more extraordinary with the Old Men of the Earth, Sea and Fire; the air-fish; an inverted, petrified ship's hull; the rainbow with its mysterious eighth colour. Despite the richness of this work, MacDonald struggled to find a publisher, so turned to more realistic fiction. The breakthrough came in 1863, with the publication of his first 'realistic' novel, *David Elginbrod*.[38] Once published, it sold steadily and, according to his son, 'Never again had he difficulty in placing a book.'[39]

He followed *David Elginbrod* with *Adela Cathcart* (1864) which brought together some of his previously rejected stories disguised as a novel. *Adela Cathcart* is a young woman suffering from an unknown illness. The illness is diagnosed by a young doctor to be a spiritual malaise, rather than a physical, and the patient is put on a regimen of story-telling. The symbolism is clear: there are some sicknesses which can only be cured by stories. The stories include a mixture of realistic narratives, parables and some of the fairy stories written before 1863.[40]

36 The title comes from Milton's *Comus*, where the Golden Key opens the doors of eternity.
37 MacDonald, George, and U.C. Knoepflmacher, *The Complete Fairy Tales*, (Penguin Classics, New York; London: Penguin, 1999) p.142
38 Initially this too was refused, until Dinah Mullock, author of the popular *John Halifax, Gentleman*, read the manuscript, told her publishers they would be fools to refuse it.
39 MacDonald, Greville, *George MacDonald and His Wife*, p.322
40 When revised the work in 1882, he removed *The Light Princess*, *The Giant's Heart* and *The Shadows*, which were, by then, available as children's stories.

His trouble in finding a publisher for his children's fiction was solved, in part, by one of closest friends. While he was writing *Phantastes* at Hastings, MacDonald was introduced to an Oxford don called Charles Dodgson. Dodgson — who was later to find fame under the pseudonym Lewis Carroll — became a close friend of the family, and the MacDonald children who were among the first to hear the draft of *Alice in Wonderland*.[41] Although they differ markedly in tone and aim, MacDonald's influence on the Alice books is profound; the same meandering dreamlike plot, the sudden changes of scenery, even the white rabbit and the talking flowers, can be found in *Phantastes*. MacDonald, too, benefitted from the success of *Alice*, for it changed the publishing landscape. Suddenly publishers were interested in fantastic literature — at least for children. So MacDonald was able to take the tales that he had smuggled into *Adela Cathcart* and publish them as *Dealings with the Fairies* (1867).

From then on, MacDonald operated what might be called a twin-track approach. He himself claimed never to write for children or adults, but 'for the childlike, whether of five, or fifty, or seventy-five.'[42] However, he did make a distinction, at least in publishing terms. His adult novels concentrated on realistic settings and plots (although not without some fantasy elements occasionally breaking through), while his true genius for fantasy found expression through his writing for children. He followed *Adela Cathcart* with *Alec Forbes of Howglen* and *Annals of a Quiet Neighbourhood*, the latter based on his experiences as a pastor in Arundel. In subsequent years he was to produce over twenty novels.[43] Critical judgement on these novels has tended to follow C.S. Lewis's view: that they are more useful as theology than fiction. Recent scholarship has led to a reappraisal. They can be repetitive and the author does tend to moralise; they sometimes exhibit all the signs of a potboiler

---

41 MacDonald, Greville, *George MacDonald and His Wife* pp.342–43

42 *The Fantastic Imagination*, see p.278

43 For a useful classification of the Scottish and English novels see Hein, Rolland, *The Harmony Within: The Spiritual Vision of George MacDonald* (Chicago: Cornerstone Press, (Revised Ed.) 1999) p.36–37

– a work produced to pay the rent. But for all that there are memorable scenes and characters, moments of rare insight and wisdom, and a generosity of spirit at work and a love of life. They are also genuine attempts to reproduce the Scottish dialect and customs.

MacDonald was now a well-respected figure in the Victorian literary scene. Among his friends he counted not only Lewis Carroll, but John Ruskin, the preacher F.D. Maurice, and Charles Kingsley. In 1867, after the birth of their eleventh child the family moved to The Retreat, in Hammersmith, a large house which had previously been the home of William Morris. In the spacious gardens they put on dramatic productions. The children were all adept actors, especially Lilia, who was often encouraged to take up acting professionally and who was to later break off an engagement because it would have meant her giving up acting. The MacDonald's version of *Pilgrim's Progress* proved so popular that they even took it on summer tours.

In 1869 he was awarded an honorary doctorate from his *alma mater*, King's College, and in the same year became the editor of a children's magazine, *Good Words for the Young*. Whilst the magazine became a useful vehicle for his own stories, MacDonald hated the role of an editor, especially when he had to refuse peoples' manuscripts. He also began to write more overtly theological writings, starting a series of books called *Unspoken Sermons* (1867, 1886 and 1889) as well as publishing *The Miracles of Our Lord* (1870).

In 1871 he returned to full-length fantasy writing, this time with a novel for children. *At The Back Of The North Wind* (1871) tells the story of Diamond, a boy born into poverty, who is taken on adventures by the North Wind. This was followed by *The Princess and the Goblin* (1872). The winter of 1872–73 was spent on a lucrative lecture tour of America, during which MacDonald became friends with Mark Twain.

George and Louisa had eleven children in all but his health – and that of many of his children – was always fragile. Their daughter Mary fell ill with TB. MacDonald had been granted a pension from the civil list and in 1877 the MacDonalds moved to Italy, hoping that the

Mediterranean climate would improve their health. They settled first in Nervi, near Genoa, where Mary, after a short period of remission, died in April. Just over a year later their fifteen year old son Maurice also died. The local church refused to let them bury him in the cemetery: he was buried in a graveyard reserved for strangers and heretics, on a rocky outcrop. MacDonald strove, as ever, to seek some understanding from these tragedies. In 1880 he published *A Book of Strife, in the Form of the Diary of an Old Soul*; a kind of diary-poem or daily devotional, with 366 stanzas. In 1883 he produced a second Curdie book. *The Princess and Curdie* (1883) is darker than its predecessor. Full of biting satire and even anger, one hesitates to call it a children's book at all. With its apocalyptic ending and its powerful, almost visionary feel, it reflects not only the troubled times MacDonald was passing through, but also his desire to escape the confines of the purely children's fantasy novel. The stream forced underground since *Phantastes* was breaking out.

They eventually settled in a large house in Bordighera which they christened Casa Coraggio – from the family motto, 'Corage! God mend al!'[44] Purchased through donations from several wealthy friends, it was to be the place where MacDonald spent most of the remainder of his life. They turned one large room into a performance space for their dramatic productions, while on Sunday and Wednesday evenings the house was open to any who wished to attend for hymn singing, a sermon, or talks on MacDonald's favourite literature. Bordighera became the kind of church MacDonald always dreamed of; where he could preach freely.

Death, however, continued to haunt the family. MacDonald's daughter Grace died in 1884, followed by his daughter-in-law, Vivenda, in 1890 and a granddaughter Octavia in 1891. In response he turned once again to fantasy. He began to compose another fairy story for adults, *Lilith*, a myth which would be the final embodiment of his spiritual and artistic vision. He finished the first draft in 1890 when perhaps the greatest trial of his life struck. In 1891, Lilia, MacDonald's favour-

---

44 An anagram of George MacDonald.

ite daughter and in many ways the emotional centre of the family, contracted tuberculosis. She died in November 1891, in her father's arms. The death was a hammer blow to MacDonald who had to be virtually dragged from the graveside. It sent him back to the text of *Lilith*. Over the next five years he radically reworked it four times, each time wrestling with it, reshaping it, enlarging it, digging deeper into the mystery and meaning of the spiritual

MacDonald in old age.

journey he had been travelling. Eventually published in 1895, *Lilith* is a dense, haunting book. In many ways it is MacDonald's masterpiece.

In 1899 George and Louisa returned to England, to a house built for them by their sons Greville and Robert. There the following year they celebrated their fiftieth wedding anniversary. Louisa died in 1901 and was buried in the Stranger's Cemetery in Bordighera, beside Grace and Lilia. MacDonald followed her on September 18, 1905, and his body was cremated and his ashes laid beside his wife's.

By the time C.S. Lewis encountered *Phantastes* on that windy railway station, MacDonald was already out of fashion. Yet in some ways he never was really *in* fashion: he was always on the edge, socially, spiritually and artistically. He was always, to use a Scottish word, 'outwith'; outside, beyond. It is this feeling of 'outwithness' which gives his work a special power and which is, I believe, why his work will continue to be read. The roll call of writers who have been influenced by his unique vision includes Robert Louis Stevenson, G.K. Chesterton, E. Nesbit, C.S. Lewis, J.R.R. Tolkien, Maurice Sendak, T.S. Eliot and W.H. Auden.[45] More recently scholarship has started to reappraise his novels – especially the Scottish novels – which many see as forerunners of the Kailyard School.

What he was, was a prophet, not in the sense of one who predicts the future, but in the biblical sense; someone who communicates a vision from God. And the end result of prophecy is action. Through his writing MacDonald wanted to change the world; he was the most practically-minded fantasy writer there has ever been. At the end of *Phantastes*, Anodos asks himself 'Could I translate the experience of my travels there into common life? This was the question.'[46] For MacDonald, it was vital that his readers ask themselves the same question.

Chesterton wrote of him, he 'could write fairy tales that made all experience a fairy-tale. He could give the real sense that everyone had the end of an elfin thread that must at last lead them into Paradise.'[47] In that sense, none of MacDonald's tales really end. As John Pridmore observed: 'The end of a MacDonald naratie often lies beyond the last page of the text.'[48] Perhaps the real end of a MacDonald story – the end he would have most desired – lies in the lives of his readers. We read MacDonald best when we finish the tale, close the book and, in the words of the Old Woman in the Cottage, 'Go... and do something worth doing.'[49]

45 Nor has it just been writers: the young Gustav Holst set one of the poems from *Phantastes* to music and later composed a suite for orchestra called *The Phantastes Suite*. He also planned an opera called The Magic Mirror' based on Cosmo's story in chapter 13. More recently the Waterboys used the poem 'Thou goest thine, and I go mine' (see p.246) as the lyrics to the title track of their album *Room to Roam*.

46 See p.271.

47 G.K. Chesterton, *The Victorian Age in Literature*, (Oxford University Press: London, 1966) p.67

48 John Pridmore, 'George MacDonald's Transfiguring Fantasy', *VII: an Anglo-American literary Review* 20. 2003.

49 See p.219.

A NOTE ON THE TEXT

The text comes from the 1905 edition, edited by Greville MacDonald with illustrations by Arthur Hughes. Errors or doubtful readings in that edition have been corrected using the first edition, published by Smith, Elder and Company in 1858.

MacDonald was always wary of explanations. In his essay 'The Fantastic Imagination' he wrote:

> A genuine work of art must mean many things; the truer its art, the more things it will mean. If my drawing, on the other hand, is so far from being a work of art that it needs *THIS IS A HORSE* written under it, what can it matter that neither you nor your child should know what it means? [1]

I hope that none of my annotations say 'This is a horse', but I am aware that we fans of MacDonald have interpretations and ideas which we wish to share. So, when it comes to the interpretation of symbols, as the Americans say, 'your mileage might vary.' What I have tried to do is explain obscure or antique words; draw attention to MacDonald's sources and show his influence on others; point to structural similarities and links within the text and show how MacDonald used certain symbols or ideas in other works. For MacDonald's works, first editions are hard to consult unless you are have access to an academic library; for the more popular works the number of editions is bewildering. For these reasons, therefore, I have limited myself to giving the chapter numbers, rather than citing any specific edition. Other works cited can be found in the bibliography on p.282. All Bible quotations are from the King James Version, since this was the version MacDonald used.

I would like to thank those who have helped me on this journey, in particular the staff of the Abderdeenshire County Record Office; the staff of the Brander Museum and Library, Huntly; Ian Blakemore at Rosley Books; Meg Blacker for the cover photo; and Robin Parry at Paternoster.

---

[1] See p.278.

George MacDonald Key Dates

1824   10 Dec; George MacDonald born at Huntley, Scotland.

1832.   Mother Helen dies

1839   MacDonald's father marries Margaret McColl.

1840   Wins bursary to King's College, Aberdeen.

1840-41; 43–45 Attends Aberdeen University

1845   Awarded MA. Moves to London to become a tutor.

1846   First poem published anonymously in Scottish Congregational Magazine.

1848.   Enters Highbury Theological College. Becomes engaged to Louisa Powell.

1850   Appointed Pastor at Arundel. November; suffers severe haemorrhage. Convalesces on Isle of Wight. Writes first draft of *Within and Without*.

1851   Mar; Marries Louisa Powell. December; translates Novalis' *Twelve Spiritual Songs.*

1852   Jan; birth of Lilia. June; church conflict leads to cut in salary.

1853.   Mar; death of brother Alec. May; resigns pastorate. July; birth of Mary Josephine. Moves to Manchester.

1854   Sept; birth of Caroline Grace

1855   *Within and Without* published. Another serious haemorrhage.

1856   Jan; birth of Greville. MacDonald spends winter in Algiers.

1857.   *Poems* published. Aug; birth of Irene. Family settles in Hastings.

1858.   June; death of MacDonald's brother John. Aug; death of father. Oct; *Phantastes* published. Nov; birth of Winifrid Louisa. Meets Charles Dodgson (Lewis Carroll).

1859   Moves to London. Oct; becomes professor of English Literature at Bedford College.

1860   Oct; birth of Ronald.

1862   July; birth of Robert Falconer.

1863   *David Elginbrod* published. Dodgson shows MacDonald family the draft of Alice. MacDonald meets John Ruskin.

1864   Feb; birth of Maurice. *Adela Cathcart* published.

1865   *Alec Forbes of Howglen* published. Sept; birth of Bernard Powell.

1867   Jan; birth of George MacKay. Family moves to The Retreat, Hammersmith.

1868   *Robert Falconer* published. MacDonald awarded honorary doctorate by Aberdeen University.

1869   Becomes editor of *Good Words for the Young.*

1871   *At the Back of the North Wind* published

1872   Lecture tour of America. *Wilfred Cumbermede* published. *The Princess and the Goblin* published.

1877   First trip to Italy. First performance of *Pilgrims Progress*. MacDonald awarded a Civil List pension.

1878   Apr; death of Mary Josephine.

1879   Mar; death of Maurice.

1880   MacDonald family move to Casa Coraggio, Bordighera.

1882   *The Princess and Curdie* published.

1884   May; death of Grace.

1890   Writes first version of *Lilith.*

1891   Nov; death of Lilia.

1895   *Lilith* published.

1897   MacDonald's health begins to deteriorate. *Salted with Fire,* his last novel is published.

1898   MacDonald lapses in silence.

1901   Mar; George and Louisa celebrate their Golden Wedding.

1902   13th Jan; death of Louisa. Buried at Bordighera.

1905   18th Sept; death of George MacDonald in Ashtead, Surrey. He is cremated and his ashes interred next to his wife at Bordighera.

GEORGE MACDONALD — MAJOR WORKS

1855   *Within and Without, a Poem*

1857   *Poems*

1858   *Phantastes: a Faerie Romance for Men and Women*

1863   *David Elginbrod* (3 volumes)

1864   *Adela Cathcart* (3 volumes)

1864   *The Portent: a story of the Inner Vision of the Highlanders commonly called the Second Sight.*

1865   *Alec Forbes of Howglen* (3 volumes)

1867   *Annals of a Quiet Neighbourhood* (3 volumes)

1867   *Dealings with the Fairies* (contains 'The Light Princess,' 'The Giant's Heart,' 'The Shadows,' 'Cross Purposes,' and 'The Golden Key')

1867   *Unspoken Sermons* 1st Series.

1867   *'The Disciple,' and Other Poems*

1868   *Guild Court* (3 volumes)

1868   *Robert Falconer* (3 volumes)

1868   *The Seaboard Parish* (3 volumes)

1868   *England's Antiphon*

1870   *The Miracles of our Lord* (1 volume)

1871   *At the Back of the North Wind*

1871   *Ranald Bannerman's Boyhood*

1871   *Works of Fancy and Imagination* (10 volumes)

1872   *The Princess and the Goblin*

1872   *The Vicar's Daughter* (3 volumes)

1872   *Wilfred Cumbermede* (3 volumes)

1873   *Gutta Percha Willie: the Working Genius*

1875   *Malcolm* (3 volumes)

1875   *The Wise Woman, a Parable* (first published serially as *A Double Story*; later published as *The Lost Princess, or The Wise Woman*)

1876   *Thomas Wingfold, Curate* (3 volumes)

1876   *St George and St Michael* (3 volumes)

1876   *Exotics: a Translation (in verse) of the Spiritual Songs of Novalis, the Hymn Book of Luther and other Poems from the German and Italian*

1877   *The Marquis of Lossie* (3 volumes)

1879   *Sir Gibbie* (3 volumes)

1879   *Paul Faber, Surgeon* (3 volumes)

1880   *A Book of Strife, in the form of the Diary of an Old Soul*

1881   *Mary Marston* (3 volumes)

PHANTASTES:

A

Faerie Romance for Men and Women.

BY

GEORGE MAC DONALD.

AUTHOR OF "WITHIN AND WITHOUT."

In good sooth, my masters, this is no door. Yet is it a little window, that
looketh upon a great world.

LONDON:
SMITH, ELDER AND CO., 65, CORNHILL.

1858.

The title page of the first edition.

PHANTASTES
A FAERIE ROMANCE FOR MEN AND WOMEN

GEORGE MACDONALD

In good sooth, my masters, this is no door.
Yet is it a little window, that looketh upon a great world.

*'Here it chaunced that upon their quest Sir Galahad and Sir Perciv-
ale rencountered in the depths of a great forest.'*
Chapter 3

PHANTASTES
A FAERIE ROMANCE

Phantastes from 'their fount' all shapes deriving,
In new habiliments can quickly dight.
FLETCHER'S PURPLE ISLAND[1]

---

1   *The Purple Island* by Phineas Fletcher (1582–1650). In this poetic fantasy Phantastes or Fancie
    is a counsellor of the mind. Fletcher was inspired by Spenser's *The Faerie Queene*, where Phan-
    tastes appears as a spinner of fancies, locked away in a chamber in the House of Temperance.

*One can imagine stories without coherence, yet with association, like dreams;
poems that are simply melodious and full of beautiful words, but also without
meaning and coherence, with, at the most, individual stanzas which are intelligible,
like fragments of the most varied things. This genuine poesie can at most have
a general allegorical meaning and an indirect effect, as music has. That is why
nature is so purely poetic, like the study of a magician or a physicist, a nursery
or a lumber- or storeroom...*

*A fairy-story is like a vision without coherence. An ensemble of wonderful things
and events, e.g., a musical fantasy, the harmonic sequence of an Aeolian harp;
nature itself.*

*In a genuine fairy-story, everything must be wonderful, mysterious, and coherent;
everything busy, each in a different way. The whole of nature must be wondrously
mixed with the whole spirit-world; here enters the time of anarchy, of lawlessness,
of freedom, the natural state of nature, the time of the world... The world of the
fairy-story is that world which is thoroughly opposed to the real world, and for
that reason so thoroughly similar, as chaos is similar to the completed creation.*

NOVALIS[1]

---

1 'Novalis' was the pseudonym of Friedrich von Hardenberg (1772–1801). He was a German
romantic poet and novelist. MacDonald was greatly influenced by Novalis; in 1851 he issued
Twelve Spiritual Songs, a privately-printed translation of some of Novalis' poems. This was Mac-
Donald's first published book. Greville MacDonald suggested that the complaint of the congregation at Arundel, that MacDonald was 'tainted with German theology', originated in his
translation of Novalis' poetry. The quotes come from *Novalis, Schriften,* edited by Ludwig Tieck
and Fr. (Karl Wilhelm Friedrich) von Schlegel, 4th edition (Berlin 1826) II, 170–71. In fact,
this edition contained some mistakes, notably in the third paragraph above where the edi-
tors put the word *zusammenhängend* (coherent) instead of *unzusammenhängend* (incoherent) as it
should be and is in the first two excerpts. For more information, and the German original, see
Appendix I (p.274).

— 1 —

A spirit. . .
The undulating woods, and silent well,
And rippling rivulet, and evening gloom,
Now deepening the dark shades, for speech assuming,
Held commune with him; as if he and it
Were all that was.

SHELLEY'S *ALASTOR.*[1]

I awoke one morning with the usual perplexity of mind which accompanies the return of consciousness. As I lay and looked through the eastern window of my room, a faint streak of peach-colour, dividing a cloud that just rose above the low swell of the horizon, announced the approach of the sun. As my thoughts, which a deep and apparently dreamless sleep had dissolved, began again to assume crystalline forms, the strange events of the foregoing night presented themselves anew to my wondering consciousness. The day before had been my one-and-twentieth birthday.[2] Among other ceremonies investing me with my legal rights, the keys of an old secretary, in which my father had kept his private papers, had been delivered up to me.[3] As soon as I was left alone, I ordered lights in the chamber where the secretary stood, the first lights that had been there for many a year; for, since my father's

---

1 *Alastor, or The Spirit of Solitude* was published in 1816. Shelley's first major poem, it tells of an unidentified poet and his search for 'strange truths in undiscovered lands.' The extract comes from ll.479–88, where the poet appears to have lost his avenging demon with the approach of death. The original has 'leaping' rivulet.
2 In Victorian Britain the age at which a man became 'adult' was 21.
3 *Secretary*: a secretaire, or what we would call today a bureau.

death, the room had been left undisturbed.[4] But, as if the darkness had been too long an inmate to be easily expelled, and had dyed with blackness the walls to which, bat-like, it had clung, these tapers served but ill to light up the gloomy hangings, and seemed to throw yet darker shadows into the hollows of the deep-wrought cornice. All the further portions of the room lay shrouded in a mystery whose deepest folds were gathered around the dark oak cabinet which I now approached with a strange mingling of reverence and curiosity. Perhaps, like a geologist, I was about to turn up to the light some of the buried strata of the human world, with its fossil remains charred by passion and petrified by tears.[5] Perhaps I was to learn how my father, whose personal history was unknown to me, had woven his web of story; how he had found the world, and how the world had left him. Perhaps I was to find only the records of lands and moneys, how gotten and how secured; coming down from strange men, and through troublous times, to me who knew little or nothing of them all.

To solve my speculations, and to dispel the awe which was fast gathering around me as if the dead were drawing near, I approached the secretary; and having found the key that fitted the upper portion, I opened it with some difficulty, drew near it a heavy high-backed chair, and sat down before a multitude of little drawers and slides and pigeon-holes. But the door of a little cupboard in the centre especially attracted my interest, as if there lay the secret of this long hidden world. Its key I found. One of the rusty hinges cracked and broke as I opened the door: it revealed a number of small pigeon-holes. These, however, being but shallow compared with the depth of those around the little cupboard, the outer ones reaching to the back of the desk, I concluded that there must be some accessible space behind; and found, indeed, that they were

---

4 Sadly, between the writing of the novel and its publication, MacDonald's father did, indeed, pass away.

5 Geology was incredibly popular in Victorian society. The Geological Society of London was founded in 1807, and the science had a wide amateur following.

formed in a separate framework, which admitted of the whole being pulled out in one piece. Behind, I found a sort of flexible portcullis of small bars of wood laid close together horizontally. After long search, and trying many ways to move it, I discovered at last a scarcely projecting point of steel on one side. I pressed this repeatedly and hard with the point of an old tool that was lying near, till at length it yielded inwards; and the little slide, flying up suddenly, disclosed a chamber — empty, except that in one corner lay a little heap of withered rose-leaves, whose long-lived scent had long since departed; and, in another, a small packet of papers, tied with a bit of ribbon, whose colour had gone with the rose-scent.[6] Almost fearing to touch them, they witnessed so mutely to the law of oblivion, I leaned

There stood on the threshold a tiny woman-form

back in my chair, and regarded them for a moment; when suddenly there stood on the threshold of the little chamber, as though she had just emerged from its depth, a tiny woman-form, as perfect in shape as if she had been a small Greek statuette roused to life and motion. Her dress was of a kind that could never grow old-fashioned, because it was simply natural: a robe plaited in a band around the neck, and confined by a belt about the waist, descended to her feet. It was only afterwards, however, that I took notice of her dress, although my surprise was by no means of so overpowering a degree as such an apparition might naturally be expected

6   The contents of the papers is not revealed. They appear to be love letters. Elsewhere in *Phantastes* MacDonald writes 'the lover [has] his secret drawer' (p.159.)

to excite. Seeing, however, as I suppose, some astonishment in my countenance, she came forward within a yard of me, and said, in a voice that strangely recalled a sensation of twilight, and reedy river banks, and a low wind, even in this deathly room, 'Anodos[7], you never saw such a little creature before, did you?'

'No,' said I; 'and indeed I hardly believe I do now.'

'Ah! that is always the way with you men; you believe nothing the first time; and it is foolish enough to let mere repetition convince you of what you consider in itself unbelievable. I am not going to argue with you, however, but to grant you a wish.'

Here I could not help interrupting her with the foolish speech, of which, however, I had no cause to repent:

'How can such a very little creature as you grant or refuse anything?'

'Is that all the philosophy you have gained in one-and twenty years?' said she. 'Form is much, but size is nothing. It is a mere matter of relation. I suppose your six-foot lordship does not feel altogether insignificant, though to others you do look small beside your old Uncle Ralph[8], who rises above you a great half-foot at least. But size is of so little consequence with me, that I may as well accommodate myself to your foolish prejudices.'

So saying, she leapt from the desk upon the floor; where she stood a tall, gracious lady, with pale face and large blue eyes. Her dark hair flowed behind, wavy but uncurled, down to her waist, and against it her form stood clear in its robe of white.

'Now,' said she, 'you will believe me.'

---

7 This word, 'Anodos', is rich with meaning. Some have seen it as meaning 'pathless' or 'on no road', but it is also Greek for 'ascent'. Plato used the word to describe the 'pathway' from the physical self to a higher plane of reality, particularly in his famous allegory of the cave. All these meanings are appropriate to the action of the novel, although a clue to MacDonald's primary meaning may lie in *Lilith*, where the Raven talks about 'old Sir Upward' (MacDonald, *Lilith* ch.1). In *Phantastes* Anodos is later called 'Sir Anodos' (chapter 10; p.130). For more connections see McGillis, '*Phantastes* and *Lilith*; Femininity and Freedom', in Raeper (Ed.), *The Gold Thread: Essays on George MacDonald*, p.32.

8 The name 'Ralph' also appears in *Lilith*, where he is the protagonist's grandfather. Old Sir Ralph 'believed in nothing he could not see or lay hold of.' (MacDonald, *Lilith* ch.1).

Overcome with the presence of a beauty which I could now perceive, and drawn towards her by an attraction irresistible as incomprehensible, I suppose I stretched out my arms towards her, for she drew back a step or two, and said:

'Foolish boy, if you could touch me, I should hurt you. Besides, I was two hundred and thirty-seven years old, last Midsummer eve; and a man must not fall in love with his grandmother, you know.'[9]

'But you are not my grandmother,' said I.

'How do you know that?' she retorted. 'I dare say you know something of your great grandfathers a good deal further back than that; but you know very little about your great grandmothers on either side. Now, to the point. Your little sister was reading a fairy-tale to you last night.'

'She was.'

'When she had finished, she said, as she closed the book, "Is there a fairy-country, brother?" You replied with a sigh, "I suppose there is, if one could find the way into it."'

'I did; but I meant something quite different from what you seem to think.'

'Never mind what I seem to think. You shall find the way into Fairy Land to-morrow. Now look in my eyes.'

Eagerly I did so. They filled me with an unknown longing. I remembered somehow that my mother died when I was a baby. I looked deeper and deeper, till they spread around me like seas, and I sank in their waters. I forgot all the rest, till I found myself at the window, whose gloomy curtains were withdrawn, and where I

---

9   This figure is the first of the idealised 'grandmother' figures in MacDonald's writing: a forerunner of the great-great-Grandmother in *The Princess and the Goblin* and *The Princess and Curdie*. In *Adela Cathcart*, MacDonald describes God as 'Him who is Father and Mother both in one' (*Adela Cathcart* vol.2. ch. 2). The earliest of these feminine depictions of God appears in MacDonald's poem 'A Hidden Life', where he imagines 'A mighty woman sat, with waiting face,/ Calm as that life whose rapt intensity/Borders on death, silent, waiting for him,/To make him grand forever with a kiss...' (MacDonald, 'A Hidden Life', *Collected Poems Vol. 1*). Typically, Anodos attempts to embrace her – to possess her. Her response may allude to a popular farce at the time, entitled *You Can't Marry Your Grandmother*. On Midsummer eve, see p.100

stood gazing on a whole heaven of stars, small and sparkling in the moonlight. Below lay a sea, still as death and hoary in the moon, sweeping into bays and around capes and islands, away, away, I knew not whither. Alas! it was no sea, but a low fog burnished by the moon.[10] 'Surely there is such a sea somewhere!' said I to myself. A low sweet voice beside me replied –

'In Fairy Land, Anodos.'

I turned, but saw no one. I closed the secretary, and went to my own room, and to bed.

All this I recalled as I lay with half-closed eyes. I was soon to find the truth of the lady's promise, that this day I should discover the road into Fairy Land.

10 In one reality, this is the fog outside his window, in another it is a sea in fairy land. In this, MacDonald draws on Novalis, who wrote, 'We are closer to things invisible than to things visible.' He will encounter the sea in Fairy land.

—2—

'Where is the stream?' cried he, with tears. 'Seest thou no its blue waves above us?'
He looked up, and lo! the blue stream was flowing gently over their heads.
NOVALIS, HEINRICH VON OFTERDINGEN[1]

While these strange events were passing through my mind, I suddenly, as one awakes to the consciousness that the sea has been moaning by him for hours, or that the storm has been howling about his window all night, became aware of the sound of running water near me; and looking out of bed, I saw that a large green marble basin, in which I was wont to wash, and which stood on a low pedestal of the same material in a corner of my room, was overflowing like a spring; and that a stream of clear water was running over the carpet, all the length of the room, finding its outlet I knew not where. And, stranger still, where this carpet, which I had myself designed to imitate a field of grass and daisies, bordered the course of the little stream, the grass-blades and daisies seemed to wave in a tiny breeze that followed the water's flow; while under the rivulet they bent and swayed with every motion of the changeful current, as if they were about to dissolve with it, and, forsaking their fixed form, become fluent as the waters.

---

1 "'Wo ist der Strom?" rief er mit Thränen. "Siehst du nicht seine blauen Wellen über uns?" Er sah hinauf, und der blaue Strom floss leise über ihrem Haupte.' This comes from a point in the novel, *Heinrich von Ofterdingen*, where Heinrich dreams that he is struggling to save his beloved Matilda, whose boat has capsized and who has been sucked into a blue whirlpool. Heinrich loses consciousness; when he wakes he finds himself in a strange country where the flowers and trees can talk. In the novel Heinrich wakes from his dream before we hear them speak; in *Phantastes*, MacDonald will show their talk.

*The branches
and leaves on the
curtain of my bed
were in motion*

My dressing-table was an old-fashioned piece of furniture of
black oak, with drawers all down the front. These were elaborately
carved in foliage, of which ivy formed the chief part. The nearer
end of this table remained just as it had been, but on the further
end a singular change had commenced. I happened to fix my eye
on a little cluster of ivy-leaves. The first of these was evidently the
work of the carver; the next looked curious; the third was unmis-
takable ivy; and just beyond it a tendril of clematis had twined

itself about the gilt handle of one of the drawers.[2] Hearing next a slight motion above me, I looked up, and saw that the branches and leaves designed upon the curtains of my bed were slightly in motion. Not knowing what change might follow next, I thought it high time to get up; and, springing from the bed, my bare feet alighted upon a cool green sward; and although I dressed in all haste, I found myself completing my toilet under the boughs of a great tree, whose top waved in the golden stream of the sunrise with many interchanging lights, and with shadows of leaf and branch gliding over leaf and branch, as the cool morning wind swung it to and fro, like a sinking sea-wave.

After washing as well as I could in the clear stream, I rose and looked around me. The tree under which I seemed to have lain all night was one of the advanced guard of a dense forest, towards which the rivulet ran. Faint traces of a footpath, much overgrown with grass and moss, and with here and there a pimpernel even, were discernible along the right bank. 'This,' thought I, 'must surely be the path into Fairy Land, which the lady of last night promised I should so soon find.' I crossed the rivulet, and accompanied it, keeping the footpath on its right bank, until it led me, as I expected, into the wood. Here I left it, without any good reason, and with a vague feeling that I ought to have followed its course: I took a more southerly direction.[3]

---

2 Anodos does not so much enter Fairy Land as find himself surrounded by it. The decorations of his chamber – some of which he has designed – have come to life. MacDonald uses a similar transformation in 'Cross Purposes', where the girl, Alice, shrinks to find that the tufts on her bedspread have turned into bushes and heather. (MacDonald, 'Cross Purposes', *Dealings with the Fairies*)

3 'The water itself, that dances and sings, and slakes the wonderful thirst... this live thing which, if I might I would have running through my room, yea babbling along my table – this water is its own self, its own truth, and is therein a truth of God.' (MacDonald *Unspoken Sermons III*, 'The Truth'.) In *Phantastes*, water is a positive force. It leads Anodos into Fairy Land, gives him the power of song, leads him to the Fairy Palace and the house of the Old Woman, revives and purifies him and even comforts him in the midst of despair. MacDonald may have had in mind the biblical image of the water of life (e.g. Rev 22.1: 'And he shewed me a pure river of water of life, clear as crystal, proceeding out of the throne of God and of the Lamb.')

—*3*—

Man doth usurp all space,
Stares thee, in rock, bush, river, in the face.
Never thine eyes behold a tree;
'Tis no sea thou seést in the sea,
'Tis but a disguised humanity.
To avoid thy fellow, vain thy plan;
All that interests a man, is man.

HENRY SUTTON[1]

The trees, which were far apart where I entered, giving free passage to the level rays of the sun, closed rapidly as I advanced, so that ere long their crowded stems barred the sunlight out, forming as it were a thick grating between me and the East. I seemed to be advancing towards a second midnight. In the midst of the intervening twilight, however, before I entered what appeared to be the darkest portion of the forest, I saw a country maiden coming towards me from its very depths. She did not seem to observe me, for she was apparently intent upon a bunch of wild flowers which she carried in her hand. I could hardly see her face; for, though she came direct towards me, she never looked up. But when we met, instead of passing, she turned and walked alongside of me for a few yards, still keeping her face downwards, and busied with her flowers. She spoke rapidly, however, all the time, in a low tone, as if talking to herself, but evidently addressing the purport

---

1   Henry Sutton (1825–1901) was a poet and journalist who was heavily influenced by the mysticism of Swedenborg. His poetry was hugely admired in his time, but he is now largely forgotten. He attended services led by MacDonald when MacDonald was living and preaching in Manchester, between February 1854 and June 1855.

of her words to me. She seemed afraid
of being observed by some lurking foe.
'Trust the Oak,' said she; 'trust the Oak, and
the Elm, and the great Beech.[2] Take care of the
Birch, for though she is honest, she is too young
not to be changeable. But shun the Ash and the
Alder; for the Ash is an ogre – you will know

I saw a country maiden coming towards me

him by his thick fingers; and the Alder will smother you with her
web of hair, if you let her near you at night.' All this was uttered
without pause or alteration of tone. Then she turned suddenly and
left me, walking still with the same unchanging gait. I could not
conjecture what she meant, but satisfied myself with thinking that it
would be time enough to find out her meaning when there was need
to make use of her warning; and that the occasion would reveal the
admonition. I concluded from the flowers that she carried, that the
forest could not be everywhere so dense as it appeared from where I
was now walking; and I was right in this conclusion. For soon I came
to a more open part, and by and by crossed a wide grassy glade,

2   Throughout *Phantastes* trees have symbolic meanings. Anodos will meet the Beech, Alder and
    Ash. The cottage where the maiden lives is bounded by four great oaks – symbol of sturdy
    trustworthiness. See p.52, p.57.

on which were several circles of brighter green. But even here I was struck with the utter stillness. No bird sang. No insect hummed. Not a living creature crossed my way. Yet somehow the whole environment seemed only asleep, and to wear even in sleep an air of expectation. The trees seemed all to have an expression of conscious mystery, as if they said to themselves, 'We could, an' if we would.'[3] They had all a meaning look about them. Then I remembered that night is the fairies' day, and the moon their sun; and I thought – Everything sleeps and dreams now: when the night comes, it will be different. At the same time I, being a man and a child of the day, felt some anxiety as to how I should fare among the elves and other children of the night who wake when mortals dream, and find their common life in those wondrous hours that flow noiselessly over the moveless death-like forms of men and women and children, lying strewn and parted beneath the weight of the heavy waves of night, which flow on and beat them down, and hold them drowned and senseless, until the ebbtide comes, and the waves sink away, back into the ocean of the dark. But I took courage and went on. Soon, however, I became again anxious, though from another cause. I had eaten nothing that day, and for an hour past had been feeling the want of food. So I grew afraid lest I should find nothing to meet my human necessities in this strange place; but once more I comforted myself with hope and went on.

Before noon, I fancied I saw a thin blue smoke rising amongst the stems of larger trees in front of me; and soon I came to an open spot of ground in which stood a little cottage, so built that the stems of four great trees formed its corners, while their branches met and intertwined over its roof, heaping a great cloud of leaves over it, up towards the heavens. I wondered at finding a human dwelling in this neighbourhood; and yet it did not look altogether human, though sufficiently so to encourage me to expect some sort of food. Seeing

3 *We could an' if we would*: We could if we desired. From Shakespeare. *Hamlet*, Act 1, Scene 5, l.184.

no door, I went round to the other side, and there I found one, wide open. A woman sat beside it, preparing some vegetables for dinner. This was homely and comforting. As I came near, she looked up, and seeing me, showed no surprise, but bent her head again over her work, and said in a low tone:

'Did you see my daughter?'

'I believe I did,' said I. 'Can you give me something to eat, for I am very hungry?'

'With pleasure,' she replied, in the same tone; 'but do not say anything more, till you come into the house, for the Ash is watching us.'

Having said this, she rose and led the way into the cottage; which, I now saw, was built of the stems of small trees set closely together, and was furnished with rough chairs and tables, from which even the bark had not been removed. As soon as she had shut the door and set a chair:

'You have fairy blood in you,' said she, looking hard at me.

'How do you know that?'

'You could not have got so far into this wood if it were not so; and I am trying to find out some trace of it in your countenance. I think I see it.'

'What do you see?'

'Oh, never mind: I may be mistaken in that.'

'But how then do you come to live here?'

'Because I too have fairy-blood in me.'

Here I, in my turn, looked hard at her; and thought I could perceive, notwithstanding the coarseness of her features, and especially the heaviness of her eyebrows, a something unusual – I could hardly call it grace, and yet it was an expression that strangely contrasted with the form of her features. I noticed too that her hands were delicately formed, though brown with work and exposure.

'I should be ill,' she continued, 'if I did not live on the borders of the fairies' country, and now and then eat of their food. And I see by your eyes that you are not quite free of the same need; though, from your education and the activity of your mind, you have felt it less than I. You may be further removed too from the fairy race.'

I remembered what the lady had said about my grandmothers.

Here she placed some bread and some milk before me, with a kindly apology for the homeliness of the fare, with which, however, I was in no humour to quarrel. I now thought it time to try to get some explanation of the strange words both of her daughter and herself.

'What did you mean by speaking so about the Ash?'

She rose and looked out of the little window. My eyes followed her; but as the window was too small to allow anything to be seen from where I was sitting, I rose and looked over her shoulder. I had just time to see, across the open space, on the edge of the denser forest, a single large ash-tree, whose foliage showed bluish, amidst the truer green of the other trees around it; when she pushed me back with an expression of impatience and terror, and then almost shut out the light from the window by setting up a large old book in it.

'In general,' said she, recovering her composure, 'there is no danger in the daytime, for then he is sound asleep; but there is something unusual going on in the woods; there must be some solemnity among the fairies to-night, for all the trees are restless, and although they cannot come awake, they see and hear in their sleep.'

'But what danger is to be dreaded from him?'

Instead of answering the question, she went again to the window and looked out, saying she feared the fairies would be interrupted by foul weather, for a storm was brewing in the west.

'And the sooner it grows dark, the sooner the Ash will be awake,' added she.

I asked her how she knew that there was any unusual excitement in the woods. She replied:

'Besides the look of the trees, the dog there is unhappy; and the eyes and ears of the white rabbit are redder than usual, and he frisks about as if he expected some fun. If the cat were at home, she would have her back up; for the young fairies pull the sparks out of her tail with bramble thorns, and she knows when they are coming. So do I, in another way.'

At this instant, a grey cat rushed in like a demon, and disappeared in a hole in the wall.

'There, I told you!' said the woman.

'But what of the ash-tree?' said I, returning once more to the subject. Here, however, the young woman, whom I had met in the morning, entered. A smile passed between the mother and daughter; and then the latter began to help her mother in little household duties.

'I should like to stay here till the evening,' I said; 'and then go on my journey, if you will allow me.'

'You are welcome to do as you please; only it might be better to stay all night, than risk the dangers of the wood then. Where are you going?'

'Nay, that I do not know,' I replied; 'but I wish to see all that is to be seen, and therefore I should like to start just at sundown.'

'You are a bold youth, if you have any idea of what you are daring; but a rash one, if you know nothing about it; and, excuse me, you do not seem very well informed about the country and its manners. However, no one comes here but for some reason, either known to himself or to those who have charge of him; so you shall do just as you wish.'

Accordingly I sat down, and feeling rather tired, and disinclined for further talk, I asked leave to look at the old book which still screened the window. The woman brought it to me directly, but not before taking another look towards the forest, and then drawing a white blind over the window. I sat down opposite to it by the table, on which I laid the great old volume, and read. It contained many

wondrous tales of Fairy Land, and olden times, and the Knights
of King Arthur's table. I read on and on, till the shades of the afternoon began to deepen; for in the midst of the forest it gloomed
earlier than in the open country. At length I came to this passage –

> 'Here it chanced, that upon their quest, Sir Galahad and Sir Per-
> civale rencountered in the depths of a great forest.[4] Now, Sir Gala-
> had was dight all in harness of silver, clear and shining; the which
> is a delight to look upon, but full hasty to tarnish, and withouten
> the labour of a ready squire, uneath to be kept fair and clean.
> And yet withouten squire or page, Sir Galahad's armour shone
> like the moon. And he rode a great white mare, whose bases and
> other housings were black, but all besprent[5] with fair lilys of silver
> sheen. Whereas Sir Percivale bestrode a red horse, with a tawny
> mane and tail; whose trappings were all to-smirched with mud
> and mire; and his armour was wondrous rosty to behold, ne could
> he by any art furbish it again; so that as the sun in his going down
> shone twixt the bare trunks of the trees, full upon the knights
> twain, the one did seem all shining with light, and the other all
> to glow with ruddy fire. Now it came about in this wise. For Sir
> Percivale, after his escape from the demon lady, when as the cross
> on the handle of his sword smote him to the heart, and he rove
> himself through the thigh[6], and escaped away, he came to a great
> wood; and, in nowise cured of his fault, yet bemoaning the same,
> the damosel of the alder tree encountered him, right fair to see;
> and with her fair words and false countenance she comforted him
> and beguiled him, until he followed her where she led him to a –'

Here a low hurried cry from my hostess caused me to look up
from the book, and I read no more.

'Look there!' she said; 'look at his fingers!'

---

4 Galahad was the purest of the Knights of the Round Table; his natural purity makes his
 armour shine. Percivale accompanied Galahad on his quest for the Holy Grail.

5 *Besprent*: sprinkled with

6 *rove himself*: stabbed himself. This tale, told in the style of Malory, is a warning. Caxton's rubric
 to Malory's *Quest of the Holy Grail*, chapter 10, book 14 called this episode 'How Syr Percyval
 for penaunce roof [rove] hymself thorough the thyghe, and how she was knowen for the
 devyl.' The story tells of Percivale's attempted seduction by a mysterious woman. He is saved
 when the shape of the handle of his sword reminds him of the cross, but he conquers his
 desire, by stabbing himself in the thigh. The 'gentilwoman' of the tale turns out to be none
 other than 'the master fyende of helle'. (Malory, Sir Thomas, *The Works of Sir Thomas Malory*,
 P.J.C. Field, Eugene Vinaver (Ed.), (Oxford: Clarendon Press, 1990) II, p.903)

Just as I had been reading in the book, the setting sun was shining through a cleft in the clouds piled up in the west; and a shadow as of a large distorted hand, with thick knobs and humps on the fingers, so that it was much wider across the fingers than across the undivided part of the hand, passed slowly over the little blind, and then as slowly returned in the opposite direction.

'He is almost awake, mother; and greedier than usual to-night.'

'Hush, child; you need not make him more angry with us than he is; for you do not know how soon something may happen to oblige us to be in the forest after nightfall.'

'But you are in the forest,' said I; 'how is it that you are safe here?'

'He dares not come nearer than he is now,' she replied; 'for any of those four oaks, at the corners of our cottage, would tear him to pieces; they are our friends. But he stands there and makes awful faces at us sometimes, and stretches out his long arms and fingers, and tries to kill us with fright; for, indeed, that is his favourite way of doing. Pray, keep out of his way to-night.'

'Shall I be able to see these things?' said I.

'That I cannot tell yet, not knowing how much of the fairy nature there is in you. But we shall soon see whether you can discern the fairies in my little garden, and that will be some guide to us.'

'Are the trees fairies too, as well as the flowers?' I asked.

'They are of the same race,' she replied; 'though those you call fairies in your country are chiefly the young children of the flower fairies. They are very fond of having fun with the thick people, as they call you; for, like most children, they like fun better than anything else.'

'Why do you have flowers so near you then? Do they not annoy you?'

'Oh, no, they are very amusing, with their mimicries of grown people, and mock solemnities. Sometimes they will act a whole play through before my eyes, with perfect composure and assurance, for they are not afraid of me. Only, as soon as they have done, they burst into peals of tiny laughter, as if it was such a joke to have been serious over anything. These I speak of, however, are the fairies of the garden. They are more staid and educated than those of the fields and woods. Of course they have near relations amongst the wild flowers, but they patronise them, and treat them as country cousins, who know nothing of life, and very little of manners. Now and then, however, they are compelled to envy the grace and simplicity of the natural flowers.'

'Do they live *in* the flowers?' I said.

'I cannot tell,' she replied. 'There is something in it I do not understand. Sometimes they disappear altogether, even from me, though I know they are near. They seem to die always with the flowers they resemble, and by whose names they are called; but whether they return to life with the fresh flowers, or, whether it be new flowers, new fairies, I cannot tell. They have as many sorts of dispositions as men and women, while their moods are yet more variable; twenty different expressions will cross their little faces in half a minute. I often amuse myself with watching them, but I have never been able to make personal acquaintance with any of them. If I speak to one, he or she looks up in my face, as if I were not worth heeding, gives a little laugh, and runs away.'

Here the woman started, as if suddenly recollecting herself, and said in a low voice to her daughter, 'Make haste – go and watch him, and see in what direction he goes.'

I may as well mention here, that the conclusion I arrived at from the observations I was afterwards able to make, was, that the flowers die because the fairies go away; not that the fairies disappear because the flowers die. The flowers seem a sort of houses for them, or outer bodies, which they can put on or off when they please. Just as you could form some idea of the nature of a man from the kind of house he built, if he followed his own taste, so you could, without seeing the fairies, tell what any one of them is like, by looking at the flower till you feel that you understand it. For just what the flower says to you, would the face and form of the fairy say; only so much more plainly as a face and human figure can express more than a flower. For the house or the clothes, though like the inhabitant or the wearer, cannot be wrought into an equal power of utterance. Yet you would see a strange resemblance, almost oneness, between the flower and the fairy, which you could not describe, but which described itself to you. Whether all the flowers have fairies, I cannot determine, any more than I can be sure whether all men and women have souls.[7]

The woman and I continued the conversation for a few minutes longer. I was much interested by the information she gave me, and astonished at the language in which she was able to convey it. It seemed that intercourse with the fairies was no bad education in itself. But now the daughter returned with the news, that the Ash had just gone away in a south-westerly direction; and, as my course seemed to lie eastward, she hoped I should be in no danger of meeting him if I departed at once.[8] I looked out of the little window, and there stood the ash-tree, to my eyes the same as before; but I believed that they knew better than I did, and prepared to go. I pulled out my purse, but to my dismay there was nothing in it. The woman with a smile begged me not to trouble myself, for money was not of the slightest use there; and as I might meet with people in my journeys whom I could not recognise to be fairies, it was well I had no money to offer, for nothing offended them so much.

'They would think,' she added, 'that you were making game of them; and that is their peculiar privilege with regard to us.' So we went together into the little garden which sloped down towards a lower part of the wood.

---

7 Each fairy seem to be some kind of anima or spirit inhabiting the flower. The comparison is drawn between the soul, which inhabits the body.

8 In Christian belief, east reflects the idea of Christ as the rising 'sun of righteousness'. Hence the orientation of churches on a west-east axis, with the altar at the eastern end.

Here, to my great pleasure, all was life and bustle. There was still light enough from the day to see a little; and the pale half-moon, halfway to the zenith, was reviving every moment

The whole garden was like a carnival, with tiny, gaily decorated forms, in groups, assemblies, processions, pairs or trios, moving stately on, running about wildly, or sauntering hither or thither. From the cups or bells of tall flowers, as from balconies, some looked down on the masses below, now bursting with laughter, now grave as owls; but even in their deepest solemnity, seeming only to be waiting for the arrival of the next laugh. Some were launched on a little marshy stream at the bottom, in boats chosen from the heaps of last year's leaves that lay about, curled and withered. These soon sank with them; whereupon they swam ashore and got others. Those who took fresh rose-leaves for their boats floated the longest; but for these they had to fight; for the fairy of the rose-tree complained bitterly that they were stealing her clothes, and defended her property bravely.

'You can't wear half you've got,' said some.

'Never you mind; I don't choose you to have them: they are my property.'

'All for the good of the community!' said one, and ran off with a great hollow leaf. But the rose-fairy sprang after him (what a beauty she was! only too like a drawing-room young lady), knocked him heels-over-head as he ran, and recovered her great red leaf. But in the meantime twenty had hurried off in different directions with others just as good; and the little creature sat down and cried, and then, in a pet, sent a perfect pink snowstorm of petals from her tree, leaping from branch to branch, and stamping and shaking and pulling. At last, after another good cry, she chose the biggest she could find, and ran away laughing, to launch her boat amongst the rest.

But my attention was first and chiefly attracted by a group of fairies near the cottage, who were talking together around what seemed a last dying primrose. They talked singing, and their talk made a song, something like this:

'Sister Snowdrop died
    Before we were born.'[9]
'She came like a bride
    In a snowy morn.'
'What's a bride?'
    'What is snow?'
'Never tried.'
    'Do not know.'

'Who told you about her?'
    'Little Primrose there
Cannot do without her.'
    'Oh, so sweetly fair!'
'Never fear,
    She will come,
Primrose dear.'
    'Is she dumb?'

'She'll come by-and-by.'
    'You will never see her.'
'She went home to die,
    Till the new year.'
'Snowdrop!' ' 'Tis no good
    To invite her.'
'Primrose is very rude,
    'I will bite her.'

'Oh, you naughty Pocket!
    'Look, she drops her head.'
'She deserved it, Rocket,
    'And she was nearly dead.'

9 Snowdrop was the name of a kitten belonging to Mary, MacDonald's second daughter. Lewis Carroll used it as the name of the kitten in *Alice Through the Looking Glass*. See Carroll, Lewis and Martin Gardner, *The Annotated Alice: Alice's Adventures in Wonderland; and, Through the Looking Glass*, (Rev. ed., London: Penguin, 1970) p.178. It was a flower which MacDonald often used as a symbol. He wrote: 'Because of our needs and aspirations, the snowdrop gives birth in our hearts to a loftier spiritual and poetic feeling than the rose, most complete in form, colour and odour. The rose is Paradise – the snowdrop is of the striving, hoping, longing Earth.' (MacDonald, *Orts*, 'Forms of Literature'.) MacDonald was later to revisit the idea of the death of plants, in the parable of the snowdrop and the rose, in *David Elginbrod*. In that story, the snowdrop is plucked by an invalid girl, upon which 'it trembled and died in her hand, which was a heavenly death for a snowdrop...' (MacDonald, *David Elginbrod*, ch. 4)

> *'To your hammock — off with you!'*
> *'And swing alone.'*
> *'No one will laugh with you.'*
> *'No, not one.'*
>
> *'Now let us moan.'*
> *'And cover her o'er.'*
> *'Primrose is gone.'*
> *'All but the flower.'*
> *'Here is a leaf.'*
> *'Lay her upon it.'*
> *'Follow in grief.'*
> *'Pocket has done it.'*
>
> *'Deeper, poor creature!*
> *Winter may come.'*
> *'He cannot reach her —*
> *That is a hum.'*[10]
> *'She is buried, the beauty!'*
> *'Now she is done.'*
> *'That was the duty.'*
> *'Now for the fun.'*

And with a wild laugh they sprang away, most of them towards the cottage. During the latter part of the song-talk, they had formed themselves into a funeral procession, two of them bearing poor Primrose, whose death Pocket had hastened by biting her stalk, upon one of her own great leaves. They bore her solemnly along some distance, and then buried her under a tree. Although I say her I saw nothing but the withered primrose-flower on its long stalk. Pocket, who had been expelled from the company by common consent, went sulkily away towards her hammock, for she was the fairy of the calceolaria, and looked rather wicked.[11] When she reached its stem, she stopped and looked round. I could not help speaking to her, for I stood near her. I said, 'Pocket, how could you be so naughty?'

---

10 *Hum*: imposition or hoax, short for 'humbug'.

11 *Calceolaria*: also called Lady's Slipper, Slipper flower, Slipperwort, Pouch Flower and Pocket-book plant; hence the name of the fairy who inhabits it: Pocket.

'I am never naughty,' she said, half-crossly, half-defiantly; 'only if you come near my hammock, I will bite you, and then you will go away.'

'Why did you bite poor Primrose?'

'Because she said we should never see Snowdrop; as if we were not good enough to look at her, and she was, the proud thing! – served her right!'

'Oh, Pocket, Pocket,' said I; but by this time the party which had gone towards the house, rushed out again, shouting and screaming with laughter. Half of them were on the cat's back, and half held on by her fur and tail, or ran beside her; till, more coming to their help, the furious cat was held fast; and they proceeded to pick the sparks out of her with thorns and pins, which they handled like harpoons. Indeed, there were more instruments at work about her than there could have been sparks in her. One little fellow who held on hard by the tip of the tail, with his feet planted on the ground at an angle of forty-five degrees, helping to keep her fast, administered a continuous flow of admonitions to Pussy.

'Now, Pussy, be patient. You know quite well it is all for your good. You cannot be comfortable with all those sparks in you; and, indeed, I am charitably disposed to believe' (here he became very pompous) 'that they are the cause of all your bad temper; so we must have them all out, every one; else we shall be reduced to the painful necessity of cutting your claws, and pulling out your eye-teeth. Quiet! Pussy, quiet!'

But with a perfect hurricane of feline curses, the poor animal broke loose, and dashed across the garden and through the hedge, faster than even the fairies could follow. 'Never mind, never mind, we shall find her again; and by that time she will have laid in a fresh stock of sparks. Hooray!' And off they set, after some new mischief.

But I will not linger to enlarge on the amusing display of these frolicsome creatures. Their manners and habits are now so well known to the world, having been so often described by eyewitnesses, that it would be only indulging self-conceit, to add my account in full to the rest.[12] I cannot help wishing, however, that my readers could see them for themselves. Especially do I desire that they should see the fairy of the daisy; a little, chubby, round-eyed child, with such innocent trust in his look! Even the most mischievous of the fairies would not tease him, although he did not belong to their set at all, but was quite a little country bumpkin. He wandered about alone, and looked at everything, with his hands in his little pockets, and a white night-cap on, the darling! He was not so beautiful as many other wild flowers I saw afterwards, but so dear and loving in his looks and little confident ways.

The fairy of the daisy

12 The Victorian fairy painting flowered (to coin a phrase) between 1840 and 1870. The interest may have stemmed from the Shakespearian revival, with elaborate productions of *A Midsummer Night's Dream*, a new interest in folklore (a term that was first used in 1846) and the publication of fairy tale collections from Germany and France – not to mention a reaction against industrialisation and increased mechanisation. Whatever the cause, the Fairy Painting became a recognised genre piece. Sir Edwin Landseer's *Scene from a Midsummer Night's Dream* (1848–57) was exhibited at the Royal Academy in 1851. It featured cherubic fairies and a white rabbit with red eyes – see p.79. (Maas, Jeremy, *Victorian Fairy Painting*, (London: Merrell Holberton, 1997, pp.87–88.)

—4—

'When bale is att hyest, boote is nyest.'

BALLAD OF SIR ALDINGAR.[1]

B y this time, my hostess was quite anxious that I should be
gone. So, with warm thanks for their hospitality, I took my
leave, and went my way through the little garden towards the
forest. Some of the garden flowers had wandered into the wood,
and were growing here and there along the path, but the trees soon
became too thick and shadowy for them. I particularly noticed
some tall lilies, which grew on both sides of the way, with large
dazzlingly white flowers, set off by the universal green. It was now
dark enough for me to see that every flower was shining with a light
of its own. Indeed it was by this light that I saw them, an inter-
nal, peculiar light, proceeding from each, and not reflected from a
common source of light as in the daytime. This light sufficed only
for the plant itself, and was not strong enough to cast any but the
faintest shadows around it, or to illuminate any of the neighbouring objects with other than the faintest tinge of its own individual

---

1 *When bale is att hyest, boote is nyest:* When evil is greatest, help is nearest. This traditional ballad
   was later included by Francis James Child in his *English and Scottish Popular Ballads.* The ballad recounts how Sir Aldingar slanders his mistress, Queen Eleanor, who is miraculously defended
   by her champion – a four-year-old child.

hue. From the lilies above mentioned, from the campanulas, from the foxgloves, and every bell-shaped flower, curious little figures shot up their heads, peeped at me, and drew back. They seemed to inhabit them, as snails their shells but I was sure some of them were intruders, and belonged to the gnomes or goblin-fairies, who inhabit the ground and earthy creeping plants. From the cups of Arum lilies, creatures with great heads and grotesque faces shot up like Jack-in-the-box, and made grimaces at me; or rose slowly and slily over the edge of the cup, and spouted water at me, slipping suddenly back, like those little soldier-crabs that inhabit the shells of sea-snails. Passing a row of tall thistles, I saw them crowded with little faces, which peeped every one from behind its flower, and drew back as quickly; and I heard them saying to each other, evidently intending me to hear, but the speaker always hiding behind his tuft, when I looked in his direction, 'Look at him! Look at him! He has begun a story without a beginning, and it will never have any end. He! he! he! Look at him!'[2]

But as I went further into the wood, these sights and sounds became fewer, giving way to others of a different character. A little forest of wild hyacinths was alive with exquisite creatures, who stood nearly motionless, with drooping necks, holding each by the stem of her flower, and swaying gently with it, whenever a low breath of wind swung the crowded floral belfry. In like manner, though differing of course in form and meaning, stood a group of harebells, like little angels waiting, ready, till they were wanted to go on some yet unknown message. In darker nooks, by the mossy roots of the trees, or in little tufts of grass, each dwelling in a globe of its own green light, weaving a network of grass and its shadows, glowed the glowworms. They were just like the glowworms of our own land, for they are fairies everywhere; worms in the day, and glowworms at night, when their own can appear, and they can be themselves

---

2 Anodos is unaware that he is inhabiting his own story.

to others as well as themselves.[3] But they had their enemies here. For I saw great strong-armed beetles, hurrying about with most unwieldy haste, awkward as elephant-calves, looking apparently for glowworms; for the moment a beetle espied one, through what to it was a forest of grass, or an underwood of moss, it pounced upon it, and bore it away, in spite of its feeble resistance. Wondering what their object could be, I watched one of the beetles, and then I discovered a thing I could not account for. But it is no use trying to account for things in Fairy Land; and one who travels there soon learns to forget the very idea of doing so, and takes everything as it comes; like a child, who, being in a chronic condition of wonder, is surprised at nothing.[4] What I saw was this. Everywhere, here and there over the ground, lay little, dark-looking lumps of something more like earth than anything else, and about the size of a chestnut. The beetles hunted in couples for these; and having found one, one of them stayed to watch it, while the other hurried to find a glow-worm. By signals, I presume, between them, the latter soon found his companion again: they then took the glowworm and held its luminous tail to the dark earthly pellet; when lo, it shot up into the air like a sky-rocket, seldom, however, reaching the height of the highest tree. Just like a rocket too, it burst in the air, and fell in a shower of the most gorgeously coloured sparks of every variety of hue; golden and red, and purple and green, and blue and rosy fires crossed and inter-crossed each other, beneath the shadowy heads, and between the columnar stems of the forest trees. They never used the same glowworm twice, I observed; but let him go, apparently uninjured by the use they had made of him.[5]

In other parts, the whole of the immediately surrounding foliage was illuminated by the interwoven dances in the air of splendidly

---

3 'God makes the glow-worm as well as the star; the light in both is divine.' (MacDonald, *Orts*, 'Essays on Some of the Forms of Literature')

4 Fairy Land has its own rules, its own laws. See Appendix 2, p.276.

5 This image is based on the Egyptian dung-beetle God *Kephri*, who, each night, pushes the sun underground from west to east, and, each morning, propels it into the sky like a rocket.

coloured fire-flies, which sped hither and thither, turned, twisted, crossed, and recrossed, entwining every complexity of intervolved motion. Here and there, whole mighty trees glowed with an emitted phosphorescent light. You could trace the very course of the great roots in the earth by the faint light that came through; and every twig, and every vein on every leaf was a streak of pale fire.

All this time, as I went through the wood, I was haunted with the feeling that other shapes, more like my own size and mien, were moving about at a little distance on all sides of me. But as yet I could discern none of them, although the moon was high enough to send a great many of her rays down between the trees, and these rays were unusually bright, and sight-giving, notwithstanding she was only a half-moon.[6] I constantly imagined, however, that forms were visible in all directions except that to which my gaze was turned; and that they only became invisible, or resolved themselves into other woodland shapes, the moment my looks were directed towards them. However this may have been, except for this feeling of presence, the woods seemed utterly bare of anything like human companionship, although my glance often fell on some object which I fancied to be a human form; for I soon found that I was quite deceived; as, the moment I fixed my regard on it, it showed plainly that it was a bush, or a tree, or a rock.

Soon a vague sense of discomfort possessed me. With variations of relief, this gradually increased; as if some evil thing were wandering about in my neighbourhood, sometimes nearer and sometimes further off, but still approaching. The feeling continued and

6   The moon is a benificent power in MacDonald's work, reflecting the much more powerful light of the Sun. MacDonald used this image elsewhere for that through which we can see the light of God. "'The face o' God's like the sun, as ye hae tellt me; for no man cud see him and live.'"... "But the mune," continued Annie, disregarding Tibbie's interruption, "maun be like the face o' Christ, for it gies licht and ye can luik at it notwithstandin'. The mune's jist like the sun wi' the ower-muckle taen oot o' 't.'" (MacDonald, *Alec Forbes*, ch.55.). 'Till we thus know Him, let us hold the Bible dear as the moon of our darkness, by which we travel towards the east; not dear as the sun whence her light cometh, and towards which we haste, that, walking in the sun himself, we may no more need the mirror that reflected his absent brightness.' (MacDonald, *Unspoken Sermons* I, 'The Higher Truth'.)

deepened, until all my pleasure in the shows of various kinds that everywhere betokened the presence of the merry fairies vanished by degrees, and left me full of anxiety and fear, which I was unable to associate with any definite object whatever. At length the thought crossed my mind with horror: 'Can it be possible that the Ash is looking for me? or that, in his nightly wanderings, his path is gradually verging towards mine?' I comforted myself, however, by remembering that he had started quite in another direction; one that would lead him, if he kept it, far apart from me; especially as, for the last two or three hours, I had been diligently journeying eastward. I kept on my way, therefore, striving by direct effort of the will against the encroaching fear; and to this end occupying my mind, as much as I could, with other thoughts. I was so far successful that, although I was conscious, if I yielded for a moment, I should be almost overwhelmed with horror, I was yet able to walk right on for an hour or more. What I feared I could not tell. Indeed, I was left in a state of the vaguest uncertainty as regarded the nature of my enemy, and knew not the mode or object of his attacks; for, somehow or other, none of my questions had succeeded in drawing a definite answer from the dame in the cottage. How then to defend myself I knew not; nor even by what sign I might with certainty recognise the presence of my foe; for as yet this vague though powerful fear was all the indication of danger I had. To add to my distress, the clouds in the west had risen nearly to the top of the skies, and they and the moon were travelling slowly towards each other. Indeed, some of their advanced guard had already met her, and she had begun to wade through a filmy vapour that gradually deepened. At length she was for a moment almost entirely obscured. When she shone out again, with a brilliancy increased by the contrast, I saw plainly on the path before me – from around which at this spot the trees receded, leaving a small space of green sward – the shadow of a large hand, with knotty joints and protuberances here and there. Especially I remarked, even in the midst of my fear, the bulbous points of the fingers. I looked hurriedly all around, but could see nothing from which such a shadow should fall. Now, however, that I had a direction, however undetermined, in which to project my apprehension, the very sense of danger and need of action over-came that stifling which is the worst property of fear. I reflected in a moment, that if this were indeed a shadow, it was useless to look for the object that cast it in any other direction than between the shadow and the moon. I looked, and peered, and intensified my vision, all to no purpose. I could see nothing of that kind, not even an ash-tree in the neighbourhood. Still the shadow remained; not steady, but moving to and fro, and once I saw the fingers close, and grind themselves close, like the claws of a wild animal, as if in uncontrollable longing for some anticipated prey.[7] There seemed but one mode left of discovering the substance of this shadow. I went forward boldly, though with an inward shudder which I would not heed, to the spot where the shadow lay, threw myself on the ground, laid my head within the form of the hand, and turned my eyes towards the moon Good heavens! what did I see? I wonder that ever I arose, and that the very shadow of the hand did not hold me where I lay until fear had frozen my brain. I saw the strangest figure; vague, shadowy, almost transparent, in the central parts, and gradu-ally deepening in substance towards the outside, until it ended in extremities capable of casting such a shadow as fell from the hand, through the awful fingers of which I now saw the moon. The hand was uplifted in the attitude of a paw about to strike its prey. But the face, which throbbed with fluctuating and pulsatory visibility – not from changes in the light it reflected, but from changes in its own conditions of reflecting power, the alterations being from within, not from without – it was horrible. I do not know how to describe it. It caused a new sensation. Just as one cannot translate a horrible odour, or a ghastly pain, or a fearful sound, into words, so

---

7 It is the Ash-tree's shadow which is the danger. At the cottage, the girl said the Ash had 'gone away in a south-westerly direction', yet Anodos saw the tree still standing there (see p.59).

I cannot describe this new form of awful hideousness. I can only try to describe something that is not it, but seems somewhat parallel to it; or at least is suggested by it. It reminded me of what I had heard of vampires; for the face resembled that of a corpse more than anything else I can think of; especially when I can conceive such a face in motion, but not suggesting any life as the source of the motion.[8] The features were rather handsome than otherwise, except the mouth, which had scarcely a curve in it. The lips were of equal thickness; but the thickness was not at all remarkable, even although they looked slightly swollen. They seemed fixedly open, but were not wide apart. Of course I did not remark these lineaments at the time: I was too horrified for that. I noted them afterwards, when the form returned on my inward sight with a vividness too intense to admit of my doubting the accuracy of the reflex. But the most awful of the features were the eyes. These were alive, yet not with life. They seemed lighted up with an infinite greed. A gnawing voracity, which devoured the devourer, seemed to be the indwelling and propelling power of the whole ghostly apparition. I lay for a few moments simply imbruted with terror; when another cloud, obscuring the moon, delivered me from the immediately paralysing effects of the presence to the vision of the object of horror, while it added the force of imagination to the power of fear within me; inasmuch as, knowing far worse cause for apprehension than before, I remained equally ignorant from what I had to defend myself, or how to take any precautions: he might be upon me in the darkness any moment. I sprang to my feet, and sped I knew not whither, only away from

8   Vampires in mid-Victorian times were not the suave, charismatic count Dracula – which was not written till 1897 – but 'cannabalistically inclined reanimated corpses', more like the zombies of modern horror films. (See Clute, John and John Grant, *The Encyclopedia of Fantasy*, (London: Orbit, 1999) p.980.) There had been a rash of 'vampire sightings' in Eastern Europe in the 18th century. Voltaire described in his *Philosophical Dictionary* 'These vampires were corpses who went out of their graves at night to suck the blood of the living...' MacDonald revisited the fear around vampires in his short story 'The Cruel Painter', where he described vampires as 'a body retaining a kind of animal life after the soul had departed.' (MacDonald, 'The Cruel Painter' in *Adela Cathcart*, Book III, ch.6, also *The Portent and Other Stories*.)

the spectre. I thought no longer of the path, and often narrowly es-
caped dashing myself against a tree, in my headlong flight of fear.

Great drops of rain began to patter on the leaves. Thunder began to mutter, then growl in the distance. I ran on. The rain fell
heavier. At length the thick leaves could hold it up no longer; and,
like a second firmament, they poured their torrents on the earth. I
was soon drenched, but that was nothing. I came to a small swollen
stream that rushed through the woods. I had a vague hope that if
I crossed this stream, I should be in safety from my pursuer; but
I soon found that my hope was as false as it was vague. I dashed
across the stream, ascended a rising ground, and reached a more
open space, where stood only great trees. Through them I directed
my way, holding eastward as nearly as I could guess, but not at all
certain that I was not moving in an opposite direction. My mind
was just reviving a little from its extreme terror, when, suddenly, a
flash of lightning, or rather a cataract of successive flashes, behind
me, seemed to throw on the ground in front of me, but far more
faintly than before, from the extent of the source of the light, the
shadow of the same horrible hand. I sprang forward, stung to yet
wilder speed; but had not run many steps before my foot slipped,
and, vainly attempting to recover myself, I fell at the foot of one of
the large trees. Half-stunned, I yet raised myself, and almost involuntarily looked back. All I saw was the hand within three feet of
my face. But, at the same moment, I felt two large soft arms thrown
round me from behind; and a voice like a woman's said: 'Do not
fear the goblin; he dares not hurt you now.' With that, the hand was
suddenly withdrawn as from a fire, and disappeared in the darkness
and the rain. Overcome with the mingling of terror and joy, I lay
for some time almost insensible. The first thing I remember is the
sound of a voice above me, full and low, and strangely reminding
me of the sound of a gentle wind amidst the leaves of a great tree.
It murmured over and over again: 'I may love him, I may love him;
for he is a man, and I am only a beech-tree.' I found I was seated on

*'I felt two large soft arms thrown round
me from behind...'*

the ground, leaning against a human form, and supported still by
the arms around me, which I knew to be those of a woman who
must be rather above the human size, and largely proportioned. I

turned my head, but without moving otherwise, for I feared lest the arms should untwine themselves; and clear, somewhat mournful eyes met mine. At least that is how they impressed me; but I could see very little of colour or outline as we sat in the dark and rainy shadow of the tree. The face seemed very lovely, and solemn from its stillness; with the aspect of one who is quite content, but waiting for something. I saw my conjecture from her arms was correct: she was above the human scale throughout, but not greatly.

'Why do you call yourself a beech-tree?' I said.

'Because I am one,' she replied, in the same low, musical, murmuring voice.[9]

'You are a woman,' I returned.

'Do you think so? Am I very like a woman then?'

'You are a very beautiful woman. Is it possible you should not know it?'

'I am very glad you think so. I fancy I feel like a woman sometimes. I do so to-night – and always when the rain drips from my hair. For there is an old prophecy in our woods that one day we shall all be men and women like you. Do you know anything about it in your region? Shall I be very happy when I am a woman? I fear not, for it is always in nights like these that I feel like one. But I long to be a woman for all that.'

I had let her talk on, for her voice was like a solution of all musical sounds. I now told her that I could hardly say whether women were happy or not. I knew one who had not been happy; and for my part, I had often longed for Fairy Land, as she now longed for the world of men.[10] But then neither of us had lived long, and perhaps people grew happier as they grew older. Only I doubted it. I could

---

9 'The poets of old Greece saw beauteous shapes/Sighed forth from out the rooted, earth-fast trees...The large-limbed, sweepy-curved, smooth-rinded beech/Gave forth the perfect woman to the night;' (MacDonald, *Within and Without* Part IV, sc.3.) The Dryads of Ancient Greece were tree-spirits. Those associated with specific trees would die if the tree died.

10 'I knew one who had not been happy...' Perhaps the woman he avoids meeting in chapter 19 (see p.215)

not help sighing. She felt the sigh, for her arms were still round me. She asked me how old I was.

'Twenty-one,' said I.

'Why, you baby!' said she, and kissed me with the sweetest kiss of winds and odours. There was a cool faithfulness in the kiss that revived my heart wonderfully. I felt that I feared the dreadful Ash no more.

'What did the horrible Ash want with me?' I said.

'I am not quite sure, but I think he wants to bury you at the foot of his tree. But he shall not touch you, my child.'

'Are all the ash-trees as dreadful as he?'

'Oh, no. They are all disagreeable selfish creatures – (what horrid men they will make, if it be true!) – but this one has a hole in his heart that nobody knows of but one or two; and he is always trying to fill it up, but he cannot. That must be what he wanted you for. I wonder if he will ever be a man. If he is, I hope they will kill him.'

'How kind of you to save me from him!'

'I will take care that he shall not come near you again. But there are some in the wood more like me, from whom, alas! I cannot protect you. Only if you see any of them very beautiful, try to walk round them.'

'What then?'

'I cannot tell you more. But now I must tie some of my hair about you, and then the Ash will not touch you. Here, cut some off. You men have strange cutting things about you.'

She shook her long hair loose over me, never moving her arms.

'I cannot cut your beautiful hair. It would be a shame.'

'Not cut my hair! It will have grown long enough before any is wanted again in this wild forest. Perhaps it may never be of any use again – not till I am a woman.' And she sighed.

As gently as I could, I cut with a knife a long tress of flowing, dark hair, she hanging her beautiful head over me. When I had finished, she shuddered and breathed deep, as one does when an acute pain, steadfastly endured without sign of suffering, is at length relaxed. She then took the hair and tied it round me, singing a strange, sweet song, which I could not understand, but which left in me a feeling like this –

> *'I saw thee ne'er before;*
> *I see thee never more;*
> *But love, and help, and pain, beautiful one,*
> *Have made thee mine, till all my years are done.'*

I cannot put more of it into words. She closed her arms about me again, and went on singing. The rain in the leaves, and a light wind that had arisen, kept her song company. I was wrapt in a trance of still delight. It told me the secret of the woods, and the flowers, and the birds. At one time I felt as if I was wandering in childhood through sunny spring forests, over carpets of primroses, anemones, and little white starry things – I had almost said creatures, and finding new wonderful flowers at every turn. At another, I lay half dreaming in the hot summer noon, with a book of old tales beside me, beneath a great beech; or, in autumn, grew sad because I trod on the leaves that had sheltered me, and received their last blessing in the sweet odours of decay; or, in a winter evening, frozen still, looked up, as I went home to a warm fireside, through the netted boughs and twigs to the cold, snowy moon, with her opal zone around her. At last I had fallen asleep; for I know nothing more that passed till I found myself lying under a superb beech-tree, in the clear light of the morning, just before sunrise. Around me was a girdle of fresh beech-leaves. Alas! I brought nothing with me out of Fairy Land, but memories – memories. The great boughs of the beech hung drooping around me. At my head rose its smooth stem, with its great sweeps of curving surface that swelled like un-developed limbs. The leaves and branches above kept on the song which had sung me asleep; only now, to my mind, it sounded like a farewell and a speedwell. I sat a long time, unwilling to go; but my unfinished story urged me on.[11] I must act and wander. With the sun well risen, I rose, and put my arms as far as they would reach around the beech-tree, and kissed it, and said good-bye. A trembling went through the leaves; a few of the last drops of the night's rain fell from off them at my feet; and as I walked slowly away, I seemed to hear in a whisper once more the words: 'I may love him, I may love him; for he is a man, and I am only a beech-tree.'

11 See the goblins' chant on p.64.

— 5 —

'And she was smooth and full, as if one gush
Of life had washed her, or as if a sleep
Lay on her eyelid, easier to sweep
Than bee from daisy.'

BEDDOES' PYGMALION.[1]

'Sche was as whyt as lylye yn May,
Or snow that sneweth yn wynterys day.'

ROMANCE OF SIR LAUNFAL.[2]

I walked on, in the fresh morning air, as if new-born. The only thing that damped my pleasure was a cloud of something between sorrow and delight that crossed my mind with the frequently returning thought of my last night's hostess. 'But then,' thought I, 'if she is sorry, I could not help it; and she has all the pleasures she ever had. Such a day as this is surely a joy to her, as much at least as to me. And her life will perhaps be the richer, for holding now within it the memory of what came, but could not stay. And if ever she is a woman, who knows but we may meet somewhere? there is plenty of room for meeting in the universe.'

---

1 Thomas Beddoes (1803–1849) was a poet of something of a gloomy, macabre bent. Of his best-known work, *Death's Jest-Book* (published posthumously) Ian Jack writes 'there are few works which leave one in such uncertainty whether the author was a madman or a visionary.' (Jack, Ian, *English Literature 1815–1832*, Oxford, OUP, 1963, p.142.) Like MacDonald he studied science at University (later becoming a doctor) and was fascinated by German literature. Much of his later life was lived in Germany; he committed suicide in Basle in 1849.

2 An Arthurian romance, written by Thomas Chestre, dating from the late 14th century. The story how Sir Launfal is loved and aided by Tryamour, a powerful fairy-maiden on condition he keeps their relationship secret. These lines come from the point when Launfal descovers Tryamour in a sumptuous pavilion.

Comforting myself thus, yet with a vague compunction, as if I ought not to have left her, I went on. There was little to distinguish the woods to-day from those of my own land; except that all the wild things, rabbits, birds, squirrels, mice, and the numberless other inhabitants, were very tame; that is, they did not run away from me, but gazed at me as I passed, frequently coming nearer, as if to examine me more closely. Whether this came from utter ignorance, or from familiarity with the human appearance of beings who never hurt them, I could not tell. As I stood once, looking up to the splendid flower of a parasite, which hung from the branch of a tree over my head, a large white rabbit cantered slowly up, put one of its little feet on one of mine, and looked up at me with its red eyes, just as I had been looking up at the flower above me. I stooped and stroked it; but when I attempted to lift it, it banged the ground with its hind feet and scampered off at a great rate, turning, however, to look at me several times before I lost sight of it.[3] Now and then, too, a dim human figure would appear and disappear, at some distance, amongst the trees, moving like a sleep-walker. But no one ever came near me. This day I found plenty of food in the forest – strange nuts and fruits I had never seen before. I hesitated to eat them; but argued that, if I could live on the air of Fairy Land, I could live on its food also. I found my reasoning correct, and the result was better than I had hoped; for it not only satisfied my hunger, but operated in such a way upon my senses that I was brought into far more complete relationship with the things around me. The human forms appeared much more dense and defined; more tangibly visible, if I may say so. I seemed to know better which direction to choose when any doubt arose. I began to feel in some degree what the birds meant in their songs, though I could not express it in words, any more than you can some landscapes. At times, to my surprise, I found myself listening attentively, and as if it were

---

3 This is clearly a forerunner of the White Rabbit in Alice – written by MacDonald's close friend Lewis Carroll. See also p.55.

no unusual thing with me, to a conversation between two squirrels or monkeys. The subjects were not very interesting, except as associated with the individual life and necessities of the little creatures: where the best nuts were to be found in the neighbourhood, and who could crack them best, or who had most laid up for the winter, and such like; only they never said where the store was. There was no great difference in kind between their talk and our ordinary human conversation. Some of the creatures I never heard speak at all, and believe they never do so, except under the impulse of some great excitement. The mice talked; but the hedgehogs seemed very phlegmatic; and though I met a couple of moles above ground several times, they never said a word to each other in my hearing. There were no wild beasts in the forest; at least, I did not see one larger than a wild cat. There were plenty of snakes, however, and I do not think they were all harmless; but none ever bit me.

Soon after mid-day I arrived at a bare rocky hill, of no great size, but very steep; and having no trees — scarcely even a bush — upon it, entirely exposed to the heat of the sun. Over this my way seemed to lie, and I immediately began the ascent. On reaching the top, hot and weary, I looked around me, and saw that the forest still stretched as far as the sight could reach on every side of me. I observed that the trees, in the direction in which I was about to descend, did not come so near the foot of the hill as on the other side, and was especially regretting the unexpected postponement of shelter, because this side of the hill seemed more difficult to descend than the other had been to climb, when my eye caught the appearance of a natural path, winding down through broken rocks and along the course of a tiny stream, which I hoped would lead me more easily to the foot. I tried it, and found the descent not at all laborious; nevertheless, when I reached the bottom, I was very tired and exhausted with the heat. But just where the path seemed to end, rose a great rock, quite overgrown with shrubs and creeping plants, some of them in full and splendid blossom: these almost concealed an opening in the rock, into which the path appeared to lead. I entered, thirsting for the shade which it promised. What was my delight to find a rocky cell, all the angles rounded away with rich moss, and every ledge and projection crowded with lovely ferns, the variety of whose forms, and groupings, and shades wrought in me like a poem; for such a harmony could not exist, except they all consented to some one end! A little well of the clearest water filled a mossy hollow in one corner. I drank, and felt as if I knew what the elixir of life must be; then threw myself on a mossy mound that lay like a couch along the inner end. Here I lay in a delicious reverie for some time; during which all lovely forms, and colours, and sounds seemed to use my brain as a common hall, where they could come and go, unbidden and unexcused. I had never imagined that such capacity for simple happiness lay in me, as was now awakened by this assembly of forms and spiritual sensations, which yet were far too vague to admit of being translated into any shape common to my own and another mind. I had lain for an hour, I should suppose, though it may have been far longer, when, the harmonious tumult in my mind having somewhat relaxed, I became aware that my eyes were fixed on a strange, time-worn bas-relief on the rock opposite to me. This, after some pondering, I concluded to represent Pygmalion, as he awaited the quickening of his statue.[4] The sculptor sat more rigid than the figure to which his eyes were turned. That seemed about to step from its pedestal and embrace the man, who waited rather than expected.

'A lovely story,' I said to myself. 'This cave, now, with the bushes cut away from the entrance to let the light in, might be such a place as he would choose, withdrawn from the notice of men, to set up his block of marble, and mould into a visible body the thought already clothed with form in the unseen hall of the sculptor's brain. And, indeed, if I mistake not,' I said, starting up, as a sudden ray

4 *Bas-relief*: a sculpted picture, which is raised from the background. In Ovid's *Metamorphosis*, Pygmalion is a sculptor who falls in love with the statue he has made. (In Ovid's version it is carved from ivory.) The goddess Aphrodite takes pity on the sculptor and brings the statue to life.

of light arrived at that moment through a crevice in the roof, and lighted up a small portion of the rock, bare of vegetation, 'this very rock is marble, white enough and delicate enough for any statue, even if destined to become an ideal woman in the arms of the sculptor.'[5]

I took my knife and removed the moss from a part of the block on which I had been lying; when, to my surprise, I found it more like alabaster than ordinary marble, and soft to the edge of the knife. In fact, it was alabaster. By an inexplicable, though by no means unusual kind of impulse, I went on removing the moss from the surface of the stone; and soon saw that it was polished, or at least smooth, throughout. I continued my labour; and after clearing a space of about a couple of square feet, I observed what caused me to prosecute the work with more interest and care than before. For the ray of sunlight had now reached the spot I had cleared, and under its lustre the alabaster revealed its usual slight transparency when polished, except where my knife had scratched the surface; and I observed that the transparency seemed to have a definite limit, and to end upon an opaque body like the more solid, white marble. I was careful to scratch no more. And first, a vague anticipation gave way to a startling sense of possibility; then, as I proceeded, one revelation after another produced the entrancing conviction, that under the crust of alabaster lay a dimly visible form in marble, but whether of man or woman I could not yet tell. I worked on as rapidly as the necessary care would permit; and when I had uncovered the whole mass, and rising from my knees, had retreated a little way, so that the effect of the whole might fall on me, I saw before me with sufficient plainness – though at the same time with considerable indistinctness, arising from the limited amount of light the place admitted, as well as from the nature of the object itself – a block of pure alabaster enclosing the form, apparently in marble, of a reposing woman. She lay on one side, with her hand under her cheek, and her face towards me; but her

5   The quest for the ideal woman will occupy Anodos for much of the rest of this story.

hair had fallen partly over her face, so that I could not see the expression of the whole. What I did see appeared to me perfectly lovely; more near the face that had been born with me in my soul, than anything I had seen before in nature or art. The actual outlines of the rest of the form were so indistinct, that the more than semi-opacity of the alabaster seemed insufficient to account for the fact; and I conjectured that a light robe added its obscurity. Numberless histories passed through my mind of change of substance from enchantment and other causes, and of imprisonments such as this before me. I thought of the Prince of the Enchanted City, half marble and half a man; of Ariel; of Niobe; of the Sleeping Beauty in the Wood; of the bleeding trees; and many other histories.[6] Even my adventure of the preceding evening with the lady of the beech-tree contributed to arouse the wild hope, that by some means life might be given to this form also, and that, breaking from her alabaster tomb, she might glorify my eyes with her presence. 'For,' I argued, 'who can tell but this cave may be the home of Marble, and this, essential Marble – that spirit of marble which, present throughout, makes it capable of being moulded into any form?[7] Then if she should awake! But how to awake her? A kiss awoke the Sleeping Beauty: a kiss cannot reach her through the incrusting alabaster.' I kneeled, however, and kissed the pale coffin; but she slept on. I bethought me of Orpheus, and the following stones; – that trees should follow his music seemed nothing surprising now.[8] Might not a song awake this form, that the glory of motion might for a time displace the loveliness of rest? Sweet sounds can go where kisses may not enter. I sat and thought.

6   *The Prince of the Enchanted City*: the King of the Black Isle from the *Arabian Nights*. He is turned into half-man, half-marble by his wife who is an enchantress after he wounded a slave whom she loved. *Ariel*: from Shakespeare's *Tempest*, where he is a sprite who has been imprisoned in a tree by Sycorax the witch. *Niobe*: In Greek myth, Niobe was turned into a stone waterfall following the death of her children. *Sleeping Beauty*: Charles Perrault's fairy tale *La Belle au Bois Dormant* was first published in 1697. *Bleeding trees*: trees which were inhabited by nymphs and which would bleed if cut. In Ovid's story of Eresichthon, King of Thrace he cuts a tree which is the home of a Dryad, which bleeds. (*Metamorphoses* 8.774).

7   i.e., the Platonic 'ideal' marble.

8   Orpheus's music was so powerful that trees and stones followed the music of his lyre.

Now, although always delighting in music, I had never been gifted with the power of song, until I entered the fairy forest. I had a voice, and I had a true sense of sound; but when I tried to sing, the one would not content the other, and so I remained silent. This morning, however, I had found myself, ere I was aware, rejoicing in a song; but whether it was before or after I had eaten of the fruits of the forest, I could not satisfy myself. I concluded it was after, however; and that the increased impulse to sing I now felt, was in part owing to having drunk of the little well, which shone like a brilliant eye in a corner of the cave.[9] I sat down on the ground by the 'antenatal tomb,'[10] leaned upon it with my face towards the head of the figure within, and sang – the words and tones coming together, and inseparably connected, as if word and tone formed one thing; or, as if each word could be uttered only in that tone, and was incapable of distinction from it, except in idea, by an acute analysis. I sang something like this: but the words are only a dull representation of a state whose very elevation precluded the possibility of remembrance; and in which I presume the words really employed were as far above these, as that state transcended this wherein I recall it:

> *'Marble woman, vainly sleeping*
> *In the very death of dreams!*
> *Wilt thou – slumber from thee sweeping,*
> *All but what with vision teems –*
> *Hear my voice come through the golden*
> *Mist of memory and hope;*
> *And with shadowy smile embolden*
> *Me with primal Death to cope?*

9 It is drinking the water which has awakend the power of creativity in Anodos.
10 A quote from Shelley, 'The Sensitive Plant' l.167 'And many an antenatal tomb/Where butterflies dream of the life to come...'

> 'Thee the sculptors all pursuing,
> Have embodied but their own;
> Round their visions, form enduring,
> Marble vestments thou hast thrown;
> But thyself, in silence winding,
> Thou hast kept eternally;
> Thee they found not, many finding —
> I have found thee: wake for me.'

As I sang, I looked earnestly at the face so vaguely revealed before me. I fancied, yet believed it to be but fancy, that through the dim veil of the alabaster, I saw a motion of the head as if caused by a sinking sigh. I gazed more earnestly, and concluded that it was but fancy. Neverthless I could not help singing again —

> 'Rest is now filled full of beauty,
> And can give thee up, I ween;
> Come thou forth, for other duty
> Motion pineth for her queen.
>
> 'Or, if needing years to wake thee
> From thy slumbrous solitudes,
> Come, sleep-walking, and betake thee
> To the friendly, sleeping woods.
>
> 'Sweeter dreams are in the forest,
> Round thee storms would never rave;
> And when need of rest is sorest,
> Glide thou then into thy cave.
>
> 'Or, if still thou choosest rather
> Marble, be its spell on me;
> Let thy slumber round me gather,
> Let another dream with thee!'

Again I paused, and gazed through the stony shroud, as if, by very force of penetrative sight, I would clear every lineament of the lovely face. And now I thought the hand that had lain under the cheek, had slipped a little downward. But then I could not be sure that I had at first observed its position accurately. So I sang again; for the longing had grown into a passionate need of seeing her alive —

'Or art thou Death, O woman? for since I
Have set me singing by thy side,
Life hath forsook the upper sky,
And all the outer world hath died.

'Yea, I am dead; for thou hast drawn
My life all downward unto thee.
Dead moon of love! let twilight dawn:
Awake! and let the darkness flee.

'Cold lady of the lovely stone!
Awake! or I shall perish here;
And thou be never more alone,
My form and I for ages near.

'But words are vain; reject them all —
They utter but a feeble part:
Hear thou the depths from which they call,
The voiceless longing of my heart.'

There arose a slightly crashing sound. Like a sudden apparition that comes and is gone, a white form, veiled in a light robe of whiteness, burst upwards from the stone, stood, glided forth, and gleamed away towards the woods. For I followed to the mouth of the cave, as soon as the amazement and concentration of delight permitted the nerves of motion again to act; and saw the white form amidst the trees, as it crossed a little glade on the edge of the forest where the sunlight fell full, seeming to gather with intenser radiance on the one object that floated rather than flitted through its lake of beams. I gazed after her in a kind of despair; found, freed, lost! It seemed useless to follow, yet follow I must. I marked the direction she took; and without once looking round to the forsaken cave, I hastened towards the forest.[11]

11 In his poem 'A Story of the Sea-Shore', MacDonald describes a room or building he had seen as a youth in a garden on the north coast of Scotland. The statue stood in 'a little room, built somehow... against the steep hill-side, /Whose top was with a circular temple crowned, ... So that, beclouded ever in the night/Of a luxuriant ivy, its low door, ... Appeared to open right into the hill.' (MacDonald, *Poems*, 1857 edition). In the room stood 'the wonder of the place... A woman-form in marble, cold and clear.' In a later version of the poem (*Poetical Works*, Vol.I) he described the place as being 'on the Moray shore'. Possibly it was Cullen House and the building — and statue — stood in the extensive gardens.

'I gazed after her in a kind of despair...'

—6—

*'Ah, let a man beware, when his wishes, fulfilled, rain down upon him, and his
happiness is unbounded.'*

FOUQUÉ: *DER ZAUBERRING*[1]

*'Thy red lips, like worms,
Travel over my cheek.'*

MOTHERWELL[2]

B ut as I crossed the space between the foot of the hill and the
forest, a vision of another kind delayed my steps. Through
an opening to the westward flowed, like a stream, the rays of
the setting sun, and overflowed with a ruddy splendour the open
space where I was. And riding as it were down this stream towards
me, came a horseman in what appeared red armour. From front-
let to tail, the horse likewise shone red in the sunset. I felt as if
I must have seen the knight before; but as he drew near, I could
recall no feature of his countenance. Ere he came up to me, however, I remembered the legend of Sir Percival in the rusty armour,
which I had left unfinished in the old book in the cottage: it was
of Sir Percival that he reminded me. And no wonder; for when
he came close up to me, I saw that, from crest to heel, the whole

---

1   *'Ach, hüte sich doch ein Mensch, wenn seine erfüllten Wünsche auf ihn herad regnen, und er so über alle Maasse
    fröhlich ist!'* Friedrich de la Motte Fouqué, German novelist (1777–1843). *Die Zaubering* ('The
    Magic Ring') was published in 1825. MacDonald greatly admired Fouqué, especially his
    novel *Undine*. In his essay 'The Fantastic Imagination', MacDonald wrote: 'Were I asked, what
    is a fairytale? I should reply, Read *Undine*: that is a fairytale... of all fairytales I know, I think
    Undine the most beautiful.' (See p.275)

2   William Motherwell, poet and journalist (1797–1835). The line comes from his poem 'The
    Demon Lady'.

surface of his armour was covered with a light rust. The golden spurs shone, but the iron greaves glowed in the sunlight. The *morning star*, which hung from his wrist, glittered and glowed with its silver and bronze.[3] His whole appearance was terrible; but his face did not answer to this appearance. It was sad, even to gloominess; and something of shame seemed to cover it. Yet it was noble and high, though thus beclouded; and the form looked lofty, although the head drooped, and the whole frame was bowed as with an inward grief. The horse seemed to share in his master's dejection, and walked spiritless and slow. I noticed, too, that the white plume on his helmet was discoloured and drooping. 'He has fallen in a joust with spears,' I said to myself; 'yet it becomes not a noble knight to be conquered in spirit because his body hath fallen.' He appeared not to observe me, for he was riding past without looking up, and started into a warlike attitude the moment the first sound of my voice reached him. Then a flush, as of shame, covered all of his face that the lifted beaver disclosed.[4] He returned my greeting with distant courtesy, and passed on. But suddenly, he reined up, sat a moment still, and then turning his horse, rode back to where I stood looking after him.

'I am ashamed,' he said, 'to appear a knight, and in such a guise; but it behoves me to tell you to take warning from me, lest the same evil, in his kind, overtake the singer that has befallen the knight. Hast thou ever read the story of Sir Percival and the' — (here he shuddered, that his armour rang) — 'Maiden of the Alder-tree?'

'In part, I have,' said I; 'for yesterday, at the entrance of this forest, I found in a cottage the volume wherein it is recorded.'

'Then take heed,' he rejoined; 'for, see my armour — I put it off; and as it befell to him, so has it befallen to me. I that was proud am humble now. Yet is she terribly beautiful — beware. Never,' he added, raising his head, 'shall this armour be furbished, but by the

---

3   *Greaves*: pieces of armour protecting the shin. *Morning-star*: a mace or a flair, with a ball at the end, studded with sharp spikes.

4   *Beaver*: is the lower portion of the face-guard of a Knight's helmet.

blows of knightly encounter, until the last speck has disappeared from every spot where the battle-axe and sword of evil-doers, or noble foes, might fall; when I shall again lift my head, and say to my squire, "Do thy duty once more, and make this armour shine."'

Before I could inquire further, he had struck spurs into his horse and galloped away, shrouded from my voice in the noise of his armour. For I called after him, anxious to know more about this fearful enchantress; but in vain – he heard me not. 'Yet,' I said to myself, 'I have now been often warned; surely I shall be well on my guard; and I am fully resolved I shall not be ensnared by any beauty, however beautiful. Doubtless, some one man may escape, and I shall be he.' So I went on into the wood, still hoping to find, in some one of its mysterious recesses, my lost lady of the marble. The sunny afternoon died into the loveliest twilight. Great bats began to flit about with their own noiseless flight, seemingly purposeless, because its objects are unseen. The monotonous music of the owl issued from all unexpected quarters in the half-darkness around me. The glow-worm was alight here and there, burning out into the great universe. The night-hawk heightened all the harmony and stillness with his oft-recurring, discordant jar.[5] Numberless unknown sounds came out of the unknown dusk; but all were of twilight-kind, oppressing the heart as with a condensed atmosphere of dreamy undefined love and longing. The odours of night arose, and bathed me in that luxurious mournfulness peculiar to them, as if the plants whence they floated had been watered with bygone tears. Earth drew me towards her bosom; I felt as if I could fall down and kiss her. I forgot I was in Fairy Land, and seemed to be walking in a perfect night of our own old nursing earth. Great stems rose about me, uplifting a thick multitudinous roof above me of branches, and twigs, and leaves – the bird and insect world uplifted over mine, with its own landscapes, its own thickets, and paths, and glades, and dwellings; its own bird-ways and insect-delights. Great

5 *Night-hawk*: night-jar.

boughs crossed my path; great roots based the tree-columns, and mightily clasped the earth, strong to lift and strong to uphold. It seemed an old, old forest, perfect in forest ways and pleasures. And when, in the midst of this ecstacy, I remembered that under some close canopy of leaves, by some giant stem, or in some mossy cave, or beside some leafy well, sat the lady of the marble, whom my songs had called forth into the outer world, waiting (might it not be?) to meet and thank her deliverer in a twilight which would veil her confusion, the whole night became one dream-realm of joy, the central form of which was everywhere present, although unbeheld. Then, remembering how my songs seemed to have called her from the marble, piercing through the pearly shroud of alabaster – 'Why,' thought I, 'should not my voice reach her now, through the ebon night that inwraps her.' My voice burst into song so spontaneously that it seemed involuntarily.

'Not a sound
But, echoing in me,
Vibrates all around
With a blind delight,
Till it breaks on Thee,
Queen of Night!

'Every tree,
O'ershadowing with gloom,
Seems to cover thee
Secret, dark, love-still'd,
In a holy room
Silence-filled.

'Let no moon
Creep up the heaven to-night;
I in darksome noon
Walking hopefully,
Seek my shrouded light –
Grope for thee!

'Darker grow
The borders of the dark!
Through the branches glow,

> *From the roof above,*
> *Star and diamond-sparks*
> *Light for love.*[6]

Scarcely had the last sounds floated away from the hearing of my own ears, when I heard instead a low delicious laugh near me. It was not the laugh of one who would not be heard, but the laugh of one who has just received something long and patiently desired – a laugh that ends in a low musical moan. I started, and, turning sideways, saw a dim white figure seated beside an intertwining thicket of smaller trees and underwood.

'It is my white lady!' I said, and flung myself on the ground beside her; striving, through the gathering darkness, to get a glimpse of the form which had broken its marble prison at my call.

'It is your white lady!' said the sweetest voice, in reply, sending a thrill of speechless delight through a heart which all the love-charms of the preceding day and evening had been tempering for this culminating hour. Yet, if I would have confessed it, there was something either in the sound of the voice, although it seemed sweetness itself, or else in this yielding which awaited no gradation of gentle approaches, that did not vibrate harmoniously with the beat of my inward music. And likewise, when, taking her hand in mine, I drew closer to her, looking for the beauty of her face, which, indeed, I found too plenteously, a cold shiver ran through me; but 'it is the marble,' I said to myself, and heeded it not.

She withdrew her hand from mine, and after that would scarce allow me to touch her. It seemed strange, after the fulness of her first greeting, that she could not trust me to come close to her. Though her words were those of a lover, she kept herself withdrawn as if a mile of space interposed between us.

'Why did you run away from me when you woke in the cave?' I said.

---

6 This is very different to the song he sung to awaken the White Lady. This is a song of desire, of hidden love. He does not want the moon to shine. He gets what he wants – cf. the Fouqué quote at the head of the chapter.

'I found myself in a little cave...'

'Did I?' she re-
turned. 'That was
very unkind of me;
but I did not know
better.'

'I wish I could see you. The night is very
dark.'

'So it is. Come to my grotto. There is light there.'

'Have you another cave, then?'

'Come and see.'

But she did not move until I rose first, and then she was on her
feet before I could offer my hand to help her. She came close to
my side, and conducted me through the wood. But once or twice,
when, involuntarily almost, I was about to put my arm around her
as we walked on through the warm gloom, she sprang away several paces, always keeping her face full towards me, and then stood
looking at me, slightly stooping, in the attitude of one who fears

some half-seen enemy. It was too dark to discern the expression of her face. Then she would return and walk close beside me again, as if nothing had happened. I thought this strange; but, besides that I had almost, as I said before, given up the attempt to account for appearances in Fairy Land, I judged that it would be very unfair to expect from one who had slept so long and had been so suddenly awakened, a behaviour correspondent to what I might unreflectingly look for. I knew not what she might have been dreaming about. Besides, it was possible that, while her words were free, her sense of touch might be exquisitely delicate.

At length, after walking a long way in the woods, we arrived at another thicket, through the intertexture of which was glimmering a pale rosy light.

'Push aside the branches,' she said, 'and make room for us to enter.'

I did as she told me.

'Go in,' she said; 'I will follow you.'

I did as she desired, and found myself in a little cave, not very unlike the marble cave. It was festooned and draperied with all kinds of green that cling to shady rocks. In the furthest corner, half-hidden in leaves, through which it glowed, mingling lovely shadows between them, burned a bright rosy flame on a little earthen lamp. The lady glided round by the wall from behind me, still keeping her face towards me, and seated herself in the furthest corner, with her back to the lamp, which she hid completely from my view. I then saw indeed a form of perfect loveliness before me. Almost it seemed as if the light of the rose-lamp shone through her (for it could not be reflected from her); such a delicate shade of pink seemed to shadow what in itself must be a marbly whiteness of hue. I discovered afterwards, however, that there was one thing in it I did not like; which was, that the white part of the eye was tinged with the same slight roseate hue as the rest of the form. It is strange that I cannot recall her features; but they, as well as her somewhat girlish figure, left on me simply and only the impression of intense loveliness. I lay down at her feet, and gazed up into her face as I lay.

She began, and told me a strange tale, which, likewise, I cannot recollect; but which, at every turn and every pause, somehow or other fixed my eyes and thoughts upon her extreme beauty; seeming always to culminate in something that had a relation, revealed or hidden, but always operative, with her own loveliness. I lay entranced. It was a tale which brings back a feeling as of snows and tempests; torrents and water-sprites; lovers parted for long, and meeting at last; with a gorgeous summer night to close up the whole. I listened till she and I were blended with the tale; till she and I were the whole history.[7] And we had met at last in this same cave of greenery, while the summer night hung round us heavy with love, and the odours that crept through the silence from the sleeping woods were the only signs of an outer world that invaded our solitude. What followed I cannot clearly remember. The succeeding horror almost obliterated it. I woke as a grey dawn stole into the cave. The damsel had disappeared; but in the shrubbery, at the mouth of the cave, stood a strange horrible object. It looked like an open coffin set up on one end; only that the part for the head and neck was defined from the shoulder-part. In fact, it was a rough representation of the human frame, only hollow, as if made of decaying bark torn from a tree.[8] It had arms, which were only slightly seamed, down from the shoulder-blade by the elbow, as if the bark had healed again from the cut of a knife. But the arms moved, and the hand and the fingers were tearing asunder a long silky tress of hair. The thing turned round — it had for a face and front those of my enchantress, but now of a pale greenish hue in the light of the morning, and with dead lustreless eyes. In the horror of the

7 Stories can intoxicate. Anodos feels himself part of this story, as with so many of the tales he hears in Fairy Land, but it is not a good or noble tale.
8 The Alder-maiden is literally hollow. Anodos has pursued love for self-satisfying ends, but such sensual, possessive, self-centred love leads only to emptiness.

moment, another fear invaded me. I put my hand to my waist, and found indeed that my girdle of beech-leaves was gone. Hair again in her hands, she was tearing it fiercely. Once more, as she turned, she laughed a low laugh, but now full of scorn and derision; and then she said, as if to a companion with whom she had been talking while I slept, 'There he is; you can take him now.' I lay still, petrified with dismay and fear; for I now saw another figure beside her, which, although vague and indistinct, I yet recognised but too well. It was the Ash-tree. My beauty was the Maid of the Alder! and she was giving me, spoiled of my only availing defence, into the hands of my awful foe. The Ash bent his Gorgon-head, and entered the cave.[9]

'The Ash shuddered and groaned...'

I could not stir. He drew near me. His ghoul-eyes and his ghastly face fascinated me. He came stooping, with the hideous hand outstretched, like a beast of prey. I had given myself up to a death of unfathomable horror, when, suddenly, and just as he was on the point

9 *Gorgon-head*: In Greek mythology, Medusa, the only mortal gorgon, had hair composed of live, venomous snakes.

of seizing me, the dull, heavy blow of an axe echoed through the wood, followed by others in quick repetition. The Ash shuddered and groaned, withdrew the outstretched hand, retreated backwards to the mouth of the cave, then turned and disappeared amongst the trees. The other walking Death looked at me once, with a careless dislike on her beautifully moulded features; then, heedless any more to conceal her hollow deformity, turned her frightful back and likewise vanished amid the green obscurity without. I lay and wept. The Maid of the Alder-tree had befooled me – nearly slain me – in spite of all the warnings I had received from those who knew my danger.

'Fight on, my men, Sir Andrew sayes,
A little Ime hurt, but yett not slaine;
He but lye downe and bleede awhile,
And then Ile rise and fight againe.'
BALLAD OF SIR ANDREW BARTON.[1]

B ut I could not remain where I was any longer, though the daylight was hateful to me, and the thought of the great, innocent, bold sunrise unendurable. Here there was no well to cool my face, smarting with the bitterness of my own tears. Nor would I have washed in the well of that grotto, had it flowed clear as the rivers of Paradise.[2] I rose, and feebly left the sepulchral cave. I took my way I knew not whither, but still towards the sunrise. The birds were singing; but not for me. All the creatures spoke a language of their own, with which I had nothing to do, and to which I cared not to find the key any more. I walked listlessly along. What distressed me most — more even than my own folly — was the perplexing question, How can beauty and ugliness dwell so near? Even with her altered complexion and her face of dislike; disenchanted of the belief that clung around her; known for a living, walking sepulchre, faithless, deluding, traitorous; I felt notwithstanding all this, that she was beautiful. Upon this I pondered with undiminished perplexity, though not without some gain. Then I began to make surmises as to the mode of my deliverance; and concluded that some hero, wandering in search of adventure, had heard how

1 Sir Andrew Barton (c. 1466 – 1511) was High Admiral of Scotland. He was a privateer, like Sir Francis Drake. He was defeated and captured in 1511 by Sir Edward Howard.
2 Significantly, the Alder-maiden's cave lacks the water of Fairy land.

the forest was infested; and, knowing it was useless to attack the evil thing in person, had assailed with his battle-axe the body in which he dwelt, and on which he was dependent for his power of mischief in the wood. 'Very likely,' I thought, 'the repentant-knight, who warned me of the evil which has befallen me, was busy retrieving his lost honour, while I was sinking into the same sorrow with himself; and, hearing of the dangerous and mysterious being, arrived at his tree in time to save me from being dragged to its roots, and buried like carrion, to nourish him for yet deeper insatiableness.' I found afterwards that my conjecture was correct. I wondered how he had fared when his blows recalled the Ash himself, and that too I learned afterwards.

I walked on the whole day, with intervals of rest, but without food; for I could not have eaten, had any been offered me; till, in the afternoon, I seemed to approach the outskirts of the forest, and at length arrived at a farm-house. An unspeakable joy arose in my heart at beholding an abode of human beings once more, and I hastened up to the door, and knocked. A kind-looking, matronly woman, still handsome, made her appearance; who, as soon as she saw me, said kindly, 'Ah, my poor boy, you have come from the wood! Were you in it last night?' I should have ill endured, the day before, to be called boy; but now the motherly kindness of the word went to my heart; and, like a boy indeed, I burst into tears. She soothed me right gently; and, leading me into a room, made me lie down on a settle, while she went to find me some refreshment. She soon returned with food, but I could not eat. She almost compelled me to swallow some wine, when I revived sufficiently to be able to answer some of her questions. I told her the whole story.

'It is just as I feared,' she said; 'but you are now for the night beyond the reach of any of these dreadful creatures. It is no wonder they could delude a child like you. But I must beg you, when my husband comes in, not to say a word about these things; for he thinks me even half crazy for believing anything of the sort. But

I must believe my senses, as he cannot believe beyond his, which give him no intimations of this kind. I think he could spend the whole of Midsummer-eve in the wood and come back with the report that he saw nothing worse than himself.[3] Indeed, good man, he would hardly find anything better than himself, if he had seven more senses given him.'

'But tell me how it is that she could be so beautiful without any heart at all – without any place even for a heart to live in.'

'I cannot quite tell,' she said; 'but I am sure she would not look so beautiful if she did not take means to make herself look more beautiful than she is. And then, you know, you began by being in love with her before you saw her beauty, mistaking her for the lady of the marble – another kind altogether, I should think. But the chief thing that makes her beautiful is this: that, although she loves no man, she loves the love of any man; and when she finds one in her power, her desire to bewitch him and gain his love (not for the sake of his love either, but that she may be conscious anew of her own beauty, through the admiration he manifests), makes her very lovely – with a self-destructive beauty, though; for it is that which is constantly wearing her away within, till, at last, the decay will reach her face, and her whole front, when all the lovely mask of nothing will fall to pieces, and she be vanished for ever. So a wise man, whom she met in the wood some years ago, and who, I think, for all his wisdom, fared no better than you, told me, when, like you, he spent the next night here, and recounted to me his adventures.'

I thanked her very warmly for her solution, though it was but partial; wondering much that in her, as in the woman I met on my first entering the forest, there should be such superiority to her apparent condition. Here she left me to take some rest; though, indeed, I was too much agitated to rest in any other way than by simply ceasing to move.

3 The night before Midsummer's day (24th June). Traditionally, a night of fairy celebration. Anodos' grandmother dates her age from Midsummer eve (see p.45).

'I could hardly believe that
there was a Fairy Land...'

In half an hour, I heard a heavy step approach and enter the
house. A jolly voice, whose slight huskiness appeared to proceed
from overmuch laughter, called out 'Betsy, the pigs' trough is quite
empty, and that is a pity. Let them swill, lass! They're of no use
but to get fat. Ha! ha! ha! Gluttony is not forbidden in their com-
mandments. Ha! ha! ha!' The very voice, kind and jovial, seemed
to disrobe the room of the strange look which all new places wear
– to disenchant it out of the realm of the ideal into that of the
actual. It began to look as if I had known every corner of it for

twenty years; and when, soon after, the dame came and fetched me to partake of their early supper, the grasp of his great hand, and the harvest-moon of his benevolent face, which was needed to light up the rotundity of the globe beneath it, produced such a reaction in me, that, for a moment, I could hardly believe that there was a Fairy Land; and that all I had passed through since I left home, had not been the wandering dream of a diseased imagination, operating on a too mobile frame, not merely causing me indeed to travel, but peopling for me with vague phantoms the regions through which my actual steps had led me. But the next moment my eye fell upon a little girl who was sitting in the chimney-corner, with a little book open on her knee, from which she had apparently just looked up to fix great inquiring eyes upon me. I believed in Fairy Land again. She went on with her reading, as soon as she saw that I observed her looking at me. I went near, and peeping over her shoulder, saw that she was reading 'The History of Graciosa and Percinet.'[4]

'Very improving book, sir,' remarked the old farmer, with a good-humoured laugh. 'We are in the very hottest corner of Fairy Land here. Ha! ha! Stormy night, last night, sir.'

'Was it, indeed?' I rejoined. 'It was not so with me. A lovelier night I never saw.'

'Indeed! Where were you last night?'

'I spent it in the forest. I had lost my way.'

'Ah! then, perhaps, you will be able to convince my good woman, that there is nothing very remarkable about the forest; for, to tell the truth, it bears but a bad name in these parts. I dare say you saw nothing worse than yourself there?'

'I hope I did,' was my inward reply; but, for an audible one, I contented myself with saying, 'Why, I certainly did see some appearances I could hardly account for; but that is nothing to be

---

4 *Graciosa and Percinet* (*Gracieuse et Percinet*) is a fairy tale by Mme d'Aulnoy (1650/51–1705). It tells of a beautiful young princess called Graciosa who is hated by her wicked step-mother, but protected by Percinet, a page-boy who is really a prince.

wondered at in an unknown wild forest, and with the uncertain light of the moon alone to go by.'

'Very true! you speak like a sensible man, sir. We have but few sensible folks round about us. Now, you would hardly credit it, but my wife believes every fairy-tale that ever was written. I cannot account for it. She is a most sensible woman in everything else.'[5]

'But should not that make you treat her belief with something of respect, though you cannot share in it yourself?'

'Yes, that is all very well in theory; but when you come to live every day in the midst of absurdity, it is far less easy to behave respectfully to it. Why, my wife actually believes the story of the "White Cat." You know it, I dare say.'[6]

'I read all these tales when a child, and know that one especially well.'

'But, father,' interposed the little girl in the chimney-corner, 'you know quite well that mother is descended from that very princess who was changed by the wicked fairy into a white cat. Mother has told me so a many times, and you ought to believe everything she says.'

'I can easily believe that,' rejoined the farmer, with another fit of laughter; 'for, the other night, a mouse came gnawing and scratching beneath the floor, and would not let us go to sleep. Your mother sprang out of bed, and going as near it as she could, mewed so infernally like a great cat, that the noise ceased instantly. I believe

---

5   The farmer is a thoroughly good-natured man, who cannot believe in the supernatural. Mac-Donald firmly believed that such people were closer to the kingdom of heaven, than many Christians. 'It is better to be an atheist who does the will of God, than a so-called Christian who does not. The atheist will not be dismissed because he said *Lord, Lord* and did not obey.' (MacDonald, *Paul Faber, Surgeon*, ch.5). Curdie is unable to see Irene's Grandmother or her beautiful rooms. '...instead of the palatial room and the beautiful woman to whose lap Irene is taken, [Curdie] sees only the bare attic and the heap of musty straw and a ray of sunlight through a hole in the roof.' (MacDonald, Greville, *George MacDonald and His Wife*, (London: G. Allen & Unwin, 1924) p.377. See also *The Princess and Curdie*, ch.22.) The farmer's honest disbelief is different to his son's sneering cynicism.

6   A fairy story by Mme d'Aulnoy. It first appeared in *Contes nouveaux ou Les Fées à la mode* (1698). The story features the queen of a kingdom of cats, who is really an enchanted princess.

the poor mouse died of the fright, for we have never heard it again. Ha! ha! ha!'

The son, an ill-looking youth, who had entered during the conversation, joined in his father's laugh; but his laugh was very different from the old man's: it was polluted with a sneer. I watched him, and saw that, as soon as it was over, he looked scared, as if he dreaded some evil consequences to follow his presumption. The woman stood near, waiting till we should seat ourselves at the table, and listening to it all with an amused air, which had something in it of the look with which one listens to the sententious remarks of a pompous child. We sat down to supper, and I ate heartily. My bygone distresses began already to look far off.

'In what direction are you going?' asked the old man.

'Eastward,' I replied; nor could I have given a more definite answer. 'Does the forest extend much further in that direction?'

'Oh! for miles and miles; I do not know how far. For although I have lived on the borders of it all my life, I have been too busy to make journeys of discovery into it. Nor do I see what I could discover. It is only trees and trees, till one is sick of them. By the way, if you follow the eastward track from here, you will pass close to what the children say is the very house of the ogre that Hop-o'-my-Thumb visited, and ate his little daughters with the crowns of gold.'[7]

'Oh, father! ate his little daughters! No; he only changed their gold crowns for nightcaps; and the great long-toothed ogre killed them in mistake; but I do not think even he ate them, for you know they were his own little ogresses.'

---

7 *Hop-o'-my-Thumb*: a story in Charles Perrault's *Contes de ma Mère L'Oye* (1697) under the title 'Le Petit Poucet'. Poverty-striken parents abandon their seven sons in the wood. The youngest son is called 'Petit Poucet' – 'little thumb', or Hop o'my Thumb in the English version. The boys are captured by an Ogre, who decides to eat them in the morning. While the children sleep, Hop changes his brothers' caps with the gold crowns of the Ogre's seven daughters. The Ogre wakes in the night and kills his daughters by mistake. (See Carpenter and Prichard, *The Oxford Companion to Children's Literature*, (Oxford: Oxford University Press, 1984) pp.259-60.)

'Well, well, child; you know all about it a great deal better than I do. However, the house has, of course, in such a foolish neighbourhood as this, a bad enough name; and I must confess there is a woman living in it, with teeth long enough, and white enough too, for the lineal descendant of the greatest ogre that ever was made. I think you had better not go near her.'

In such talk as this the night wore on. When supper was finished, which lasted some time, my hostess conducted me to my chamber.

'If you had not had enough of it already,' she said, 'I would have put you in another room, which looks towards the forest; and where you would most likely have seen something more of its inhabitants. For they frequently pass the window, and even enter the room sometimes. Strange creatures spend whole nights in it, at certain seasons of the year. I am used to it, and do not mind it. No more does my little girl, who sleeps in it always. But this room looks southward towards the open country, and they never show themselves here; at least I never saw any.'

I was somewhat sorry not to gather any experience that I might have, of the inhabitants of Fairy Land; but the effect of the farmer's company, and of my own later adventures, was such, that I chose rather an undisturbed night in my more human quarters; which, with their clean white curtains and white linen, were very inviting to my weariness.

In the morning I awoke refreshed, after a profound and dreamless sleep. The sun was high, when I looked out of the window, shining over a wide, undulating, cultivated country. Various garden-vegetables were growing beneath my window. Everything was radiant with clear sunlight. The dew-drops were sparkling their busiest; the cows in a near-by field were eating as if they had not been at it all day yesterday; the maids were singing at their work as they passed to and fro between the out-houses: I did not believe in Fairy Land. I went down, and found the family already at breakfast. But before I entered the room where they sat, the little girl came to me,

I did not believe in Fairy Land

and looked up in my face, as though she wanted to say something to me. I stooped towards her; she put her arms round my neck, and her mouth to my ear, and whispered –

'A white lady has been flitting about the house all night.'

'No whispering behind doors!' cried the farmer; and we entered together. 'Well, how have you slept? No bogies, eh?'[8]

'Not one, thank you; I slept uncommonly well.'

'I am glad to hear it. Come and breakfast.'

After breakfast, the farmer and his son went out; and I was left alone with the mother and daughter.

'When I looked out of the window this morning,' I said, 'I felt almost certain that Fairy Land was all a delusion of my brain; but whenever I come near you or your little daughter, I feel differently. Yet I could persuade myself, after my last adventures, to go back, and have nothing more to do with such strange beings.'

'How will you go back?' said the woman.

'Nay, that I do not know.'

'Because I have heard, that, for those who enter Fairy Land, there is no way of going back. They must go on, and go through it. How, I do not in the least know.'

8 *Bogies*: (also known as bogles, bugs, bugaboos). In Scottish folklore a class of sprites who frighten and endanger humans.

'That is quite the impression on my own mind. Something compels me to go on, as if my only path was onward, but I feel less inclined this morning to continue my adventures.'

'Will you come and see my little child's room? She sleeps in the one I told you of, looking towards the forest.'

'Willingly,' I said.

So we went together, the little girl running before to open the door for us. It was a large room, full of old-fashioned furniture, that seemed to have once belonged to some great house. The window was built with a low arch, and filled with lozenge-shaped panes. The wall was very thick, and built of solid stone. I could see that part of the house had been erected against the remains of some old castle or abbey, or other great building; the fallen stones of which had probably served to complete it. But as soon as I looked out of the window, a gush of wonderment and longing flowed over my soul like the tide of a great sea. Fairy Land lay before me, and drew me towards it with an irresistible attraction. The trees bathed their great heads in the waves of the morning, while their roots were planted deep in gloom; save where on the borders the sunshine broke against their stems, or swept in long streams through their avenues, washing with brighter hue all the leaves over which it flowed; revealing the rich brown of the decayed leaves and fallen pine-cones, and the delicate greens of the long grasses and tiny forests of moss that covered the channel over which it passed in motionless rivers of light. I turned hurriedly to bid my hostess farewell without further delay. She smiled at my haste, but with an anxious look.

'You had better not go near the house of the ogre, I think. My son will show you into another path, which will join the first beyond it.'

Not wishing to be headstrong or too confident any more, I agreed; and having taken leave of my kind entertainers, went into the wood, accompanied by the youth. He scarcely spoke as we went along; but he led me through the trees till we struck upon a path. He told me to follow it, and, with a muttered 'good morning' left me.

—8—

'I am a part of the part, which at first was the whole.'
                    GOETHE – MEPHISTOPHELES IN FAUST[1]

My spirits rose as I went deeper; into the forest; but I could not regain my former elasticity of mind. I found cheerfulness to be like life itself – not to be created by any argument. Afterwards I learned, that the best way to manage some kinds of painfill thoughts, is to dare them to do their worst; to let them lie and gnaw at your heart till they are tired; and you find you still have a residue of life they cannot kill. So, better and worse, I went on, till I came to a little clearing in the forest. In the middle of this clearing stood a long, low hut, built with one end against a single tall cypress, which rose like a spire to the building.[2] A vague misgiving crossed my mind when I saw it; but I must needs go closer, and look through a little half-open door, near the opposite end from the cypress. Window I saw none. On peeping in, and looking towards the further end, I saw a lamp burning, with a dim, reddish flame, and the head of a woman, bent downwards, as if reading by its light. I could see nothing more for a few moments. At length, as my eyes got used to the dimness of the place, I saw that the part of the rude building near me was used for household purposes; for several rough utensils lay here and there, and a bed stood in the corner. An irresistible attraction caused me to enter.

1   'Ich bin ein Theil des Theils, der anfangs alles war.' Johann Wolfgang von Goethe (1749–1832) was a poet, philosopher, scientist, novelist, playwright and critic.
2   The Cypress which forms a spire on this 'church' is a tree associated with death and gloom. Cypresses are found in many cemeteries; Greeks and Romans put sprigs of cypress in coffins and tombs.

The woman never raised her face, the upper part of which alone I could see distinctly; but, as soon as I stepped within the threshold, she began to read aloud, in a low and not altogether unpleasing voice, from an ancient little volume which she held open with one hand on the table upon which stood the lamp. What she read was something like this:

'So, then, as darkness had no beginning, neither will it ever have an end. So, then, is it eternal. The negation of aught else, is its affirmation. Where the light cannot come, there abideth the darkness. The light doth but hollow a mine out of the infinite extension of the darkness. And ever upon the steps of the light treadeth the darkness; yea, springeth in fountains and wells amidst it, from the secret channels of its mighty sea. Truly, man is but a passing flame, moving unquietly amid the surrounding rest of night; without which he yet could not be, and whereof he is in part compounded.'[3]

As I drew nearer, and she read on, she moved a little to turn a leaf of the dark old volume, and I saw that her face was sallow and slightly forbidding. Her forehead was high, and her black eyes repressedly quiet. But she took no notice of me. This end of the cottage, if cottage it could be called, was destitute of furniture, except the table with the lamp, and the chair on which the woman sat. In one corner was a door, apparently of a cupboard in the wall, but which might lead to a room beyond. Still the irresistible desire which had made me enter the building urged me: I must open that

---

3 With its language reminiscent of the Authorised Version, the 'Bible' the woman reads from resembles an inversion of language found in John's gospel and letters (see, for example, John 1.1–5, 1 Jn 1.5; 2.8ff etc.) In one of his *Unspoken Sermons*, based on 1 John 1.5, MacDonald wrote: 'If God be light, what more, what else can I seek than God, than God himself! Away with your doctrines! Away with your salvation from the "justice" of a God whom it is a horror to imagine! Away with your iron cages of false metaphysics! I am saved – for God is light!' (MacDonald, *Unspoken Sermons III* 'Light'). The reference to man as a 'passing flame' brings to mind the service for Burial of the Dead ('Man that is born of woman hath but a short time to live, and is full of misery. He cometh up and is cut down like a flower: he fleeth as it were a shadow, and never continueth in one stay... In the midst of life we are in death.') This is a place linked with darkness, sin and death; a 'Church of Darkness' as it is called later (see p.129).

door, and see what was beyond it. I approached, and laid my hand on the rude latch. Then the woman spoke, but without lifting her head or looking at me: 'You had better not open that door.' This was uttered quite quietly; and she went on with her reading, partly in silence, partly aloud; but both modes seemed equally intended for herself alone. The prohibition, however, only increased my desire to see; and as she took no further notice, I gently opened the door to its full width, and looked in. At first, I saw nothing worthy of attention. It seemed a common closet, with shelves on each hand, on which stood various little necessaries for the humble uses of a cottage. In one corner stood one or two brooms, in another a hatchet and other common tools; showing that it was in use every hour of the day for household purposes. But, as I looked, I saw that there were no shelves at the back, and that an empty space went in further; its termination appearing to be a faintly glimmering wall or curtain, somewhat less, however, than the width and height of the doorway where I stood. But, as I continued looking, for a few seconds, towards this faintly luminous limit, my eyes came into true relation with their object. All at once, with such a shiver as when one is suddenly conscious of the presence of another in a room where he has, for hours, considered himself alone, I saw that the seemingly luminous extremity was a sky, as of night, beheld through the long perspective of a narrow, dark passage, through what, or built of what, I could not tell. As I gazed, I clearly discerned two or three stars glimmering faintly in the distant blue.[4] But, suddenly, and as if it had been running fast from a far distance for this very point, and had turned the corner without abating its swiftness, a dark figure sped into and along the passage from the blue opening at the remote end. I started back and shuddered, but kept looking, for I could not help it. On and on it came, with a speedy approach but delayed arrival; till, at last, through the many gradations of ap-

4 Reminiscent of the cave of the immortals, see Introduction, p.17. A glimpse, perhaps, into eternity.

*'A runner with ghostly
feet...'*

proach, it seemed to come within the sphere of myself, rushed up
to me, and passed me into the cottage. All I could tell of its appearance was, that it seemed to be a dark human figure. Its motion was
entirely noiseless, and might be called a gliding, were it not that it
appeared that of a runner, but with ghostly feet. I had moved back
yet a little to let him pass me, and looked round after him instantly.
I could not see him.

'Where is he?' I said, in some alarm, to the woman, who still sat
reading.

'There, on the floor, behind you,' she said, pointing with her arm
half-outstretched, but not lifting her eyes. I turned and looked,

but saw nothing. Then with a feeling that there was yet something behind me, I looked round over my shoulder; and there, on the ground, lay a black shadow, the size of a man. It was so dark, that I could see it in the dim light of the lamp, which shone full upon it, apparently without thinning at all the intensity of its hue.

'I told you,' said the woman, 'you had better not look into that closet.'

'What is it?' I said, with a growing sense of horror.

'It is only your shadow that has found you,' she replied. Everybody's shadow is ranging up and down looking for him. I believe you call it by a different name in your world: yours has found you, as every person's is almost certain to do who looks into that closet, especially after meeting one in the forest, whom I dare say you have met.'[5]

Here, for the first time, she lifted her head, and looked full at me: her mouth was full of long, white, shining teeth; and I knew that I was in the house of the ogre. I could not speak, but turned

---

5 The shadow is one of the key symbols in *Phantastes*. The old woman says that in our world we call it 'by a different name' and there has been much scholarly debate over what that name is. For Woolf, the Shadow represented 'pessimistic and cycnical disillusionment' (Woolf, *The Golden Key*, p.67); for Raeper it is the blighting effect of reality (Raeper, *George Mac-Donald*, p.149); David Robb calls it a form of dejection or despair (Robb, *George MacDonald*, pp.83–84). It can, of course, contain something of all of these meanings, but, apart from the significant clues in *Phantastes*, there are other points when MacDonald clarifies the symbol. In *Unspoken Sermons*, he writes: 'Self, I have not to consult you, but him whose idea is the soul of you, and of which as yet you are all unworthy. I have to do, not with you, but with the source of you, by whom it is that any moment you exist – the Causing of you, not the caused you… If I were to mind what you say, I should soon be sick of you; even now I am ever and anon disgusted with your paltry, mean face, which I meet at every turn. No! let me have the company of the Perfect One, not of you! … I will not make a friend of the mere shadow of my own being! Good-bye, Self! I deny you, and will do my best every day to leave you behind me.' (MacDonald, *Unspoken Sermons II*, 'Self-denial'). In his novel *St George and St Michael* he wrote: 'Shall I tell thee who hath possessed thee? – for the demon hath a name that is known amongst men, though it frighteneth few, and draweth many, alas! His name is Self, and he is the shadow of thy own self.' (MacDonald, *St. George and St. Michael*, ch.47.) The shadow is 'self', not as in our identity, but as in our selfishness or self-centredness. As the book progresses, Anodos will, repeatedly, face the challenge of defeating himself. As Hein wrote, 'For him [MacDonald] what people must pit their spiritual energies against is the inferior selves of their beings, the undersides of their natures. The enemy is within us, is indeed ourselves.' (Hein, *The Harmony Within*, p.76).

and left the house, with the shadow at my heels. 'A nice sort of valet to have,' I said to myself bitterly, as I stepped into the sunshine, and, looking over my shoulder, saw that it lay yet blacker in the full blaze of the sunlight. Indeed, only when I stood between it and the sun, was the blackness at all diminished. I was so bewildered – stunned – both by the event itself and its suddenness, that I could not at all realise to myself what it would be to have such a constant and strange attendance; but with a dim conviction that my present dislike would soon grow to loathing, I took my dreary way through the wood.

'O lady! we receive but what we give,
And in our life alone does nature live:
Ours is her wedding garment, ours her shroud!

❋ ❋ ❋

Ah! from the soul itself must issue forth,
A light, a glory, a fair luminous cloud,
Enveloping the Earth —
And from the soul itself must there be sent
A sweet and potent voice of its own birth,
Of all sweet sounds the life and element!'

COLERIDGE[1]

From this time, until I arrived at the palace of Fairy Land, I can attempt no consecutive account of my wanderings and adventures. Everything, henceforward, existed for me in its relation to my attendant. What influence he exercised upon everything into contact with which I was brought, may be understood from a few detached instances. To begin with this very day on which he first joined me: after I had walked heartlessly along for two or three hours, I was very weary, and lay down to rest in a most delightful part of the forest, carpeted with wild flowers. I lay for half an hour in a dull repose, and then got up to pursue my way. The flowers on the spot where I had lain were crushed to the earth: but I saw that they would soon lift their heads and rejoice again in the sun and air. Not so those on which my shadow had lain. The

---

1 Samuel Taylor Coleridge (1772–1834). The lines come from 'Dejection: An Ode', written 1802.

very outline of it could be traced in the withered lifeless grass, and the scorched and shrivelled flowers which stood there, dead, and hopeless of any resurrection. I shuddered, and hastened away with sad forebodings.

In a few days, I had reason to dread an extension of its baleful influences from the fact, that it was no longer confined to one position in regard to myself. Hitherto, when seized with an irresistible desire to look on my evil demon (which longing would unaccountably seize me at any moment, returning at longer or shorter intervals, sometimes every minute), I had to turn my head backwards, and look over my shoulder; in which position, as long as I could retain it, I was fascinated. But one day, having come out on a clear grassy hill, which commanded a glorious prospect, though of what I cannot now tell, my shadow moved round, and came in front of me. And, presently, a new manifestation increased my distress. For it began to coruscate, and shoot out on all sides a radiation of dim shadow. These rays of gloom issued from the central shadow as from a black sun, lengthening and shortening with continual change. But wherever a ray struck, that part of earth, or sea, or sky, became void, and desert, and sad to my heart. On this, the first development of its new power, one ray shot out beyond the rest, seeming to lengthen infinitely, until it smote the great sun on the face, which withered and darkened beneath the blow. I turned away and went on. The shadow retreated to its former position; and when I looked again, it had drawn in all its spears of darkness, and followed like a dog at my heels.[2]

Once, as I passed by a cottage, there came out a lovely fairy child, with two wondrous toys, one in each hand. The one was the tube through which the fairy-gifted poet looks when he be-

---

2 The power of the shadow increases with the attention that Anodos gives it. The more he gazes on it, the greater it grows. Here it even blots out the sun. 'Love indeed is the highest in all truth; and the pressure of a hand, a kiss, the caress of a child, will do more to save sometimes than the wisest argument, even rightly understood. Love alone is wisdom, love alone is power; and where love seems to fail it is where self has stepped between and dulled the potency of its rays.' (MacDonald, *Paul Faber*, ch.36).

holds the same thing everywhere; the other that through which he looks when he combines into new forms of loveliness those images of beauty which his own choice has gathered from all regions wherein he has travelled. Round the child's head was an aureole of emanating rays. As I looked at him in wonder and delight, round crept from behind me the something dark, and the child stood in my shadow. Straightway he was a commonplace boy, with a rough broad-brimmed straw hat, through which brim the sun shone from behind. The toys he carried were a multiplying-glass and a kaleidoscope. I sighed and departed.[3]

One evening, as a great silent flood of western gold flowed through an avenue in the woods, down the stream, just as when I saw him first, came the sad knight, riding on his chestnut steed. But his armour did not shine half so red as when I saw him first. Many a blow of mighty sword and axe, turned aside by the strength of his mail, and glancing adown the surface, had swept from its path the fretted rust, and the glorious steel had answered the kindly blow with the thanks of returning light. These streaks and spots made his armour look like the floor of a forest in the sunlight. His forehead was higher than before, for the contracting wrinkles were nearly gone; and the sadness that remained on his face was the sadness of a dewy summer twilight, not that of a frosty autumn morn. He, too, had met the Alder-maiden as I, but he had plunged into the torrent of mighty deeds, and the stain was nearly washed away. No shadow followed him. He had not entered the dark house; he had not had time to open the closet door. 'Will he ever look in?' I said to myself. 'Must his shadow find him some day?' But I could not answer my own questions.

We travelled together for two days, and I began to love him. It was plain that he suspected my story in some degree; and I saw him once or twice looking curiously and anxiously at my attendant

3 *Multiplying glass*: a lens cut into numerous facets so as to make one object appear many times – like the eyes of a fly. Anodos loses that childlike sense of wonder.; under the influence of the shadow, these fairy objects are merely toys.

gloom, which all this time had remained very obsequiously behind me; but I offered no explanation, and he asked none. Shame at my neglect of his warning, and a horror which shrunk from even alluding to its cause, kept me silent; till, on the evening of the second day, some noble words from my companion roused all my heart; and I was at the point of falling on his neck, and telling him the whole story; seeking, if not for helpful advice, for of that I was hopeless, yet for the comfort of sympathy – when round slid the shadow and inwrapt my friend; and I could not trust him. The glory of his brow vanished; the light of his eye grew cold; and I held my peace. The next morning we parted.

But the most dreadful thing of all was, that I now began to feel something like satisfaction in the presence of the shadow. I began to be rather vain of my attendant, saying to myself, 'In a land like this, with so many illusions everywhere, I need his aid to disenchant the things around me. He does away with all appearances, and shows me things in their true colour and form. And I am not one to be fooled with the vanities of the common crowd. I will not see beauty where there is none. I will dare to behold things as they are. And if I live in a waste instead of a paradise, I will live knowing where I live.' But of this a certain exercise of his power which soon followed quite cured me, turning my feelings towards him once more into loathing and distrust. It was thus:

One bright noon, a little maiden joined me, coming through the wood in a direction at right angles to my path. She came along singing and dancing, happy as a child, though she seemed almost a woman. In her hands – now in one, now in another – she carried a small globe, bright and clear as the purest crystal. This seemed at once her plaything and her greatest treasure. At one moment, you would have thought her utterly careless of it, and at another, overwhelmed with anxiety for its safety. But I believe she was taking care of it all the time, perhaps not least when least occupied about it. She stopped by me with a smile, and bade me good day with the sweetest voice. I felt a wonderful liking to the child – for she produced on me more the impression of a child, though my understanding told me differently. We talked a little, and then walked on together in the direction I had been pursuing. I asked her about the globe she carried, but getting no definite answer, I held out my hand to take it. She drew back, and said, but smiling almost invitingly the while,

'The maiden came along singing and dancing, happy as a child...'

'You must not touch it;' – then, after a moment's pause – 'Or if you do, it must be very gently.' I touched it with a finger. A slight vibratory motion arose in it, accompanied, or perhaps manifested, by a faint sweet sound. I touched it again, and the sound increased. I touched it the third time: a tiny torrent of harmony rolled out of the little globe. She would not let me touch it any more.

We travelled on together all that day. She left me when twilight came on; but next day, at noon, she met me as before, and again we travelled till evening. The third day she came once more at noon, and we walked on together. Now, though we had talked about a great many things connected with Fairy Land, and the life she had led hitherto, I had never been able to learn anything about the globe. This day, however, as we went on, the shadow glided round and inwrapt the maiden. It could not change her. But my desire to know about the globe, which in his gloom began to waver as with an inward light, and to shoot out flashes of many-coloured flame, grew irresistible. I put out both my hands and laid hold of it. It began to sound as before. The sound rapidly increased, till it grew a low tempest of harmony, and the globe trembled, and quivered, and throbbed between my hands. I had not the heart to pull it away from the maiden, though I held it in spite of her attempts to take it from me; yes, I shame to say, in spite of her prayers, and, at last, her tears. The music went on growing in, intensity and complication of tones, and the globe vibrated and heaved; till at last it burst in our hands, and a black vapour broke upwards from out of it; then turned, as if blown sideways, and enveloped the maiden, hiding even the shadow in its blackness. She held fast the fragments, which I abandoned, and fled from me into the forest in the direction whence she had come, wailing like a child, and crying, 'You have broken my globe; my globe is broken – my globe is broken!' I followed her, in the hope of comforting her; but had not pursued her far, before a sudden cold gust of wind bowed the tree-tops above us, and swept through their stems around us; a great cloud overspread the day, and a fierce tempest came on, in which I lost sight of her. It lies heavy on my heart to this hour. At night, ere I fall asleep, often, whatever I may be thinking about, I suddenly hear her voice, crying out, 'You have broken my globe; my globe is broken; ah, my globe!'[4]

---

4 There is an undeniably sexual undertone to this event. But just as the shadow makes the wonderful mundane, turns friendship to mistrust, replaces idealism with realism, so love is replaced by lust. The girl becomes an object to be used. MacDonald, although working within the conventions of the Victorian world, was not coy about sex and its potential both for good and evil.

Here I will mention one more strange thing; but whether this peculiarity was owing to my shadow at all, I am not able to assure myself. I came to a village, the inhabitants of which could not at first
sight be distinguished from the dwellers in our land. They rather
avoided than sought my company, though they were very pleasant
when I addressed them. But at last I observed, that whenever I
came within a certain distance of any one of them, which distance,
however, varied with different individuals, the whole appearance of
the person began to change; and this change increased in degree as
I approached. When I receded to the former distance, the former
appearance was restored. The nature of the change was grotesque,
following no fixed rule. The nearest resemblance to it that I know,
is the distortion produced in your countenance when you look at
it as reflected in a concave or convex surface — say, either side of a
bright spoon. Of this phenomenon I first became aware in rather
a ludicrous way. My host's daughter was a very pleasant pretty girl,
who made herself more agreeable to me than most of those about
me. For some days my companion-shadow had been less obtrusive
than usual; and such was the reaction of spirits occasioned by the
simple mitigation of torment, that, although I had cause enough
besides to be gloomy, I felt light and comparatively happy. My impression is, that she was quite aware of the law of appearances that
existed between the people of the place and myself, and had resolved to amuse herself at my expense; for one evening, after some
jesting and raillery, she, somehow or other, provoked me to attempt
to kiss her. But she was well defended from any assault of the kind.
Her countenance became, of a sudden, absurdly hideous; the pretty
mouth was elongated and otherwise amplified sufficiently to have
allowed of six simultaneous kisses. I started back in bewildered
dismay; she burst into the merriest fit of laughter, and ran from the
room. I soon found that the same undefinable law of change operated between me and all the other villagers; and that, to feel I was
in pleasant company, it was absolutely necessary for me to discover

and observe the right focal distance between myself and each one with whom I had to do. This done, all went pleasantly enough. Whether, when I happened to neglect this precaution, I presented to them an equally ridiculous appearance, I did not ascertain; but I presume that the alteration was common to the approximating parties. I was likewise unable to determine whether I was a necessary party to the production of this strange transformation, or whether it took place as well, under the given circumstances, between the inhabitants themselves.[5]

5 This grotesque vision is reminiscent of Swift's disgust at humans following his time with the Houyhnms in *Gulliver's Travels*. This may reflect MacDonald's dislike of the superficialities of 'society', the way that politeness and distance must be maintained. In an unpublished work written before *Phantastes* his hero enters a literary soirée and feels a similar distaste: 'When he arrived he found the rooms quite up to the ordinary degree of crush and discomfort. Across the chaos of female cones and male obelisks, bowing and grinning, each with a veil of conventional fibre over the face through which ever and anon a real thought and feeling peered and disappeared, he saw no one for some time that he knew...' (MacDonald, Greville, *George MacDonald and His Wife*, p.321).

—10—

'From Eden's bowers the full-fed rivers flow,
To guide the outcasts to the land of woe:
Our Earth one little toiling streamlet yields,
To guide the wanderers to the happy fields.'[1]

After leaving this village, where I had rested for nearly a week, I travelled through a desert region of dry sand and glittering rocks, peopled principally by goblin-fairies.[2] When I first entered their domains, and, indeed, whenever I fell in with another tribe of them, they began mocking me with offered handfuls of gold and jewels, making hideous grimaces at me, and performing the most antic homage, as if they thought I expected reverence, and meant to humour me like a maniac. But ever, as soon as one cast his eyes on the shadow behind me, he made a wry face, partly of pity, partly of contempt, and looked ashamed, as if he had been caught doing something inhuman; then, throwing down his handful of gold, and ceasing all his grimaces, he stood aside to let me pass in peace, and made signs to his companions to do the like. I had no inclination to observe them much, for the shadow was in my heart as well as at my heels. I walked listlessly and almost hopelessly along, till I arrived one day at a small spring; which, bursting cool from the heart of a sun-heated rock, flowed somewhat southwards from the direction I had been taking. I drank of this spring,

---

1 I have not been able to trace this verse in any of MacDonald's other books of poetry. The verse refers to the four rivers originating in Eden, (Genesis 2.10–14) and Adam and Eve's expulsion (Genesis 3.24). Happy fields refers to Elysium or the Elysian fields - in classical mythology the home of the blessed after death.

2 Goblins, in MacDonald's fairy tales are always malevolent creatures, representatives of our lower selves and desires. This may be why they pay such respect to the shadow.

'The goblins performed the most antic homage...'

and found myself wonderfully refreshed. A kind of love to the cheerful little stream arose in my heart. It was born in a desert; but it seemed to say to itself, 'I will flow, and sing, and lave my banks, till I make my desert a paradise.' I thought I could not do better than follow it, and see what it made of it. So down with the stream I went, over rocky lands, burning with sunbeams. But the rivulet flowed not far, before a few blades of grass appeared on its banks, and then, here and there, a stunted bush. Sometimes it disappeared altogether under ground; and after I had wandered some distance, as near as I could guess, in the direction it seemed to take, I would suddenly hear it again, singing, sometimes far away to my right or left, amongst new rocks, over which it made new cataracts of watery melodies. The verdure on its banks increased as it flowed; other streams joined it; and at last, after many days' travel, I found myself, one gorgeous summer evening, resting by the side of a broad river, with a glorious horse-chestnut tree towering above me, and dropping its blossoms, milk-white and rosy-red, all about me. As I sat, a gush of joy sprang forth in my heart, and over flowed at my eyes. Through my tears, the whole landscape glimmered in such bewildering loveliness, that I felt as if I were entering Fairy Land for the first time, and some loving hand were waiting to cool my head, and a loving word to warm my heart.[3] Roses, wild roses, everywhere! So plentiful were they, they not only perfumed the air, they seemed to dye it a faint rose-hue. The colour floated abroad with the scent, and clomb, and spread, until the whole west blushed and glowed with the gathered incense of roses. And my heart fainted with longing in my bosom. Could I but see the Spirit of the Earth, as I saw once the in-dwelling woman of the beech-tree, and my beauty of the pale marble, I should be content. Content! – Oh, how gladly would I die of the light of her eyes! Yea, I would cease to be, if that would bring me one word of love from the one mouth. The twilight sank around, and infolded me with sleep. I slept as I had not slept for months. I did not awake till late in the morning; when, refreshed in body and mind, I rose as from the death that wipes out the sadness of life, and then dies itself in the new morrow. Again I followed the stream; now climbing a steep rocky bank that hemmed it in; now wading through long grasses and wild flowers in its path; now through meadows; and anon through woods that crowded down to the very lip of the water.

At length, in a nook of the river, gloomy with the weight of overhanging foliage, and still and deep as a soul in which the torrent eddies of pain have hollowed a great gulf, and then, subsiding in violence, have left it full of a motionless, fathomless sorrow – I saw a little boat lying. So still was the water here, that the boat needed no fastening. It lay as if some one had just stepped ashore, and would in a moment return. But as there were no signs of presence, and no track through the thick bushes; and, moreover, as I was in Fairy Land where one does very much as he pleases, I forced my way to the brink, stepped into the boat, pushed it, with the help

---

3 Once again, water which comes to the aid of Anodos. The beauty of nature surrounding him allows him to cry and it is his sorrow which allows him once again to see Fairy Land again. The imagery is reminiscent of Isaiah 'The wilderness and the solitary place shall be glad for them; and the desert shall rejoice, and blossom as the rose... Then the eyes of the blind shall be opened, and the ears of the deaf shall be unstopped. Then shall the lame man leap as an hart, and the tongue of the dumb sing: for in the wilderness shall waters break out, and streams in the desert.' (Isaiah 35.1–5)

of the tree-branches, out into the stream, lay down in the bottom, and let my boat and me float whither the stream would carry us.[4] I seemed to lose myself in the great flow of sky above me unbroken in its infinitude, except when now and then, coming nearer the shore at a bend in the river, a tree would sweep its mighty head silently above mine, and glide away back into the past, never more to fling its shadow over me. I fell asleep in this cradle, in which mother Nature was rocking her weary child; and while I slept, the sun slept not, but went round his arched way. When I awoke, he slept in the waters, and I went on my silent path beneath a round silvery moon. And a pale moon looked up from the floor of the great blue cave that lay in the abysmal silence beneath.

Why are all reflections lovelier than what we call the reality? – not so grand or so strong, it may be, but always lovelier? Fair as is the gliding sloop on the shining sea, the wavering, trembling, unresting sail below is fairer still. Yea, the reflecting ocean itself, reflected in the mirror, has a wondrousness about its waters that somewhat vanishes when I turn towards itself. All mirrors are magic mirrors. The commonest room is a room in a poem when I turn to the glass. (And this reminds me, while I write, of a strange story which I read in the fairy palace, and of which I will try to make a feeble memorial in its place.)[5] In whatever way it may be accounted for, of one thing we may be sure, that this feeling is no cheat; for there is no cheating in nature and the simple unsought feelings of the soul. There must be a truth involved in it, though we may but in part lay hold

4 There are two boat journeys in *Phantastes*, both of which take Anodos from a place of sorrow, to a place of healing and transformation. It is his response to pain and sadness which leads him forward through this journey. It is not joy which 'unfolds the deepest truth' but 'white-robed Sorrow' (see p.127).

5 cf. 2 Corinthians 3.18. MacDonald saw mirrors as not only reflecting, but also holding, or receiving reality. 'Paul never thought of the mirror as reflecting, as throwing back the rays of light from its surface; he thought of it as receiving, taking into itself, the things presented it... When I see the face of my friend in a mirror, the mirror seems to hold it in itself, to surround the visage with its liquid embrace. The countenance is *there* – down there in the depth of the mirror.' (MacDonald *Unspoken Sermons III*, 'The Mirrors of the Lord.') This theme is developed in the 'strange story' which begins in chapter 13. See p.148 ff.

'The Fairy Palace in the moonlight...'

of the meaning. Even the memories of past pain are beautiful; and past delights, though beheld only through clefts in the grey clouds of sorrow, are lovely as Fairy Land. But how have I wandered into the deeper fairyland of the soul, while as yet I only float towards the fairy palace of Fairy Land! The moon, which is the lovelier memory or reflex of the down-gone sun, the joyous day seen in the faint mirror of the brooding night, had rapt me away.

I sat up in the boat. Gigantic forest trees were about me; through which, like a silver snake, twisted and twined the great river. The little waves, when I moved in the boat, heaved and fell with a plash as of molten silver, breaking the image of the moon into a thousand morsels, fusing again into one, as the ripples of laughter die into the still face of joy. The sleeping woods, in undefined massiveness; the water that flowed in its sleep; and, above all, the enchantress moon, which had cast them all, with her pale eye, into the charmed slumber, sank into my soul, and I felt as if I had died in a dream, and should never more awake.

From this I was partly aroused by a glimmering of white, that, through the trees on the left, vaguely crossed my vision, as I gazed upwards. But the trees again hid the object; and at the moment, some strange melodious bird took up its song, and sang, not an ordinary bird-song, with constant repetitions of the same melody, but what sounded like a continuous strain, in which one thought was expressed, deepening in intensity as evolved in progress. It sounded like a welcome already overshadowed with the coming farewell. As in all sweetest music, a tinge of sadness was in every note. Nor do we know how much of the pleasures even of life we owe to the intermingled sorrows. Joy cannot unfold the deepest truths, although deepest truth must be deepest joy. Cometh white-robed Sorrow, stooping and wan, and flingeth wide the doors she may not enter. Almost we linger with Sorrow for very love.

As the song concluded the stream bore my little boat with a gentle sweep round a bend of the river; and lo! on a broad lawn, which rose from the water's edge with a long green slope to a clear elevation from which the trees receded on all sides, stood a stately palace glimmering ghostly in the moonshine: it seemed to be built throughout of the whitest marble. There was no reflection of moonlight from windows – there seemed to be none; so there was no cold glitter; only, as I said, a ghostly shimmer. Numberless shadows tempered the shine, from column and balcony and tower. For everywhere galleries ran along the face of the buildings; wings were extended in many directions; and numberless openings, through which the moonbeams vanished into the interior, and which served both for doors and windows, had their separate balconies in front, communicating with a common gallery that rose on its own pillars. Of course, I did not discover all this from the river, and in the moonlight. But, though I was there for many days, I did not succeed in mastering the inner topography of the building, so extensive and complicated was it.[6]

Here I wished to land, but the boat had no oars on board. However, I found that a plank, serving for a seat, was unfastened, and with that I brought the boat to the bank and scrambled on shore. Deep soft turf sank beneath my feet, as I went up the ascent towards the palace. When I reached it, I saw that it stood on a great platform of marble, with an ascent, by broad stairs of the same, all round it. Arrived on the platform, I found there was an extensive outlook over the forest, which, however, was rather veiled than revealed by the moonlight. Entering by a wide gateway, but without gates, into an inner court, surrounded on all sides by great marble pillars supporting galleries above, I saw a large fountain of porphyry[7] in the middle, throwing up a lofty column of water, which fell, with a noise as of the fusion of all sweet sounds, into a basin beneath; overflowing which, it ran into a single channel towards the

6 The image of the labyrinthine castle or palace was a favourite device of MacDonald's. 'MacDonald in his writings often uses the metaphor of a castle for the human mind, symbolising the many rooms or facets of the psyche.' (Hein, *The Harmony Within*, p.53).

7 'Porphyry' is a beautiful red stone, usually highly polished.

interior of the building. Although the moon was by this time so low in the west, that not a ray of her light fell into the court, over the height of the surrounding buildings; yet was the court lighted by a second reflex from the sun of other lands. For the top of the column of water, just as it spread to fall, caught the moonbeams, and like a great pale lamp, hung high in the night air, threw a dim memory of light (as it were) over the court below. This court was paved in diamonds of white and red marble. According to my custom since I entered Fairy Land, of taking for a guide whatever I first found moving in any direction, I followed the stream from the basin of the fountain. It led me to a great open door, beneath the ascending steps of which it ran through a low arch and disappeared. Entering here, I found myself in a great hall, surrounded with white pillars, and paved with black and white. This I could see by the moonlight, which, from the other side, streamed through open windows into the hall. Its height I could not distinctly see. As soon as I entered, I had the feeling so common to me in the woods, that there were others there besides myself, though I could see no one, and heard no sound to indicate a presence. Since my visit to the Church of Darkness, my power of seeing the fairies of the higher orders had gradually diminished, until it had almost ceased.[8] But I could frequently believe in their presence while unable to see them. Still, although I had company, and doubtless of a safe kind, it seemed rather dreary to spend the night in an empty marble hall, however beautiful, especially as the moon was near the going down, and it would soon be dark. So I began at the place where I entered, and walked round the hall, looking for some door or passage that might lead me to a more hospitable chamber. As I walked, I was deliciously haunted with the feeling that behind some one of the seemingly innumerable pillars, one who loved me was waiting for me. Then I thought she was following me from pillar to pillar as I

8 The Church of Darkness is the cottage of the Ogress, though it was not identifed as such at the time. See p.109 ff.

went along; but no arms came out of the faint moonlight, and no sigh assured me of her presence.

At length I came to an open corridor, into which I turned; notwithstanding that, in doing so, I left the light behind. Along this I walked with outstretched hands, groping my way, till, arriving at another corridor, which seemed to strike off at right angles to that in which I was, I saw at the end a faintly glimmering light, too pale even for moonshine, resembling rather a stray phosphorescence. However, where everything was white, a little light went a great way. So I walked on to the end, and a long corridor it was. When I came up to the light, I found that it proceeded from what looked like silver letters upon a door of ebony; and, to my surprise even in the home of wonder itself, the letters formed the words, *The Chamber of Sir Anodos.* Although I had as yet no right to the honours of a knight, I ventured to conclude that the chamber was indeed intended for me; and, opening the door without hesitation, I entered.[9] Any doubt as to whether I was right in so doing, was soon dispelled. What to my dark eyes seemed a blaze of light, burst upon me. A fire of large pieces of some sweet-scented wood, supported by dogs of silver,[10] was burning on the hearth, and a bright lamp stood on a table, in the midst of a plentiful meal, apparently awaiting my arrival. But what surprised me more than all, was, that the room was in every respect a copy of my own room, the room whence the little stream from my basin had led me into Fairy Land. There was the very carpet of grass and moss and daisies, which I had myself designed; the curtains of pale blue silk, that fell like a cataract over the windows; the old-fashioned bed, with the chintz furniture, on which I had slept from boyhood. 'Now I shall sleep,' I said to myself. 'My shadow dares not come here.'

I sat down to the table, and began to help myself to the good things before me with confidence. And now I found, as in many

9   The title is prophetic. See p.237.

10 *Dogs of silver*: fire dogs or andirons; metal supports with a horizontal bar to hold wood in a fireplace.

instances before, how true the fairy tales are; for I was waited on, all the time of my meal, by invisible hands. I had scarcely to do more than look towards anything I wanted, when it was brought me, just as if it had come to me of itself. My glass was kept filled with the wine I had chosen, until I looked towards another bottle or decanter; when a fresh glass was substituted, and the other wine supplied. When I had eaten and drank more heartily and joyfully than ever since I entered Fairy Land, the whole was removed by several attendants, of whom some were male and some female, as I thought I could distinguish from the way the dishes were lifted from the table, and the motion with which they were carried out of the room. As soon as they were all taken away, I heard a sound as of the shutting of a door, and knew that I was left alone. I sat long by the fire, meditating, and wondering how it would all end; and when at length, wearied with thinking, I betook myself to my own bed, it was half with a hope that, when I awoke in the morning, I should awake not only in my own room, but in my own castle also; and that I should walk, out upon my own native soil, and find that Fairy Land was, after all, only a vision of the night. The sound of the falling waters of the fountain floated me into oblivion.

— 11 —

'A wilderness of building, sinking far
And self-withdrawn into a wondrous depth,
Far sinking into splendour — without end!
Fabric it seemed of diamond and of gold,
With alabaster domes, and silver spires,
And blazing terrace upon terrace, high
Uplifted.'

WORDSWORTH[1]

But when, after a sleep, which, although dreamless, yet left behind it a sense of past blessedness, I awoke in the full morning, I found, indeed, that the room was still my own; but that it looked abroad upon an unknown landscape of forest and hill and dale on the one side – and on the other, upon the marble court, with the great fountain, the crest of which now flashed glorious in the sun, and cast on the pavement beneath a shower of faint shadows from the waters that fell from it into the marble basin below.

Agreeably to all authentic accounts of the treatment of travellers in Fairy Land, I found by my bedside a complete suit of fresh clothing, just such as I was in the habit of wearing; for, though varied sufficiently from the one removed, it was yet in complete accordance with my tastes. I dressed myself in this, and went out. The whole palace shone like silver in the sun. The marble was partly dull and partly polished; and every pinnacle, dome, and turret

---

1 From 'The Excursion' II.836–42. The original has 'boundless depth' rather than 'wondrous depth.'

'*Too dazzling for earthly eyes...*'

ended in a ball, or cone, or cusp of silver. It was like frost-work, and too dazzling, in the sun, for earthly eyes like mine.

I will not attempt to describe the environs, save by saying, that all the pleasures to be found in the most varied and artistic arrangement of wood and river, lawn and wild forest, garden and shrubbery, rocky hill and luxurious vale; in living creatures wild and tame, in gorgeous birds, scattered fountains, little streams, and reedy lakes — all were here. Some parts of the palace itself I shall have occasion to describe more minutely.

For this whole morning I never thought of my demon shadow; and not till the weariness which supervened on delight brought it again to my memory, did I look round to see if it was behind me: it was scarcely discernible. But its presence, however faintly revealed, sent a pang to my heart, for the pain of which, not all the beauties around me could compensate. It was followed, however, by the comforting reflection that, peradventure, I might here find the magic word of power to banish the demon and set me free, so that I should no longer be a man beside myself. The Queen of Fairy Land, thought I, must dwell here: surely she will put forth her power to deliver me, and send me singing through the further gates of her country back to my own land. 'Shadow of me!' I said;

'which art not me, but which representest thyself to me as me; here I may find a shadow of light which will devour thee, the shadow of darkness! Here I may find a blessing which will fall on thee as a curse, and damn thee to the blackness whence thou hast emerged unbidden.' I said this, stretched at length on the slope of the lawn above the river; and as the hope arose within me, the sun came forth from a light fleecy cloud that swept across his face; and hill and dale, and the great river winding on through the still mysterious forest, flashed back his rays as with a silent shout of joy; all nature lived and glowed; the very earth grew warm beneath me; a magnificent dragon-fly went past me like an arrow from a bow, and a whole concert of birds burst into choral song.

The heat of the sun soon became too intense even for passive support. I therefore rose, and sought the shelter of one of the arcades. Wandering along from one to another of these, wherever my heedless steps led me, and wondering everywhere at the simple magnificence of the building, I arrived at another hall, the roof of which was of a pale blue, spangled with constellations of silver stars, and supported by porphyry pillars of a paler red than ordinary. – In this house (I may remark in passing), silver seemed everywhere preferred to gold; and such was the purity of the air, that it showed nowhere signs of tarnishing. – The whole of the floor of this hall, except a narrow path behind the pillars, paved with black, was hollowed into a huge basin, many feet deep, and filled with the purest, most liquid and radiant water. The sides of the basin were white marble, and the bottom was paved with all kinds of refulgent stones, of every shape and hue. In their arrangement, you would have supposed, at first sight, that there was no design, for they seemed to lie as if cast there from careless and playful hands; but it was a most harmonious confusion; and as I looked at the play of their colours, especially when the waters were in motion, I came at last to feel as if not one little pebble could be displaced, with out injuring the effect of the whole. Beneath this floor of the water, lay the reflection of the blue inverted roof, fretted with its silver stars, like a second deeper sea, clasping and upholding the first. The fairy bath was probably fed from the fountain in the court. Led by an irresistible desire, I undressed, and plunged into the water. It clothed me as with a new sense and its object both in one. The waters lay so close to me, they seemed to enter and revive my heart. I rose to the surface, shook the water from my hair, and swam as in a rainbow, amid the coruscations of the gems below seen through the agitation caused by my motion. Then, with open eyes, I dived, and swam beneath the surface. And here was a new wonder. For the basin, thus beheld, appeared to extend on all sides like a sea, with here and there groups as of ocean rocks, hollowed by ceaseless billows into wondrous caves and grotesque pinnacles. Around the caves grew sea-weeds of all hues, and the corals glowed between; while far off, I saw the glimmer of what seemed to be creatures of human form at home in the waters. I thought I had been enchanted; and that when I rose to the surface, I should find myself miles from land, swimming alone upon a heaving sea; but when my eyes emerged from the waters, I saw above me the blue spangled vault, and the red pillars around. I dived again, and found myself once more in the heart of a great sea. I then arose, and swam to the edge, where I got out easily, for the water reached the very brim, and, as I drew near washed in tiny waves over the black marble border. I dressed, and went out, deeply refreshed.

And now I began to discern faint, gracious forms, here and there throughout the building. Some walked together in earnest conversation. Others strayed alone. Some stood in groups, as if looking at and talking about a picture or a statue. None of them heeded me. Nor were they plainly visible to my eyes. Sometimes a group, or single individual, would fade entirely out of the realm of my vision as I gazed. When evening came, and the moon arose, clear as a round of a horizon-sea when the sun hangs over it in the west, I began to see them all more plainly; especially when they came between me and the moon; and yet more especially, when I myself was in the shade. But, even then, I sometimes saw only the passing wave of a white robe; or a lovely arm or neck gleamed by in the moonshine; or white feet went walking alone over the moony sward. Nor, I grieve to say, did I ever come much nearer to these glorious beings, or ever look upon the Queen of the Fairies herself. My destiny ordered otherwise.

In this palace of marble and silver, and fountains and moonshine, I spent many days; waited upon constantly in my room with everything desirable, and bathing daily in the fairy bath. All this time I was little troubled with my demon shadow I had a vague feeling that he was somewhere about the palace; but it seemed as if the hope that I should in this place be finally freed from his hated presence, had sufficed to banish him for a time. How and where I found him, I shall soon have to relate.

The third day after my arrival, I found the library of the palace; and here, all the time I remained, I spent most of the middle of the day. For it was, not to mention far greater attractions, a luxurious retreat from the noontide sun. During the mornings and afternoons, I wandered about the lovely neighbourhood, or lay, lost in delicious day-dreams, beneath some mighty tree on the open lawn. My evenings were by-and-by spent in a part of the palace, the account of which, and of my adventures in connection with it, I must yet postpone for a little.

The library was a mighty hall, lighted from the roof, which was formed of something like glass, vaulted over in a single piece, and stained throughout with a great mysterious picture in gorgeous colouring.[2] The walls were lined from floor to roof with books and books: most of them in ancient bindings, but some in strange new fashions which I had never seen, and which, were I to make the

---

2   The library is an important image in MacDonald's work. The world of books is a place where God can be encountered. '...the very outside of a book had a charm to me. It was a kind of sacrament – an outward and visible sign of an inward and spiritual grace; as, indeed, what on God's earth is not?' (MacDonald, *The Portent*, ch.7.)

attempt, I could ill describe. All around the walls, in front of the books, ran galleries in rows, communicating by stairs. These galleries were built of all kinds of coloured stones; all sorts of marble and granite, with porphyry, jasper, lapis lazuli, agate, and various others, were ranged in wonderful melody of successive colours.[3] Although the material, then, of which these galleries and stairs were built, rendered necessary a certain degree of massiveness in the construction, yet such was the size of the place, that they seemed to run along the walls like cords. Over some parts of the library, descended curtains of silk of various dyes, none of which I ever saw lifted while I was there; and I felt somehow that it would be presumptuous in me to venture to look within them. But the use of the other books seemed free; and day after day I came to the library, threw myself on one of the many sumptuous eastern carpets, which lay here and there on the floor, and read, and read, until weary; if that can be designated as weariness, which was rather the faintness of rapturous delight; or until, sometimes, the failing of the light invited me to go abroad, in the hope that a cool gentle breeze might have arisen to bathe, with an airy invigorating bath, the limbs which the glow of the burning spirit within had withered no less than the glow of the blazing sun without. One peculiarity of these books, or at least most of those I looked into, I must make a somewhat vain attempt to describe.

If, for instance, it was a book of metaphysics I opened, I had scarcely read two pages before I seemed to myself to be pondering over discovered truth, and constructing the intellectual machine whereby to communicate the discovery to my fellow men. With some books, however, of this nature, it seemed rather as if the process was removed yet a great way further back; and I was trying to find the root of a manifestation, the spiritual truth whence a material vision sprang; or to combine two propositions, both apparently true, either at once or in different remembered moods, and

3   MacDonald was, according to his son Ronald, always very fond of gemstones. 'In precious stones he took a delight almost barbaric, but enriched by the knowledge of an amateur.' (Ronald MacDonald, *From a Northern Window*, pp.45-46.)

to find the point in which their invisibly converging lines would unite in one, revealing a truth higher than either and differing from both; though so far from being opposed to either, that it was that whence each derived its life and power. Or if the book was one of travels, I found myself the traveller. New lands, fresh experiences, novel customs, rose around me. I walked, I discovered, I fought, I suffered, I rejoiced in my success. Was it a history? I was the chief actor therein. I suffered my own blame; I was glad in my own praise. With a fiction it was the same. Mine was the whole story. For I took the place of the character who was most like myself, and his story was mine; until, grown weary with the life of years condensed in an hour, or arrived at my deathbed, or the end of the volume, I would awake, with a sudden bewilderment, to the consciousness of my present life, recognising the walls and roof around me, and finding I joyed or sorrowed only in a book. If the book was a poem, the words disappeared, or took the subordinate position of an accompaniment to the succession of forms and images that rose and vanished with a soundless rhythm, and a hidden rime.[4]

In one, with a mystical title, which I cannot recall, I read of a world that is not like ours. The wondrous account, in such a feeble, fragmentary way as is possible to me, I would willingly impart. Whether or not it was all a poem, I cannot tell; but, from the impulse I felt, when I first contemplated writing it, to break into rime, to which impulse I shall give way if it comes upon me again, I think it must have been, partly at least, in verse.

---

4   In Fairy Land art and life are interchangeable. Anodos is already in a story with no end (see p.66). Here he starts to inhabit the stories of other people, identifying with their tales. This is both a comment about the transformational power of stories and also about the idea that all human life is a story (see Introduction, p.19ff.).

—12—

Chained is the Spring. The night-wind bold
Blows over the hard earth;
Time is not more confused and cold,
Nor keeps more wintry mirth.
Yet blow, and roll the world about;
Blow, Time — blow, winter's Wind!
Through chinks of Time, heaven peepeth out,
And Spring the frost behind.

G. E. M.[1]

They who believe in the influences of the stars over the fates of men, are, in feeling at least, nearer the truth than they who regard the heavenly bodies as related to them merely by a common obedience to an external law. All that man sees has to do with man.[2] Worlds cannot be without an intermundane relationship. The community of the centre of all creation suggests an interradiating connection and dependence of the parts. Else a grander idea is conceivable than that which is already imbodied. The blank, which is only a forgotten life, lying behind the consciousness, and the misty splendour, which is an undeveloped life, lying before it, may be full of

---

1 Although the poem appears in the *Poetical Works of George MacDonald* (1893) under the title 'The Wind of the World', it is not by MacDonald. 'G.E.M.' is actually Greville Ewing Matheson, a close friend of George MacDonald. (See MacDonald, Greville, *George MacDonald and His Wife*, p.157.) A selection of Matheson's poems appeared, alongside those of George MacDonald and his brother John in *A Threefold Cord*, published in 1883. However none of the poems were assigned to individual authors, which may account for its inclusion in *Poetical Works*.

2 In an article written in 1853, MacDonald wrote 'Nor can there be anything human that is not, in some connexion or other admissable into art. The widest idea of art must comprehend all things.' (MacDonald, *Orts*, 'Browning's "Christmas Eve"'.)

mysterious revelations of other connexions with the worlds around us, than those of science and poetry. No shining belt or gleaming moon, no red and green glory in a self-encircling twin-star, but has a relation with the hidden things of a man's soul, and, it may be, with the secret history of his body as well. They are portions of the living house wherein he abides.

> Through the realms of the monarch Sun
> Creeps a world, whose course had begun,
> On a weary path with a weary pace,
> Before the Earth sprang forth on her race:
> But many a time the Earth had sped
> Around the path she still must tread,
> Ere the elder planet, on leaden wing,
> Once circled the court of the planet's king.
>
> There, in that lonely and distant star,
> The seasons are not as our seasons are;
> But many a year hath Autumn to dress
> The trees in their matron loveliness;
> As long hath old Winter in triumph to go
> O'er beauties dead in his vaults below;
> And many a year the Spring doth wear
> Combing the icicles from her hair;
> And Summer, dear Summer, hath years of June,
> With large white clouds, and cool showers at noon:
> And a beauty that grows to a weight like grief,
> Till a burst of tears is the heart's relief.
>
> Children, born when Winter is king,
> May never rejoice in the hoping Spring;
> Though their own heart-buds are bursting with joy,
> And the child hath grown to the girl or boy;
> But may die with cold and icy hours
> Watching them ever in place of flowers.
> And some who awake from their primal sleep,
> When the sighs of Summer through forests creep,
> Live, and love, and are loved again;
> Seek for pleasure, and find its pain;
> Sink to their last, their forsaken sleeping,
> With the same sweet odours around them creeping.

Now the children, there, are not born as the children are born in worlds nearer to the sun. For they arrive no one knows how. A maiden, walking alone, hears a cry: for even there a cry is the first utterance; and searching about, she findeth, under an overhanging rock, or within a clump of bushes, or, it may be, betwixt gray stones on the side of a hill, or in any other sheltered and unexpected spot, a little child. This she taketh tenderly, and beareth home with joy, calling out, 'Mother, mother' — if so be that her mother lives — 'I have got a baby — I have found a child!' All the household gathers round to see; — *'Where is it? What is it like? Where did you find it?'* and such-like questions, abounding. And thereupon she relates the whole story of the discovery; for by the circumstances, such as season of the year, time of the day, condition of the air, and such like, and, especially, the peculiar and never-repeated aspect of the heavens and earth at the time, and the nature of the place of shelter wherein it is found, is determined, or at least indicated, the nature of the child thus discovered. Therefore, at certain seasons, and in certain states of the weather, according, in part, to their own fancy, the young women go out to look for children. They generally avoid seeking them, though they cannot help sometimes finding them, in places and with circumstances uncongenial to their peculiar likings. But no sooner is a child found, than its claim for protection and nurture obliterates all feeling of choice in the matter. Chiefly, however, in the season of summer, which lasts so long, coming as it does after such long intervals; and mostly in the warm evenings, about the middle of twilight; and principally in the woods and along the river banks, do the maidens go looking for children just as children look for flowers. And ever as the child grows, yea, more and more as he advances in years, will his face indicate to those who understand the spirit of Nature, and her utterances in the face of the world, the nature of the place of his birth, and the other circumstances thereof; whether a clear morning sun guided his mother to the nook whence issued the boy's low cry; or at eve the lonely

*In the woods and along the river banks,
do the maidens go looking for children*

maiden (for the same woman never finds a second, at least while the first lives) discovers the girl by the glimmer of her white skin, lying in a nest like that of the lark, amid long encircling grasses, and the upward-gazing eyes of the lowly daisies; whether the storm bowed the forest trees around, or the still frost fixed in silence the else flowing and babbling stream.

After they grow up, the men and women are but little together. There is this peculiar difference between them, which likewise distinguishes the women from those of the earth. The men alone have arms; the women have only wings. Resplendent wings are they, wherein they can shroud themselves from head to foot in a panoply of glistering glory. By these wings alone, it may frequently be judged in what seasons, and under what aspects, they were born. From those that came in winter, go great white wings, white as snow; the edge of every feather shining like the sheen of silver, so that they flash and glitter like frost in the sun. But underneath, they are tinged with a faint pink or rose-colour. Those born in spring have wings of a brilliant green, green as grass; and towards the edges the feathers are enamelled like the surface of the grass-blades. These again are white within. Those that are born in summer have wings of a deep rose-colour, lined with pale gold. And those born in autumn have purple wings, with a rich brown on the inside. But these colours are modified and altered in all varieties, corresponding to the mood of the day and hour, as well as the season of the year; and sometimes I found the various colours so intermingled, that I could not determine even the season, though doubtless the hieroglyphic could be deciphered by more experienced eyes. One splendour, in particular, I remember – wings of deep carmine, with an inner down of warm gray, around a form of brilliant whiteness. She had been found as the sun went down through a low sea-fog, casting crimson along a broad sea-path into a little cave on the shore, where a bathing maiden saw her lying.

But though I speak of sun and fog, and sea and shore, the world there is in some respects very different from the earth whereon men live. For instance, the waters reflect no forms. To the unaccustomed eye they appear, if undisturbed, like the surface of a dark metal, only that the latter would reflect indistinctly, whereas they reflect not at all, except light which falls immediately upon them. This has a great effect in causing the landscapes to differ from those on the earth. On the stillest evening, no tall ship on the sea sends a long wavering reflection almost to the feet of him on shore; the face of no maiden brightens at its own beauty in a still forest-well. The sun and moon alone make a glitter on the surface. The sea is like a sea of death, ready to ingulf and never to reveal: a visible shadow of oblivion. Yet the women sport in its waters like gorgeous sea-birds. The men more rarely enter them. But, on the contrary, the sky reflects everything beneath it, as if it were built of water like ours. Of course, from its concavity there is some distortion of the reflected objects; yet wondrous combinations of form are often to be seen in the overhanging depth. And then it is not shaped so much like a round dome as the sky of the earth, but, more of an egg-shape, rises to a great towering height in the middle, appearing far more lofty than the other. When the stars come out at night, it shows a mighty cupola, 'fretted with golden fires,'[3] wherein there is room for all tempests to rush and rave.

One evening in early summer, I stood with a group of men and women on a steep rock that overhung the sea.[4] They were all questioning me about my world and the ways thereof. In making reply to one of their questions, I was compelled to say that children are not born in the Earth as with them. Upon this I was assailed with a whole battery of inquiries, which at first I tried to avoid; but, at last, I was compelled, in the vaguest manner I could invent, to make some approach to the subject in question. Immediately a dim notion of what I meant, seemed to dawn in the minds of most of the women. Some of them folded their great wings all around them, as they generally do when in the least offended, and stood erect and motionless. One spread out her rosy pinions, and flashed from the promontory into the gulf at its foot. A great light shone in the eyes of one maiden, who turned and walked slowly away, with her purple and white wings half dispread behind her. She was found, the next morning, dead beneath a withered tree on a bare hill-side, some miles inland. They buried her where she lay, as is their custom; for, before they die, they instinctively search for a spot like the

3 Shakespeare, *Hamlet* Act II, sc ii, l.301
4 Anodos has literally entered the world of this story.

place of their birth, and having found one that satisfies them, they lie down, fold their wings around them, if they be women, or cross their arms over their breasts, if they are men, just as if they were going to sleep; and so sleep indeed. The sign or cause of coming death is an indescribable longing for something, they know not what, which seizes them, and drives them into solitude, consuming them within, till the body fails. When a youth and a maiden look too deep into each other's eyes, this longing seizes and possesses them; but instead of drawing nearer to each other, they wander away, each alone, into solitary places, and die of their desire. But it seems to me, that thereafter they are born babes upon our earth: where, if, when grown, they find each other, it goes well with them; if not, it will seem to go ill. But of this I know nothing. When I told them that the women on the Earth had not wings like them, but arms, they stared, and said how bold and masculine they must look; not knowing that their wings, glorious as they are, are but undeveloped arms.

But see the power of this book, that, while recounting what I can recall of its contents, I write as if myself had visited the far-off planet, learned its ways and appearances, and conversed with its men and women. And so, while writing, it seemed to me that I had.

The book goes on with the story of a maiden, who, born at the close of autumn, and living in a long, to her endless winter, set out at last to find the regions of spring; for, as in our earth, the seasons are divided over the globe. It begins something like this:

> She watched them dying for many a day,
> Dropping from off the old trees away,
> One by one; or else in a shower
> Crowding over the withered flower
> For as if they had done some grievous wrong,
> The sun, that had nursed them and loved them so long,
> Grew weary of loving, and, turning back,
> Hastened away on his southern track;
> And helplessly hung each shrivelled leaf,
> Faded away with an idle grief.

And the gusts of wind, sad Autumn's sighs,
Mournfully swept through their families;
Casting away with a helpless moan
All that he yet might call his own,
As the child, when his bird is gone for ever,
Flingeth the cage on the wandering river.
And the giant trees, as bare as Death,
Slowly bowed to the great Wind's breath;
And groaned with trying to keep from groaning
Amidst the young trees bending and moaning.
And the ancient planet's mighty sea
Was heaving and falling most restlessly,
And the tops of the waves were broken and white,
Tossing about to ease their might;
And the river was striving to reach the main,
And the ripple was hurrying back again.
Nature lived in sadness now;
Sadness lived on the maiden's brow,
As she watched, with a fixed, half-conscious eye,
One lonely leaf that trembled on high,
Till it dropped at last from the desolate bough —
Sorrow, oh, sorrow! 'tis winter now.
And her tears gushed forth, though it was but a leaf,
For little will loose the swollen fountain of grief:
When up to the lip the water goes,
It needs but a drop, and it overflows.
Oh! many and many a dreary year
Must pass away ere the buds appear:
Many a night of darksome sorrow
Yield to the light of a joyless morrow,
Ere birds again, on the clothed trees,
Shall fill the branches with melodies.
She will dream of meadows with wakeful streams;
Of wavy grass in the sunny beams;
Of hidden wells that soundless spring,
Hoarding their joy as a holy thing;
Of founts that tell it all day long
To the listening woods, with exultant song;
She will dream of evenings that die into nights,
Where each sense is filled with its own delights,
And the soul is still as the vaulted sky,
Lulled with an inner harmony;
And the flowers give out to the dewy night,

Changed into perfume, the gathered light;
And the darkness sinks upon all their host,
Till the sun sail up on the eastern coast —
She will wake and see the branches bare,
Weaving a net in the frozen air.

The story goes on to tell how, at last, weary with wintriness, she travelled towards the southern regions of her globe, to meet the spring on its slow way northwards; and how, after many sad adventures, many disappointed hopes, and many tears, bitter and fruitless, she found at last, one stormy afternoon, in a leafless forest, a single snowdrop growing betwixt the borders of the winter and spring. She lay down beside it and died. I almost believe that a child, pale and peaceful as a snowdrop, was born in the Earth within a fixed season from that stormy afternoon.[5]

---

5 Once again we have a story where sadness brings development, where the snowdrop – Mac-Donald's flower of hope (see p.61) – leads her through death to life in a new world.

—13—

'I saw a ship sailing upon the sea
Deeply laden as ship could be;
But not so deep as in love I am
For I care not whether I sink or swim.'

OLD BALLAD[1]

'But Love is such a Mystery
I cannot find it out:
For when I think I'm best resolv'd,
I then am in most doubt.'

SIR JOHN SUCKLING[2]

One story I will try to reproduce. But, alas! it is like trying to reconstruct a forest out of broken branches and withered leaves. In the fairy book, everything was just as it should be, though whether in words or something else, I cannot tell. It glowed and flashed the thoughts upon the soul, with such a power that the medium disappeared from the consciousness, and it was occupied only with the things themselves. My representation of it must resemble a translation from a rich and powerful language, capable of embodying the thoughts of a splendidly developed people, into the meagre and half-articulate speech of a savage tribe. Of course, while I read it, I was Cosmo, and his history was mine. Yet, all the time, I seemed to have a kind of double consciousness, and

---

1   This appears to be a version of the ballad 'The Water is Wide' although I have not been able to trace it in this version exactly. 'The Water is Wide' is based on 'Waly, Waly, gin Love be bonny', a folk song dating from the 1600s and probably originating in the Scottish borders.
2   Sir John Suckling (1609–1642) Cavalier poet. The lines are from 'I prithee send me back my heart.'

the story a double meaning. Sometimes it seemed only to represent a simple story of ordinary life, perhaps almost of universal life; wherein two souls, loving each other and longing to come nearer, do, after all, but behold each other as in a glass darkly.[3]

As through the hard rock go the branching silver veins; as into the solid land run the creeks and gulfs from the unresting sea; as the lights and influences of the upper worlds sink silently through the earth's atmosphere; so doth Faerie invade the world of men, and sometimes startle the common eye with an association as of cause and effect, when between the two no connecting links can be traced.

Cosmo von Wehrstahl was a student at the University of Prague.[4] Though of a noble family, he was poor, and prided himself upon the independence that poverty gives; for what will not a man pride himself upon, when he cannot get rid of it? A favourite with his fellow students, he yet had no companions; and none of them had ever crossed the threshold of his lodging in the top of one of the highest houses in the old town. Indeed, the secret of much of that complaisance which recommended him to his fellows, was the thought of his unknown retreat, whither in the evening he could betake himself and indulge undisturbed in his own studies and reveries. These studies, besides those subjects necessary to his course

---

3 I Corinthians 13.12. 'For now we see through a glass, darkly; but then face to face: now I know in part; but then shall I know even as also I am known.' On MacDonald's view of mirrors, see p.125; *Introduction* p.15.

4 Prague had a reputation for mystical sciences. When Rudolph II moved his court there he filled the city with astrologers, astronomers, scholars, alchemists and all manner of mystics. Prague's reputation continued up to the twentieth century when the Surrealist André Breton called Prague the magic capital of Europe. In setting this story in Prague, MacDonald is echoing the German romantics like Hoffman, who set their stories in University towns. For example, *The Golden Pot*, which MacDonald was reading the summer before working on *Phantastes*, features the adventures of the student Anselmus in Dresden. MacDonald was to use Prague as a setting again for his short story 'The Cruel Painter', which was included in *Adela Cathcart* in 1864. The hero of that story, Karl von Wolkenlicht, is also a student. (MacDonald, *Adela Cathcart*, Book III, ch.6.) Cosmo was a name with significance for MacDonald, probably related to the Greek word, *kosmos*, world. The name appears as Cosmo Warlock in *Castle Warlock*, and Cosmo Cupples in *Alec Forbes of Howglen*. (See Soto, Fernando. 'Cosmos and Diamonds: Naming and Connoting in MacDonald's Works' *North Wind*, 20. 2001, p.30–42)

at the University, embraced some less commonly known and approved; for in a secret drawer lay the works of Albertus Magnus and Cornelius Agrippa[5], along with others less read and more abstruse. As yet, however, he had followed these researches only from curiosity, and had turned them to no practical purpose.

His lodging consisted of one large low-ceiled room, singularly bare of furniture; for besides a couple of wooden chairs, a couch which served for dreaming on both by day and night, and a great press of black oak[6], there was very little in the room that could be called furniture. But curious instruments were heaped in the corners; and in one stood a skeleton, half-leaning against the wall, half-supported by a string about its neck. One of its hands, all of fingers, rested on the heavy pommel of a great sword that stood beside it. Various weapons were scattered about over the floor. The walls were utterly bare of adornment; for the few strange things, such as a large dried bat with wings dispread, the skin of a porcupine, and a stuffed sea-mouse,[7] could hardly be reckoned as such. But although his fancy delighted in vagaries like these, he indulged his imagination with far different fare. His mind had never yet been filled with an absorbing passion; but it lay like a still twilight open to any wind, whether the low breath that wafts but odours, or the storm that bows the great trees till they strain and creak. He saw everything as through a rose-coloured glass. When he looked from his window on the street below, not a maiden passed but she moved as in a story, and drew his thoughts after her till she disappeared in the vista. When he walked in the streets, he always felt as if reading a tale, into which he sought to weave every face of interest that went

5 *Albertus Magnus* (c.1193–1280) also known as Albert the Great, was a medieval monk, philosopher and scientist. After his death many legends grew about his skills as an alchemist and magician. He did write on alchemy but there is little evidence that he ever tried any experiements. He is credited with the discovery of the element arsenic. *Cornelius Agrippa*, or Heinrich Cornelius Agrippa von Netelsheim (1486–1535). A German writer and philosopher, who wrote on a range of occult subjects. He, too, was credited after his death with magical powers.

6 *Press*: a large cupboard for clothes or books.

7 *Sea-mouse*: *Aphrodita aculeata*. A kind of marine worm, covered in dense hairs.

by; and every sweet voice swept his soul as with the wing of a passing angel. He was in fact a poet without words; the more absorbed and endangered, that the springing-waters were dammed back into his soul, where, finding no utterance, they grew, and swelled, and undermined. He used to lie on his hard couch, and read a tale or a poem, till the book dropped from his hand; but he dreamed on, he knew not whether awake or asleep, until the opposite roof grew upon his sense, and turned golden in the sunrise. Then he arose too; and the impulses of vigorous youth kept him ever active, either in study or in sport, until again the close of the day left him free; and the world of night, which had lain drowned in the cataract of the day, rose up in his soul, with all its stars, and dim-seen phantom shapes. But this could hardly last long. Some one form must sooner or later step within the charmed circle, enter the house of life, and compel the bewildered magician to kneel and worship.

One afternoon, towards dusk, he was wandering dreamily in one of the principal streets, when a fellow student roused him by a slap on the shoulder, and asked him to accompany him into a little back alley to look at some old armour which he had taken a fancy to possess. Cosmo was considered an authority in every matter pertaining to arms, ancient or modern. In the use of weapons, none of the students could come near him; and his practical acquaintance with some had principally contributed to establish his authority in reference to all. He accompanied him willingly. They entered a narrow alley, and thence a dirty little court, where a low arched door admitted them into a heterogeneous assemblage of everything musty, and dusty, and old, that could well be imagined. His verdict on the armour was satisfactory, and his companion at once concluded the purchase. As they were leaving the place, Cosmo's eye was attracted by an old mirror of an elliptical shape, which leaned against the wall, covered with dust. Around it was some curious carving, which he could see but very indistinctly by the glimmering light which the owner of the shop carried in his hand. It was this carving that attracted his attention; at least so it appeared to him. He left the place, however, with his friend, taking no further notice of it. They walked together to the main street, where they parted and took opposite directions.

No sooner was Cosmo left alone, than the thought of the curious old mirror returned to him. A strong desire to see it more plainly arose within him, and he directed his steps once more towards the shop. The owner opened the door when he knocked, as if he had expected him. He was a little, old, withered man, with a hooked nose, and burning eyes constantly in a slow restless motion, and looking here and there as if after something that eluded them. Pretending to examine several other articles, Cosmo at last approached the mirror, and requested to have it taken down.

'Take it down yourself, master; I cannot reach it,' said the old man.

Cosmo took it down carefully, when he saw that the carving was indeed delicate and costly, being both of admirable design and execution; containing withal many devices which seemed to embody some meaning to which he had no clue. This, naturally, in one of his tastes and temperament, increased the interest he felt in the old mirror; so much, indeed, that he now longed to possess it, in order to study its frame at his leisure. He pretended, however, to want it only for use; and saying he feared the plate could be of little service, as it was rather old, he brushed away a little of the dust from its face, expecting to see a dull reflection within. His surprise was great when he found the reflection brilliant, revealing a glass not only uninjured by age, but wondrously clear and perfect (should the whole correspond to this part) even for one newly from the hands of the maker. He asked carelessly what the owner wanted for the thing. The old man replied by mentioning a sum of money far beyond the reach of poor Cosmo, who proceeded to replace the mirror where it had stood before.

'You think the price too high?' said the old man.

'I do not know that it is too much for you to ask,' replied Cosmo; 'but it is far too much for me to give.'

The old man held up his light towards Cosmo's face. 'I like your look,' said he.

Cosmo could not return the compliment. In fact, now he looked closely at him for the first time, he felt a kind of repugnance to him, mingled with a strange feeling of doubt whether a man or a woman stood before him.

'What is your name?' he continued.

'Cosmo von Wehrstahl.'

'Ah, ah! I thought as much. I see your father in you. I knew your father very well, young sir. I dare say in some odd corners of my house, you might find some old things with his crest and cipher upon them still. Well, I like you: you shall have the mirror at the fourth part of what I asked for it; but upon one condition.'

'What is that?' said Cosmo; for, although the price was still a great deal for him to give, he could just manage it; and the desire to possess the mirror had increased to an altogether unaccountable degree, since it had seemed beyond his reach.

'That if you should ever want to get rid of it again, you will let me have the first offer.'

'Certainly,' replied Cosmo, with a smile; adding, 'a moderate condition indeed.'

'On your honour?' insisted the seller.

'On my honour,' said the buyer; and the bargain was concluded.

'I will carry it home for you,' said the old man, as Cosmo took it in his hands.

'No, no; I will carry it myself,' said he; for he had a peculiar dislike to revealing his residence to any one, and more especially to this person, to whom he felt every moment a greater antipathy.

'Just as you please,' said the old creature, and muttered to himself as he held his light at the door to show him out of the court: 'Sold for the sixth time! I wonder what will be the upshot of it this time. I should think my lady had enough of it by now!' Cosmo carried his prize carefully home. But all the way he had an uncomfortable feeling that he was watched and dogged. Repeatedly he looked about, but saw nothing to justify his suspicions. Indeed, the streets were too crowded and too ill lighted to expose very readily a careful spy, if such there should be at his heels. He reached his lodging in safety, and leaned his purchase against the wall, rather relieved, strong as he was, to be rid of its weight; then, lighting his pipe, threw himself on the couch, and was soon lapt in the folds of one of his haunting dreams.

He returned home earlier than usual the next day, and fixed the mirror to the wall, over the hearth, at one end of his long room. He then carefully wiped away the dust from its face, and, clear as the water of a sunny spring, the mirror shone out from beneath the envious covering. But his interest was chiefly occupied with the curious carving of the frame. This he cleaned as well as he could with a brush; and then he proceeded to a minute examination of its various parts, in the hope of discovering some index to the intention of the carver. In this, however, he was unsuccessful; and, at length, pausing with some weariness and disappointment, he gazed vacantly for a few moments into the depth of the reflected room. But ere long he said, half aloud: 'What a strange thing a mirror is! and what a wondrous affinity exists between it and a man's imagination! For this room of mine, as I behold it in the glass, is the same, and yet not the same.[8] It is not the mere representation of the room I live in, but it looks just as if I were reading about it in a story I like. All its commonness has disappeared. The mirror has lifted it out of the region of fact into the realm of art; and the very representing of it to me has clothed with interest that which was otherwise hard and bare; just as one sees with delight upon the stage the representation of a character from which one would escape in life as from something unendurably wearisome. But is it

8   This passage echoes – or mirrors – the text on p.125.

not rather that art rescues nature from the weary and sated regards
of our senses, and the degrading injustice of our anxious everyday
life, and, appealing to the imagination, which dwells apart, reveals
Nature in some degree as she really is, and as she represents herself
to the eye of the child, whose every-day life, fearless and unambi-
tious, meets the true import of the wonder-teeming world around
him, and rejoices therein without questioning? That skeleton, now
– I almost fear it, standing there so still, with eyes only for the
unseen, like a watch-tower looking across all the waste of this busy
world into the quiet regions of rest beyond. And yet I know every
bone and every joint in it as well as my own fist. And that old battle-axe looks as if any moment it might be caught up by a mailed
hand, and, borne forth by the mighty arm, go crashing through
casque, and skull, and brain, invading the Unknown with yet another bewildered ghost. I should like to live in that room if I could
only get into it.'[9]

Scarcely had the half-moulded words floated from him, as he
stood gazing into the mirror, when, striking him as with a flash
of amazement that fixed him in his posture, noiseless and un-
announced, glided suddenly through the door into the reflected
room, with stately motion, yet reluctant and faltering step, the
graceful form of a woman, clothed all in white. Her back only
was visible as she walked slowly up to the couch in the further end
of the room, on which she laid herself wearily, turning towards
him a face of unutterable loveliness, in which suffering, and dislike,
and a sense of compulsion, strangely mingled with the beauty. He
stood without the power of motion for some moments, with his
eyes irrecoverably fixed upon her; and even after he was conscious
of the ability to move, he could not summon up courage to turn
and look on her, face to face, in the veritable chamber in which he
stood. At length, with a sudden effort, in which the exercise of the

9 'Oh, Kitty, how nice it would be if we could only get through into Looking-glass House! I'm
  sure it's got, oh! such beautiful things in it!' (Carroll, *Through the Looking Glass*, ch.1.) On the
  influence of MacDonald on Carroll, see *Introduction* p.26.

will
was
s o

'She lay with closed eyes, whence two tears were just welling...'

pure, that it seemed involuntary, he turned his face to the couch. It
was vacant. In bewilderment, mingled with terror, he turned again
to the mirror: there, on the reflected couch, lay the exquisite lady-
form. She lay with closed eyes, whence two large tears were just
welling from beneath the veiling lids; still as death, save for the
convulsive motion of her bosom.[10]

Cosmo himself could not have described what he felt. His emo-
tions were of a kind that destroyed consciousness, and could never
be clearly recalled. He could not help standing yet by the mirror,
and keeping his eyes fixed on the lady, though he was painfully
aware of his rudeness, and feared every moment that she would
open hers, and meet his fixed regard. But he was, ere long, a little
relieved; for, after a while, her eyelids slowly rose, and her eyes remained uncovered, but unemployed for a time; and when, at length,

10 This is Cosmo's 'white lady'. She is a somnambule – a sleep walker, mesmerised into a trance-
like state. Hoffman's story *Der Magnetiseur* (1814) feautures a number of fiendish hypnotists.
MacDonald went to see the Polish hypnotist Zamoiski while he was living in Hastings, and
used him as the model for the sinister Von Funkelstein in *David Elginbrod*.

they began to wander about the room, as if languidly seeking to make some acquaintance with her environment, they were never directed towards him: it seemed nothing but what was in the mirror could affect her vision; and, therefore, if she saw him at all, it could only be his back, which, of necessity, was turned towards her in the glass. The two figures in the mirror could not meet face to face, except he turned and looked at her, present in his room; and, as she was not there, he concluded that if he were to turn towards the part in his room corresponding to that in which she lay, his reflection would either be invisible to her altogether, or at least it must appear to her to gaze vacantly towards her, and no meeting of the eyes would produce the impression of spiritual proximity. By-and-by her eyes fell upon the skeleton, and he saw her shudder and close them. She did not open them again, but signs of repugnance continued evident on her countenance. Cosmo would have removed the obnoxious thing at once, but he feared to discompose her yet more by the assertion of his presence which the act would involve. So he stood and watched her. The eyelids yet shrouded the eyes, as a costly case the jewels within; the troubled expression gradually faded from the countenance, leaving only a faint sorrow behind; the features settled into an unchanging expression of rest; and by these signs, and the slow regular motion of her breathing, Cosmo knew that she slept. He could now gaze on her without embarrassment. He saw that her figure, dressed in the simplest robe of white, was worthy of her face; and so harmonious, that either the delicately moulded foot, or any finger of the equally delicate hand, was an index to the whole. As she lay, her whole form manifested the relaxation of perfect repose. He gazed till he was weary, and at last seated himself near the new-found shrine, and mechanically took up a book, like one who watches by a sick-bed. But his eyes gathered no thoughts from the page before him. His intellect had been stunned by the bold contradiction, to its face, of all its experience, and now lay passive, without assertion, or speculation, or even conscious astonishment; while his imagination sent one wild dream of blessedness after another coursing through his soul. How long he sat he knew not; but at length he roused himself, rose, and, trembling in every portion of his frame, looked again into the mirror. She was gone. The mirror reflected faithfully what his room presented, and nothing more. It stood there like a golden setting whence the central jewel has been stolen away – like a night-sky without the glory of its stars. She had carried with her all the strangeness of the reflected room. It had sunk to the level of the one without. But when the first pangs of his disappointment had passed, Cosmo began to comfort himself with the hope that she might return, perhaps the next evening, at the same hour. Resolving that if she did, she should not at least be scared by the hateful skeleton, he removed that and several other articles of questionable appearance into a recess by the side of the hearth, whence they could not possibly cast any reflection into the mirror; and having made his poor room as tidy as he could, sought the solace of the open sky and of a night wind that had begun to blow, for he could not rest where he was. When he returned, somewhat composed, he could hardly prevail with himself to lie down on his bed; for he could not help feeling as if she had lain upon it; and for him to lie there now would be something like sacrilege. However, weariness prevailed; and laying himself on the couch, dressed as he was, he slept till day.

With a beating heart, beating till he could hardly breathe, he stood in dumb hope before the mirror, on the following evening. Again the reflected room shone as through a purple vapour in the gathering twilight. Everything seemed waiting like himself for a coming splendour to glorify its poor earthliness with the presence of a heavenly joy. And just as the room vibrated with the strokes of the neighbouring church bell, announcing the hour of six, in glided the pale beauty, and again laid herself on the couch. Poor Cosmo nearly lost his senses with delight. She was there once more!

Her eyes sought the corner where the skeleton had stood, and a faint gleam of satisfaction crossed her face, apparently at seeing it empty. She looked suffering still, but there was less of discomfort expressed in her countenance than there had been the night before. She took more notice of the things about her, and seemed to gaze with some curiosity on the strange apparatus standing here and there in her room. At length, however, drowsiness seemed to over-take her, and again she fell asleep. Resolved not to lose sight of her this time, Cosmo watched the sleeping form. Her slumber was so deep and absorbing that a fascinating repose seemed to pass conta-giously from her to him as he gazed upon her; and he started as if from a dream, when the lady moved, and, without opening her eyes, rose, and passed from the room with the gait of a somnambulist.

Cosmo was now in a state of extravagant delight. Most men have a secret treasure somewhere. The miser has his golden hoard; the virtuoso his pet ring; the student his rare book; the poet his favourite haunt; the lover his secret drawer; but Cosmo had a mir-ror with a lovely lady in it.[11] And now that he knew by the skeleton, that she was affected by the things around her, he had a new object in life: he would turn the bare chamber in the mirror into a room such as no lady need disdain to call her own. This he could effect only by furnishing and adorning his. And Cosmo was poor. Yet he possessed accomplishments that could be turned to account; although, hitherto, he had preferred living on his slender allowance, to increasing his means by what his pride considered unworthy of his rank. He was the best swordsman in the University; and now he offered to give lessons in fencing and similar exercises, to such as chose to pay him well for the trouble. His proposal was heard with surprise by the students; but it was eagerly accepted by many; and soon his instructions were not confined to the richer students, but were anxiously sought by many of the young nobility of Prague and its neighbourhood. So that very soon he had a good deal of

11 He is already thinking of the lady as his possession.

money at his command. The first thing he did was to remove his apparatus and oddities into a closet in the room. Then he placed his bed and a few other necessaries on each side of the hearth, and parted them from the rest of the room by two screens of Indian fabric. Then he put an elegant couch for the lady to lie upon, in the corner where his bed had formerly stood; and, by degrees, every day adding some article of luxury, converted it, at length, into a rich boudoir. Every night, about the same time, the lady entered. The first time she saw the new couch, she started with a half-smile; then her face grew very sad, the tears came to her eyes, and she laid herself upon the couch, and pressed her face into the silken cushions, as if to hide from everything. She took notice of each addition and each change as the work proceeded; and a look of acknowledgment, as if she knew that some one was ministering to her, and was grateful for it, mingled with the constant look of suffering. At length, after she had lain down as usual one evening, her eyes fell upon some paintings with which Cosmo had just finished adorning the walls. She rose, and to his great delight, walked across the room, and proceeded to examine them carefully, testifying much pleasure in her looks as she did so. But again the sorrowful, tearful expression returned, and again she buried her face in the pillows of her couch. Gradually, however, her countenance had grown more composed; much of the suffering manifest on her first appearance had vanished, and a kind of quiet, hopeful expression had taken its place; which, however, frequently gave way to an anxious, troubled look, mingled with something of sympathetic pity.

Meantime, how fared Cosmo? As might be expected in one of his temperament, his interest had blossomed into love, and his love – shall I call it *ripened*, or – *withered* into passion. But, alas! he loved a shadow. He could not come near her, could not speak to her, could not hear a sound from those sweet lips, to which his longing eyes would cling like bees to their honey-founts. Ever and anon he sang to himself:

'I shall die for love of the maiden;'

and ever he looked again, and died not, though his heart seemed ready to break with intensity of life and longing. And the more he did for her, the more he loved her; and he hoped that, although she never appeared to see him, yet she was pleased to think that one unknown would give his life to her. He tried to comfort himself over his separation from her, by thinking that perhaps some day she would see him and make signs to him, and that would satisfy him; 'for,' thought he, 'is not this all that a loving soul can do to enter into communion with another? Nay, how many who love never come nearer than to behold each other as in a mirror; seem to know and yet never know the inward life; never enter the other soul; and part at last, with but the vaguest notion of the universe on the borders of which they have been hovering for years? If I could but speak to her, and knew that she heard me, I should be satisfied.' Once he contemplated painting a picture on the wall, which should, of necessity, convey to the lady a thought of himself; but, though he had some skill with the pencil, he found his hand tremble so much when he began the attempt, that he was forced to give it up.

'Who lives, he dies; who dies, he is alive.'[12]

One evening, as he stood gazing on his treasure, he thought he saw a faint expression of self-consciousness on her countenance, as if she surmised that passionate eyes were fixed upon her. This grew; till at last the red blood rose over her neck, and cheek, and brow. Cosmo's longing to approach her became almost delirious. This night she was dressed in an evening costume, resplendent with diamonds. This could add nothing to her beauty, but it presented it in a new aspect; enabled her loveliness to make a new manifestation of itself in a new embodiment. For essential beauty is infinite; and,

---

12 This line is missing from the 1858 edition. The line is reminiscent of Jesus' words, 'he that believeth in me, though he were dead, yet shall he live: And whosoever liveth and believeth in me shall never die.' John 11.25–26.

as the soul of Nature needs an endless succession of varied forms to embody her loveliness, countless faces of beauty springing forth, not any two the same, at any one of her heart-throbs; so the individual form needs an infinite change of its environments, to enable it to uncover all the phases of its loveliness. Diamonds glittered from amidst her hair, half hidden in its luxuriance, like stars through dark rain-clouds; and the bracelets on her white arms flashed all the colours of a rainbow of lightnings, as she lifted her snowy hands to cover her burning face. But her beauty shone down all its adornment. 'If I might have but one of her feet to kiss,' thought Cosmo, 'I should be content.' Alas! he deceived himself, for passion is never content. Nor did he know that there are two ways out of her enchanted house. But, suddenly, as if the pang had been driven into his heart from without, revealing itself first in pain, and afterwards in definite form, the thought darted into his mind, 'She has a lover somewhere. Remembered words of his bring the colour on her face now. I am nowhere to her. She lives in another world all day, and all night, after she leaves me. Why does she come and make me love her, till I, a strong man, am too faint to look upon her more?' He looked again, and her face was pale as a lily. A sorrowful compassion seemed to rebuke the glitter of the restless jewels, and the slow tears rose in her eyes. She left her room sooner this evening than was her wont. Cosmo remained alone, with a feeling as if his bosom had been suddenly left empty and hollow, and the weight of the whole world was crushing in its walls. The next evening, for the first time since she began to come, she came not.

And now Cosmo was in wretched plight. Since the thought of a rival had occurred to him, he could not rest for a moment. More than ever he longed to see the lady face to face. He persuaded himself that if he but knew the worst he would be satisfied; for then he could abandon Prague, and find that relief in constant motion, which is the hope of all active minds when invaded by distress. Meantime he waited with unspeakable anxiety for the next night, hoping she would return: but she did not appear. And now he fell really ill. Rallied by his fellow students on his wretched looks, he ceased to attend the lectures. His engagements were neglected. He cared for nothing. The sky, with the great sun in it, was to him a heartless, burning desert. The men and women in the streets were mere puppets, without motives in themselves, or interest to him. He saw them all as on the ever-changing field of a *camera obscura*.[13] She — she alone and altogether — was his universe, his well of life, his incarnate good. For six evenings she came not. Let his absorbing passion, and the slow fever that was consuming his brain, be his excuse for the resolution which he had taken and begun to execute, before that time had expired.

Reasoning with himself, that it must be by some enchantment connected with the mirror, that the form of the lady was to be seen in it, he determined to attempt to turn to account what he had hitherto studied principally from curiosity. 'For,' said he to himself, 'if a spell can force her presence in that glass (and she came unwillingly at first), may not a stronger spell, such as I know, especially with the aid of her half-presence in the mirror, if ever she appears again, compel her living form to come to me here? If I do her wrong, let love be my excuse. I want only to know my doom from her own lips.' He never doubted, all the time, that she was a real earthly woman; or, rather, that there was a woman, who, somehow or other, threw this reflection of her form into the magic mirror.

He opened his secret drawer, took out his books of magic, lighted his lamp, and read and made notes from midnight till three in the morning, for three successive nights. Then he replaced his books; and the next night went out in quest of the materials necessary for the conjuration. These were not easy to find; for, in love-charms and all incantations of this nature, ingredients are employed scarcely fit to be mentioned, and for the thought even of

13 *Camera obscura*: (Latin, 'Dark chamber') A kind of room, with a small hole in one side. Light would enter through this pin-hole and display the scene onto a wall or piece of paper. In the nineteenth century room-sized camera obscura flourished at seaside resorts and scenic views.

which, in connexion with her, he could only excuse himself on the score of his bitter need. At length he succeeded in procuring all he required; and on the seventh evening from that on which she had last appeared, he found himself prepared for the exercise of unlawful and tyrannical power.

He cleared the centre of the room; stooped and drew a circle of red on the floor, around the spot where he stood; wrote in the four quarters mystical signs, and numbers which were all powers of seven or nine;[14] examined the whole ring carefully, to see that no smallest break had occurred in the circumference; and then rose from his bending posture. As he rose, the church clock struck seven; and, just as she had appeared the first time, reluctant, slow, and stately, glided in the lady. Cosmo trembled; and when, turning, she revealed a countenance worn and wan, as with sickness or inward trouble, he grew faint, and felt as if he dared not proceed. But as he gazed on the face and form, which now possessed his whole soul, to the exclusion of all other joys and griefs, the longing to speak to her, to know that she heard him, to hear from her one word in return, became so unendurable, that he suddenly and hastily resumed his preparations. Stepping carefully from the circle, he put a small brazier into its centre. He then set fire to its contents of charcoal, and while it burned up, opened his window and seated himself, waiting, beside it.

It was a sultry evening. The air was full of thunder. A sense of luxurious depression filled the brain. The sky seemed to have grown heavy, and to compress the air beneath it. A kind of purplish tinge pervaded the atmosphere, and through the open window came the scents of the distant fields, which all the vapours of the city could not quench. Soon the charcoal glowed. Cosmo sprinkled upon it the incense and other substances which he had compounded, and, stepping within the circle, turned his face from the brazier and

14 Mystical numbers. Pythagoras thought seven the perfect number; seven was a sacred number for the Israelites, Babylonians, Egyptians and other ancient races. Nine – the trinity of trinities – was also seen as significant.

towards the mirror. Then, fixing his eyes upon the face of the lady, he began with a trembling voice to repeat a powerful incantation. He had not gone far, before the lady grew pale; and then, like a returning wave, the blood washed all its banks with its crimson tide, and she hid her face in her hands. Then he passed to a conjuration stronger yet. The lady rose and walked uneasily to and fro in her room. Another spell; and she seemed seeking with her eyes for some object on which they wished to rest. At length it seemed as if she suddenly espied him; for her eyes fixed themselves full and wide upon his, and she drew gradually, and somewhat unwillingly, close to her side of the mirror, just as if his eyes had fascinated her. Cosmo had never seen her so near before. Now at least, eyes met eyes; but he could not quite understand the expression of hers. They were full of tender entreaty, but there was something more that he could not interpret. Though his heart seemed to labour in his throat, he would allow no delight or agitation to turn him from his task. Looking still in her face, he passed on to the mightiest charm he knew. Suddenly the lady turned and walked out of the door of her reflected chamber. A moment after she entered his room with veritable presence; and, forgetting all his precautions, he sprang from the charmed circle, and knelt before her. There she stood, the living lady of his passionate visions, alone beside him, in a thundery twilight, and the glow of a magic fire.

'Why,' said the lady, with a trembling voice, 'didst thou bring a poor maiden through the rainy streets alone?'

'Because I am dying for love of thee; but I only brought thee from the mirror there.'

'Ah, the mirror!' and she looked up at it, and shuddered. 'Alas! I am but a slave, while that mirror exists. But do not think it was the power of thy spells that drew me; it was thy longing desire to see me, that beat at the door of my heart, till I was forced to yield.'

'Canst thou love me then?' said Cosmo, in a voice calm as death, but almost inarticulate with emotion.

'I do not know,' she replied sadly; 'that I cannot tell, so long as I am bewildered with enchantments. It were indeed a joy too great, to lay my head on thy bosom and weep to death; for I think thou lovest me, though I do not know; – but –'

Cosmo rose from his knees.

'I love thee as – nay, I know not what – for since I have loved thee, there is nothing else.' He seized her hand: she withdrew it.

'No, better not; I am in thy power, and therefore I may not.'

She burst into tears, and kneeling before him in her turn, said –

'Cosmo, if thou lovest me, set me free, even from thyself; break the mirror.'

'And shall I see thyself instead?'

'That I cannot tell, I will not deceive thee; we may never meet again.'

A fierce struggle arose in Cosmo's bosom. Now she was in his power. She did not dislike him at least; and he could see her when he would. To break the mirror would be to destroy his very life to banish out of his universe the only glory it possessed. The whole world would be but a prison, if he annihilated the one window that looked into the paradise of love. Not yet pure in love, he hesitated.

With a wail of sorrow the lady rose to her feet. 'Ah! he loves me not; he loves me not even as I love him; and alas! I care more for his love than even for the freedom I ask.'

'I will not wait to be willing,' cried Cosmo; and sprang to the corner where the great sword stood.

Meantime it had grown very dark; only the embers cast a red glow through the room. He seized the sword by the steel scabbard, and stood before the mirror; but as he heaved a great blow at it with the heavy pommel, the blade slipped half-way out of the scabbard, and the pommel struck the wall above the mirror. At that moment, a terrible clap of thunder seemed to burst in the very room beside them; and ere Cosmo could repeat the blow, he fell senseless on the hearth. When he came to himself, he found that the lady and the mirror had both disappeared. He was seized with a brain fever, which kept him to his couch for weeks.

When he recovered his reason, he began to think what could have become of the mirror. For the lady, he hoped she had found her way back as she came; but as the mirror involved her fate with its own, he was more immediately anxious about that. He could not think she had carried it away. It was much too heavy, even if it had not been too firmly fixed in the wall, for her to remove it. Then again, he remembered the thunder; which made him believe that it was not the lightning, but some other blow that had struck him down. He concluded that, either by supernatural agency, he having exposed himself to the vengeance of the demons in leaving the circle of safety, or in some other mode, the mirror had probably found its way back to its former owner; and, horrible to think of, might have been by this time once more disposed of, delivering up the lady into the power of another man; who, if he used his power no worse than he himself had done, might yet give Cosmo abundant cause to curse the selfish indecision which prevented him from shattering the mirror at once. Indeed, to think that she whom he loved, and who had prayed to him for freedom, should be still at the mercy, in some degree, of the possessor of the mirror, and was at least exposed to his constant observation, was in itself enough to madden a chary lover.

Anxiety to be well retarded his recovery; but at length he was able to creep abroad. He first made his way to the old broker's, pretending to be in search of something else. A laughing sneer on the creature's face convinced him that he knew all about it; but he could not see it amongst his furniture, or get any information out of him as to what had become of it. He expressed the utmost surprise at hearing it had been stolen, a surprise which Cosmo saw at once to be counterfeited; while, at the same time, he fancied that the old wretch was not at all anxious to have it mistaken for genuine. Full of distress, which he concealed as well as he could, he made many searches, but with no avail. Of course

he could ask no questions; but he kept his ears awake for any re-
motest hint that might set him in a direction of search. He never
went out without a short heavy hammer of steel about him, that
he might shatter the mirror the moment he was made happy by
the sight of his lost treasure, if ever that blessed moment should
arrive. Whether he should see the lady again, was now a thought
altogether secondary, and postponed to the achievement of her
freedom. He wandered here and there, like an anxious ghost, pale
and haggard; gnawed ever at the heart, by the thought of what she
might be suffering – all from his fault.

One night, he mingled with a crowd that filled the rooms of one
of the most distinguished mansions in the city; for he accepted
every invitation, that he might lose no chance, however poor, of ob-
taining some information that might expedite his discovery. Here
he wandered about, listening to every stray word that he could
catch, in the hope of a revelation. As he approached some ladies
who were talking quietly in a corner, one said to another: 'Have you
heard of the strange illness of the Princess von Hohenweiss?'

'Yes; she has been ill for more than a year now. It is very sad for
so fine a creature to have such a terrible malady. She was better for
some weeks lately, but within the last few days the same attacks
have returned, apparently accompanied with more suffering than
ever. It is altogether an inexplicable story.'

'Is there a story connected with her illness?'

'I have only heard imperfect reports of it; but it is said that she
gave offence some eighteen months ago to an old woman who had
held an office of trust in the family, and who, after some incoherent
threats, disappeared. This peculiar affection followed soon after.
But the strangest part of the story is its association with the loss of
an antique mirror, which stood in her dressing-room, and of which
she constantly made use.'

Here the speaker's voice sank to a whisper; and Cosmo, although
his very soul sat listening in his ears, could hear no more. He trem-

bled too much to dare to address the ladies, even if it had been advisable to expose himself to their curiosity. The name of the Princess was well known to him, but he had never seen her; except indeed it was she, which now he hardly doubted, who had knelt before him on that dreadful night. Fearful of attracting attention, for, from the weak state of his health, he could not recover an appearance of calmness, he made his way to the open air, and reached his lodgings; glad in this, that he at least knew where she lived, although he never dreamed of approaching her openly, even if he should be happy enough to free her from her hateful bondage. He hoped, too, that as he had unexpectedly learned so much, the other and far more important part might be revealed to him ere long.

'Have you seen Steinwald lately?'

'No, I have not seen him for some time. He is almost a match for me at the rapier, and I suppose he thinks he needs no more lessons.'

'I wonder what has become of him. I want to see him very much. Let me see; the last time I saw him he was coming out of that old broker's den, to which, if you remember, you accompanied me once, to look at some armour. That is fully three weeks ago.'

This hint was enough for Cosmo. Von Steinwald was a man of influence in the court, well known for his reckless habits and fierce passions. The very possibility that the mirror should be in his possession was hell itself to Cosmo. But violent or hasty measures of any sort were most unlikely to succeed. All that he wanted was an opportunity of breaking the fatal glass; and to obtain this he must bide his time. He revolved many plans in his mind, but without being able to fix upon any.

At length, one evening, as he was passing the house of Von Steinwald, he saw the windows more than usually brilliant. He watched for a while, and seeing that company began to arrive, hastened home, and dressed as richly as he could, in the hope of mingling with the guests unquestioned: in effecting which, there could be no difficulty for a man of his carriage.

In a lofty, silent chamber, in another part of the city, lay a form more like marble than a living woman.[15] The loveliness of death seemed frozen upon her face, for her lips were rigid, and her eyelids closed. Her long white hands were crossed over her breast, and no breathing disturbed their repose. Beside the dead, men speak in whispers, as if the deepest rest of all could be broken by the sound of a living voice. Just so, though the soul was evidently beyond the reach of all intimations from the senses, the two ladies, who sat beside her, spoke in the gentlest tones of subdued sorrow.

'She has lain so for an hour.'

'This cannot last long, I fear.'

'How much thinner she has grown within the last few weeks! If she would only speak, and explain what she suffers, it would be better for her. I think she has visions in her trances, but nothing can induce her to refer to them when she is awake.'

'Does she ever speak in these trances?'

'I have never heard her; but they say she walks sometimes, and once put the whole household in a terrible fright by disappearing for a whole hour, and returning drenched with rain, and almost dead with exhaustion and fright. But even then she would give no account of what had happened.'

A scarce audible murmur from the yet motionless lips of the lady here startled her attendants. After several ineffectual attempts at articulation, the word '*Cosmo!*' burst from her. Then she lay still as before; but only for a moment. With a wild cry, she sprang from the couch erect on the floor, flung her arms above her head, with clasped and straining hands, and, her wide eyes flashing with light,

15 Cosmo has awoken his own marble woman.

called aloud, with a voice exultant as that of a spirit bursting from a sepulchre, 'I am free! I am free! I thank thee!' Then she flung herself on the couch, and sobbed; then rose, and paced wildly up and down the room, with gestures of mingled delight and anxiety. Then turning to her motionless attendants – 'Quick, Lisa, my cloak and hood!' Then lower – 'I must go to him. Make haste, Lisa! You may come with me, if you will.'

In another moment they were in the street, hurrying along towards one of the bridges over the Moldau. The moon was near the zenith, and the streets were almost empty. The Princess soon outstripped her attendant, and was half-way over the bridge, before the other reached it.

'Are you free, lady? The mirror is broken: are you free?'

The words were spoken close beside her, as she hurried on. She turned; and there, leaning on the parapet in a recess of the bridge, stood Cosmo, in a splendid dress, but with a white and quivering face. 'Cosmo! – I am free – and thy servant for ever. I was coming to you now.'

'And I to you, for Death made me bold; but I could get no further. Have I atoned at all? Do I love you a little – truly?'

'Ah, I know now that you love me, my Cosmo; but what do you say about death?'

He did not reply. His hand was pressed against his side. She looked more closely: the blood was welling from between the fingers. She flung her arms around him with a faint bitter wail.

When Lisa came up, she found her mistress kneeling above a wan dead face, which smiled on in the spectral moonbeams.

And now I will say no more about these wondrous volumes; though I could tell many a tale out of them, and could, perhaps, vaguely represent some entrancing thoughts of a deeper kind which I found within them. From many a sultry noon till twilight, did I sit in that grand hall, buried and risen again in these old books.[16] And I trust I have carried away in my soul some of the exhalations of their undying leaves. In after hours of deserved or needful sorrow, portions of what I read there have often come to me again, with an unexpected comforting; which was not fruitless, even though the comfort might seem in itself groundless and vain.

16 Books offer the readert the chance to be reborn; to experience death and rebirth, the ultimate transformation.

—14—

Your gallery
Have we pass'd through, not without much content
In many singularities; but we saw not
That which my daughter came to look upon,
The statue of her mother.

WINTER'S TALE.[1]

It seemed to me strange, that all this time I had heard no music in the fairy palace. I was convinced there must be music in it, but that my sense was as yet too gross to receive the influence of those mysterious motions that beget sound. Sometimes I felt sure, from the way the few figures of which I got such transitory glimpses passed me, or glided into vacancy before me, that they were moving to the law of music; and, in fact, several times I fancied for a moment that I heard a few wondrous tones coming I knew not whence. But they did not last long enough to convince me that I had heard them with the bodily sense. Such as they were, however, they took strange liberties with me, causing me to burst suddenly into tears, of which there was no presence to make me ashamed, or casting me into a kind of trance of speechless delight, which, passing as suddenly, left me faint and longing for more.

1 Shakespeare, *The Winter's Tale*, Act V, Scene 3, lines 9–14. This is the final scene of the play, where Hermione, the Queen thought to be dead, pretends to be a statue and returns to life. Her return to life is accompanied by music.

Now, on an evening, before I had been a week in the palace, I was wandering through one lighted arcade and corridor after another. At length I arrived, through a door that closed behind me, in another vast hall of the palace. It was filled with a subdued crimson light; by which I saw that slender pillars of black, built close to walls of white marble, rose to a great height, and then, dividing into innumerable divergent arches, supported a roof, like the walls, of white marble, upon which the arches intersected intricately, forming a fretting of black upon the white, like the network of a skeleton-leaf. The floor was black. Between several pairs of the pillars upon every side, the place of the wall behind was occupied by a crimson curtain of thick silk, hanging in heavy and rich folds. Behind each of these curtains burned a powerful light, and these were the sources of the glow that filled the hall.[2] A peculiar delicious odour pervaded the place. As soon as I entered, the old inspiration seemed to return to me, for I felt a strong impulse to sing; or rather, it seemed as if some one else was singing a song in my soul, which wanted to come forth at my lips, imbodied in my breath. But I kept silence; and feeling somewhat overcome by the red light and the perfume, as well as by the emotion within me, and seeing at one end of the hall a great crimson chair, more like a throne than a chair, beside a table of white marble, I went to it, and, throwing myself in it, gave myself up to a succession of images of bewildering beauty, which passed before my inward eye, in a long and occasionally crowded train. Here I sat for hours, I suppose; till, returning somewhat to myself, I saw that the red light had paled away, and felt a cool gentle breath gliding over my forehead. I rose and left the hall with unsteady steps, finding my way with some difficulty to my own chamber, and faintly remembering, as I went, that only in the marble cave, before I found the sleeping statue, had I ever had a similar experience.

After this, I repaired every morning to the same hall; where I sometimes sat in the chair and dreamed deliciously, and sometimes

2   This hall is later called 'The White Hall of Phantasy' – see p.181.

walked up and down over the black floor. Sometimes I acted within myself a whole drama, during one of these perambulations; sometimes walked deliberately through the whole epic of a tale; sometimes ventured to sing a song, though with a shrinking fear of I knew not what. I was astonished at the beauty of my own voice as it rang through the place, or rather crept undulating, like a serpent of sound, along the walls and roof of this superb music-hall. Entrancing verses arose within me as of their own accord, chanting themselves to their own melodies, and requiring no addition of music to satisfy the inward sense. But, ever in the pauses of these, when the singing mood was upon me, I seemed to hear something like the distant sound of multitudes of dancers, and felt as if it was the unheard music, moving their rhythmic motion, that within me blossomed in verse and song. I felt, too, that could I but see the dance, I should, from the harmony of complicated movements, not of the dancers in relation to each other merely, but of each dancer individually in the manifested plastic power that moved the consenting harmonious form, understand the whole of the music on the billows of which they floated and swung.

At length, one night, suddenly, when this feeling of dancing came upon me, I bethought me of lifting one of the crimson curtains, and looking if, perchance, behind it there might not be hid some other mystery, which might at least remove a step further the bewilderment of the present one. Nor was I altogether disappointed. I walked to one of the magnificent draperies, lifted a corner, and peeped in. There, burned a great, crimson, globe-shaped light, high in the cubical centre of another hall, which might be larger or less than that in which I stood, for its dimensions were not easily perceived, seeing that floor and roof and walls were entirely of black marble. The roof was supported by the same arrangement of pillars radiating in arches, as that of the first hall; only, here, the pillars and arches were of dark red. But what absorbed my delighted gaze, was an innumerable assembly of white marble statues, of every form, and in multitudinous posture, filling the hall throughout. These stood, in the ruddy glow of the great lamp, upon pedestals of jet black. Around the lamp shone in golden letters, plainly legible from where I stood, the two words –

TOUCH NOT![3]

There was in all this, however, no solution to the sound of dancing; and now I was aware that the influence on my mind had ceased. I did not go in that evening, for I was weary and faint, but I hoarded up the expectation of entering, as of a great coming joy.

Next night I walked, as on the preceding, through the hall. My mind was filled with pictures and songs, and therewith so much absorbed, that I did not for some time think of looking within the curtain I had last night lifted. When the thought of doing so occurred to me first, I happened to be within a few yards of it. I became conscious, at the same moment, that the sound of dancing had been for some time in my ears. I approached the curtain quickly, and, lifting it, entered the black hall. Everything was still as death. I should have concluded that the sound must have proceeded from some other more distant quarter, which conclusion its faintness would, in ordinary circumstances, have necessitated from the first; but there was a something about the statues that caused me still to remain in doubt. As I said, each stood perfectly still upon its black pedestal: but there was about every one a certain air, not of motion, but as if it had just ceased from movement; as if the rest were not altogether of the marbly stillness of thousands of years. It was as if the peculiar atmosphere of each had yet a kind of invisible tremulousness; as if its agitated wavelets had not yet subsided into a perfect calm. I had the suspicion that they had anticipated my appearance, and had sprung, each, from the living joy of the dance, to the death-silence and blackness of its isolated pedestal, just before I entered. I walked across the central hall to the curtain opposite

3   The prohibition echoes the words of Anodos's grandmother at the beginning of the story. Anodos's besetting sin in the book is his desire to touch, to hold, to possess.

the one I had lifted, and, entering there, found all the appearances similar; only that the statues were different, and differently grouped. Neither did they produce on my mind that impression — of motion just expired, which I had experienced from the others. I found that behind every one of the crimson curtains was a similar hall, similarly lighted, and similarly occupied. The next night, I did not allow my thoughts to be absorbed as before with inward images, but crept stealthily along to the furthest curtain in the hall, from behind which, likewise, I had formerly seemed to hear the sound of dancing. I drew aside its edge as suddenly as I could, and, looking in, saw that the utmost stillness pervaded the vast place. I walked in, and passed through it to the other end. There I found that it communicated with a circular corridor, divided from it only by two rows of red columns. This corridor, which was black, with red niches holding statues, ran entirely about the statue-halls, forming a communication between the further ends of them all; further, that is, as regards the central hall of white whence they all diverged like radii, finding their circumference in the corridor. Round this corridor I now went, entering all the halls, of which there were twelve, and finding them all similarly constructed, but filled with quite various statues, of what seemed both ancient and modern sculpture. After I had simply walked through them, I found myself sufficiently tired to long for rest, and went to my own room.

In the night I dreamed that, walking close by one of the curtains, I was suddenly seized with the desire to enter, and darted in. This time I was too quick for them. All the statues were in motion, statues no longer, but men and women — all shapes of beauty that ever sprang from the brain of the sculptor, mingled in the convolutions of a complicated dance. Passing through them to the further end, I almost started from my sleep on beholding, not taking part in the dance with the others, nor seemingly endued with life like them, but standing in marble coldness and rigidity upon a black pedestal in the extreme left corner — my lady of the cave; the marble beauty who sprang from her tomb or her cradle at the call of my songs. While I gazed in speechless astonishment and admiration, a dark shadow, descending from above like the curtain of a stage, gradually hid her entirely from my view. I felt with a shudder that this shadow was perchance my missing demon, whom I had not seen for days. I awoke with a stifled cry.

Of course, the next evening I began my journey through the halls (for I knew not to which my dream had carried me), in the hope of proving the dream to be a true one, by discovering my marble beauty upon her black pedestal. At length, on reaching the tenth hall, I thought I recognised some of the forms I had seen dancing in my dream; and to my bewilderment, when I arrived at the extreme corner on the left, there stood, the only one I had yet seen, a vacant pedestal. It was exactly in the position occupied, in my dream, by the pedestal on which the white lady stood. Hope beat violently in my heart. 'Now,' said I to myself, 'if yet another part of the dream would but come true, and I should succeed in surprising these forms in their nightly dance; it might be the rest would follow, and I should see on the pedestal my marble queen. Then surely if my songs sufficed to give her life before, when she lay in the bonds of alabaster, much more would they be sufficient then to give her volition and motion, when she alone of assembled crowds of marble forms, would be standing rigid and cold.'

But the difficulty was, to surprise the dancers. I had found that a premeditated attempt at surprise, though executed with the utmost care and rapidity, was of no avail. And, in my dream, it was effected by a sudden thought suddenly executed. I saw, therefore, that there was no plan of operation offering any probability of success, but this: to allow my mind to be occupied with other thoughts, as I wandered around the great centre-hall; and so wait till the impulse to enter one of the others should happen to arise in me just at the moment when I was close to one of the crimson curtains. For I hoped that if I entered any one of the twelve halls at the right moment, that would as it were give me the right of entrance to all the others, seeing they all had communication behind. I would not diminish the hope of the right chance, by supposing it necessary that a desire to enter should awake within me, precisely when I was close to the curtains of the tenth hall.

At first the impulses to see recurred so continually, in spite of the crowded imagery that kept passing through my mind, that they formed too nearly a continuous chain, for the hope that any one of them would succeed as a surprise. But as I persisted in banishing them, they recurred less and less often; and after two or three, at considerable intervals, had come when the spot where I happened to be was unsuitable, the hope strengthened, that soon one might arise just at the right moment; namely, when, in walking round the hall, I should be close to one of the curtains.

At length the right moment and the impulse coincided. I darted into the ninth hall. It was full of the most exquisite moving forms. The whole space wavered and swam with the involutions of an intricate dance. It seemed to break suddenly as I entered, and all made one or two bounds towards their pedestals; but, apparently on finding that they were thoroughly overtaken, they returned to their employment (for it seemed with them earnest enough to be called such) without further heeding me. Somewhat impeded by the floating crowd, I made what haste I could towards the bottom of the hall; whence, entering the corridor, I turned towards the tenth. I soon arrived at the corner I wanted to reach, for the corridor was comparatively empty; but, although the dancers here, after a little confusion, altogether disregarded my presence, I was dismayed at beholding, even yet, a vacant pedestal. But I had a conviction that she was near me. And as I looked at the pedestal, I thought I saw upon it, vaguely revealed as if through overlapping folds of drapery, the indistinct outlines of white feet. Yet there was no sign of drapery or concealing shadow whatever. But I remembered the descending shadow in my dream. And I hoped still in the power of my songs; thinking that what could dispel alabaster, might likewise be capable of dispelling what concealed my beauty now, even if it were the demon whose darkness had overshadowed all my life.

—15—

Alexander: When will you finish Campaspe?
Apelles: Never finish: for always in absolute beauty there is somewhat above art.
LYLY'S *CAMPASPE*[1]

And now, what song should I sing to unveil my Isis, if indeed she was present unseen? I hurried away to the white hall of Phantasy, heedless of the innumerable forms of beauty that crowded my way: these might cross my eyes, but the unseen filled my brain. I wandered long, up and down the silent space: no songs came. My soul was not still enough for songs. Only in the silence and darkness of the soul's night, do those stars of the inward firmament sink to its lower surface from the singing realms beyond, and shine upon the conscious spirit. Here all effort was unavailing. If they came not, they could not be found.

Next night, it was just the same. I walked through the red glimmer of the silent hall; but lonely as there I walked, as lonely trod my soul up and down the halls of the brain. At last I entered one of the statue-halls. The dance had just commenced, and I was delighted to find that I was free of their assembly. I walked on till I came to the sacred corner. There I found the pedestal just as I had left it, with the faint glimmer as of white feet still resting on the dead black. As soon as I saw it, I seemed to feel a presence which longed to become visible; and, as it were, called to me to gift it with self-manifestation, that it might shine on me. The power of song came to me. But the moment my voice, though I sang low and soft,

---

1 John Lyly (c.1554–1606) was a dramatist and prose writer. *Alexander and Campaspe* was a play presented at court in 1584-85. It tells of a love triangle between Alexander the Great, Campaspe, a young Theban captive, and Apelles, the painter who paints her portrait.

stirred the air of the hall, the dancers started; the quick interweaving crowd shook, lost its form, divided; each figure sprang to its pedestal, and stood, a self-evolving life no more, but a rigid, life-like, marble shape, with the whole form composed into the expression of a single state or act. Silence rolled like a spiritual thunder through the grand space. My song had ceased, scared at its own influences. But I saw in the hand of one of the statues close by me, a harp whose chords yet quivered. I remembered that as she bounded past me, her harp had brushed against my arm; so the spell of the marble had not infolded it. I sprang to her, and with a gesture of entreaty, laid my hand on the harp. The marble hand, probably from its contact with the uncharmed harp, had strength enough to relax its hold, and yield the harp to me. No other motion indicated life. Instinctively I struck the chords and sang. And not to break upon the record of my song, I mention here, that as I sang the first four lines, the loveliest feet became clear upon the black pedestal; and ever as I sang, it was as if a veil were being lifted up from before the form, but an invisible veil, so that the statue appeared to grow before me, not so much by evolution, as by infinitesimal degrees of added height. And, while I sang, I did not feel that I stood by a statue, as indeed it appeared to be, but that a real woman-soul was revealing itself by successive stages of imbodiment, and consequent manifestatlon and expression.

> *Feet of beauty, firmly planting*
> *Arches white on rosy heel!*
> *Whence the life-spring, throbbing, panting,*
> *Pulses upward to reveal!*
> *Fairest things know least despising;*
> *Foot and earth meet tenderly:*
> *'Tis the woman, resting, rising*
> *Upward to sublimity,*
>
> *Rise the limbs, sedately sloping,*
> *Strong and gentle, full and free;*
> *Soft and slow, like certain hoping,*
> *Drawing nigh the broad firm knee.*

'I sprang to her, and laid
my hand on the harp...'

Up to speech! As up to roses
　Pants the life from leaf to flower,
So each blending change discloses,
　Nearer still, expression's power.

Lo! fair sweeps, white surges, twining
　Up and outward fearlessly!
Temple columns, close combining,
　Lift a holy mystery.
Heart of mine! what strange surprises
　Mount aloft on such a stair!
Some great vision upward rises,
　Curving, bending, floating fair.

Bands and sweeps, and hill and hollow
　Lead my fascinated eye;
Some apocalypse will follow,
　Some new world of deity.
Zoned unseen, and outward swelling,
　With new thoughts and wonders rife,
Queenly majesty foretelling,
　See the expanding house of life!

Sudden heaving, unforbidden
　Sighs eternal, still the same —
Mounts of snow have summits hidden
　In the mists of uttered flame.
But the spirit, dawning nearly
　Finds no speech for earnest pain;
Finds a soundless sighing merely —
　Builds its stairs, and mounts again.

Heart, the queen, with secret hoping,
　Sendeth out her waiting pair;
Hands, blind hands, half blindly groping,
　Half inclasping visions rare;
And the great arms, heartways bending;
　Might of Beauty, drawing home
There returning, and re-blending,
　Where from roots of love they roam.

Build thy slopes of radiance beamy
  Spirit, fair with womanhood!
Tower thy precipice, white-gleamy,
  Climb unto the hour of good.
Dumb space will be rent asunder,
  Now the shining column stands
Ready to be crowned with wonder
  By the builder's joyous hands.

All the lines abroad are spreading,
  Like a fountain's falling race.
Lo, the chin, first feature, treading,
  Airy foot to rest the face!
Speech is nigh; oh, see the blushing,
  Sweet approach of lip and breath!
Round the mouth dim silence, hushing,
  Waits to die ecstatic death.

Span across in treble curving,
  Bow of promise, upper lip!
Set them free, with gracious swerving;
  Let the wing-words float and dip.
Dumb art thou? O Love immortal,
  More than words thy speech must be;
Childless yet the tender portal
  Of the home of melody.

Now the nostrils open fearless,
  Proud in calm unconsciousness,
Sure it must be something peerless
  That the great Pan would express!
Deepens, crowds some meaning tender,
  In the pure, dear lady-face.
Lo, a blinding burst of splendour! —
  'Tis the free soul's issuing grace.

Two calm lakes of molten glory
  Circling round unfathomed deeps!
Lightning-flashes, transitory,
  Cross the gulfs where darkness sleeps.
This the gate, at last, of gladness,
  To the outward striving me:
In a rain of light and sadness,
  Out its loves and longings flee!

With a presence I am smitten
  Dumb, with a foreknown surprise;
Presence greater yet than written
  Even in the glorious eyes.
Through the gulfs, with inward gazes,
  I may look till I am lost;
Wandering deep in spirit-mazes,
  In a sea without a coast.

Windows open to the glorious!
  Time and space, oh, far beyond!
Woman, ah! thou art victorious,
  And I perish, overfond.
Springs aloft the yet Unspoken
  In the forehead's endless grace,
Full of silences unbroken;
  Infinite, unfeatured face.

Domes above, the mount of wonder;
  Height and hollow wrapt in night;
Hiding in its caverns under
  Woman-nations in their might.
Passing forms, the highest Human
  Faints away to the Divine
Features none, of man or woman,
  Can unveil the holiest shine.

Sideways, grooved porches only
  Visible to passing eye,
Stand the silent, doorless, lonely
  Entrance-gates of melody.
But all sounds fly in as boldly,
  Groan and song, and kiss and cry
At their galleries, lifted coldly,
  Darkly, 'twixt the earth and sky.

Beauty, thou art spent, thou knowest
  So, in faint, half-glad despair,
From the summit thou o'erflowest
  In a fall of torrent hair;
Hiding what thou hast created
  In a half-transparent shroud:
Thus, with glory soft-abated,
  Shines the moon through vapoury cloud.

—16—

Ev'n the Styx, which ninefold her infoldeth
   Hems not Ceres' daughter in its flow;
But she grasps the apple — ever holdeth
   Her, sad Orcus, down below.

SCHILLER, *DAS IDEAL UND DAS LEBEN*[1]

E ver as I sang, the veil was uplifted; ever as I sang, the signs of life grew; till, when the eyes dawned upon me, it was with that sunrise of splendour which my feeble song attempted to re-imbody. The wonder is, that I was not altogether overcome, but was able to complete my song as the unseen veil continued to rise. This ability came solely from the state of mental elevation in which I found myself. Only because uplifted in song, was I able to endure the blaze of the dawn. But I cannot tell whether she looked more of statue or more of woman; she seemed removed into that region of phantasy where all is intensely vivid, but nothing clearly defined. At last, as I sang of her descending hair, the glow of soul faded away, like a dying sunset. A lamp within had been extinguished, and the house of life shone blank in a winter morn. She was a statue once more — but visible, and that was much gained. Yet the revulsion from

---

1   '*Selbst der Styx, der neunfach sie umwindet, Wehrt die Rückkehr Ceres Tochter nicht: Nach dem Apfel greift sie, und es bindet Ewig sie des Orkus Pflicht.*' Friedrich Schiller (1759–1805) was a German dramatist and poet. *Das Ideal und das Leben* (Ideal and Life) is a philosophical poem written in 1796. *Styx*: the river that, according to classical mythology, flowed reound hell. *Ceres*: the Roman name for mother earth, or the corn goddess and Ceres' daughter is Proserpine or Persephone, the goddess of springtime. *Orcus*: the Latin name for hell. Persephone was abducted by Pluto, god of the underworld. Although released by Jupiter, she was forced to spend six months of every year in hell, because she had eaten of the fruit of the underworld. the myth illustrates the changing of the seasons.

hope and
fruition was
such, that, unable to
restrain myself, I sprang
to her, and, in defiance of
the law of the place, flung my
arms around her, as if I would tear
her from the grasp of a visible Death,
and lifted her from the pedestal down
to my heart. But no sooner had her feet
ceased to be in contact with the black

'A white figure gleamed past me, wringing her hands...'

pedestal, than she shuddered and trembled all over; then, writhing from my arms,
before I could tighten their hold, she sprang into the corridor, with
the reproachful cry, 'You should not have touched me!' darted behind one of the exterior pillars of the circle, and disappeared.[2] I
followed almost as fast; but ere I could reach the pillar, the sound
of a closing door, the saddest of all sounds sometimes, fell on my
ear; and, arriving at the spot where she had vanished, I saw, lighted
by a pale yellow lamp which hung above it, a heavy, rough door,
altogether unlike any others I had seen in the palace; for they were

2 Once again Anodos seeks to touch her – although this time from different motives: he wants
   to rescue her. But he has broken the law and there is an Eden-like expulsion from paradise.

all of ebony, or ivory, or covered with silver-plates, or of some odorous wood, and very ornate; whereas this seemed of old oak, with heavy nails and iron studs. Notwithstanding the precipitation of my pursuit, I could not help reading, in silver letters beneath the lamp: '*No one enters here without the leave of the Queen.*' But what was the Queen to me, when I followed my white lady? I dashed the door to the wall and sprang through. Lo! I stood on a waste windy hill. Great stones like tombstones stood all about me. No door, no palace was to be seen. A white figure gleamed past me, wringing her hands, and crying, 'Ah! you should have sung to me; you should have sung to me!' and disappeared behind one of the stones. I followed. A cold gust of wind met me from behind the stone; and when I looked, I saw nothing but a great hole in the earth, into which I could find no way of entering. Had she fallen in? I could not tell. I must wait for the daylight. I sat down and wept, for there was no help.

17

First, I thought, almost despairing,
    This must crush my spirit now;
Yet I bore it, and am bearing —
    Only do not ask me how.

HEINE[1]

W hen the daylight came, it brought the possibility of action, but with it little of consolation. With the first visible increase of light, I gazed into the chasm, but could not, for more than an hour, see sufficiently well to discover its nature. At last I saw it was almost a perpendicular opening, like a roughly excavated well, only very large. I could perceive no bottom; and it was not till the sun actually rose, that I discovered a sort of natural staircase, in many parts little more than suggested, which led round and round the gulf, descending spirally into its abyss. I saw at once that this was my path; and without a moment's hesitation, glad to quit the sunlight, which stared at me most heartlessly, I commenced my tortuous descent. It was very difficult. In some parts I had to cling to the rocks like a bat. In one place, I dropped from the track down upon the next returning spire of the stair; which being broad in this particular portion, and standing out from the wall at right angles, received me upon my feet safe,

---

1 'Anfangs wollt' ich fast verzagen, Und ich glaubt' ich trüg' es nie, Und ich hab' es doch getragen, — Aber fragt mich nur nicht: wie?' Heinrich Heine (1797–1856) was a German poet and journalist. A Jew who converted to Christianity, his books were later burned by the Nazis. Many years later, at the site of one of these immolations, a line from his 1821 play *Almansor* was engraved in the ground: 'Where they burn books, they will ultimately also burn people.'

though somewhat stupefied by the shock. After descending a great way, I found the stair ended at a narrow opening which entered the rock horizontally. Into this I crept, and, having entered, had just room to turn round. I put my head out into the shaft by which I had come down, and surveyed the course of my descent. Looking up, I saw the stars; although the sun must by this time have been high in the heavens. Looking below, I saw that the sides of the shaft went sheer down, smooth as glass; and far beneath me, I saw the reflection of the same stars I had seen in the heavens when I looked up.[2] I turned again, and crept inwards some distance, when the passage widened, and I was at length able to stand and walk upright. Wider and loftier grew the way; new paths branched off on every side; great open halls appeared; till at last I found myself wandering on through an underground country, in which the sky was of rock, and instead of trees and flowers, there were only fantastic rocks and stones. And ever as I went, darker grew my thoughts, till at last I had no hope whatever of finding the white lady: I no longer called her to myself my white lady. Whenever a choice was necessary, I always chose the path which seemed to lead downwards.

At length I began to find that these regions were inhabited. From behind a rock a peal of harsh grating laughter, full of evil humour, rang through my ears, and, looking round, I saw a queer, goblin creature, with a great head and ridiculous features, just such as those described, in German histories and travels, as Kobolds.[3] 'What do you want with me?' I said. He pointed at me with a long forefinger, very thick at the root, and sharpened to a point, and answered, 'He!

---

2 In chapter 20 of *The Pickwick Papers*, Charles Dickens referred to the popular idea that being 'placed at the bottom of a reasonably deep well' affords the 'opportunity of perceiving the stars in the daytime.' The idea that at the bottom of a deep well, one could see the stars during daylight dates back to Aristotle (*On the Generation of Animals* Book 5, ch. 1). Pliny supported the idea, as did many Muslim scientists. Observatories in Europe and the Middle East were said to have observation wells. Modern experiments have failed to endorse the theory.

3 *Kobold*: the German goblin or mine spirit. From the Greek *kobalos* – a mischievous, evil spirit. These goblins, and the mine they inhabit, are the forerunners of those in MacDonald's *The Princess and the Goblin*.

he! he! what do you want here?' Then, changing his tone, he continued, with mock humility – 'Honoured sir, vouchsafe to withdraw
from thy slaves the lustre of thy august presence, for thy slaves cannot
support its brightness.' A second appeared, and struck in: 'You are so
big, you keep the sun from us. We can't see for you, and we're so cold.'
Thereupon arose, on all sides, the most terrific uproar of laughter,
from voices like those of children in volume, but scrannel and harsh
as those of decrepit age, though, unfortunately, without its weakness.
The whole pandemonium of fairy devils, of all varieties of fantastic
ugliness, both in form and feature, and of all sizes from one to four
feet, seemed to have suddenly assembled about me. At length, after
a great babble of talk among themselves, in a language unknown to
me, and after seemingly endless gesticulation, consultation, elbow-
nudging, and unmitigated peals of laughter, they formed into a circle
about one of their number, who scrambled upon a stone, and, much
to my surprise, and somewhat to my dismay, began to sing, in a voice
corresponding in its nature to his talking one, from beginning to
end, the song with which I had brought the light into the eyes of the
white lady. He sang the same air too; and, all the time, maintained a
face of mock entreaty and worship; accompanying the song with the
travestied gestures of one playing on the lute.[4] The whole assembly
kept silence, except at the close of every verse, when they roared,
and danced, and shouted with laughter, and flung themselves on the
ground, in real or pretended convulsions of delight. When he had
finished, the singer threw himself from the top of the stone, turning
heels over head several times in his descent; and when he did alight, it
was on the top of his head, on which he hopped about, making the
most grotesque gesticulations with his legs in the air. Inexpressible
laughter followed, which broke up in a shower of tiny stones from in-

4   That the kobolds know the exact words of Anodos's song implies that they are part of him;
    they are, in a sense, his own demons. The kobolds mock Anodos with his apparent failure and
    with his deepest fear – that someone else will have 'his' white lady. It is only when he accepts
    this that they fall silent. This episode mirrors the goblins' mockery of Anodos in chapter 10
    (p.122). Both events take place in a dry, rocky landscape; one above ground and one below.
    Both journeys end in a magical boat ride to a place of healing.

numerable hands. They could not materially injure me, although they cut me on the head and face. I attempted to run away, but they all rushed upon me, and, laying hold of every part that afforded a grasp, held me tight. Crowding about me like bees, they shouted an insect-swarm of exasperating speeches up into my face, among which the most frequently recurring were —

They all rushed upon me, and held me tight

'You shan't have her; you shan't have her; he! he! he! She's for a better man; how he'll kiss her! how he'll kiss her!'

The galvanic torrent of this battery of malevolence stung to life within me a spark of nobleness, and I said aloud, 'Well, if he is a better man, let him have her.'

They instantly let go their hold of me, and fell back a step or two, with a whole broadside of grunts and humphs, as of unexpected and disappointed approbation. I made a step or two forward, and a lane was instantly opened for me through the midst of the grinning little antics, who bowed most politely to me on every side as I passed. After I had gone a few yards, I looked back, and saw them all standing quite still, looking after me, like a great school of boys; till suddenly one turned round, and with a loud whoop, rushed into the midst of the others. In an instant, the whole was one writhing and tumbling heap of contortion, reminding me of the live pyramids of intertwined snakes of which travellers make report. As soon as one was worked out of the mass, he bounded off a few paces, and then, with a somersault and a run, threw himself gyrating into the air, and descended with all his weight on the summit of the heaving and struggling chaos of fantastic figures. I left them still busy at this fierce and apparently aimless amusement. And as I went, I sang —

> *If a nobler waits for thee,*
> *I will weep aside;*
> *It is well that thou should'st be,*
> *Of the nobler, bride.*
>
> *For if love builds up the home,*
> *Where the heart is free,*
> *Homeless yet the heart must roam,*
> *That has not found thee.*
>
> *One must suffer: I, for her*
> *Yield in her my part*
> *Take her, thou art worthier —*
> *Still I be still, my heart!*
>
> *Gift ungotten! largess high*
> *Of a frustrate will!*
> *But to yield it lovingly*
> *Is a something still.*

Then a little song arose of itself in my soul; and I felt for the moment, while it sank sadly within me, as if I was once more walking up and down the white hall of Phantasy in the Fairy Palace. But this lasted no longer than the song; as will be seen.

> *Do not vex thy violet*
> *Perfume to afford:*
> *Else no odour thou wilt get*
> *From its little hoard.*

In thy lady's gracious eyes
Look not thou too long;
Else from them the glory flies,
And thou dost her wrong.

Come not thou too near the maid,
Clasp her not too wild;
Else the splendour is allayed,
And thy heart beguiled.

A crash of laughter, more discordant and deriding than any I had yet heard, invaded my ears. Looking on in the direction of the sound, I saw a little elderly woman, much taller, however, than the goblins I had just left, seated upon a stone by the side of the path. She rose, as I drew near, and came forward to meet me. She was very plain and commonplace in appearance, without being hideously ugly. Looking up in my face with a stupid sneer, she said: 'Isn't it a pity you haven't a pretty girl to walk all alone with you through this sweet country? How different everything would look? wouldn't it? Strange that one can never have what one would like best! How the roses would bloom and all that, even in this infernal hole! wouldn't they, Anodos? Her eyes would light up the old cave, wouldn't they?'

'That depends on who the pretty girl should be,' replied I.

'Not so very much matter that,' she answered; 'look here.'

I had turned to go away as I gave my reply, but now I stopped and looked at her. As a rough unsightly bud might suddenly blossom into the most lovely flower; or rather, as a sunbeam bursts through a shapeless cloud, and transfigures the earth; so burst a face of resplendent beauty, as it were through the unsightly visage of the woman, destroying it with light as it dawned through it. A summer sky rose above me, gray with heat; across a shining slumberous landscape, looked from afar the peaks of snow-capped mountains; and down from a great rock beside me fell a sheet of water mad with its own delight.

'Stay with me,' she said, lifting up her exquisite face, and looking full in mine.

I drew back. Again the infernal laugh grated upon my ears; again the rocks closed in around me, and the ugly woman looked at me with wicked, mocking hazel eyes. 'You shall have your reward,' said she. 'You shall see your white lady again.'

'That lies not with you,' I replied, and turned and left her.

She followed me with shriek upon shriek of laughter, as I went on my way.

I may mention here, that although there was always light enough to see my path and a few yards on every side of me, I never could find out the source of this sad sepulchral illumination.

18

In the wind's uproar, the sea's raging grim, And the sighs that are born in him.
                                                                    HEINE[1]

> *From dreams of bliss shall men awake*
> *One day, but not to weep:*
> *The dreams remain; they only break*
> *The mirror of the sleep.*

                                        JEAN PAUL, HESPERUS[2]

How I got through this dreary part of my travels, I do not know. I do not think I was upheld by the hope that any moment the light might break in upon me; for I scarcely thought about that. I went on with a dull endurance, varied by moments of uncontrollable sadness; for more and more the conviction grew upon me that I should never see the white lady again. It may seem strange that one with whom I had held so little communion should have so engrossed my thoughts; but benefits conferred awaken love in some minds, as surely as benefits received in others. Besides being delighted and proud that *my* songs had called the beautiful creature to life, the same fact caused me to feel a tenderness unspeakable for her, accompanied with a kind

---

1 '*Im Sausen des Windes, im Brausen des Meers, Und im Seufzen der eigenen Brust.*' On Heine, see p.188 n.1.

2 '*Ja, es wird zwar ein anderes Zeitalter kommen, wo es Licht wird, und wo der Mensch aus erhabnen Traümen erwacht, und die Traüme — weider findet, weil er nichts verlor als den Schlaf.*' Jean Paul was the pseudonym of the German novelist Johann Paul Friedrich Richter (1763–1825). *Hesperus* was written in 1795. Here, MacDonald has put a line from a prose work into verse, and also added a reference to 'the mirror' which is not in the original. (See William Webb, 'George MacDonald and Jean Paul: An Introduction', *North Wind* 14, 1995, pp.65–71).

of feeling of property in her; for so the goblin Selfishness would reward the angel Love. When to all this is added, an overpowering sense of her beauty, and an unquestioning conviction that this was a true index to inward loveliness, it may be understood how it came to pass that my imagination filled my whole soul with the play of its own multitudinous colours and harmonies around the form which yet stood, a gracious marble radiance, in the midst of its white hall of phantasy. The time passed by unheeded; for my thoughts were busy. Perhaps this was also in part the cause of my needing no food, and never thinking how I should find any, during this subterraneous part of my travels. How long they endured I could not tell, for I had no means of measuring time; and when I looked back, there was such a discrepancy between the decisions of my imagination and my judgment, as to the length of time that had passed, that I was bewildered, and gave up all attempts to arrive at any conclusion on the point.

A gray mist continually gathered behind me. When I looked back towards the past, this mist was the medium through which my eyes had to strain for a vision of what had gone by; and the form of the white lady had receded into an unknown region. At length the country of rock began to close again around me, gradually and slowly narrowing, till I found myself walking in a gallery of rock once more, both sides of which I could touch with my outstretched hands. It narrowed yet, until I was forced to move carefully, in order to avoid striking against the projecting pieces of rock. The roof sank lower and lower, until I was compelled, first to stoop, and then to creep on my hands and knees. It recalled terrible dreams of childhood; but I was not much afraid, because I felt sure that this was my path, and my only hope of leaving Fairy Land, of which I was now almost weary.[3]

At length, on getting past an abrupt turn in the passage, through which I had to force myself, I saw, a few yards ahead of me, the

3 This is the imagery of second birth. Anodos is reduced to a state of childlike dependence.

A wintry sea, bare, and waste, and gray

long-forgotten daylight shining through a small opening, to which the path, if path it could now be called, led me. With great difficulty I accomplished these last few yards, and came forth to the day. I stood on the shore of a wintry sea, with a wintry sun just a few feet above its horizon-edge. It was bare, and waste, and gray.[4] Hundreds of hopeless waves rushed constantly shorewards, falling exhausted upon a beach of great loose stones, that seemed to stretch miles and miles in both directions. There was nothing for the eye but mingling shades of gray; nothing for the ear but the rush of the coming, the roar of the breaking, and the moan of the retreating wave. No rock lifted up a sheltering severity above the dreariness around; even that from which I had myself emerged rose scarcely a

4 "'Winter," he went on, "does not belong to death, although the outside of it looks like death. Beneath the snow, the grass is growing. Below the frost, the roots are warm and alive. Winter is only a spring too weak and feeble for us to see that it is living. The cold does for all things what the gardener has sometimes to do for valuable trees: he must half kill them before they will bear any fruit. Winter is in truth the small beginnings of the spring.'" (MacDonald, *Adela Cathcart* Book I, ch.2.) This wasteland, which appears so desolate and despairing, will bring a new birth for Anodos. Robb suggests this scene is a response to Arnold's poem, *Dover Beach*. According to MacDonald's son, Matthew Arnold was an 'intimate' friend of his father's. (MacDonald, Greville, *George MacDonald and his Wife*, p.300.) However, *Dover Beach* was not published till 1867. There are only two extant letters from Arnold to MacDonald, the earliest of which dates from 1868 (*Letters of Matthew Arnold*, Vol 3, p.242). Nevertheless, it is interesting to contrast MacDonald's attitude with Arnold's. For Arnold, the beach was a place without hope; for MacDonald it was a point where hope springs into life again. (See Robb, *George MacDonald*, pp.80–83).

foot above the opening by which I had reached the dismal day, more dismal even than the tomb I had left. A cold, death-like wind swept across the shore, seeming to issue from a pale mouth of cloud upon the horizon. Sign of life was nowhere visible. I wandered over the stones, up and down the beach, a human imbodiment of the nature around me. The wind increased; its keen waves flowed through my soul; the foam rushed higher up the stones; a few dead stars began to gleam in the east; the sound of the waves grew louder and yet more despairing. A dark curtain of cloud was lifted up, and a pale blue rent shone between its foot and the edge of the sea, out from which rushed an icy storm of frozen wind, that tore the waters into spray as it passed, and flung the billows in raving heaps upon the desolate shore. I could bear it no longer.

'I will not be tortured to death,' I cried; 'I will meet it half-way. The life within me is yet enough to bear me up to the face of Death, and then I die unconquered.'

Before it had grown so dark, I had observed, though without any particular interest, that on one part of the shore a low platform of rock seemed to run out far into the midst of the breaking waters. Towards this I now went, scrambling over smooth stones, to which scarce even a particle of sea-weed clung; and having found it, I got on it, and followed its direction, as near as I could guess, out into the tumbling chaos. I could hardly keep my feet against the wind and sea. The waves repeatedly all but swept me off my path; but I kept on my way, till I reached the end of the low promontory, which, in the fall of the waves, rose a good many feet above the surface, and, in their rise, was covered with their waters. I stood one moment and gazed into the heaving abyss beneath me; then plunged headlong into the mounting wave below. A blessing, like the kiss of a mother, seemed to alight on my soul; a calm, deeper than that which accompanies a hope deferred, bathed my spirit. I sank far into the waters, and sought not to return. I felt as if once more the great arms of the beech-tree were around me, soothing me after the miseries I had passed through, and telling me, like a little sick child, that I should be better to-morrow. The waters of themselves lifted me, as with loving arms, to the surface. I breathed again, but did not unclose my eyes. I would not look on the wintry sea, and the pitiless gray sky.[5] Thus I floated, till something gently touched me. It was a little boat floating beside me. How it came there I could not tell; but it rose and sank on the waters, and kept touching me in its fall, as if with a human will to let me know that help was by me. It was a little gay-coloured boat, seemingly covered with glistering scales like those of a fish, all of brilliant rainbow hues. I scrambled into it, and lay down in the bottom, with a sense of exquisite repose. Then I drew over me a rich, heavy, purple cloth that was beside me; and, lying still, knew, by the sound of the waters, that my little bark was fleeting rapidly onwards. Finding, however, none of that stormy motion which the sea had manifested when I beheld it from the shore, I opened my eyes; and, looking first up, saw above me the deep violet sky of a warm southern night; and then, lifting my head, saw that I was sailing fast upon a summer sea, in the last border of a southern twilight. The aureole of the sun yet shot the extreme faint tips of its longest rays above the horizon-waves, and withdrew them not. It was a perpetual twilight. The stars, great and earnest, like children's eyes, bent down lovingly towards the waters; and the reflected stars within seemed to float up, as if longing to meet their embraces. But when I looked down, a new wonder met my view. For, vaguely revealed beneath the wave, I floated above my whole Past. The fields of my childhood flitted by; the halls of my youthful labours; the streets of great cities where I had dwelt; and the assemblies of men and women wherein I had wearied myself

5   MacDonald used the sea as a symbol of death in other works. In *The Golden Key*, Mossy and Tangle 'taste of death' when they plunge into the bath of the Old Man of the Sea, described as 'a basin hollowed out of rock, and half-full of the clearest sea-water.' (MacDonald, *The Golden Key*.) Elsewhere, MacDonald writes of death as 'that region into which, as into a wave-less sea, all the rivers of life rush and are silent. Is it the sea of death? No. The sea of life – a life too keen, too refined, for our senses to know it, and therefore we call it death – because we cannot lay hold upon it.' (MacDonald, *Annals of a Quiet Neighbourhood*, ch.29.)

seeking for rest.[6] But so indistinct were the visions, that sometimes I thought I was sailing on a shallow sea, and that strange rocks and forests of sea-plants beguiled my eye, sufficiently to be transformed, by the magic of the phantasy, into well-known objects and regions. Yet, at times, a beloved form seemed to lie close beneath me in sleep; and the eyelids would tremble as if about to forsake the conscious eye; and the arms would heave upwards, as if in dreams they sought for a satisfying presence. But these motions might come only from the heaving of the waters between those forms and me. Soon I fell asleep, overcome with fatigue and delight. In dreams of unspeakable joy – of restored friendships; of revived embraces; of love which said it had never died; of faces that had vanished long ago, yet said with smiling lips that they knew nothing of the grave; of pardons implored, and granted with such bursting floods of love, that I was almost glad I had sinned – thus I passed through this wondrous twilight.[7] I awoke with the feeling that I had been kissed and loved to my heart's content; and found that my boat was floating motionless by the grassy shore of a little island.

6 This may be autobiographical. It reflects MacDonald's own journey, from the fields around his childhood home of Huntly, to cities like Aberdeen, London and Manchester. The Assemblies of men and women may refer to the churches, or to places like University and the Highbury College where he trained as a pastor.

7 This is a potent image of forgiveness – the bliss is such that it almost – almost – makes the sin worthwhile. The idea links in with MacDonald's belief in the power of apparently evil events to transform and shape us.

19

*'In still rest, in changeless simplicity, I bear, uninterrupted, the consciousness of
the whole of Humanity within me.'*

SCHLEIERMACHER, MONOLOGEN[1]

*'. . . such a sweetness, such a grace,
In all thy speech appear,
That what to th'eye a beauteous face,
That thy tongue is to the ear.'*

COWLEY[2]

The water was deep to the very edge; and I sprang from the little boat upon a soft grassy turf. The island seemed rich with a profusion of all grasses and low flowers. All delicate lowly things were most plentiful; but no trees rose skywards, not even a bush overtopped the tall grasses, except in one place near the cottage I am about to describe, where a few plants of the gum-cistus,[3] which drops every night all the blossoms that the day brings forth, formed a kind of natural arbour. The whole island lay open to the sky and sea. It rose nowhere more than a few feet above the level of the waters, which flowed deep all around its border. Here there seemed to be neither tide nor storm. A sense of persistent calm and fulness arose in the mind at the sight of the slow, pulse-like rise and fall of the deep, clear, unrippled waters

---

1 'In stiller Ruhe, in wechselloser Einfalt führ ich ununterbrochen das Bewusstseyn der ganzen Menschheit in mir.' Friedrich Schleiermacher, German theologian and philosopher (1768 – 1834). *Monologen* ('Soliloquies') was published in 1800.

2 Abraham Cowley (1618–67) poet. The lines come from his poem 'The Mistress'.

3 *Gum-cistus*: commonly known as rock roses.

against the bank of the island, for shore it could hardly be called, being so much more like the edge of a full, solemn river. As I walked over the grass towards the cottage, which stood at a little distance from the bank, all the flowers of childhood looked at me with perfect child-eyes out of the grass. My heart, softened by the dreams through which it had passed, overflowed in a sad, tender love towards them. They looked to me like children impregnably fortified in a helpless confidence. The sun stood half-way down the western sky, shining very soft and golden; and there grew a second world of shadows amidst the world of grasses and wild flowers.

The cottage was square, with low walls, and a high pyramidal roof thatched with long reeds, of which the withered blossoms hung over all the eaves. It is noticeable that most of the buildings I saw in Fairy Land were cottages.[4] There was no path to a door, nor, indeed, was there any track worn by footsteps in the island.[5] The cottage rose right out of the smooth turf. It had no windows that I could see; but there was a door in the centre of the side facing me, up to which I went. I knocked, and the sweetest voice I had ever heard said, 'Come in.' I entered. A bright fire was burning on a hearth in the centre of the earthern floor, and the smoke found its way out at an opening in the centre of the pyramidal roof. Over the fire hung a little pot, and over the pot bent a woman-face, the most wonderful, I thought, that I had ever beheld. For it was older than any countenance I had ever looked upon. There was not a spot in which a wrinkle could lie, where a wrinkle lay not. And the skin was ancient and brown, like old parchment. The woman's form was tall and spare: and when she stood up to welcome me, I saw that she was straight as an arrow. Could that voice of sweetness have issued from those lips of age? Mild as they were, could they be the portals

4 MacDonald generally associates holiness with simplicity. The cottages in *Phantastes* are all the homes of good people and all places where Anodos can find rest. The exception – the church of darkness – is described as a 'hut.' Anodos is ambivalent about its status: '...the cottage, if cottage it could be called...' see p.109.

5 This is Anodos's 'own' island; no-one else has been here before him, just as he had his own room in the Fairy Palace.

whence flowed such melody? But the moment I saw her eyes, I no longer wondered at her voice: they were absolutely young – those of a woman of five-and-twenty, large, and of a clear gray. Wrinkles had beset them all about; the eyelids themselves were old, and heavy, and worn; but the eyes were very incarnations of soft light.[6] She held out her hand to me, and the voice of sweetness again greeted me, with the single word, 'Welcome.' She set an old wooden chair for me, near the fire, and went on with her cooking. A wondrous sense of refuge and repose came upon me. I felt like a boy who has got home from school, miles across the hills, through a heavy storm of wind and snow. Almost, as I gazed on her, I sprang from my seat to kiss those old lips. And when, having finished her cooking, she brought some of the dish she had prepared, and set it on a little table by me, covered with a snow-white cloth, I could not help laying my head on her bosom, and bursting into happy tears. She put her arms round me, saying, 'Poor child; poor child!'[7]

As I continued to weep, she gently disengaged herself, and, taking a spoon, put some of the food (I did not know what it was) to my lips, entreating me most endearingly to swallow it. To please her, I made an effort, and succeeded. She went on feeding me like a baby, with one arm round me, till I looked up in her face and smiled: then she gave me the spoon and told me to eat, for it would do me good. I obeyed her, and found myself wonderfully refreshed. Then she drew near the fire an old-fashioned couch that was in the cottage, and making me lie down upon it, sat at my feet, and began to sing. Amazing store of old ballads rippled from her lips, over the pebbles of ancient tunes; and the voice that sang was sweet as the voice of a tuneful maiden that singeth ever from very fulness of

---

6 The old woman with the young eyes is the first real embodiment of MacDonald's grandmother-God figures. She is not his own great-grandmother of chap.1, but a different, far greater figure. This archetype reappears as the Grandmother in *The Princess and the Goblin*, the Old Woman in *The Golden Key*.

7 As hinted at by his womb-like emergence from the tunnel (see p.194), Anodos has returned to a childish state – almost, indeed, the state of a baby, unable to feed himself. He has been reborn.

song. The songs were almost all sad, but with a sound of comfort. One I can faintly recall. It was something like this:[8]

Sir Aglovaile through the churchyard rode;
Sing, All alone I lie:
Little recked he where'er he yode,
All alone, up in the sky.
Swerved his courser, and plunged with fear
All alone I lie:
His cry might have wakened the dead men near,
All alone, up in the sky.

The very dead that lay at his feet,
Lapt in the mouldy winding-sheet.

But he curbed him and spurred him, until he stood
Still in his place, like a horse of wood,

With nostrils uplift, and eyes wide and wan;
But the sweat in streams from his fetlocks ran.

A ghost grew out of the shadowy air,
And sat in the midst of her moony hair.

In her gleamy hair she sat and wept;
In the dreamful moon they lay and slept;

The shadows above, and the bodies below,
Lay and slept in the moonbeams slow.

And she sang, like the moan of an autumn wind
Over the stubble left behind:

Alas, how easily things go wrong!
A sigh too much, or a kiss too long,
And there follows a mist and a weeping rain,
And life is never the same again.
Alas, how hardly things go right!
'Tis hard to watch on a summer night,
For the sigh will come and the kiss will stay,
And the summer night is a winter day.

'Oh, lovely ghosts my heart is woes
To see thee weeping and wailing so.

Oh, lovely ghost,' said the fearless knight,
'Can the sword of a warrior set it right?

Or prayer of bedesman, praying mild,
As a cup of water a feverish child,

Sooth thee at last, in dreamless mood
To sleep the sleep a dead lady should?

Thine eyes they fill me with longing sore,
As if I had known thee for evermore.

Oh, lovely ghost, I could leave the day
To sit with thee in the moon away

If thou wouldst trust me, and lay thy head
To rest on a bosom that is not dead.'

The lady sprang up with a strange ghost-cry,
And she flung her white ghost-arms on high:

And she laughed a laugh that was not gay,
And it lengthened out till it died away;

And the dead beneath turned and moaned,
And the yew-trees above they shuddered and groaned.

'Will he love me twice with a love that is vain?
Will he kill the poor ghost yet again?

I thought thou wert good; but I said, and wept:
'Can I have dreamed who have not slept?'

And I knew, alas! or ever I would,
Whether I dreamed, or thou wert good.

When my baby died, my brain grew wild.
I awoke, and found I was with my child.'

8   The Ballad of Sir Aglovaile is another reflection of Anodos's story. Just as the Cosmo story reflected his first meeting with the white lady, where he wanted to possess her, this ballad reflects on his second meeting, where he wants to protect her.

'Show me the child thou callest mine...'

'If thou art the ghost of my Adelaide,
How is it? Thou wert but a village maid,

And thou seemest an angel lady white,
Though thin, and wan, and past delight.'

The lady smiled a flickering smile,
And she pressed her temples hard the while.

'Thou seest that Death for a woman can
Do more than knighthood for a man.'

'But show me the child thou callest mine,
Is she out to-night in the ghost's sunshine?'

'In St. Peter's Church she is playing on,
At hide-and-seek, with Apostle John.

When the moonbeams right through the window go,
Where the twelve are standing in glorious show,

She says the rest of them do not stir,
But one comes down to play with her.

Then I can go where I list, and weep,
For good St. John my child will keep.'

'Thy beauty filleth the very air,
Never saw I a woman so fair.'

'Come, if thou darest, and sit by my side;
But do not touch me, or woe will betide.

Alas, I am weak: I might well know
This gladness betokens some further woe.

Yet come. It will come. I will bear it. I can.
For thou lovest me yet — though but as a man.'

The knight dismounted in earnest speed;
Away through the tombstones thundered the steed,

And fell by the outer wall, and died.
But the knight he kneeled by the lady's side;

Kneeled beside her in wondrous bliss,
Rapt in an everlasting kiss:
Though never his lips come the lady nigh,
And his eyes alone on her beauty lie.

All the night long, till the cock crew loud,
He kneeled by the lady, lapt in her shroud.

And what they said, I may not say:
Dead night was sweeter than living day.

How she made him so blissful glad
Who made her and found her so ghostly sad,

I may not tell; but it needs no touch
To make them blessed who love so much.

'Come every night, my ghost, to me;
And one night I will come to thee.

'Tis good to have a ghostly wife:
She will not tremble at clang of strife;

She will only hearken, amid the din,
Behind the door, if he cometh in.'

And this is how Sir Aglovaile
Often walked in the moonlight pale.

And oft when the crescent but thinned the gloom,
Full orbed moonlight filled his room;

And through beneath his chamber door,
Fell a ghostly gleam on the outer floor;

And they that passed, in fear averred
That murmured words they often heard.

'Twas then that the eastern crescent shone
Through the chancel window, and good St. John

Played with the ghost-child all the night,
And the mother was free till the morning light,

And sped through the dawning night, to stay
With Aglovaile till the break of day.

And their love was a rapture, lone and high,
And dumb as the moon in the topmost sky.

One night Sir Aglovaile, weary, slept
And dreamed a dream wherein he wept.

A warrior he was, not often wept he,
But this night he wept full bitterly.

He woke — beside him the ghost-girl shone
Out of the dark: 'twas the eve of St. John.

He had dreamed a dream of a still, dark wood,
Where the maiden of old beside him stood;

But a mist came down, and caught her away,
And he sought her in vain through the pathless day,

Till he wept with the grief that can do no more,
And thought he had dreamt the dream before.

From bursting heart the weeping flowed on;
And lo! beside him the ghost-girl shone;

Shone like the light on a harbour's breast,
Over the sea of his dream's unrest;

Shone like the wondrous, nameless boon,
That the heart seeks ever, night or noon:

Warnings forgotten, when needed most,
He clasped to his bosom the radiant ghost.

She wailed aloud, and faded, and sank.
With upturn'd white face, cold and blank,

In his arms lay the corpse of the maiden pale,
And she came no more to Sir Aglovaile.

Only a voice, when winds were wild,
Sobbed and wailed like a chidden child.

> *Alas, how easily things go wrong!*
> *A sigh too much, or a kiss too long,*
> *And there follows a mist and a weeping rain,*
> *And life is never the same again.*

This was one of the simplest of her songs, which, perhaps, is the cause of my being able to remember it better than most of the others. While she sung, I was in Elysium,[9] with the sense of a rich soul upholding, embracing, and overhanging mine, full of all plenty and bounty. I felt as if she could give me everything I wanted; as if I should never wish to leave her, but would be content to be sung to and fed by her, day after day, as years rolled by. At last I fell asleep while she sang.

When I awoke, I knew not whether it was night or day. The fire had sunk to a few red embers, which just gave light enough to show me the woman standing a few feet from me, with her back towards me, facing the door by which I had entered. She was weeping, but very gently and plentifully. The tears seemed to come freely from her heart. Thus she stood for a few minutes; then, slowly turning at right angles to her former position, she faced another of the four sides of the cottage. I now observed, for the first time, that here was a door likewise; and that, indeed, there was one in the centre of every side of the cottage. When she looked towards the second door, her

9   *Elysium*: in Greek mythology the place assigned to the blessed after death.

tears ceased to flow, but sighs took their place. She often closed her eyes as she stood; and every time she closed her eyes, a gentle sigh seemed to be born in her heart, and to escape at her lips. But when her eyes were open, her sighs were deep and very sad, and shook her whole frame. Then she turned towards the third door, and a cry as of fear or suppressed pain broke from her; but she seemed to heart-en herself against the dismay, and to front it steadily; for, although I often heard a slight cry, and sometimes a moan, yet she never moved or bent her head, and I felt sure that her eyes never closed. Then she turned to the fourth door, and I saw her shudder, and then stand still as a statue; till at last she turned towards me and approached the fire. I saw that her face was white as death. But she gave one look upwards, and smiled the sweetest, most child-innocent smile; then heaped fresh wood on the fire, and, sitting down by the blaze, drew her wheel near her, and began to spin.[10] While she spun, she mur-mured a low strange song, to which the hum of wheel made a kind of infinite symphony.[11] At length she paused in her spinning and singing, and glanced towards me, like a mother who looks whether or not her child gives signs of waking. She smiled when she saw that my eyes were open. I asked her whether it was day yet. She answered, 'It is always day here, so long as I keep my fire burning.'

I felt wonderfully refreshed; and a great desire to see more of the island awoke within me. I rose, and saying that I wished to look about me, went towards the door by which I had entered.

10 There are four doors in the cottage. The first, which is never specifically named, is associated with weeping, then there is 'the door of Sighs', 'the door of Dismay' and 'the door of the Timeless' which is the worst of all. The old woman's look upwards may reflect Christ's words in John's gospel '...Father, if thou be willing, remove this cup from me: nevertheless not my will, but thine, be done.' (Luke 22.42)

11 The great-great-Grandmother in the Curdie books has a spinning wheel. When Curdie visits her, he opens the door to see 'the great sky, and the stars' and in the distance a 'great wheel of fire, turning and turning, and flashing out blue lights.' He finds that '...the great revolving wheel in the sky was the princess's spinning-wheel, near the other end of the room, turning very fast... Then the lady began to sing, and her wheel spun an accompaniment to her song... Oh! the sweet sounds of that spinning wheel! Now they were gold, now silver, now grass, now palm trees, now ancient cities, now rubies, now mountain brooks, now peacock's feathers, now clouds, now snowdrops, and now mid-sea islands,' (MacDonald, *The Princess and Curdie*, ch. 8.)

'Stay a moment,' said my hostess, with some trepidation in her voice. 'Listen to me. You will not see what you expect when you go out of that door. Only remember this: whenever you wish to come back to me, enter wherever you see this mark.'

She held up her left hand between me and the fire. Upon the palm, which appeared almost transparent, I saw, in dark red, a mark like this ⤸ which I took care to fix in my mind.[12]

She then kissed me, and bade me good-bye with a solemnity that awed me; and bewildered me too, seeing I was only going out for a little ramble in an island, which I did not believe larger than could easily be compassed in a few hours' walk at most. As I went she resumed her spinning.

I opened the door, and stepped out. The moment my foot touched the smooth sward, I seemed to issue from the door of an old barn on my father's estate, where, in the hot afternoons, I used to go and lie amongst the straw, and read. It seemed to me now that I had been asleep there. At a little distance in the field, I saw two of my brothers at play.[13] The moment they caught sight of me, they called out to me to come and join them, which I did; and we played together as we had done years ago, till the red sun went down in the west, and the gray fog began to rise from the river. Then we went home together with a strange happiness. As we went, we heard the continually renewed larum of a landrail[14] in the long grass. One of my brothers and I separated to a little distance, and each commenced running towards the part whence the sound appeared to come, in the hope of approaching the spot where the bird was, and so getting at least a sight of it, if we should not be able to capture the little creature. My father's voice recalled us from

12 The mark does not appear to have any precedent. It seems to have been an entirely invented symbol. The fact that it is a stigmata, on her hand is an obvious allusion to Christ.
13 MacDonald had four brothers, but he was closest to John and Alec. Alec died in 1853 (see Introduction pp.21–22) and John in 1858, just before *Phantastes* was published.
14 *Larum*: alarm call. *Landrail*: corncrake.

trampling down the rich long grass, soon to be cut down and laid aside for the winter.[15] I had quite forgotten all about Fairy Land, and the wonderful old woman, and the curious red mark.

My favourite brother and I shared the same bed. Some childish dispute arose between us; and our last words, ere we fell asleep, were not of kindness, notwithstanding the pleasures of the day. When I woke in the morning, I missed him. He had risen early, and had gone to bathe in the river. In another hour, he was brought home drowned. Alas! alas! if we had only gone to sleep as usual, the one with his arm about the other! Amidst the horror of the moment, a strange conviction flashed across my mind, that I had gone through the very same once before.[16]

I rushed out of the house, I knew not why, sobbing and crying bitterly. I ran through the fields in aimless distress, till, passing the old barn, I caught sight of a red mark on the door. The merest trifles sometimes rivet the attention in the deepest misery; the intellect has so little to do with grief. I went up to look at this mark, which I did not remember ever to have seen before. As I looked at it, I thought I would go in and lie down amongst the straw, for I was very weary with running about and weeping. I opened the door; and there in the cottage sat the old woman as I had left her, at her spinning-wheel.

'I did not expect you quite so soon,' she said, as I shut the door behind me. I went up to the couch, and threw myself on it with that fatigue wherewith one awakes from a feverish dream of hopeless grief.

The old woman sang:

---

15 Writing to his Father in June 1853, soon after the death of his brother Alec, MacDonald recalled running with Alec 'through the long grass on a warm summer night, trying to catch the corn scraich [i.e. corncrake], till recalled by you and reprimanded for trampling down the grass.' (Hein, *George MacDonald: Victorian Mythmaker*, p.41).

16 When *Phantastes* was written MacDonald had lost three of his six brothers. John McKay died in infancy, when George was six; James (b.1826) died when George was 10; and Alec (b.1827) died in 1853. See Introduction pp.21–22.

> *The great sun, benighted,*
> *May faint from the sky;*
> *But love, once uplighted,*
> *Will never more die.*
>
> *Form, with its brightness,*
> *From eyes will depart:*
> *It walketh, in whiteness,*
> *The halls of the heart.*

Ere she had ceased singing, my courage had returned. I started from the couch, and, without taking leave of the old woman, opened the door of Sighs, and sprang into what should appear.

I stood in a lordly hall, where, by a blazing fire on the hearth, sat a lady, waiting, I knew, for some one long desired. A mirror was near me, but I saw that my form had no place within its depths, so I feared not that I should be seen.[17] The lady wonderfully resembled my marble lady, but was altogether of the daughters of men, and I could not tell whether or not it was she. It was not for me she waited. The tramp of a great horse rang through the court without. It ceased, and the clang of armour told that his rider alighted, and the sound of his ringing heels approached the hall. The door opened; but the lady waited, for she would meet her lord alone. He strode in: she flew like a home-bound dove into his arms, and nestled on the hard steel. It was the knight of the soiled armour. But now the armour shone like polished glass; and strange to tell, though the mirror reflected not my form, I saw a dim shadow of myself in the shining steel.[18]

'O my beloved, thou art come, and I am blessed.'

Her soft fingers speedily overcame the hard clasp of his helmet; one by one she undid the buckles of his armour; and she toiled under the weight of the mail, as she would carry it aside. Then she unclasped his greaves, and unbuckled his spurs; and once more she

17 Another magic mirror. This time the mirror reveals that Anodos is invisible to the other people in the scene.
18 Anodos is both reflected in and a reflection of the knight. He will have to travel the same journey and fight the same kind of battles as the knight, albeit their fates are different.

sprang into his arms, and laid her head where she could now feel the beating of his heart. Then she disengaged herself from his embrace, and, moving back a step or two, gazed at him. He stood there a mighty form, crowned with a noble head, where all sadness had disappeared, or had been absorbed in solemn purpose. Yet I suppose that he looked more thoughtful than the lady had expected to see him, for she did not renew her caresses, although his face glowed with love, and the few words he spoke were as mighty deeds for strength; but she led him towards the hearth, and seated him in an ancient chair, and set wine before him, and sat at his feet.

'I am sad,' he said, 'when I think of the youth whom I met twice in the forests of Fairy Land; and who, you say, twice, with his songs, roused you from the death-sleep of an evil enchantment. There was something noble in him, but it was a nobleness of thought, and not of deed. He may yet perish of vile fear.'

'Ah!' returned the lady, 'you saved him once, and for that I thank you; for may I not say that I somewhat loved him? But tell me how you fared, when you struck your battle-axe into the ash-tree, and he came and found you; for so much of the story you had told me, when the beggar-child came and took you away.'[19]

'As soon as I saw him,' rejoined the knight, 'I knew that earthly arms availed not against such as he; and that my soul must meet him in its naked strength. So I unclasped my helm, and flung it on the ground; and, holding my good axe yet in my hand, gazed at him with steady eyes. On he came, a horror indeed, but I did not flinch. Endurance must conquer, where force could not reach. He came nearer and nearer, till the ghastly face was close to mine. A shudder as of death ran through me; but I think I did not move, for he seemed to quail, and retreated. As soon as he gave back, I struck one more sturdy blow on the stem of his tree, that the forest

19 MacDonald is playing with the time-frame of the book. This section looks back to Anodos's two encounters with the white lady (chapters 5 and 16), the Knight's two meetings with Anodos (chapters 6 and 9) and the Knight's fight with the Ash (chapter 6). But it also looks forward to the adventure with the 'beggar-child' related in chapter 23.

rang; and then looked at him again. He writhed and grinned with rage and apparent pain, and again approached me, but retreated sooner than before. I heeded him no more, but hewed with a will at the tree, till the trunk creaked, and the head bowed, and with a crash it fell to the earth. Then I looked up from my labour, and lo! the spectre had vanished, and I saw him no more; nor ever in my wanderings have I heard of him again.'

'Well struck! well withstood! my hero,' said the lady.

'But,' said the knight, somewhat troubled, 'dost thou love the youth still?'

'Ah!' she replied, 'how can I help it? He woke me from worse than death; he loved me. I had never been for thee, if he had not sought me first. But I love him not as I love thee. He was but the moon of my night; thou art the sun of my day, O beloved.'[20]

'Thou art right,' returned the noble man. 'It were hard, indeed, not to have some love in return for such a gift as he hath given thee. I, too, owe him more than words can speak.'

Humbled before them, with an aching and desolate heart, I yet could not restrain my words:

'Let me, then, be the moon of thy night still, O woman! And when thy day is beclouded, as the fairest days will be, let some song of mine comfort thee, as an old, withered, half-forgotten thing, that belongs to an ancient mournful hour of uncompleted birth, which yet was beautiful in its time.'

They sat silent, and I almost thought they were listening. The colour of the lady's eyes grew deeper and deeper; the slow tears grew, and filled them, and overflowed. They rose, and passed, hand in hand, close to where I stood; and each looked towards me in passing. Then they disappeared through a door which closed behind them; but, ere it closed, I saw that the room into which it opened was a rich chamber, hung with gorgeous arras. I stood with an ocean of sighs frozen in my bosom. I could remain no longer.

20 Anodos as a reflection of the knight again.

She was near me, and I could not see her; near me in the arms of one loved better than I, and I would not see her, and I would not be by her. But how to escape from the nearness of the best beloved? I had not this time forgotten the mark; for the fact that I could not enter the sphere of these living beings kept me aware that, for me, I moved in a vision, while they moved in life. I looked all about for the mark, but could see it nowhere; for I avoided looking just where it was. There the dull red cipher glowed, on the very door of their secret chamber. Struck with agony, I dashed it open, and fell at the feet of the ancient woman, who still spun on, the whole dissolved ocean of my sighs bursting from me in a storm of tearless sobs.[21] Whether I fainted or slept, I do not know; but, as I returned to consciousness, before I seemed to have power to move, I heard the woman singing, and could distinguish the words:

> *O light of dead and of dying days!*
> *O Love! in thy glory go,*
> *In a rosy mist and a moony maze,*
> *O'er the pathless peaks of snow.*
>
> *But what is left for the cold gray soul,*
> *That moans like a wounded dove?*
> *One wine is left in the broken bowl! —*
> *'Tis — To love, and love, and love.*

Now I could weep. When she saw me weeping, she sang:

> *Better to sit at the waters' birth,*
> *Than a sea of waves to win;*
> *To live in the love that floweth forth,*
> *Than the love that cometh in.*
>
> *Be thy heart a well of love, my child,*
> *Flowing, and free, and sure;*
> *For a cistern of love, though undefiled,*
> *Keeps not the spirit pure.*

---

21 Anodos is forced to confront the very thing he hates and fears most — the intimacy of the knight and the white lady.

I rose from the earth, loving the white lady as I had never loved her before.

Then I walked up to the door of Dismay, and opened it, and went out. And lo! I came forth upon a crowded street, where men and women went to and fro in multitudes. I knew it well; and, turning to one hand, walked sadly along the pavement. Suddenly I saw approaching me, a little way off, a form well known to me (*well-known!* — alas, how weak the word!) in the years when I thought my boyhood was left behind, and shortly before I entered the realm of Fairy Land.[22] Wrong and Sorrow had gone together, hand-in-hand as it is well they do. Unchangeably dear was that face. It lay in my heart as a child lies in its own white bed; but I could not meet her.

'Anything but that,' I said, and, turning aside, sprang up the steps to a door, on which I fancied I saw the mystic sign. I entered — not the mysterious cottage, but her home. I rushed wildly on, and stood by the door of her room.

'She is out,' I said, 'I will see the old room once more.'

I opened the door gently, and stood in a great solemn church. A deep-toned bell, whose sounds throbbed and echoed and swam through the empty building, struck the hour of midnight. The moon shone through the windows of the clerestory,[23] and enough of the ghostly radiance was diffused through the church to let me see, walking with a stately, yet somewhat trailing and stumbling step, down the opposite aisle, for I stood in one of the transepts, a figure dressed in a white robe, whether for the night, or for that longer night which lies too deep for the day, I could not tell. Was it she? and was this her chamber? I crossed the church, and followed. The figure stopped, seemed to ascend as it were a high bed, and lay down. I reached the place where it lay, glimmering white. The bed was a tomb. The light was too ghostly to see clearly, but I passed my hand over the face and the hands and the feet, which were all

22 Anodos entered Fairy Land when he was 21, see p.41. As with the other doors he is forced to confront the pains of his past.

23 *Clerestory*: from 'clear storey', i.e. the upper part of a large church above the nave, choir, etc.

bare. They were cold – they were marble, but I knew them. It grew dark. I turned to retrace my steps, but found, ere long, that I had wandered into what seemed a little chapel. I groped about, seeking the door. Everything I touched belonged to the dead. My hands fell on the cold effigy of a knight who lay with his legs crossed and his sword broken beside him. He lay in his noble rest, and I lived on in ignoble strife. I felt for the left hand and a certain finger; I found there the ring knew: he was one of my own ancestors.[24] I was in the chapel over the burial-vault of my race. I called aloud: 'If any of the dead are moving here, let them take pity upon me, for I, alas! am still alive; and let some dead woman comfort me, for I am a stranger in the land of the dead, and see no light.' A warm kiss alighted on my lips through the dark. And I said, 'The dead kiss well; I will not be afraid.' And a great hand was reached out of the dark, and grasped mine for a moment, mightily and tenderly. I said to myself: 'The veil between, though very dark, is very thin.'

Groping my way further, I stumbled over the heavy stone that covered the entrance of the vault: and, in stumbling, descried upon the stone the mark, glowing in red fire. I caught the great ring. All my effort could not have moved the huge slab; but it opened the door of the cottage, and I threw myself once more, pale and speechless, on the couch beside the ancient dame. She sang once more:

> *Thou dreamest: on a rock thou art,*
> *High o'er the broken wave;*
> *Thou fallest with a fearful start*
> *But not into thy grave;*
> *For, waking in the morning's light,*
> *Thou smilest at the vanished night*
>
> *So wilt thou sink, all pale and dumb,*
> *Into the fainting gloom;*
> *But ere the coming terrors come,*
> *Thou wak'st – where is the tomb?*
> *Thou wak'st – the dead ones smile above,*
> *With hovering arms of sleepless love.*

24 Another marble woman and another knight – this time from Anodos's life in the 'real' world.

She paused; then sang again:

> *We weep for gladness, weep for grief;*
> *The tears they are the same;*
> *We sigh for longing, and relief;*
> *The sighs have but one name,*
>
> *And mingled in the dying strife,*
> *Are moans that are not sad*
> *The pangs of death are throbs of life,*
> *Its sighs are sometimes glad.*
>
> *The face is very strange and white:*
> *It is Earth's only spot*
> *That feebly flickers back the light*
> *The living seeth not.*

I fell asleep, and slept a dreamless sleep, for I know not how long. When I awoke, I found that my hostess had moved from where she had been sitting, and now sat between me and the fourth door. I guessed that her design was to prevent my entering there. I sprang from the couch, and darted past her to the door. I opened it at once and went out. All I remember is a cry of distress from the woman: 'Don't go there, my child! Don't go there!' But I was gone.

I knew nothing more; or, if I did, I had forgot it all when I awoke to consciousness, lying on the floor of the cottage, with my head in the lap of the woman, who was weeping over me, and stroking my hair with both hands, talking to me as a mother might talk to a sick and sleeping, or a dead child. As soon as I looked up and saw her, she smiled through her tears; smiled with withered face and young eyes, till her countenance was irradiated with the light of the smile. Then she bathed my head and face and hands in an icy cold, colourless liquid, which smelt a little of damp earth. Immediately I was able to sit up. She rose and put some food before me. When I had eaten, she said: 'Listen to me, my child. You must leave me directly!'

'Leave you!' I said. 'I am so happy with you. I never was so happy in my life.'

'But you must go,' she rejoined sadly. 'Listen! What do you hear?'

'I hear the sound as of a great throbbing of water.'

'Ah! you do hear it? Well, I had to go through that door – the door of the Timeless' (and she shuddered as she pointed to the fourth door) – 'to find you; for if I had not gone, you would never have entered again; and because I went, the waters around my cottage will rise and rise, and flow and come, till they build a great firmament of waters over my dwelling.[25] But as long as I keep my fire burning, they cannot enter. I have fuel enough for years; and after one year they will sink away again, and be just as they were before you came. I have not been buried for a hundred years now.' And she smiled and wept.

'Alas! alas!' I cried. 'I have brought this evil on the best and kindest of friends, who has filled my heart with great gifts.'

'Do not think of that,' she rejoined. 'I can bear it very well. You will come back to me some day, I know. But I beg you, for my sake, my dear child, to do one thing. In whatever sorrow you may be, however inconsolable and irremediable it may appear, believe me that the old woman in the cottage, with the young eyes' (and she smiled), 'knows something, though she must not always tell it, that would quite satisfy you about it, even in the worst moments of your distress. Now you must go.'

'But how can I go, if the waters are all about, and if the doors all lead into other regions and other worlds?'

'This is not an island,' she replied; 'but is joined to the land by a narrow neck; and for the door, I will lead you myself through the right one.'

25 The door of the Timeless is the only door from which Anodos cannot rescue himself. Given that he has to be rescued by the old woman, and that, as a result of going through the door he has to leave this place of happiness, the door may signify sin and wickedness. (McInnis, Jeff, *Shadows and Chivalry*, p.115). The rising of the floodwaters recalls God's decision in Genesis to send a flood to destroy mankind because 'the wickedness of man was great in the earth, and that every imagination of the thoughts of his heart was only evil continually.' (Genesis 6.5).

She took my hand, and led me through the third door;[26] where-upon I found myself standing in the deep grassy turf on which I had landed from the little boat, but upon the opposite side of the cottage. She pointed out the direction I must take, to find the isthmus and escape the rising waters.[27]

Then putting her arms around me, she held me to her bosom; and as I kissed her, I felt as if I were leaving my mother for the first time, and could not help weeping bitterly. At length she gently pushed me away, and with the words, 'Go, my son, and do something worth doing,' turned back, and, entering the cottage, closed the door behind her.[28]

I felt very desolate as I went.

---

26 The third door was the door of Dismay – also the door where Anodos entered his own tomb.

27 *Isthmus:* Narrow strip of land, with water on both sides, connecting two largee bodies of land.

28 The chapter ends with two of the key statements of the book; that there is always a reason for evil 'that would quite satisfy you' and that the response to Christ is to 'go... and do something worth doing.'

20

'Thou hadst no fame; that which thou didst like good
Was but thy appetite that swayed thy blood
For that time to the best; for as a blast
That through a house comes, usually doth cast
Things out of order, yet by chance may come
And blow some one thing to his proper room,
So did thy appetite, and not thy zeal,
Sway thee by chance to do some one thing well.'
                    FLETCHER, THE FAITHFUL SHEPHERDESS[1]

'The noble hart that harbours vertuous thought
And is with childe of glorious great intent,
Can never rest, until it forth have brought
Th' eternall brood of glorie excellent.'

                         SPENSER, THE FAERIE QUEENE[2].

I had not gone very far before I felt that the turf beneath my feet was soaked with the rising waters. But I reached the isthmus in safety. It was rocky, and so much higher than the level of the peninsula, that I had plenty of time to cross. I saw on each side of me the water rising rapidly, altogether without wind, or violent

1 John Fletcher (1579 – 1625). Jacobean playwright. *The Faithful Shepherdess* was, according to its author, a 'pastoral tragicomedy'. The production, in 1608, was a failure, which Fletcher put down to his audience's preconceived expectations: they wanted the conventional dances and comedy and murders, but he delivered 'a representation of familiar people'.

2 Edmund Spenser (c.1522 – 1599). *The Fairie Queene*, with its ornate allegory and symbolism, was a key influence on *Phantastes*. Phantastes is, in fact, a character in Spenser's poem, an 'endless spinner of fantasies, locked away in a dark chamber within the House of Temperance.' (Raeper, *George MacDonald*, p.144).

motion, or broken waves, but as if a slow strong fire were glowing beneath it. Ascending a steep acclivity, I found myself at last in an open, rocky country. After travelling for some hours, as nearly in a straight line as I could, I arrived at a lonely tower, built on the top of a little hill, which overlooked the whole neighbouring country. As I approached, I heard the clang of an anvil; and so rapid were the blows, that I despaired of making myself heard till a pause in the work should ensue. It was some minutes before a cessation took place; but when it did, I knocked loudly, and had not long to wait; for, a moment after, the door was partly opened by a noble-looking youth, half-undressed, glowing with heat, and begrimed with the blackness of the forge. In one hand he held a sword, so lately from the furnace that it yet shone with a dull fire. As soon as he saw me, he threw the door wide open, and standing aside, invited me very cordially to enter. I did so; when he shut and bolted the door most carefully, and then led the way inwards. He brought me into a rude hall, which seemed to occupy almost the whole of the ground floor of the little tower, and which I saw was now being used as a workshop. A huge fire roared on the hearth, beside which was an anvil. By the anvil stood, in similar undress, and in a waiting attitude, hammer in hand, a second youth, tall as the former, but far more slightly built. Reversing the usual course of perception in such meetings, I thought them, at first sight, very unlike; and at the second glance, knew that they were brothers. The former, and apparently the elder, was muscular and dark, with curling hair, and large hazel eyes, which sometimes grew wondrously soft. The second was slender and fair, yet with a countenance like an eagle, and an eye which, though pale blue, shone with an almost fierce expression. He stood erect, as if looking from a lofty mountain crag, over a vast plain outstretched below. As soon as we entered the hall, the elder turned to me, and I saw that a glow of satisfaction shone on both their faces. To my surprise and great pleasure, he addressed me thus:

'Brother, will you sit by the fire and rest, till we finish this part of our work?'

I signified my assent; and, resolved to await any disclosure they might be inclined to make, seated myself in silence near the hearth.

The elder brother then laid the sword in the fire, covered it well over, and when it had attained a sufficient degree of heat, drew it out and laid it on the anvil, moving it carefully about, while the younger, with a succession of quick smart blows, appeared either to be welding it, or hammering one part of it to a consenting shape with the rest. Having finished, they laid it carefully in the fire; and, when it was very hot indeed, plunged it into a vessel full of some liquid, whence a blue flame sprang upwards, as the glowing steel entered. There they left it; and drawing two stools to the fire, sat down, one on each side of me.

'We are very glad to see you, brother. We have been expecting you for some days,' said the dark-haired youth.

'I am proud to be called your brother,' I rejoined; 'and you will not think I refuse the name, if I desire to know why you honour me with it?'

'Ah! then he does not know about it,' said the younger. 'We thought you had known of the bond betwixt us, and the work we have to do together. You must tell him, brother, from the first.'

So the elder began:

'Our father is king of this country. Before we were born, three giant brothers had appeared in the land. No one knew exactly when, and no one had the least idea whence they came. They took possession of a ruined castle that had stood unchanged and un-occupied within the memory of any of the country people. The vaults of this castle had remained uninjured by time, and these, I presume, they made use of at first. They were rarely seen, and never offered the least injury to any one; so that they were regarded in the neighbourhood as at least perfectly harmless, if not rather

benevolent beings. But it began to be observed, that the old castle had assumed somehow or other, no one knew when or how, a
somewhat different look from what it used to have. Not only were
several breaches in the lower part of the walls built up, but actually some of the battlements which yet stood, had been repaired,
apparently to prevent them from falling into worse decay, while
the more important parts were being restored. Of course, every
one supposed the giants must have a hand in the work, but no one
ever saw them engaged in it. The peasants became yet more uneasy,
after one, who had concealed himself, and watched all night, in
the neighbourhood of the castle, reported that he had seen, in full
moonlight, the three huge giants working with might and main, all
night long, restoring to their former position some massive stones,
formerly steps of a grand turnpike stair,[3] a great portion of which
had long since fallen, along with part of the wall of the round
tower in which it had been built. This wall they were completing,
foot by foot, along with the stair. But the people said they had no
just pretext for interfering: although the real reason for letting the
giants alone was, that everybody was far too much afraid of them
to interrupt them.

'At length, with the help of a neighbouring quarry, the whole of
the external wall of the castle was finished. And now the country
folks were in greater fear than before. But for several years the giants
remained very peaceful. The reason of this was afterwards supposed
to be the fact, that they were distantly related to several good people
in the country; for, as long as these lived, they remained quiet; but
as soon as they were all dead the real nature of the giants broke out.
Having completed the outside of their castle, they proceeded, by
spoiling the country houses around them, to make a quiet luxurious
provision for their comfort within. Affairs reached such a pass, that
the news of their robberies came to my father's ears; but he, alas!
was so crippled in his resources, by a war he was carrying on with a

---

3 *Turnpike stair:* spiral or winding staircase.

neighbouring prince, that he could only spare a very few men, to attempt the capture of their stronghold. Upon these the giants issued in the night, and slew every man of them. And now, grown bolder by success and impunity, they no longer confined their depredations to property, but began to seize the persons of their distinguished neighbours, knights and ladies, and hold them in durance, the misery of which was heightened by all manner of indignity, until they were redeemed by their friends, at an exorbitant ransom. Many knights have adventured their overthrow, but to their own instead; for they have all been slain, or captured, or forced to make a hasty retreat. To crown their enormities, if any man now attempts their destruction, they, immediately upon his defeat, put one or more of their captives to a shameful death, on a turret in sight of passers-by; so that they have been much less molested of late; and we, although we have burned, for years, to attack these demons and destroy them, dared not, for the sake of their captives, risk the adventure, before we should have reached at least our earliest manhood. Now, however, we are preparing for the attempt; and the grounds of this preparation are these. Having only the resolution, and not the experience necessary for the undertaking, we went and consulted a lonely woman of wisdom, who lives not very far from here, in the direction of the quarter from which you have come. She received us most kindly, and gave us what seems to us the best of advice. She first inquired what experience we had had in arms. We told her we had been well exercised from our boyhood, and for some years had kept ourselves in constant practice, with a view to this necessity.

"'But you have not actually fought for life and death?" said she.

'We were forced to confess we had not.

"'So much the better in some respects," she replied. "Now listen to me. Go first and work with an armourer, for as long time as you find needful to obtain a knowledge of his craft; which will not be long, seeing your hearts will be all in the work. Then go to some lonely tower, you two alone. Receive no visits from man or woman.

There forge for yourselves every piece of armour that you wish to wear, or to use, in your coming encounter. And keep up your exercises. As, however, two of you can be no match for the three giants, I will find you, if I can, a third brother, who will take on himself the third share of the fight, and the preparation. Indeed, I have already seen one who will, I think, be the very man for your fellowship, but it will be some time before he comes to me. He is wandering now without an aim.[4] I will show him to you in a glass, and, when he comes, you will know him at once. If he will share your endeavours, you must teach him all you know, and he will repay you well, in present song, and in future deeds."

'She opened the door of a curious old cabinet that stood in the room. On the inside of this door was an oval convex mirror.[5] Looking in it for some time, we at length saw reflected the place where we stood, and the old dame seated in her chair. Our forms were not reflected. But at the feet of the dame lay a young man, yourself, weeping.

"'Surely this youth will not serve our ends," said I, "for he weeps."

'The old woman smiled. "Past tears are present strength," said she.

"'Oh!" said my brother, "I saw you weep once over an eagle you shot."

"'That was because it was so like you, brother," I replied; "but indeed, this youth may have better cause for tears than that — I was wrong."

"'Wait a while," said the woman; "if I mistake not, he will make you weep till your tears are dry for ever. Tears are the only cure for weeping. And you may have need of the cure, before you go forth to fight the giants. You must wait for him, in your tower, till he comes.'

'Now if you will join us, we will soon teach you to make your armour; and we will fight together, and work together, and love

4 One meaning of 'Anodos' is 'pathless' or 'aimless'. (See p.44)
5 Another mirror, this time showing the interior of the Old Woman's cottage. It appears to show Anodos's return from the door of Sighs (p.214).

each other as never three loved before. And you will sing to us, will you not?'

'That I will, when I can,' I answered; 'but it is only at times that the power of song comes upon me. For that I must wait; but I have a feeling that if I work well, song will not be far off to enliven the labour.'

This was all the compact made: the brothers required nothing more, and I did not think of giving anything more. I rose, and threw off my upper garments.

'I know the uses of the sword,' I said. 'I am ashamed of my white hands beside yours so nobly soiled and hard; but that shame will soon be wiped away.'

'No, no; we will not work to-day. Rest is as needful as toil. Bring the wine, brother; it is your turn to serve to-day.'

The younger brother soon covered a table with rough viands, but good wine; and we ate and drank heartily, beside our work. Before the meal was over, I had learned all their story. Each had something in his heart which made the conviction, that he would victoriously perish in the coming conflict, a real sorrow to him. Otherwise they thought they would have lived enough. The causes of their trouble were respectively these:

While they wrought with an armourer, in a city famed for workmanship in steel and silver, the elder had fallen in love with a lady as far beneath him in real rank, as she was above the station he had as apprentice to an armourer. Nor did he seek to further his suit by discovering himself; but there was simply so much manhood about him, that no one ever thought of rank when in his company. This is what his brother said about it. The lady could not help loving him in return. He told her when he left her, that he had a perilous adventure before him, and that when it was achieved, she would either see him return to claim her, or hear that he had died with honour. The younger brother's grief arose from the fact, that, if they were both slain, his old father, the king, would be childless. His love for

his father was so exceeding, that to one unable to sympathise with
it, it would have appeared extravagant. Both loved him equally at
heart; but the love of the younger had been more developed, because his thoughts and anxieties had not been otherwise occupied.
When at home, he had been his constant companion; and, of late,
had ministered to the infirmities of his growing age. The youth
was never weary of listening to the tales of his sire's youthful adventures; and had not yet in the smallest degree lost the conviction,
that his father was the greatest man in the world. The grandest tri-
umph possible to his conception was, to return to his father, laden
with the spoils of one of the hated giants. But they both were in
some dread, lest the thought of the loneliness of these two might
occur to them, in the moment when decision was most necessary,
and disturb, in some degree, the self-possession requisite for the
success of their attempt. For, as I have said, they were yet untried
in actual conflict. 'Now,' thought I, 'I see to what the powers of my
gift must minister.' For my own part, I did not dread death, for I
had nothing to care to live for; but I dreaded the encounter because
of the responsibility connected with it. I resolved however to work
hard, and thus grow cool, and quick, and forceful.

The time passed away in work and song, in talk and ramble,
in friendly fight and brotherly aid. I would not forge for myself
armour of heavy mail like theirs, for I was not so powerful as they,
and depended more for any success I might secure, upon nimbleness
of motion, certainty of eye, and ready response of hand. Therefore
I began to make for myself a shirt of steel plates and rings; which
work, while more troublesome, was better suited to me than the
heavier labour. Much assistance did the brothers give me, even after, by their instructions, I was able to make some progress alone.
Their work was in a moment abandoned, to render any required
aid to mine. As the old woman had promised, I tried to repay them
with song; and many were the tears they both shed over my ballads
and dirges. The songs they liked best to hear were two which I

The time passed away in work and song

made for them. They were not half so good as many others I knew, especially some I had learned from the wise woman in the cottage; but what comes nearest to our needs we like the best.

I

The king sat on his throne
Glowing in gold and red;
The crown in his right hand shone,
And the gray hairs crowned his head.

His only son walks in,
And in walls of steel he stands:
Make me, O father, strong to win,
With the blessing of holy hands.'

He knelt before his sire,
Who blessed him with feeble smile
His eyes shone out with a kingly fire,
But his old lips quivered the while.

'Go to the fight, my son,
Bring back the giant's head;
And the crown with which my brows have done,
Shall glitter on thine instead.'

'My father, I seek no crowns,
But unspoken praise from thee;
For thy people's good, and thy renown,
I will die to set them free.'

The king sat down and waited there,
And rose not, night nor day;
Till a sound of shouting filled the air,
And cries of a sore dismay.

Then like a king he sat once more,
With the crown upon his head;
And up to the throne the people bore
A mighty giant dead.

And up to the throne the people bore
A pale and lifeless boy.
The king rose up like a prophet of yore,
In a lofty, deathlike joy.

He put the crown on the chilly brow:
'Thou should'st have reigned with me
But Death is the king of both, and now
I go to obey with thee.

'Surely some good in me there lay,
To beget the noble one.'
The old man smiled like a winter day,
And fell beside his son.

II

'O lady, thy lover is dead,' they cried;
'He is dead, but hath slain the foe;
He hath left his name to be magnified
In a song of wonder and woe.'

'Alas! I am well repaid,' said she,
'With a pain that stings like joy:
For I feared, from his tenderness to me,
That he was but a feeble boy.

'Now I shall hold my head on high,
The queen among my kind;
If ye hear a sound, 'tis only a sigh
For a glory left behind.'[6]

The first three times I sang these songs they both wept passionately. But after the third time, they wept no more. Their eyes shone, and their faces grew pale, but they never wept at any of my songs again.

---

6 Anodos's songs strengthen the warriors, but also mirror the story and act as prophecies of what will happen.

—21—

I put my life in my hands.

THE BOOK OF JUDGES[1]

A t length, with much toil and equal delight, our armour was finished. We armed each other, and tested the strength of the defence, with many blows of loving force. I was inferior in strength to both my brothers, but a little more agile than either; and upon this agility, joined to precision in hitting with the point of my weapon, I grounded my hopes of success in the ensuing combat. I likewise laboured to develop yet more the keenness of sight with which I was naturally gifted; and, from the remarks of my companions, I soon learned that my endeavours were not in vain.

The morning arrived on which we had determined to make the attempt, and succeed or perish – perhaps both. We had resolved to fight on foot; knowing that the mishap of many of the knights

1 'And when I saw that ye delivered me not, I put my life in my hands, and passed over against the children of Ammon, and the Lord delivered them into my hand: wherefore then are ye come up unto me this day, to fight against me?' (Judges 12.3). Jephthah is remonstrating with the 'men of Ephraim' who did not come to his aid against the Ammonites.

who had made the attempt, had resulted from the fright of their horses at the appearance of the giants; and believing with Sir Gawain, that, though mare's sons might be false to us, the earth would never prove a traitor.[2] But most of our preparations were, in their immediate aim at least, frustrated.

We rose, that fatal morning, by daybreak. We had rested from all labour the day before, and now were fresh as the lark. We bathed in cold spring water, and dressed ourselves in clean garments, with a sense of preparation, as for a solemn festivity. When we had broken our fast, I took an old lyre, which I had found in the tower and had myself repaired, and sung for the last time the two ballads of which I have said so much already. I followed them with this, for a closing song:

> *Oh, well for him who breaks his dream*
> *With the blow that ends the strife*
> *And, waking, knows the peace that flows*
> *Around the pain of life!*
>
> *We are dead, my brothers! Our bodies clasp,*
> *As an armour, our souls about;*
> *This hand is the battle-axe I grasp,*
> *And this my hammer stout.*
>
> *Fear not, my brothers, for we are dead;*
> *No noise can break our rest;*
> *The calm of the grave is about the head,*
> *And the heart heaves not the breast.*
>
> *And our life we throw to our people back,*
> *To live with, a further store;*
> *We leave it them, that there be no lack*
> *In the land where we live no more.*
>
> *Oh, well for him who breaks his dream*
> *With the blow that ends the strife*
> *And, waking, knows the peace that flows*
> *Around the noise of life!*

2 Malory, *Morte D'Arthur* Book 20. The Siege of Benwick. Gawain's horse is cut from under him during his final fight against Launcelot.

As the last few tones of the instrument were following, like a dirge, the death of the song, we all sprang to our feet. For, through one of the little windows of the tower, towards which I had looked as I sang, I saw, suddenly rising over the edge of the slope on which our tower stood, three enormous heads. The brothers knew at once, by my looks, what caused my sudden movement. We were utterly unarmed, and there was no time to arm. But we seemed to adopt the same resolution simultaneously; for each caught up his favourite weapon, and, leaving his defence behind, sprang to the door. I snatched up a long rapier, abruptly, but very finely pointed, in my sword-hand, and in the other a sabre; the elder brother seized his heavy battle-axe; and the younger, a great, two-handed sword, which he wielded in one hand like a feather. We had just time to get clear of the tower, embrace and say good-bye, and part to some little distance, that we might not encumber each other's motions, ere the triple giant-brotherhood drew near to attack us. They were about twice our height, and armed to the teeth. Through the visors of their helmets their monstrous eyes shone with a horrible ferocity. I was in the middle position, and the middle giant approached me. My eyes were busy with his armour, and I was not a moment in settling my mode of attack. I saw that his body-armour was somewhat clumsily made, and that the overlappings in the lower part had more play than necessary; and I hoped that, in a fortunate moment, some joint would open a little, in a visible and accessible part. I stood till he came near enough to aim a blow at me with the mace, which has been, in all ages, the favourite weapon of giants, when, of course, I leaped aside, and let the blow fall upon the spot where I had been standing. I expected this would strain the joints of his armour yet more. Full of fury, he made at me again; but I kept him busy, constantly eluding his blows, and hoping thus to fatigue him. He did not seem to fear any assault from me, and I attempted none as yet; but while I watched his motions in order to avoid his blows, I, at the same time, kept equal watch upon those joints of his armour, through some one of which I hoped to reach his life. At length, as if somewhat fatigued, he paused a moment, and drew himself slightly up; I bounded forward, foot and hand, ran my rapier right through to the armour of his back, let go the hilt, and passing under his right arm, turned as he fell, and flew at him with my sabre. At one happy blow I divided the band of his helmet, which fell off, and allowed me, with a second cut across the eyes, to blind him quite; after which I clove his head, and turned, uninjured, to see how my brothers had fared. Both the giants were down, but so were my brothers. I flew first to the one and then to the other couple. Both pairs of combatants were dead, and yet locked together, as in the death-struggle. The elder had buried his battle-axe in the body of his foe, and had fallen beneath him as he fell. The giant had strangled him in his own death-agonies. The younger had nearly hewn off the left leg of his enemy; and, grappled with in the act, had, while they rolled together on the earth, found for his dagger a passage betwixt the gorget and cuirass of the giant, and stabbed him mortally in the throat. The blood from the giant's throat was yet pouring over the hand of his foe, which still grasped the hilt of the dagger sheathed in the wound. They lay silent. I, the least worthy, remained the sole survivor in the lists.

As I stood exhausted amidst the dead, after the first worthy deed of my life, I suddenly looked behind me, and there lay the Shadow, black in the sunshine. I went into the lonely tower, and there lay the useless armour of the noble youths – supine as they. Ah, how sad it looked! It was a glorious death, but it was death. My songs could not comfort me now. I was almost ashamed that I was alive, when they, the true-hearted, were no more. And yet I breathed freer to think that I had gone through the trial, and had not failed. And perhaps I may be forgiven, if some feelings of pride arose in my bosom, when I looked down on the mighty form that lay dead by my hand.[3]

3 The Shadow's reappearance may be linked with Anodos's feeling of pride.

'After all, however,' I said to myself, and my heart sank, 'it was only skill. Your giant was but a blunderer.'

I left the bodies of friends and foes, peaceful enough when the death-fight was over, and, hastening to the country below, roused the peasants. They came with shouting and gladness, bringing waggons to carry the bodies. I resolved to take the princes home to their father, each as he lay, in the arms of his country's foe. But first I searched the giants, and found the keys of their castle, to which I repaired, followed by a great company of the people. It was a place of wonderful strength. I released the prisoners, knights and ladies, all in a sad condition, from the cruelties and neglects of the giants. It humbled me to see them crowding round me with thanks, when in truth the glorious brothers, lying dead by their lonely tower, were those to whom the thanks belonged. I had but aided in carrying out the thought born in their brain, and uttered in visible form before ever I laid hold thereupon. Yet I did count myself happy to have been chosen for their brother in this great dead. After a few hours spent in refreshing and clothing the prisoners, we all commenced our journey towards the capital. This was slow at first; but, as the strength and spirits of the prisoners returned, it became more rapid; and in three days we reached the palace of the king. As we entered the city gates, with the huge bulks lying each on a waggon drawn by horses, and two of them inextricably intertwined with the dead bodies of their princes, the people raised a shout and then a cry, and followed in multitudes the solemn procession.

I will not attempt to describe the behaviour of the grand old king. Joy and pride in his sons overcame his sorrow at their loss. On me he heaped every kindness that heart could devise or hand execute. He used to sit and question me, night after night, about everything that was in any way connected with them and their preparations. Our mode of life, and relation to each other, during the time we spent together, was a constant theme. He entered into the minutest details of the construction of the armour, even to

We reached the palace of the king

a peculiar mode of riveting some of the plates, with unwearying interest. This armour I had intended to beg of the king, as my sole memorials of the contest; but, when I saw the delight he took in contemplating it, and the consolation it appeared to afford him in his sorrow, I could not ask for it; but, at his request, left my own, weapons and all, to be joined with theirs in a trophy, erected in the grand square of the palace. The king, with gorgeous ceremony, dubbed me knight with his own old hand, in which trembled the sword of his youth.[4]

During the short time I remained, my company was, naturally, much courted by the young nobles. I was in a constant round of gaiety and diversion, notwithstanding that the court was in mourning. For the country was so rejoiced at the death of the giants, and so many of their lost friends had been restored to the nobility and men of wealth, that the gladness surpassed the grief. 'Ye have indeed left your lives to your people, my great brothers!' I said.

But I was ever and ever haunted by the old shadow, which I had not seen all the time that I was at work in the tower. Even in the society of the ladies of the court, who seemed to think it only their duty to make my stay there as pleasant to me as possible, I could not help being conscious of its presence, although it might not be annoying me at the time. At length, somewhat weary of uninterrupted pleasure, and nowise strengthened thereby, either in body or mind, I put on a splendid suit of armour of steel inlaid with silver, which the old king had given me, and, mounting the horse on which it had been brought to me, took my leave of the palace, to visit the distant city in which the lady dwelt, whom the elder prince had loved. I anticipated a sore task, in conveying to her the news of his glorious fate: but this trial was spared me, in a manner as strange as anything that had happened to me in Fairy Land.

---

4 He has finally become Sir Anodos. (See p.130).

—22—

No one has my form but the I.

SCHOPPE, IN JEAN PAUL'S TITAN[1]

Joy's a subtil elf.

I think man's happiest when he forgets himself.

CYRIL TOURNEUR, THE REVENGER'S TRAGEDY[2]

On the third day of my journey, I was riding gently along a road, apparently little frequented, to judge from the grass that grew upon it. I was approaching a forest. Everywhere in Fairy Land forests are the places where one may most certainly expect adventures. As I drew near, a youth, unarmed, gentle, and beautiful, who had just cut a branch from a yew growing on the skirts of the wood, evidently to make himself a bow,[3] met me, and thus accosted me:

'Sir knight, be careful as thou ridest through this forest; for it is said to be strangely enchanted, in a sort which even those who have been witnesses of its enchantment can hardly describe.'

I thanked him for his advice, which I promised to follow, and rode on. But the moment I entered the wood, it seemed to me that, if enchantment there was, it must be of a good kind; for the Shadow, which had been more than usually dark and distressing, since I

---

1 *'Niemand hat meine Gestalt als der Ich.'* On Jean Paul, see p.195. *Titan* (1800-1803) was his most ambitious novel, which took him ten years to write.

2 Cyril Tourneur (1575–1626). English dramatist. In fact, *The Revenger's Tragedy*, which was published anonymously in 1607, is now generally agreed to be the work of Thomas Middleton (1580–1627).

3 Longbows were traditionally made from yew. The yew, because of its longevity, is associated with immortality and can be found in many country churchyards.

had set out on this journey, suddenly disappeared.[4] I felt a wonderful elevation of spirits, and began to reflect on my past life, and especially on my combat with the giants, with such satisfaction, that I had actually to remind myself, that I had only killed one of them; and that, but for the brothers, I should never have had the idea of attacking them, not to mention the smallest power of standing to it. Still I rejoiced, and counted myself amongst the glorious knights of old; having even the unspeakable presumption – my shame and self-condemnation at the memory of it are such, that I write it as the only and sorest penance I can perform – to think of myself (will the world believe it?) as side by side with Sir Galahad![5] Scarcely had the thought been born in my mind, when, approaching me from the left, through the trees, I espied a resplendent knight, of mighty size, whose armour seemed to shine of itself, without the sun. When he drew near, I was astonished to see that this armour was like my own; nay, I could trace, line for line, the correspondence of the inlaid silver to the device on my own. His horse, too, was like mine in colour, form, and motion; save that, like his rider, he was greater and fiercer than his counterpart. The knight rode with beaver up. As he halted right opposite to me in the narrow path, barring my way, I saw the reflection of my countenance in the centre plate of shining steel on his breastplate. Above it rose the same face – his face – only, as I have said, larger and fiercer. I was bewildered. I could not help feeling some admiration of him, but it was mingled with a dim conviction that he was evil, and that I ought to fight with him.

'Let me pass,' I said.

'When I will,' he replied.

Something within me said: 'Spear in rest, and ride at him! else thou art for ever a slave.'

4 The Shadow disappears because this wood is pure self; it will return in its purest form, as Anodos himself.

5 'The love of the praise of men, the desire of fame, the pride that takes offence, the puffing-up of knowledge, these and every other form of Protean self-worship – we must get rid of them all. We must be free.' (MacDonald, *Unspoken Sermons II*, 'The Cause of Spiritual Stupidity'.)

I tried, but my arm trembled so much, that I could not couch my lance. To tell the truth, I, who had overcome the giant, shook like a coward before this knight. He gave a scornful laugh, that echoed through the wood, turned his horse, and said, without looking round, 'Follow me.'

I obeyed, abashed and stupefied. How long he led, and how long I followed, I cannot tell. 'I never knew misery before,' I said to myself. 'Would that I had at least struck him, and had had my death-blow in return! Why, then, do I not call to him to wheel and defend himself? Alas! I know not why, but I cannot. One look from him would cow me like a beaten hound.' I followed, and was silent.

At length we came to a dreary square tower, in the middle of a dense forest. It looked as if scarce a tree had been cut down to make room for it. Across the very door, diagonally, grew the stem of a tree, so large that there was just room to squeeze past it in order to enter. One miserable square hole in the roof was the only visible suggestion of a window. Turret or battlement, or projecting masonry of any kind, it had none. Clear and smooth and massy, it rose from its base, and ended with a line straight and unbroken. The roof, carried to a centre from each of the four walls, rose slightly to the point where the rafters met. Round the base lay several little heaps of either bits of broken branches, withered and peeled, or half-whitened bones; I could not distinguish which. As I approached, the ground sounded hollow beneath my horse's hoofs. The knight took a great key from his pocket, and reaching past the stem of the tree, with some difficulty opened the door. 'Dismount,' he commanded. I obeyed. He turned my horse's head away from the tower, gave him a terrible blow with the flat side of his sword, and sent him madly tearing through the forest.

'Now,' said he, 'enter, and take your companion with you.'

I looked round: knight and horse had vanished, and behind me lay the horrible shadow. I entered, for I could not help myself; and the shadow followed me. I had a terrible conviction that the knight and he were one. The door closed behind me.

Now I was indeed in pitiful plight. There was literally nothing in the tower but my shadow and me. The walls rose right up to the roof; in which, as I had seen from without, there was one little square opening. This I now knew to be the only window the tower possessed. I sat down on the floor, in listless wretchedness. I think I must have fallen asleep, and have slept for hours; for I suddenly became aware of existence, in observing that the moon was shining through the hole in the roof. As she rose higher and higher, her light crept down the wall over me, till at last it shone right upon my head. Instantaneously the walls of the tower seemed to vanish away like a mist.[6] I sat beneath a beech, on the edge of a forest, and the open country lay, in the moonlight, for miles and miles around me, spotted with glimmering houses and spires and towers. I thought with myself, 'Oh, joy! it was only a dream; the horrible narrow waste is gone, and I wake beneath a beech-tree, perhaps one that loves me, and I can go where I will.' I rose, as I thought, and walked about, and did what I would, but ever kept near the tree; for always, and, of course, since my meeting with the woman of the beech-tree far more than ever, I loved that tree. So the night wore on. I waited for the sun to rise, before I could venture to renew my journey. But as soon as the first faint light of the dawn appeared, instead of shining upon me from the eye of the morning, it stole like a fainting ghost through the little square hole above my head; and the walls came out as the light grew, and the glorious night was swallowed up of the hateful day. The long dreary day passed. My shadow lay black on the floor. I felt no hunger, no need of food. The night came. The moon shone. I watched her light slowly descending the wall, as I might have watched, adown the sky, the long, swift approach of a helping angel. Her rays touched me, and I was free. Thus night after

6   The moon brings hope – the hope that this reality is not all, that there is life beyond the walls of the castle.

night passed away. I should have died but for this. Every night the conviction returned, that I was free. Every morning I sat wretchedly disconsolate. At length, when the course of the moon no longer permitted her beams to touch me, the night was dreary as the day. When I slept, I was somewhat consoled by my dreams; but all the time I dreamed, I knew that I was only dreaming. But one night, at length, the moon, a mere shred of pallor, scattered a few thin ghostly rays upon me; and I think I fell asleep and dreamed. I sat in an autumn night before the vintage, on a hill overlooking my own castle. My heart sprang with joy. Oh, to be a child again, innocent, fearless, without shame or desire! I walked down to the castle. All were in consternation at my absence. My sisters were weeping for my loss. They sprang up and clung to me, with incoherent cries, as I entered. My old friends came flocking round me. A gray light shone on the roof of the hall. It was the light of the dawn shining through the square window of my tower. More earnestly than ever, I longed for freedom after this dream; more drearily than ever, crept on the next wretched day. I measured by the sunbeams, caught through the little window in the trap of my tower, how it went by, waiting only for the dreams of the night.

About noon, I started as if something foreign to all my senses and all my experience, had suddenly invaded me; yet it was only the voice of a woman singing. My whole frame quivered with joy, surprise, and the sensation of the unforeseen. Like a living soul, like an incarnation of Nature, the song entered my prison-house. Each tone folded its wings, and laid itself, like a caressing bird, upon my heart. It bathed me like a sea; inwrapt me like an odorous vapour; entered my soul like a long draught of clear spring-water; shone upon me like essential sunlight; soothed me like a mother's voice and hand. Yet, as the clearest forest-well tastes sometimes of the bitterness of decayed leaves, so to my weary, prisoned heart, its cheerfulness had a sting of cold, and its tenderness unmanned me with the faintness of long-departed joys. I wept half-bitterly, half-luxuriously; but not long. I dashed away the tears, ashamed of a weakness which I thought I had abandoned. Ere I knew, I had walked to the door, and seated myself with my ears against it, in order to catch every syllable of the revelation from the unseen outer world. And now I heard each word distinctly. The singer seemed to be standing or sitting near the tower, for the sounds indicated no change of place. The song was something like this:

> *The sun, like a golden knot on high,*
> *Gathers the glories of the sky,*
> *And binds them into a shining tent,*
> *Roofing the world with the firmament.*
> *And through the pavilion the rich winds blow,*
> *And through the pavilion the waters go.*
> *And the birds for joy, and the trees for prayer,*
> *Bowing their heads in the sunny air,*
> *And for thoughts, the gently talking springs,*
> *That come from the centre with secret things —*
> *All make a music, gentle and strong,*
> *Bound by the heart into one sweet song.*
> *And amidst them all, the mother Earth*
> *Sits with the children of her birth;*
> *She tendeth them all, as a mother hen*
> *Her little ones round her, twelve or ten:*
> *Oft she sitteth, with hands on knee,*
> *Idle with love for her family.*
> *Go forth to her from the dark and the dust,*
> *And weep beside her, if weep thou must;*
> *If she may not hold thee to her breast,*
> *Like a weary infant, that cries for rest*
> *At least she will press thee to her knee,*
> *And tell a low, sweet tale to thee,*
> *Till the hue to thy cheek and the light to thine eye,*
> *Strength to thy limbs, and courage high*
> *To thy fainting heart, return amain,*
> *And away to work thou goest again.*
> *From the narrow desert, O man of pride,*
> *Come into the house, so high and wide.*

Hardly knowing what I did, I opened the door. Why had I not done so before? I do not know.

At first I could see no one; but when I had forced myself past the tree which grew across the entrance, I saw, seated on the ground, and leaning against the tree, with her back to my prison, a beautiful woman. Her countenance seemed known to me, and yet unknown. She looked at me and smiled, when I made my appearance.

I saw, leaning against the tree, a beautiful woman.

'Ah! were you the prisoner there? I am very glad I have wiled you out.'

'Do you know me then?'

'Do you not know me? But you hurt me, and that, I suppose, makes it easy for a man to forget. You broke my globe. Yet I thank you. Perhaps I owe you many thanks for breaking it. I took the pieces, all black, and wet with crying over them, to the Fairy Queen. There was no music and no light in them now. But she took them from me, and laid them aside; and made me go to sleep in a great hall of white, with black pillars, and many red curtains.[7] When I woke in the morning, I went to her, hoping to have my globe again, whole and sound; but she sent me away without it, and I have not seen it since. Nor do I care for it now. I have something so much better. I do not need the globe to play to me; for I can sing. I could not sing at all before. Now I go about everywhere through Fairy Land, singing till my heart is like to break, just like my globe, for very joy at my own songs. And wherever I go, my songs do good, and deliver people. And now I have delivered you, and I am so happy.'

She ceased, and the tears came into her eyes.

All this time, I had been gazing at her; and now fully recognised the face of the child, glorified in the countenance of the woman. I was ashamed and humbled before her; but a great weight was lifted from my thoughts. I knelt before her, and thanked her, and begged her to forgive me.

'Rise, rise,' she said; 'I have nothing to forgive; I thank you. But now I must be gone, for I do not know how many may be waiting for me, here and there, through the dark forests; and they cannot come out till I come.'

She rose, and with a smile and a farewell, turned and left me. I dared not ask her to stay; in fact, I could hardly speak to her. Between her and me, there was a great gulf. She was uplifted, by sorrow

---

7 This is the White Hall of Phantasy of chapter 14 (see p.174).

and well-doing, into a region I could hardly hope ever to enter.[8] I watched her departure, as one watches a sunset. She went like a radiance through the dark wood, which was henceforth bright to me, from simply knowing that such a creature was in it. She was bearing the sun to the unsunned spots. The light and the music of her broken globe were now in her heart and her brain. As she went, she sang; and I caught these few words of her song; and the tones seemed to linger and wind about the trees after she had disappeared:

> *Thou goest thine, and I go mine —*
> *Many ways we wend;*
> *Many days, and many ways,*
> *Ending in one end.*
>
> *Many a wrong, and its curing song;*
> *Many a road, and many an inn;*
> *Room to roam, but only one home*
> *For all the world to win.*

And so she vanished. With a sad heart, soothed by humility, and the knowledge of her peace and gladness, I bethought me what now I should do. First, I must leave the tower far behind me, lest, in some evil moment, I might be once more caged within its horrible walls. But it was ill walking in my heavy armour; and besides I had now no right to the golden spurs and the resplendent mail, fitly dulled with long neglect. I might do for a squire; but I honoured knighthood too highly, to call myself any longer one of the noble brotherhood. I stripped off all my armour, piled it under the tree, just where the lady had been seated, and took my unknown way, eastward through

8 "'How am I then to rise into that higher region, that empyrean of love?' And, beginning straightway to try to love his neighbour, he finds that the empyrean of which he spoke is no more to be reached in itself than the law was to be reached in itself. As he cannot keep the law without first rising into the love of his neighbour, so he cannot love his neighbour without first rising higher still. The whole system of the universe works upon this law – the driving of things upward towards the centre. The man who will love his neighbour can do so by no immediately operative exercise of the will. It is the man fulfilled of God from whom he came and by whom he is, who alone can as himself love his neighbour who came from God too and is by God too.' (MacDonald, *Unspoken Sermons I*, 'Love Thy Neighbour')

the woods. Of all my weapons, I carried only a short axe in my hand. Then first I knew the delight of being lowly; of saying to myself, 'I am what I am, nothing more.' 'I have failed,' I said, 'I have lost myself – would it had been my shadow.' I looked round: the shadow was nowhere to be seen. Ere long, I learned that it was not myself, but only my shadow, that I had lost.[9] I learned that it is better, a thousand-fold, for a proud man to fall and be humbled, than to hold up his head in his pride and fancied innocence. I learned that he that will be a hero, will barely be a man; that he that will be nothing but a doer of his work, is sure of his manhood. In nothing was my ideal lowered, or dimmed, or grown less precious; I only saw it too plainly, to set myself for a moment beside it. Indeed, my ideal soon became my life; whereas, formerly, my life had consisted in a vain attempt to behold, if not my ideal in myself, at least myself in my ideal. Now, however, I took, at first, what perhaps was a mistaken pleasure, in despising and degrading myself. Another self seemed to arise, like a white spirit from a dead man, from the dumb and trampled self of the past.[10] Doubtless, this self must again die and be buried, and again, from its tomb, spring a winged child; but of this my history as yet bears not the record.[11] Self will come to life even in the slaying of self; but there is ever something deeper and stronger than it, which will emerge at last from the unknown abysses of the soul: will it be as a solemn gloom, burning with eyes? or a clear morning after the rain? or a smiling child, that finds itself nowhere, and everywhere?

9   'This love of our neighbour is the only door out of the dungeon of self, where we mope and mow, striking sparks, and rubbing phosphorescences out of the walls, and blowing our own breath in our own nostrils, instead of issuing to the fair sunlight of God, the sweet winds of the universe... To have himself, to know himself, to enjoy himself, he calls life; whereas, if he would forget himself, tenfold would be his life in God and his neighbours.' (MacDonald *Unspoken Sermons I*, 'Love Thy Neighbour')

10 'The Self, when it finds it cannot have honour because of its gifts, because of the love lavished upon it, because of its conquests, and the "golden opinions bought from all sorts of people," will please itself with the thought of its abnegations, of its unselfishness, of its devotion to God, of its forsakings for his sake.' (MacDonald *Unspoken Sermons II*, 'Self-denial')

11 'With every morn my life afresh must break/The crust of self, gathered about me fresh.' (MacDonald, *Diary of an Old Soul*, Oct 10).

23

High erected thought, seated in a heart of courtesy.
SIR PHILIP SIDNEY[1]

A sweet attractive kinde of grace,
A full assurance given by lookes,
Continuall comfort in a face,
The lineaments of Gospel bookes.
MATTHEW ROYDON, ON SIR PHILIP SIDNEY[2]

I had not gone far, for I had but just lost sight of the hated tower, when a voice of another sort, sounding near or far, as the trees permitted or intercepted its passage, reached me. It was a full, deep, manly voice, but withal clear and melodious. Now it burst on the ear with a sudden swell, and anon, dying away as suddenly, seemed to come to me across a great space. Nevertheless, it drew nearer; till, at last, I could distinguish the words of the song, and get transient glimpses of the singer, between the columns of the trees. He came nearer, dawning upon me like a growing thought. He was a knight, armed from head to heel, mounted upon a strange-looking beast, whose form I could not understand. The words which I heard him sing were like these:

> *Heart be stout,*
> *   And eye be true;*
> *Good blade out!*
> *   And ill shall rue.*

1 Sir Philip Sidney (1554–1586). The quote comes from *Defence of Poesy*.
2 Matthew Roydon (c.1550–1622). From 'An Elegie; or Friend's Passion for his Astrophill'. In the first edition of *Phantastes* this quote was attributed to Edmund Spenser.

Courage, horse!
 Thou lackst no skill;
Well thy force
 Hath matched my will.

For the foe
 With fiery breath,
At a blow,
 It still in death.

Gently, horse!
 Tread fearlessly;
'Tis his corse
 That burdens thee.

The sun's eye
 Is fierce at noon;
Thou and I
 Will rest full soon.

And new strength
 New work will meet;
Till, at length,
 Long rest is sweet.

And now horse and rider had arrived near enough for me to see, fastened by the long neck to the hinder part of the saddle, and trailing its hideous length on the ground behind, the body of a great dragon. It was no wonder that, with such a drag at his heels, the horse could make but slow progress, notwithstanding his evident dismay. The horrid, serpent-like head, with its black tongue, forked with red, hanging out of its jaws, dangled against the horse's side. Its neck was covered with long blue hair, its sides with scales of green and gold. Its back was of corrugated skin, of a purple hue. Its belly was similar in nature, but its colour was leaden, dashed with blotches of livid blue. Its skinny, bat-like wings and its tail were of a dull gray. It was strange to see how so many gorgeous colours, so many curving lines, and such beautiful things as wings and hair and scales, combined to form the horrible creature, intense in ugliness.

'Fastened to the saddle was the body of a great dragon...'

The knight was passing me with a salutation; but, as I walked towards him, he reined up, and I stood by his stirrup. When I came near him, I saw to my surprise and pleasure likewise, although a sudden pain, like a birth of fire, sprang up in my heart, that it was the knight of the soiled armour, whom I knew before, and whom I had seen in the vision, with the lady of the marble. But I could have thrown my arms around him, because she loved him. This discovery only strengthened the resolution I had formed, before I recognised him, of offering myself to the knight, to wait upon him as a squire, for he seemed to be unattended. I made my request in as few words as possible. He hesitated for a moment, and looked at me thoughtfully. I saw that he suspected who I was, but that he continued uncertain of his suspicion. No doubt he was soon convinced of its truth; but all the time I was with him, not a word crossed his lips with reference to what he evidently concluded I wished to leave unnoticed, if not to keep concealed.

'Squire and knight should be friends,'said he: 'can you take me by the hand?' And he held out the great gauntleted right hand. I grasped it willingly and strongly. Not a word more was said. The knight gave the sign to his horse, which again began his slow march, and I walked beside and a little behind.

We had not gone very far before we arrived at a little cottage; from which, as we drew near, a woman rushed out with the cry:

'My child! my child! have you found my child?'

'I have found her,' replied the knight, 'but she is sorely hurt. I was forced to leave her with the hermit, as I returned. You will find her there, and I think she will get better. You see I have brought you a present. This wretch will not hurt you again.' And he undid the creature's neck, and flung the frightful burden down by the cottage door.

The woman was now almost out of sight in the wood; but the husband stood at the door, with speechless thanks in his face.

'You must bury the monster,' said the knight. 'If I had arrived a moment later, I should have been too late. But now you need not fear, for such a creature as this very rarely appears, in the same part, twice during a lifetime.'

'Will you not dismount and rest you, Sir Knight?' said the peasant, who had, by this time, recovered himself a little. 'That I will, thankfully,' said he; and, dismounting, he gave the reins to me, and told me to unbridle the horse, and lead him into the shade. 'You need not tie him up,' he added; 'he will not run away.'

When I returned, after obeying his orders, and entered the cottage, I saw the knight seated, without his helmet, and talking most familiarly with the simple host. I stood at the open door for a moment, and, gazing at him, inwardly justified the white lady in preferring him to me. A nobler countenance I never saw. Loving-kindness beamed from every line of his face. It seemed as if he would repay himself for the late arduous combat, by indulging in all the gentleness of a womanly heart. But when the talk ceased for a moment, he seemed to fall into a reverie. Then the exquisite curves of the upper lip vanished. The lip was lengthened and compressed at the same moment. You could have told that, within the lips, the teeth were firmly closed. The whole face grew stern and determined, all but fierce; only the eyes burned on like a holy sacrifice, uplift on a granite rock.

The woman entered, with her mangled child in her arms. She was pale as her little burden. She gazed, with a wild love and despairing tenderness, on the still, all but dead face, white and clear from loss of blood and terror.

The knight rose. The light that had been confined to his eyes, now shone from his whole countenance. He took the little thing in his arms, and, with the mother's help, undressed her, and looked to her wounds. The tears flowed down his face as he did so. With tender hands he bound them up, kissed the pale cheek, and gave her back to her mother. When he went home, all his tale would be of the grief and joy of the parents; while to me, who had looked on, the gracious countenance of the armed man, beaming from the panoply of steel, over the seemingly dead child, while the powerful hands turned it and shifted it, and bound it, if possible even more gently than the mother's, formed the centre of the story.

After we had partaken of the best they could give us, the knight took his leave, with a few parting instructions to the mother as to how she should treat the child.

I brought the knight his steed, held the stirrup while he mounted, and then followed him through the wood. The horse, delighted to be free of his hideous load, bounded beneath the weight of man and armour, and could hardly be restrained from galloping on. But the knight made him time his powers to mine, and so we went on for an hour or two. Then the knight dismounted, and compelled me to get into the saddle, saying: 'Knight and squire must share the labour.'

Holding by the stirrup, he walked along by my side, heavily clad as he was, with apparent ease. As we went, he led a conversation, in which I took what humble part my sense of my condition would permit me.

'Somehow or other,' said he, 'notwithstanding the beauty of this country of Faerie, in which we are, there is much that is wrong in it. If there are great splendours, there are corresponding horrors; heights and depths; beautiful women and awful fiends; noble men and weaklings. All a man has to do, is to better what he can. And if he will settle it with himself, that even renown and success are in themselves of no great value, and be content to be defeated, if so be that the fault is not his; and so go to his work with a cool brain and a strong will, he will get it done; and fare none the worse in the end, that he was not burdened with provision and precaution.'

'But he will not always come off well,' I ventured to say.

'Perhaps not,' rejoined the knight, 'in the individual act; but the result of his lifetime will content him.'

'So it will fare with you, doubtless,' thought I; 'but for me —'

Venturing to resume the conversation after a pause, I said, hesitatingly:

'May I ask for what the little beggar-girl wanted your aid, when she came to your castle to find you?' He looked at me for a moment in silence, and then said —

'I cannot help wondering how you know of that; but there is something about you quite strange enough to entitle you to the privilege of the country; namely, to go unquestioned.[3] I, however, being only a man, such as you see me, am ready to tell you anything you like to ask me, as far as I can. The little beggar-girl came into the hall where I was sitting, and told me a very curious story, which I can only recollect very vaguely, it was so peculiar. What I can recall is, that she was sent to gather wings. As soon as she had gathered a pair of wings for herself, she was to fly away, she said, to the country she came from; but where that was, she could give no information. She said she had to beg her wings from the butterflies and moths; and wherever she begged, no one refused her. But she needed a great many of the wings of butterflies and moths to make a pair for her; and so she had to wander about day after day, looking for butterflies, and night after night, looking for moths; and then she begged for their wings. But the day before, she had come into a part of the forest, she said, where there were multitudes of splendid butterflies flitting about, with wings which were just fit to make the eyes in the shoulders of hers; and she knew she could have as many of them as she liked for the asking; but as soon as she began to beg, there came a great creature right up to her, and threw her down, and walked over her. When she got up, she saw the wood was full of these beings stalking about, and seeming to have nothing to do with each other. As soon as ever she began to beg, one of them walked over her; till at last in dismay, and in grow-

---

3 Anodos knows of it, of course, because he heard them talk about it when he went through the door of Sighs (ch. 19, p.211)

ing horror of the senseless creatures, she had run away to look for somebody to help her. I asked her what they were like. She said, like great men, made of wood, without knee-or elbow-joints, and without any noses or mouths or eyes in their faces.[4] I laughed at the little maiden, thinking she was making child's game of me; but, although she burst out laughing too, she persisted in asserting the truth of her story.

'"Only come, knight, come and see; I will lead you."

'So I armed myself, to be ready for anything that might happen, and followed the child; for, though I could make nothing of her story, I could see she was a little human being in need of some help or other. As she walked before me, I looked attentively at her. Whether or not it was from being so often knocked down and walked over, I could not tell, but her clothes were very much torn, and in several places her white skin was peeping through. I thought she was hump-backed; but on looking more closely, I saw, through the tatters of her frock – do not laugh at me – a bunch on each shoulder, of the most gorgeous colours. Looking yet more closely, I saw that they were of the shape of folded wings, and were made of all kinds of butterfly-wings and moth-wings, crowded together like the feathers on the individual butterfly pinion; but, like them, most beautifully arranged, and producing a perfect harmony of colour and shade. I could now more easily believe the rest of her story; especially as I saw, every now and then, a certain heaving motion in

4   Robert Louis Stevenson, cited this passage in a letter to his cousin Bob: 'Here is another complaint I bring against our country. I try to learn the truth, and their grim-faced dummies, their wooden effigies and creeds dead years ago at heart, come round me, like the wooden men in *Phantastes*, and I may cut at them and prove them faulty and mortal, but yet they can stamp the life out of me.' (Gray, Donald. '"Amicable Infidelity," "Grim-faced Dummies" and Rondels, RLS on George MacDonald' *North Wind*, 23, 2004, p.23.) Stevenson described himself as having 'had great pleasure from his [MacDonald's] works' and may have had the wooden men in mind when writing *Jekyll and Hyde*: '...then came the horrible part of the thing; for the man trampled calmly over the child's body and left her screaming on the ground. It sounds nothing to hear but it was hellish to see. It wasn't like a man; it was like some damned Juggernaut.' (Stevenson, Robert Louis, *The Strange Case of Dr Jekyll and Mr Hyde, and Other Stories*, Harmondsworth: Penguin Books, 1979, p.31.)

the wings, as if they longed to be uplifted and outspread. But beneath her scanty garments complete wings could not be concealed, and indeed, from her own story, they were yet unfinished.

'After walking for two or three hours (how the little girl found her way, I could not imagine), we came to a part of the forest, the very air of which was quivering with the motions of multitudes of resplendent butterflies; as gorgeous in colour, as if the eyes of peacocks' feathers had taken to flight, but of infinite variety of hue and form, only that the appearance of some kind of eye on each wing predominated. "There they are, there they are!" cried the child, in a tone of victory mingled with terror. Except for this tone, I should have thought she referred to the butterflies, for I could see nothing else. But at that moment an enormous butterfly, whose wings had great eyes of blue surrounded by confused cloudy heaps of more dingy colouring, just like a break in the clouds on a stormy day towards evening, settled near us. The child instantly began murmuring: "Butterfly, butterfly, give me your wings"; when, the moment after, she fell to the ground, and began crying as if hurt. I drew my sword and heaved a great blow in the direction in which the child had fallen. It struck something, and instantly the most grotesque imitation of a man became visible. You see this Fairy Land is full of oddities and all sorts of incredibly ridiculous things, which a man is compelled to meet and treat as real existences, although all the time he feels foolish for doing so. This being, if being it could be called, was like a block of wood roughly hewn into the mere outlines of a man; and hardly so, for it had but head, body, legs, and arms – the head without a face, and the limbs utterly formless.[5] I had hewn off one of its legs, but the two portions moved on as best they could, quite independent of each other; so that I

5   These senseless creatures are unfeeling, unbending, inflexible. There is a strong social undercurrent to this scene. The beggar-girl has to beg, but the wooden men oppress her, march over her, without even noticing her beauty. Hein sees them as cultic leaders, so stuck in their ways they can only be defeated by upsetting them, turning them on their heads. They are literally blockheads. (Hein, *The Harmony Within*, p.109.)

had done no good. I ran after it, and clove it in twain from the head downwards; but it could not be convinced that its vocation was not to walk over people; for, as soon as the little girl began her begging again, all three parts came bustling up; and if I had not interposed my weight between her and them, she would have been trampled again under them. I saw that something else must be done. If the wood was full of the creatures, it would be an endless work to chop them so small that they could do no injury; and then, besides, the parts would be so numerous, that the butterflies would be in danger from the drift of flying chips. I served this one so, however; and then told the girl to beg again, and point out the direction in which one was coming. I was glad to find, however, that I could now see him myself, and wondered how they could have been invisible before. I would not allow him to walk over the child; but while I kept him off, and she began begging again, another appeared; and it was all I could do, from the weight of my armour, to protect her from the stupid, persevering efforts of the two. But suddenly the right plan occurred to me. I tripped one of them up, and, taking him by the legs, set him up on his head, with his heels against a tree. I was delighted to find he could not move. Meantime the poor child was walked over by the other, but it was for the last time. Whenever one appeared, I followed the same plan – tripped him up and set him on his head; and so the little beggar was able to gather her wings without any trouble, which occupation she continued for several hours in my company.'

'What became of her?' I asked.

'I took her home with me to my castle, and she told me all her story; but it seemed to me, all the time, as if I were hearing a child talk in its sleep. I could not arrange her story in my mind at all, although it seemed to leave hers in some certain order of its own. My wife –'

Here the knight checked himself, and said no more. Neither did I urge the conversation farther.

Thus we journeyed for several days, resting at night in such shelter as we could get; and when no better was to be had, lying in the forest under some tree, on a couch of old leaves.

I loved the knight more and more. I believe never squire served his master with more care and joyfulness than I. I tended his horse; I cleaned his armour; my skill in the craft enabled me to repair it when necessary; I watched his needs; and was well repaid for all by the love itself which I bore him.

'This,' I said to myself, 'is a true man. I will serve him, and give him all worship, seeing in him the imbodiment of what I would fain become. If I cannot be noble myself, I will yet be servant to his nobleness.' He, in return, soon showed me such signs of friendship and respect, as made my heart glad; and I felt that, after all, mine would be no lost life, if I might wait on him to the world's end, although no smile but his should greet me, and no one but him should say, 'Well done! he was a good servant!' at last. But I burned to do something more for him than the ordinary routine of a squire's duty permitted.

One afternoon, we began to observe an appearance of roads in the wood. Branches had been cut down, and openings made, where footsteps had worn no path below. These indications increased as we passed on, till, at length, we came into a long, narrow avenue, formed by felling the trees in its line, as the remaining roots evidenced.[6] At some little distance, on both hands, we observed signs of similar avenues, which appeared to converge with ours, towards one spot. Along these we indistinctly saw several forms moving, which seemed, with ourselves, to approach the common centre. Our path brought us, at last, up to a wall of yew-trees, growing close together, and intertwining their branches so, that nothing could be seen beyond it. An opening was cut in it like a door, and all the wall was trimmed smooth and perpendicular. The knight

6 This is an unnatural place – the trees have been felled in order to create it.

dismounted, and waited till I had provided for his horse's comfort; upon which we entered the place together.

It was a great space, bare of trees, and enclosed by four walls of yew, similar to that through which we had entered. These trees grew to a very great height, and did not divide from each other till close to the top, where their summits formed a row of conical battlements all around the walls. The space contained was a parallelogram of great length. Along each of the two longer sides of the interior, were ranged three ranks of men, in white robes, standing silent and solemn, each with a sword by his side, although the rest of his costume and bearing was more priestly than soldierly. For some distance inwards, the space between these opposite rows was filled with a company of men and women and children, in holiday attire. The looks of all were directed inwards, towards the further end. Far beyond the crowd, in a long avenue, seeming to narrow in the distance, went the long rows of the white-robed men. On what the attention of the multitude was fixed, we could not tell, for the sun had set before we arrived, and it was growing dark within. It grew darker and darker. The multitude waited in silence. The stars began to shine down into the enclosure, and they grew brighter and larger every moment. A wind arose, and swayed the pinnacles of the tree-tops; and made a strange sound, half like music, half like moaning, through the close branches and leaves of the tree-walls. A young girl who stood beside me, clothed in the same dress as the priests, bowed her head, and grew pale with awe.

The knight whispered to me, 'How solemn it is! Surely they wait to hear the voice of a prophet. There is something good near!'

But I, though somewhat shaken by the feeling expressed by my master, yet had an unaccountable conviction that here was something bad. So I resolved to be keenly on the watch for what should follow. Suddenly a great star, like a sun, appeared high in the air over the temple, illuminating it throughout; and a great song arose from the men in white, which went rolling round and round the building, now receding to the end, and now approaching, down the other side, the place where we stood. For some of the singers were regularly ceasing, and the next to them as regularly taking up the song, so that it crept onwards with gradations produced by changes which could not themselves be detected, for only a few of those who were singing ceased at the same moment. The song paused; and I saw a company of six of the white-robed men walk up the centre of the human avenue, surrounding a youth gorgeously attired beneath his robe of white, and wearing a chaplet of flowers on his head. I followed them closely, with my keenest observation; and, by accompanying their slow progress with my eyes, I was able to perceive more clearly what took place when they arrived at the other end. I knew that my sight was so much more keen than that of most people, that I had good reason to suppose I should see more than the rest could, at such a distance. At the farther end a throne stood upon a platform, high above the heads of the surrounding priests. To this platform I saw the company begin to ascend, apparently by an inclined plane or gentle slope. The throne itself was elevated again, on a kind of square pedestal, to the top of which led a flight of steps. On the throne sat a majestic-looking figure, whose posture seemed to indicate a mixture of pride and benignity, as he looked down on the multitude below. The company ascended to the foot of the throne, where they all kneeled for some minutes; then they rose and passed round to the side of the pedestal upon which the throne stood. Here they crowded close behind the youth, putting him in the foremost place, and one of them opened a door in the pedestal, for the youth to enter. I was sure I saw him shrink back, and those crowding behind pushed him in.[7] Then, again, arose a burst of song from the multitude in white, which lasted some time. When it ceased, a new company of seven commenced its march up the

---

7   This is a church which literally devours its worshippers. It is an artificial place, creating its effects through the 'really grand accompaniments' rather than the goodness of its leaders and acolytes. It has the appearance of holiness or spiritual depth, but it is all just 'effects'. What is really evil about this place is that it abuses the trust of the worshippers.

centre. As they advanced, I looked up at my master: his noble countenance was full of reverence and awe. Incapable of evil himself, he
could scarcely suspect it in another, much less in a multitude such
as this, and surrounded with such appearances of solemnity. I was
certain it was the really grand accompaniments that overcame him;
that the stars overhead, the dark towering tops of the yew-trees, and
the wind that, like an unseen spirit, sighed through their branches,
bowed his spirit to the belief, that in all these ceremonies lay some
great mystical meaning which, his humility told him, his ignorance
prevented him from understanding.

More convinced than before, that there was evil here, I could
not endure that my master should be deceived; that one like him,
so pure and noble, should respect what, if my suspicions were true,
was worse than the ordinary deceptions of priestcraft. I could not
tell how far he might be led to countenance, and otherwise support
their doings, before he should find cause to repent bitterly of his
error. I watched the new procession yet more keenly, if possible,
than the former. This time, the central figure was a girl; and, at the
close, I observed, yet more indubitably, the shrinking back, and the
crowding push. What happened to the victims, I never learned; but
I had learned enough, and I could bear it no longer. I stooped, and
whispered to the young girl who stood by me, to lend me her white
garment. I wanted it, that I might not be entirely out of keeping
with the solemnity, but might have at least this help to passing unquestioned. She looked up, half-amused and half-bewildered, as if
doubting whether I was in earnest or not. But in her perplexity, she
permitted me to unfasten it, and slip it down from her shoulders.
I easily got possession of it; and, sinking down on my knees in the
crowd, I rose apparently in the habit of one of the worshippers.
Giving my battle-axe to the girl, to hold in pledge for the return
of her stole, for I wished to test the matter unarmed, and, if it was
a man that sat upon the throne, to attack him with hands bare,
as I supposed his must be, I made my way through the crowd to

the front, while the singing yet continued, desirous of reaching the platform while it was unoccupied by any of the priests. I was permitted to walk up the long avenue of white robes unmolested, though I saw questioning looks in many of the faces as I passed. I presume my coolness aided my passage; for I felt quite indifferent as to my own fate; not feeling, after the late events of my history, that I was at all worth taking care of; and enjoying, perhaps, something of an evil satisfaction, in the revenge I was thus taking upon the self which had fooled me so long. When I arrived on the platform, the song had just ceased, and I felt as if all were looking towards me. But instead of kneeling at its foot, I walked right up the stairs to the throne, laid hold of a great wooden image that seemed to sit upon it, and tried to hurl it from its seat. In this I failed at first, for I found it firmly fixed. But in dread lest, the first shock of amazement passing away, the guards would rush upon me before I had effected my purpose, I strained with all my might; and, with a noise as of the cracking, and breaking, and tearing of rotten wood, something gave way, and I hurled the image down the steps.[8] Its displacement revealed a great hole in the throne, like the hollow of a decayed tree, going down apparently a great way. But I had no time to examine it, for, as I looked into it, up out of it rushed a great brute, like a wolf, but twice the size, and tumbled me headlong with itself, down the steps of the throne. As we fell, however, I caught it by the throat, and the moment we reached the platform,

8 'How terribly, then, have the theologians misrepresented God in the measures of the low and showy, not the lofty and simple humanities! Nearly all of them represent him as a great King on a grand throne, thinking how grand he is, and making it the business of his being and the end of his universe to keep up his glory, wielding the bolts of a Jupiter against them that take his name in vain. They would not allow this, but follow out what they say, and it comes much to this... The simplest peasant who loves his children and his sheep were – no, not a truer, for the other is false, but – a true type of our God beside that monstrosity of a monarch.' (MacDonald, *Unspoken Sermons I*, 'The Child in the Midst'). MacDonald mistrusted any theology or religious system which placed the judgmental God above the merciful Christ. 'Eh, grannie! think o' the face o' that man o' sorrows, that never said a hard word till a sinfu' wuman, or a despised publican: was he thinkin' aboot's ain glory, think ye? An we have no richt to saw we ken God save in the face o' Christ Jesus. What ever's no like Christ is no like God.' (MacDonald *Robert Falconer*, Book III, ch. 5).

a struggle commenced, in which I soon got uppermost, with my hand upon its throat, and knee upon its heart. But now arose a wild cry of wrath and revenge and rescue. A universal hiss of steel, as every sword was swept from its scabbard, seemed to tear the very air in shreds. I heard the rush of hundreds towards the platform on which I knelt. I only tightened my grasp of the brute's throat. His eyes were already starting from his head, and his tongue was hanging out. My anxious hope was, that, even after they had killed me, they would be unable to undo my gripe of his throat, before the monster was past breathing. I therefore threw all my will, and force, and purpose, into the grasping hand. I remember no blow. A faintness came over me, and my consciousness departed.

24

We are ne'er like angels till our passions die.

DEKKER[1]

This wretched Inn, where we scarce stay to bait,
We call our Dwelling-Place:
We call one Step a Race:
But angels in their full enlightened state,
Angels, who Live, and know what 'tis to Be,
Who all the nonsense of our language see,
Who speak things, and our words, their ill-drawn pictures,
    scorn,

When we, by a foolish figure, say,
Behold an old man dead! then they
Speak properly, and cry, Behold a man-child born!

COWLEY[2]

I was dead, and right content. I lay in my coffin, with my hands folded in peace. The knight, and the lady I loved, wept over me. Her tears fell on my face.

'Ah!' said the knight, 'I rushed amongst them like a madman. I hewed them down like brushwood. Their swords battered on me like hail, but hurt me not. I cut a lane through to my friend. He was dead. But he had throttled the monster, and I had to cut the handful out of its throat, before I could disengage and carry off his body. They dared not molest me as I brought him back.'

1   Thomas Dekker (c. 1572 – 1632). Elizabethan dramatist and writer. The quote comes from his play *The Honest Whore* Part 2. Act 1. Sc. 2
2   Abraham Cowley (1618 – 1667). English poet. The lines come from his poem 'Life' (1656).

I was dead, and right content

'He has died well,' said the lady.

My spirit rejoiced. They left me to my repose. I felt as if a cool hand had been laid upon my heart, and had stilled it. My soul was like a summer evening, after a heavy fall of rain, when the drops are yet glistening on the trees in the last rays of the down-going sun, and the wind of the twilight has begun to blow. The hot fever of life had gone by, and I breathed the clear mountain-air of the land of Death.[3] I had never dreamed of such blessedness. It was not that I had in any way ceased to be what I had been. The very fact that anything can die, implies the existence of something that cannot die; which must either take to itself another form, as when the seed that is sown dies, and arises again; or, in conscious existence, may, perhaps, continue to lead a purely spiritual life. If my passions were dead, the souls of the passions, those essential mysteries of the spirit which had imbodied themselves in the passions, and had given to them all their glory and wonderment, yet lived, yet glowed, with a pure, undying fire. They rose above their vanishing earthly garments, and disclosed themselves angels of light. But oh, how beautiful beyond the old form! I lay thus for a time, and lived as it were an unradiating existence; my soul a motionless lake, that received all things and gave nothing back; satisfied in still contemplation, and spiritual consciousness.

Ere long, they bore me to my grave. Never tired child lay down in his white bed, and heard the sound of his playthings being laid aside for the night, with a more luxurious satisfaction of repose than I knew, when I felt the coffin settle on the firm earth, and heard the sound of the falling mould upon its lid. It has not the same hollow rattle within the coffin, that it sends up to the edge of the grave. They buried me in no graveyard. They loved me too much for that, I thank them; but they laid me in the grounds of their own castle,

---

3   "'You have tasted of death now," said the Old Man. "Is it good?"

"It is good," said Mossy. "It is better than life."

"No," said the Old Man. "It is only more life.'" (MacDonald, *The Golden Key*)

amid many trees; where, as it was spring-time, were growing prim-roses, and blue-bells, and all the families of the woods.

Now that I lay in her bosom, the whole earth, and each of her many births, was as a body to me, at my will. I seemed to feel the great heart of the mother beating into mine, and feeding me with her own life, her own essential being and nature. I heard the foot-steps of my friends above, and they sent a thrill through my heart. I knew that the helpers had gone, and that the knight and the lady remained, and spoke low, gentle, tearful words of him who lay be-neath the yet wounded sod. I rose into a single large primrose that grew by the edge of the grave, and from the window of its humble, trusting face, looked full in the countenance of the lady. I felt that I could manifest myself in the primrose; that it said a part of what I wanted to say; just as in the old time, I had used to betake myself to a song for the same end. The flower caught her eye. She stooped and plucked it, saying, 'Oh, you beautiful creature!' and, lightly kiss-ing it, put it in her bosom. It was the first kiss she had ever given me. But the flower soon began to wither, and I forsook it.[4]

It was evening. The sun was below the horizon; but his rosy beams yet illuminated a feathery cloud, that floated high above the world. I arose, I reached the cloud; and, throwing myself upon it, floated with it in sight of the sinking sun. He sank, and the cloud grew gray; but the grayness touched not my heart. It carried its rose-hue within; for now I could love without needing to be loved again. The moon came gliding up with all the past in her wan face. She changed my couch into a ghostly pallor, and threw all the earth below as to the bottom of a pale sea of dreams. But she could not make me sad. I knew now, that it is by loving, and not by being loved, that one can come nearest the soul of another; yea, that, where two love, it is the loving of each other, and not the being loved by each other, that originates and perfects and assures their

---

4 The poem sung by the flowers talked of the death of Primrose (see p.61). Here another Primrose has died, but with a kiss, rather than a bite.

blessedness. I knew that love gives to him that loveth, power over any soul beloved, even if that soul know him not, bringing him inwardly close to that spirit; a power that cannot be but for good; for in proportion as selfishness intrudes, the love ceases, and the power which springs therefrom dies. Yet all love will, one day, meet with its return. All true love will, one day, behold its own image in the eyes of the beloved, and be humbly glad. This is possible in the realms of lofty Death. 'Ah! my friends,' thought I, 'how I will tend you, and wait upon you, and haunt you with my love.'

My floating chariot bore me over a great city. Its faint dull sound steamed up into the air – a sound – how composed? 'How many hopeless cries,' thought I, 'and how many mad shouts go to make up the tumult, here so faint where I float in eternal peace, knowing that they will one day be stilled in the surrounding calm, and that despair dies into infinite hope, and the seeming impossible there, is the law here! But, O pale-faced women, and gloomy-browed men, and forgotten children, how I will wait on you, and minister to you, and, putting my arms about you in the dark, think hope into your hearts, when you fancy no one is near![5] Soon as my senses have all come back, and have grown accustomed to this new blessed life, I will be among you with the love that healeth.'

With this, a pang and a terrible shudder went through me; a writhing as of death convulsed me; and I became once again conscious of a more limited, even a bodily and earthly life.

---

5 MacDonald was well-used to such squalor in cities such as Manchester, Aberdeen and London. On visiting Edinburgh in 1855 he wrote to his wife, 'But the Canongate and the Cowgate! oh such houses! oh filth! and misery! and smells! and winding common stairs! and greated unglazed windows on all the landings! and squalid figures looking down from two, three, four, five, six, seven stories!... Some of the dark closes and entries swarming, children or grown people perhaps, almost falling away from the outlines definiteness of the human.' (MacDonald, Greville, *George MacDonald and His Wife*, p.229)

—25—

Our life is no dream; but it ought to become one, and perhaps will.

NOVALIS[1]

And on the ground, which is my modres gate,
I knocke with my staf; erlich and late,
And say to hire, Leve mother, let me in.

CHAUCER, THE PARDONERES TALE[2]

Sinking from such a state of ideal bliss, into the world of shadows which again closed around and infolded me, my first dread was, not unnaturally, that my own shadow had found me again, and that my torture had commenced anew. It was a sad revulsion of feeling. This, indeed, seemed to correspond to what we think death is, before we die. Yet I felt within me a power of calm endurance to which I had hitherto been a stranger. For, in truth, that I should be able if only to think such things as I had been thinking, was an unspeakable delight. An hour of such peace made the turmoil of a lifetime worth striving through.

I found myself lying in the open air, in the early morning, before sunrise. Over me rose the summer heaven, expectant of the sun. The clouds already saw him, coming from afar; and soon every

---

1 *'Unser Leben ist kein Traum, aber es soll und wird viellicht einer werden'.* On Novalis, see p.40. Taken from Novalis's *Fragmente vermischten Inhalts*, in the edition of Novalis's work published in Berlin by Schlegel and Tieck in 1802. This was one of MacDonald's favourite quotes and occurs in several of his books. Significantly, it was the last line of MacDonald's final work of fantasy, *Lilith*.

2 Chaucer (c. 1343 – c.1400). English author and poet. The quote comes from ll.729–31. In the tale they are spoken by an old man who wants to die.

dewdrop would rejoice in his individual presence within it. I lay motionless for a few minutes; and then slowly rose and looked about me. I was on the summit of a little hill; a valley lay beneath, and a range of mountains closed up the view upon that side. But, to my horror, across the valley, and up the height of the opposing mountains, stretched, from my very feet, a hugely expanding shade. There it lay, long and large, dark and mighty. I turned away with a sick despair; when lo! I beheld the sun just lifting his head above the eastern hill, and the shadow that fell from me, lay only where his beams fell not. I danced for joy. It was only the natural shadow, that goes with every man who walks in the sun. As he arose, higher and higher, the shadow-head sank down the side of the opposite hill, and crept in across the valley towards my feet.

A valley lay beneath me

Now that I was so joyously delivered from this fear, I saw and recognised the country around me. In the valley below, lay my own castle, and the haunts of my childhood were all about me hastened home. My sisters received me with unspeakable joy; but I suppose they observed some change in me, for a kind of respect, with a slight touch of awe in it, mingled with their joy, and made me ashamed. They had been in great distress about me. On the morning of my disappearance, they had found the floor of my room flooded; and, all that day, a wondrous and nearly impervious mist had hung about the castle and grounds. I had been gone, they told me, twenty-one days. To me it seemed twenty-one years.[3] Nor could I yet feel quite secure in my new experiences. When, at night, I lay down once more in my own bed, I did not feel at all sure that when I awoke, I should not find myself in some mysterious region of Fairy Land. My dreams were incessant and perturbed; but when I did awake, I saw clearly that I was in my own house.

My mind soon grew calm; and I began the duties of my new position, somewhat instructed, I hoped, by the adventures that had befallen me in Fairy Land. Could I translate the experience of my travels there, into common life? This was the question. Or must I live it all over again, and learn it all over again, in the other forms that belong to the world of men, whose experience yet runs parallel to that of Fairy Land? These questions I cannot answer yet. But I fear.

Even yet, I find myself looking round sometimes with anxiety, to see whether my shadow falls right away from the sun or no. I have never yet discovered any inclination to either side. And if I am not unfrequently sad, I yet cast no more of a shade on the earth, than most men who have lived in it as long as I. I have a strange feeling sometimes, that I am a ghost, sent into the world to minister to my fellow men, or, rather, to repair the wrongs I have already done. May the world be brighter for me, at least in those portions of it, where my darkness falls not.

Thus I, who set out to find my Ideal, came back rejoicing that I had lost my Shadow.

---

3 One day for each year of his life. Anodos's story in Fairy Land is linked, therefore, to the story of his own life. He has, of course, dreamed of this reunion (ch.22, p.242)

When the thought of the blessedness I experienced, after my death in Fairy Land, is too high for me to lay hold upon it and hope in it, I often think of the wise woman in the cottage, and of her solemn assurance that she knew something too good to be told. When I am oppressed by any sorrow or real perplexity, I often feel as if I had only left her cottage for a time, and would soon return out of the vision, into it again. Sometimes, on such occasions, I find myself, unconsciously almost, looking about for the mystic mark of red, with the vague hope of entering her door, and being comforted by her wise tenderness. I then console my-self by saying: 'I have come through the door of Dismay; and the way back from the world into which that has led me, is through my tomb. Upon that the red sign lies, and I shall find it one day, and be glad.'[4]

I will end my story with the relation of an incident which befell me a few days ago. I had been with my reapers, and, when they ceased their work at noon, I had lain down under the shadow of a great, ancient beech-tree, that stood on the edge of the field. As I lay, with my eyes closed, I began to listen to the sound of the leaves overhead. At first, they made sweet inarticulate music alone; but, by-and-by, the sound seemed to begin to take shape, and to be gradually moulding itself into words; till, at last, I seemed able to distinguish these, half-dissolved in a little ocean of circumfluent tones: 'A great good is coming – is coming – is coming to thee, Anodos'; and so over and over again.[5] I fancied that the sound reminded me of the voice of the ancient woman, in the cottage that was four-square. I opened my eyes, and, for a moment, almost believed that I saw her face, with its many wrin-kles and its young eyes, looking at me from between two hoary

4 The door of Dismay was the third of the doors in the house of the Old Woman, and the door which resulted in Anodos 'dying'; entering his family tomb. MacDonald wrote to his wife that 'We seek not death, but still we climb the stair where death is one wide landing to the rooms above.' (MacDonald, Greville, *George MacDonald and His Wife*, p.485)

5 Reminiscent of Julian of Norwich; '...All shall be well, and all shall be well, and all manner of thing shall be well.' Significantly, Anodos is lying under a beech tree.

branches of the beech overhead. But when I looked more keenly, I saw only twigs and leaves, and the infinite sky, in tiny spots, gazing through between. Yet I know that good is coming to me – that good is always coming; though few have at all times the simplicity and the courage to believe it. What we call evil, is the only and best shape, which, for the person and his condition at the time, could be assumed by the best good. And so, *Farewell.*

THE END

APPENDIX 1
Excerpts from Novalis[1]

Es lassen sich Erzählungen ohne Zusammenhang, jedoch mit Association, wie Träume, denken; Gedichte, die bloss wohlklingend und voll schöner Worte sind, aber auch ohne allen Sinn und Zusammenhang, höchstens einzelne Strophen verständlich, wie Bruchstücke aus den verschiedenartigsten Dingen. Diese wahre Poesie kann höchstens einen allegorischen Sinn im Grossen, und eine indirecte Wirkung, wie Musik haben. Darum ist die Natur so rein poetisch, wie die Stube eines Zauberers, eines Physikers, eine Kinderstube, eine Polter-und Vorrathskammer.

Ein Mährchen ist wie ein Traumbild ohne Zusammenhang. Ein Ensemble wunderbarer Dinge und Begebenheiten, z. B. eine Musikalische Phantasie, die harmonischen Folgen einer Aeolsharfe, die Natur selbst.

In einem echten Mährchen muss alles wunderbar, geheimnissvoll und zusammenhängend[2] *sein; alles belebt, jeder*[3] *auf eine andere Art. Die ganze Natur muss wunderlich mit der ganzen Geisterwelt gemischt sein; hier tritt die Zeit der Anarchie, der Gesetzlosigkeit, Freiheit, der Naturstand der Natur, die Zeit von*[4] *der Welt ein…Die Welt des Mährchens ist die, der Welt der Wahrheit durchaus entgegengesetzte, und eben darum ihr so durchaus ähnlich, wie das Chaos der vollendeten Schöpfung ähnlich ist. – NOVALIS.*

---

1 These are the German extracts from Novalis which, untranslated, originally prefaced *Phantastes* (see p.40). The excerpt is taken from an edition of Novalis's work edited by Ludwig Tieck and Fr. (Karl Wilhelm Friedrich) von Schlegel. There were some mistakes in the editorial transcriptions (see below) which meant that the passage included by MacDonald was not actually what appeared in the original of Novalis's *Heinrich von Ofterdingen*.

2 In Novalis: 'unzusammenhängend' i.e. 'incoherent'.

3 In Novalis: 'jedes' i.e. 'everything'.

4 In Novalis: 'vor', not 'von'.

APPENDIX 2
THE FANTASTIC IMAGINATION[1]

That we have in English no word corresponding to the German *Mährchen*, drives us to use the word *Fairytale*, regardless of the fact that the tale may have nothing to do with any sort of fairy. The old use of the word *Fairy*, by Spenser at least, might, however, well be adduced, were justification or excuse necessary where *need must*.

Were I asked, what is a fairytale? I should reply, *Read Undine: that is a fairytale; then read this and that as well, and you will see what is a fairytale.* Were I further begged to describe the *fairytale*, or define what it is, I would make answer, that I should as soon think of describing the abstract human face, or stating what must go to constitute a human being. A fairytale is just a fairytale, as a face is just a face; and of all fairytales I know, I think *Undine* the most beautiful.

Many a man, however, who would not attempt to define *a man*, might venture to say something as to what a man ought to be: even so much I will not in this place venture with regard to the fairytale, for my long past work in that kind might but poorly instance or illustrate my now more matured judgment. I will but say some things helpful to the reading, in right-minded fashion, of such fairytales as I would wish to write, or care to read.

Some thinkers would feel sorely hampered if at liberty to use no forms but such as existed in nature, or to invent nothing save in accordance with the laws of the world of the senses; but it must not therefore be imagined that they desire escape from the region of law. Nothing lawless can show the least reason why it should exist, or could at best have more than an appearance of life.

---

1 This essay first appeared as the introduction to the American edition of *The Light Princess*, published by Puttnams, New York, 1893. It was then included in *A Dish of Orts*, Sampson Low, Marston & Co. Edenbridge, Kent 1893. It contains the clearest outline of his views of fairy stories and fantasy.

The natural world has its laws, and no man must interfere with them in the way of presentment any more than in the way of use; but they themselves may suggest laws of other kinds, and man may, if he pleases, invent a little world of his own, with its own laws; for there is that in him which delights in calling up new forms – which is the nearest, perhaps, he can come to creation. When such forms are new embodiments of old truths, we call them products of the Imagination; when they are mere inventions, however lovely, I should call them the work of the Fancy: in either case, Law has been diligently at work.

His world once invented, the highest law that comes next into play is, that there shall be harmony between the laws by which the new world has begun to exist; and in the process of his creation, the inventor must hold by those laws. The moment he forgets one of them, he makes the story, by its own postulates, incredible. To be able to live a moment in an imagined world, we must see the laws of its existence obeyed. Those broken, we fall out of it. The imagination in us, whose exercise is essential to the most temporary submission to the imagination of another, immediately, with the disappearance, of Law, ceases to act. Suppose the gracious creatures of some childlike region of Fairyland talking either cockney or Gascon! Would not the tale, however lovelily begun, sink at once to the level of the Burlesque – of all forms of literature the least worthy? A man's inventions may be stupid or clever, but if he do not hold by the laws of them, or if he make one law jar with another, he contradicts himself as an inventor, he is no artist. He does not rightly consort his instruments, or he tunes them in different keys. The mind of man is the product of live Law; it thinks by law, it dwells in the midst of law, it gathers from law its growth; with law, therefore, can it alone work to any result. Inharmonious, unconsorting ideas will come to a man, but if he try to use one of such, his work will grow dull, and he will drop it from mere lack of interest. Law is the soil in which alone beauty will grow; beauty is the only stuff in which Truth can be clothed; and you may, if you will, call Imagination the tailor that cuts her garments to fit her, and Fancy his journeyman that puts the pieces of them together, or perhaps at most embroiders their button-holes. Obeying law, the maker works like his creator; not obeying law, he is such a fool as heaps a pile of stones and calls it a church.

In the moral world it is different: there a man may clothe in new forms, and for this employ his imagination freely, but he must invent nothing. He may not, for any purpose, turn its laws upside down. He must not meddle with the relations of live souls. The laws of the spirit of man must hold, alike in this world and in any world he may invent. It were no offence to suppose a world in which everything repelled instead of attracted the things around it; it would be wicked to write a tale representing a man it called good as always doing bad things, or a man it called bad as always doing good things: the notion itself is absolutely lawless. In physical things a man may invent; in moral things he must obey – and take their laws with him into his invented world as well.

'You write as if a fairytale were a thing of importance: must it have a meaning?'

It cannot help having some meaning; if it have proportion and harmony it has vitality, and vitality is truth. The beauty may be plainer in it than the truth, but without the truth the beauty could not be, and the fairytale would give no delight. Everyone, however, who feels the story, will read its meaning after his own nature and development: one man will read one meaning in it, another will read another.

'If so, how am I to assure myself that I am not reading my own meaning into it, but yours out of it?'

Why should you be so assured? It may be better that you should read your meaning into it. That may be a higher operation of your intellect than the mere reading of mine out of it: your meaning may be superior to mine.

'Suppose my child ask me what the fairytale means, what am I to say?'

If you do not know what it means, what is easier than to say so? If you do see a meaning in it, there it is for you to give him. A genuine work of art must mean many things; the truer its art, the more things it will mean. If my drawing, on the other hand, is so far from being a work of art that it needs *THIS IS A HORSE* written under it, what can it matter that neither you nor your child should know what it means? It is there not so much to convey a meaning as to wake a meaning. If it do not even wake an interest, throw it aside. A meaning may be there, but it is not for you. If, again, you do not know a horse when you see it, the name written under it will not serve you much. At all events, the business of the painter is not to teach zoology.

But indeed your children are not likely to trouble you about the meaning. They find what they are capable of finding, and more would be too much. For my part, I do not write for children, but for the childlike, whether of five, or fifty, or seventy-five.

A fairytale is not an allegory. There may be allegory in it, but it is not an allegory. He must be an artist indeed who can, in any mode, produce a strict allegory that is not a weariness to the spirit. An allegory must be Mastery or Moorditch.

A fairytale, like a butterfly or a bee, helps itself on all sides, sips at every wholesome flower, and spoils not one. The true fairytale is, to my mind, very like the sonata. We all know that a sonata means something; and where there is the faculty of talking with suitable vagueness, and choosing metaphor sufficiently loose, mind may approach mind, in the interpretation of a sonata, with the result of a more or less contenting consciousness of sympathy. But if two or three men sat down to write each what the sonata meant to him, what approximation to definite idea would be the result? Little enough — and that little more than needful. We should find it had roused related, if not identical, feelings, but probably not one common thought. Has the sonata therefore failed? Had it undertaken to convey, or ought it to be expected to impart anything defined, anything notionally recognizable?

'But words are not music; words at least are meant and fitted to carry a precise meaning!'

It is very seldom indeed that they carry the exact meaning of any user of them! And if they can be so used as to convey definite meaning, it does not follow that they ought never to carry anything else. Words are live things that may be variously employed to various ends. They can convey a scientific fact, or throw a shadow of her child's dream on the heart of a mother. They are things to put together like the pieces of a dissected map, or to arrange like the notes on a stave. Is the music in them to go for nothing? It can hardly help the definiteness of a meaning: is it therefore to be disregarded? They have length, and breadth, and outline: have they nothing to do with depth? Have they only to describe, never to impress? Has nothing any claim to their use but the definite? The cause of a child's tears may be altogether undefinable: has the mother therefore no antidote for his vague misery? That may be strong in colour which has no evident outline. A fairytale, a sonata, a gathering storm, a limitless night, seizes you and sweeps you away: do you begin at once to wrestle with it and ask whence its power over you, whither it is carrying you? The law of each is in the mind of its composer; that law makes one man feel this way, another man feel that way. To one the sonata is a world of odour and beauty, to another of soothing only and sweetness. To one, the cloudy rendezvous is a wild dance, with a terror at its heart; to another, a majestic march of heavenly hosts, with Truth in their centre pointing their course, but as yet restraining her voice. The greatest forces lie in the region of the uncomprehended.

I will go farther. – The best thing you can do for your fellow, next to rousing his conscience, is – not to give him things to think about, but to wake things up that are in him; or say, to make him think things for himself. The best Nature does for us is to work in us such moods in which thoughts of high import arise. Does any aspect of Nature wake but one thought? Does she ever suggest only one definite thing? Does she make any two men in the same place at the same moment think the same thing? Is she therefore a failure, because she is not definite? Is it nothing that she rouses the something deeper than the understanding – the power that underlies thoughts? Does she not set feeling, and so thinking at work? Would it be better that she did this after one fashion and not after many fashions? Nature is mood-engendering, thought-provoking: such ought the sonata, such ought the fairytale to be.

'But a man may then imagine in your work what he pleases, what you never meant!'

Not what he pleases, but what he can. If he be not a true man, he will draw evil out of the best; we need not mind how he treats any work of art! If he be a true man, he will imagine true things; what matter whether I meant them or not? They are there none the less that I cannot claim putting them there! One difference between God's work and man's is, that, while God's work cannot mean more than he meant, man's must mean more than he meant. For in everything that God has made, there is layer upon layer of ascending significance; also he expresses the same thought in higher and higher kinds of that thought: it is God's things, his embodied thoughts, which alone a man has to use, modified and adapted to his own purposes, for the expression of his thoughts; therefore he cannot help his words and figures falling into such combinations in the mind of another as he had himself not foreseen, so many are the thoughts allied to every other thought, so many are the relations involved in every figure, so many the facts hinted in every symbol. A man may well himself discover truth in what he wrote; for he was dealing all the time with things that came from thoughts beyond his own.

'But surely you would explain your idea to one who asked you?'

I say again, if I cannot draw a horse, I will not write *THIS IS A HORSE* under what I foolishly meant for one. Any key to a work of imagination would be nearly, if not quite, as absurd. The tale is there, not to hide, but to show: if it show nothing at your window, do not open your door to it; leave it out in the cold. To ask me to explain, is to say, 'Roses! Boil them, or we won't have them!' My tales may not be roses, but I will not boil them.

So long as I think my dog can bark, I will not sit up to bark for him.

If a writer's aim be logical conviction, he must spare no logical pains, not merely to be understood, but to escape being misunderstood; where his object is to move by suggestion, to cause to imagine, then let him assail the soul of his reader as the wind assails an aeolian harp. If there be music in my reader, I would gladly wake it. Let fairytale of mine go for a firefly that now flashes, now is dark, but may flash again. Caught in a hand which does not love its kind, it will turn to an insignificant, ugly thing, that can neither flash nor fly.

The best way with music, I imagine, is not to bring the forces of our intellect to bear upon it, but to be still and let it work on that part of us for whose sake it exists. We spoil countless precious things by intellectual greed. He who will be a man, and will not be a child, must — he cannot help himself — become a little man, that is, a dwarf. He will, however, need no consolation, for he is sure to think himself a very large creature indeed.

If any strain of my 'broken music' make a child's eyes flash, or his mother's grow for a moment dim, my labour will not have been in vain.

BIBLIOGRAPHY

The main works of MacDonald I have used in preparing this edition are:

MacDonald, George, *At the Back of the North Wind*, (New edn., London: Blackie & Son, 1900)

—, *A Book of Strife in the Form of the Diary of an Old Soul*, (New edn., London: Allen & Unwin, 1924)

—, *A Dish of Orts: Chiefly Papers on the Imagination and on Shakespeare*, (London: George Newnes, 1905)

—, *Lilith - First and Final*, (Whitethorn: Johannesen, 1994)

—, *Lilith: A Variorum Edition*, (Whitethorn: Johannesen, 1997)

—, and Greville MacDonald, *Lilith: A Romance*, (London: G. Allen & Unwin, ltd, 1924)

—, *Phantastes: A Faerie Romance*, (London: Smith, Elder & Co., 1858)

—, *Phantastes: A Faerie Romance*, (Everyman's Libr, 732; London: Dent, 1916)

—, *The Poetical Works of George MacDonald*, (Fine-paper edn., London: Chatto & Windus, 1915)

—, *Poems*, original ms. dated June 1856, in the possession of the George MacDonald Collection, Aberdeenshire Library and Information Service.

—, *Poems*, (London: Longman, Brown, Green, Longmans and Roberts, 1857)

—, *The Portent, and Other Stories*, (London: A.C. Fifield, 1924)

—, *The Princess and Curdie*, (New edn., London: Blackie & Son, 1912)

—, *The Princess and the Goblin*, (New edn., London: Blackie & Son, 1912)

—, *Unspoken Sermons, Series I, II & III*, (Whitethorn: Johannesen, 1997)

—, and U. C. Knoepflmacher, *The Complete Fairy Tales*, (Penguin Classics, New York/ London: Penguin, 1999)

—, *Within and Without*, original mss. 1851; revised 1854; in the possession of the George MacDonald Collection, Aberdeenshire Library and Information Service.

LETTERS

MacDonald, George, and C. S Lewis, *George MacDonald: An Anthology*, (London: G. Bles, 1946)

MacDonald, George, and Glenn Edward Sadler, *An Expression of Character: The Letters of George MacDonald*, (Grand Rapids: Eerdmans, 1994)

MacDonald, Greville, *George MacDonald and His Wife*, (London: G. Allen & Unwin, 1924)

SECONDARY SOURCES

Arnold, Matthew, and Cecil Y Lang, *The Letters of Matthew Arnold*, (Victorian Literature and Culture Series, Charlottesville/London: University Press of Virginia, 1996)

Auden, W. H, and Edward Mendelson, *The Complete Works of W.H. Auden. Vol 3: Prose and Travel Books in Prose and Verse*, (London: Faber and Faber, 1996)

Blackall, Eric A, *The Novels of the German Romantics*, (Ithaca/London: Cornell University Press, 1983)

Boice, Daniel. 'A Kind of Sacrament: Books and Libraries in the Fiction of George MacDonald' *Studies in Scottish Literature* 27, 1992

Briggs, Katharine Mary, *A Dictionary of Fairies: Hobgoblins, Brownies, Bogies, and Other Supernatural Creatures*, (London: Penguin, 1977)

Bulloch, John Malcolm, *A Centennial Bibliography of George MacDonald*, (Aberdeen: The University Press, 1925)

Carpenter, Humphrey, and Mari Prichard, *The Oxford Companion to Children's Literature*, (Oxford: Oxford University Press, 1984)

Carroll, Lewis, and Martin Gardner, *The Annotated Alice: Alice's Adventures in Wonderland; and, Through the Looking Glass*, (Rev. edn., London: Penguin, 1970)

Chesterton, G. K, *The Victorian Age in Literature*, (Oxford Paperbacks University Series, 8; London: Oxford University Press, 1966)

Clute, John, and John Grant, *The Encyclopedia of Fantasy*, (London: Orbit, 1999)

Dearborn, Kerry, *Baptized Imagination: The Theology of George MacDonald*, (Ashgate Studies in Theology, Imagination, and the Arts, Aldershot: Ashgate, 2006)

Docherty, John. 'A Note on the Structure and Conclusion of *Phantastes*' *North Wind* 7, 1988

—, *The Literary Products of the Lewis Carroll-George MacDonald Friendship*, (Lewiston, N.Y ; Lampeter: Mellen, 1995)

Gunther, Adrian. 'The Structure of George MacDonald's *Phantastes*' *North Wind* 12, 1993

Hein, Rolland, *George MacDonald: Victorian Mythmaker*, (Whitethorn, California: Johannesen, 1999)

—, *The Harmony Within: The Spiritual Vision of George MacDonald*, (Chicago: Cornerstone Press, (Revised edn.) 1999)

Hoffmann, E. T. A, and Ritchie Robertson, *The Golden Pot and Other Tales*, (Oxford: Oxford University Press, 2000)

Holbrook, David, *A Study of George MacDonald and the Image of Woman*, (Studies in British Literature, v. 45; Lewiston, N.Y./Lampeter: Mellen, 2000)

Howard, Susan. E. 'In Search of Spiritual Maturity: George MacDonald's *Phantastes*,' *Extrapolation* 30 (3), 1989

Hutton, Muriel. 'The George MacDonald Collection' *Yale University Library Gazette* 51, 1976

Lewis, C. S, *Surprised By Joy: The Shape of My Early Life*, (London: Geoffrey Bles, 1955)

Maas, Jeremy, *Victorian Fairy Painting*, (London: Merrell Holberton, 1997)

MacDonald, Ronald, *From a Northern Window: A Personal Remembrance of George MacDonald*, (Masterline series; v. 1; Eureka, Calif: Sunrise Books, 1989)

McGillis, Roderick, *For the Childlike: George MacDonald's Fantasies for Children*, (Metuchen, N.J/London: Children's Literature Association Scarecrow, 1992)

McInnis, Jeff, *Shadows and Chivalry: C.S. Lewis and George MacDonald on Suffering, Evil, and Goodness*, (Studies in Christian History and Thought, Milton Keynes: Paternoster, 2007)

Manlove, C.M. 'Circularity in Fantasy: George MacDonald' in *The Impulse of Fantasy Literature* (Kent, Ohio: Kent State University Press, 1983) pp.70–92.

—, 'George MacDonald's Fairy Tales' in *Christian Fantasy from 1200 to the Present* (Notre Dame: University of Notre Dame Press, 1992) pp.164-82.

Prickett, Stephen, *Romanticism and Religion: The Tradition of Coleridge and Wordsworth in the Victorian Church*, (Cambridge: Cambridge University Press, 1976)

—, *Victorian Fantasy*, (Hassocks, Sussex: Harvester Press, 1979)

Pridmore, John. 'George MacDonald's Transfiguring Fantasy' *VII: an Anglo-American literary review* 20. 2003

Raeper, William, *George MacDonald*, (Tring: Lion, 1987)

—, *The Gold Thread: Essays on George MacDonald*, (Edinburgh: Edinburgh University Press, 1990)

Robb, David S, *George MacDonald*, (Scottish Writers, 11; Edinburgh: Scottish Academic Press, 1987)

Shaberman, R. B, *George MacDonald: A Bibliographical Study*, (Winchester Detroit: St. Paul's Bibliographies Omingraphics, 1990)

Soto, Fernando. 'Mirrors in MacDonald's *Phantastes*: A Reflexive Structure' *North wind* 23, 2004

—, 'Cosmos and Diamonds: Naming and Connoting in MacDonald's Works' *North Wind* 20, 2001, pp.30–42

Stevenson, Robert Louis, *The Strange Case of Dr Jekyll and Mr Hyde, and Other Stories*, (Harmondsworth: Penguin Books, 1979)

Sutton, Max Keith. 'The Psychology of the Self in MacDonald's *Phantastes*' *VII: an Anglo-American literary review* 5. 1984

Tolkien, J. R. R, *Tree and Leaf*, (London: Allen & Unwin, 1974)

Webb, William, 'George MacDonald and Jean Paul' *North Wind*, 14, 1995

Wolff, Robert Lee, *The Golden Key: A Study of the Fiction of George MacDonald*, (New Haven: Yale University Press, 1961)

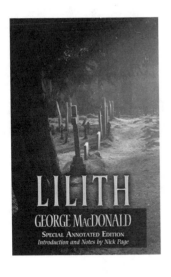

Lilith

(Special Edition)

George MacDonald

*With introduction and notes
by Nick Page*

Mr. Vane owns a library that seems to be haunted by a ghostly, raven-like, former librarian. This wraith comes and goes between the library and a parallel universe and Vane learns that his own father had visited this strange alternative world and is there right now. Following Mr Raven, the librarian, into this world through a mirror, Vane embarks on the first of several journeys into another dimension, each journey taking him deeper into the mystery of evil and its ultimate eclipse.

Lilith, first published in 1895, is considered among the darkest and most profound of MacDonald's works. The result of intensive re-working and rewriting, the book is MacDonald's ultimate meditation on issues of goodness, evil, life, death and salvation.

'Lilith is equal if not superior to the best of Poe.' – **W. H. Auden** (1907-1973), poet and author

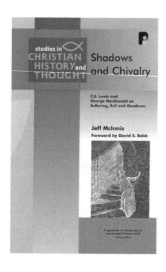

Shadows and Chivalry

Pain, Suffering, Evil and Goodness in the Works of George MacDonald and C.S. Lewis

Jeff McInnis

McInnis studies the influence of George MacDonald on C.S. Lewis. Beginning with the authors' early experiences of suffering and their literary reactions to it, McInnis shows how MacDonald's writings helped transform Lewis from an imaginative doubter and escapist into a believer in the reality of God and his goodness. While other books have only mentioned the fact that Lewis called MacDonald his 'master', and that MacDonald's *Phantastes* helped 'baptize' Lewis' imagination, this study traces the overall effect of MacDonald's works on Lewis' thought and imagination.

'A genuinely enriching read for any earnest Christian Mind.' – **Rolland Hein**

'A book that henceforth will be indispensable to all students of C.S. Lewis.' – **David Lyle Jeffrey**

Jeff McInnis is an English Instructor at Panola College, Carthage, Texas

978-1-84227-430-9